TRAITORS GATE

TRAITORS GATE

Jeffrey Archer is one of the world's bestselling authors, with sales of over 275 million copies in 115 countries and 48 languages.

Famous for his discipline as a writer who works on up to fourteen drafts of each book, Jeffrey also brings a vast amount of insider knowledge to his books. Whether it's his own career in politics, his passionate interest in art, or the wealth of fascinating background detail – inspired by the extraordinary network of friends he has built over a lifetime at the heart of Britain's establishment – his novels provide a fascinating glimpse into a range of closed worlds.

A member of the House of Lords, the author is married to Dame Mary Archer, Chair of the Science Museum Group, and they have two sons, two granddaughters and three grandsons. He splits his time between London, Grantchester in Cambridge, and Mallorca, where he writes the first draft of each new novel.

www.jeffreyarcher.co.uk

Also by Jeffrey Archer

THE WILLIAM WARWICK NOVELS
Nothing Ventured
Hidden in Plain Sight
Turn a Blind Eye
Over My Dead Body
Next in Line

THE CLIFTON CHRONICLES
Only Time Will Tell
The Sins of the Father
Best Kept Secret
Be Careful What You Wish For
Mightier than the Sword
Cometh the Hour
This Was a Man

NOVELS
Not a Penny More, Not a Penny Less
Shall We Tell the President?
Kane and Abel
The Prodigal Daughter
First Amongst Equals
A Matter of Honour
As the Crow Flies
Honour Amongst Thieves
The Fourth Estate
The Eleventh Commandment
Sons of Fortune
False Impression
The Gospel According to Judas
(with the assistance of Professor Francis J. Moloney)
A Prisoner of Birth
Paths of Glory
Heads You Win

SHORT STORIES
A Quiver Full of Arrows
A Twist in the Tale
Twelve Red Herrings
The Collected Short Stories
To Cut a Long Story Short
Cat O'Nine Tales
And Thereby Hangs a Tale
Tell Tale
The Short, the Long and the Tall

PLAYS
Beyond Reasonable Doubt
Exclusive
The Accused
Confession
Who Killed the Mayor?

PRISON DIARIES
Volume One – Belmarsh: Hell
Volume Two – Wayland: Purgatory
Volume Three – North Sea Camp: Heaven

SCREENPLAYS
Mallory: Walking Off the Map
False Impression

Jeffrey Archer

TRAITORS GATE

HarperCollins*Publishers*

HarperCollins*Publishers* Ltd
1 London Bridge Street,
London SE1 9GF

www.harpercollins.co.uk

HarperCollins*Publishers*
Macken House,
39/40 Mayor Street Upper,
Dublin 1 D01 C9W8

First published by HarperCollins*Publishers* 2023
8

Interior images:
Image p.255: Author: Haiward, Gulielmus; Gascoyne, J / Source/Shelfmark: Maps.Crace.8.42, A True and exact draught of the Tower Liberties, surveyed in the year 1397 by Gulielmus Haiward and J. Gascoyne
Credit: British Library, London, UK © British Library Board. All Rights Reserved/Bridgeman Images
Image p.257: Thomas Blood and his accomplices making their escape after stealing the Crown of Charles II, 1793 (engraving) (b&w photo)
Credit: Private Collection/Bridgeman Images

A catalogue record for this book is available from the British Library

ISBN: 978-0-00-847437-9 (HB)
ISBN: 978-0-00-860738-8 (US-only HB)
ISBN: 978-0-00-864819-0 (Special sale-only)
ISBN: 978-0-00-847438-6 (TPB)
ISBN: 978-0-00-852324-4 (IN)

Typeset in New Caledonia LT Std by
Palimpsest Book Production Ltd, Falkirk, Stirlingshire

Printed and bound in the UK using 100% Renewable Electricity
at CPI Group (UK) Ltd

To Alan Gard,
Master Jeweller

BOOK I

'Uneasy lies the head that wears a crown.'

William Shakespeare,
Henry IV, Part II

CHAPTER 1

TUESDAY 22 OCTOBER 1996

COMMANDER HAWKSBY PULLED OPEN THE bottom drawer of his desk and took out two dice, although he was not a gambling man.

Superintendent William Warwick and Inspector Ross Hogan remained standing as the Hawk, like a Vegas croupier, shook the dice vigorously in his right hand before tossing them onto his desk and waiting for them to settle.

'Five and two,' said William. The Hawk raised an eyebrow as he waited for William and Ross to confirm the relevance of the two numbers. 'Five, sir,' said William, 'means that when we leave the palace, we'll be taking the longer Embankment route.'

'And the two, Inspector?' demanded Commander Hawksby, switching his attention to Ross.

'The password is "Traitors Gate".'

The Hawk nodded before checking his watch. 'Better get

moving,' he said. 'Can't afford to keep the Lord Chamberlain waiting.' He bent down and put the dice back in the bottom drawer of his desk for another year.

William and Ross quickly left the office as the commander picked up his phone and dialled a number that wasn't in any phone book. It was answered after one ring. 'Five and two,' he said.

'Five and two,' repeated the voice on the other end of the line before the phone went dead.

William and Ross marched along the corridor, past the lift, and jogged down two sets of stairs to the ground floor of Scotland Yard. They didn't stop moving until they'd reached the entrance, where they saw Constable Danny Ives seated behind the wheel of a dark grey Land Rover, not their usual mode of transport, but appropriate for the occasion.

'Good morning, sir,' said Danny as William climbed into the back of the car.

'Morning, Danny,' William replied as Ross joined him.

Superintendent Warwick and Constable Ives had joined the force a decade before, in the same intake as fledgling recruits, and it had taken the perpetual constable some time to stop calling his boss by his old nickname 'choirboy', and call him 'sir' instead. It had taken considerably longer for him to mean it.

Danny switched on the engine and eased the unfamiliar vehicle into first gear before moving off. He didn't need to be told where they were going. After all, it wasn't every day they visited Buckingham Palace.

He never exceeded the speed limit, as they didn't want anyone to notice them, though on the journey back to the palace, they would touch sixty, sometimes seventy mph in one of the busiest capitals on earth.

Danny came to a halt at the top of Whitehall and glanced up at Britain's legendary naval hero perched on his column. When the lights turned green, he swung left, drove under Admiralty Arch and proceeded slowly along the Mall, his destination now in sight.

When they reached the imposing marble statue of Queen Victoria, every other vehicle turned right or left of the palace, while they headed for the entrance, where once again Danny came to a halt. An Irish guardsman stepped forward as the back window of the Land Rover purred down. He examined Superintendent Warwick's warrant card, placed a tick next to his name, and stood aside to allow the head of Royalty Protection to enter the grounds. Danny spotted a grey armoured Jaguar parked in the far corner of the courtyard and drew up behind it. Nothing changes, he thought when he saw Phil Harris, the Lord Chamberlain's driver, standing to attention by the back door waiting for his boss.

Danny got out of the car and walked across to join his old mate. 'Morning, Phil.'

'Good morning, Danny,' Harris replied. Although the two men met only twice a year, they had become friends. Lord Chamberlains might be replaced from time to time, but Phil Harris had served three holders of that high office during the past eleven years, and Danny had almost as much service under his belt.

'I presume you know which route we'll be taking?' asked Danny.

'Number five,' said Phil.

'And the password?'

'Number two. Your commander had briefed my boss even before you'd left the Yard.'

'I've just spotted His Lordship,' whispered Danny as the

head of the royal household came striding across the courtyard towards them like the old soldier he'd been. Harris opened the back door of the Jaguar while Danny quickly returned to the Land Rover. The Lord Chamberlain, a courteous man who never paraded his rank, gave William a wave before slipping into the back of his car.

The little convoy swept out of an unmarked side entrance onto the Mall and headed for Trafalgar Square. No outriders, no sirens, no blue lights. They didn't want to alert any curious onlookers, something they wouldn't be able to avoid on the journey back from the Tower.

Danny followed, and although he kept his distance, he would never allow another vehicle to slip in between him and the Lord Chamberlain's armoured car.

William picked up the phone in his armrest and dialled a number he called only twice a year.

'Chief Yeoman Warder,' announced a voice.

'We should be with you in about fifteen minutes,' said William.

'Everything's been prepared and is ready for you,' responded the Chief Yeoman Warder.

'I can see no reason for any hold-ups,' William commented, before replacing the phone in the armrest. He would call again only if there was an emergency and there hadn't been one in the past five years.

'How are the kids?' asked Ross, interrupting his thoughts.

'Growing up far too quickly,' responded William as they drove on to the Embankment. 'Artemisia is top of her class, but she will burst into tears whenever she comes second.'

'Just like her mother,' said Ross. 'And Peter?'

'He's just been made a prefect and expects to be school captain next year.'

'Clearly lacks your ambition,' said Ross, grinning. 'What about my beloved Jojo?'

'Your daughter's in love with Prince Harry and has already written to Buckingham Palace inviting him to tea.'

'I know,' sighed Ross. 'She asked me to deliver the letter.' Ross felt a moment of guilt as he thought about why his daughter still lived with Beth and William. But since his wife's death, they'd both agreed he couldn't do his job properly while trying to bring up Jojo as a single parent. They'd turned out to be wonderful foster parents. But he never admitted to anyone just how much he missed her.

'Time to think about what *we're* meant to be delivering,' said William.

Ross snapped out of his reverie and began to concentrate on the task ahead. Danny had to run a red light as they passed Somerset House to make sure he didn't lose contact with the Lord Chamberlain's Jaguar. Nothing would have pleased Phil Harris more than to show he could outwit Danny.

They didn't take a left into the heart of the city – a square mile policed by another force, who were unaware of their presence – but continued on through the underpass and didn't stop again until they emerged onto Upper Thames Street, coming to a halt at the next traffic light, the Tower of London now in sight.

When the Jaguar swung across the intersection, Danny followed it down St Katharine's Way with only the Thames in front of him. They finally took a sharp right and came to a halt in front of the East Gate of the Tower. A barrier automatically rose.

The duty warder stepped out of the sentry box and marched across to the Lord Chamberlain's car.

'Good morning, Phil,' the warder said. 'Password?'

'Traitors Gate,' Harris responded. The warder turned and

nodded, and the two vast wooden gates that barred their way slowly parted.

Both vehicles continued the last leg of their journey unimpeded by the public as the Tower was closed for the day, so they had only a couple of dozen Yeoman Warders and the eight resident ravens to keep them company. Danny drove beside the Thames for another hundred yards before turning right and proceeding over the east drawbridge – originally built for horses, not cars. The two cars swept under the Queen Elizabeth Archway and up the steep slope towards the Jewel House, where they saw the Jewel House Warder standing to attention beside General Sir Harry Stanley KCVO, the Resident Governor and Keeper of the Crown Jewels.

Phil Harris brought the car to a halt, leapt out and opened the back door for his boss. The two men, who also met only twice a year, shook hands. After a cursory greeting and the minimum of small talk, the Governor led his guest down the short path towards the Jewel House.

'Morning, Walter,' said Harris, giving the Chief Yeoman Warder a warm smile before putting the boot in. 'Another bad year for the Gunners.'

'Don't remind me,' responded the Chief Yeoman Warder before he followed his boss into the Jewel House, slamming the door firmly behind him.

William got out of the back of the Land Rover and waited. He often wondered what went on behind those closed doors guarded by a cadre of Yeoman Warders known as 'The Partisans', a dozen men who were prepared for an emergency that hadn't happened since 1671.

Once the Jewel House door had been locked, Harris returned to his car and continued with the annual routine. He drove a small semi-circle, with Danny following close behind, to ensure they were ready to move and move quickly when the time came for them to depart. They were joined by five outriders from the Special Escort Group, who usually only accompanied members of the Royal Family, the Prime Minister and foreign heads of state, but the Imperial State Crown and Sword of State were symbols of Her Majesty's authority and required the same protection. Once the two cars and escort were all in place, Harris got out of the lead car, opened the boot and waited. William's eyes never left the Jewel House as he too waited for the door to open and General Stanley to reappear, accompanied by the most valuable treasures in the kingdom.

Three men entered the Jewel House but five emerged a few minutes later. The two Jewel House Warders led the way, each carrying a black leather case with the insignia EIIR inscribed on the lid in gold. One of the boxes resembled a viola case and contained the Sword of State, while the other held the Imperial State Crown that had been placed on the head of Queen Elizabeth II by the Archbishop of Canterbury during her coronation ceremony in 1953 and would once again be worn by Her Majesty the next day when she delivered the Queen's Speech to the House of Lords at eleven thirty in the forenoon, to quote the official proceedings.

The final person to emerge from the Jewel House was the Lord Chamberlain himself who, once he'd seen the two black boxes securely locked in the boot of the armoured Jaguar, took his place in the back of the car. He nodded, to acknowledge that the second half of the operation could begin.

The Chief Yeoman Warder sprang to attention and saluted as the escort party moved off and neither he nor the Resident Governor left their posts until the little convoy was out of sight.

• • •

A taxi drove down the wrong side of the road as it approached the Savoy Hotel. Miles Faulkner had forgotten this was the only street in London where you can drive on the right without fear of being pulled over.

It was nearly five years since Miles had been in London. A man who divided opinion – he considered himself as an international businessman, while the police thought him a crook – he'd ended up serving a few years at Her Majesty's pleasure. After leaving prison, having served four years for fraud, Miles had left England and purchased a luxury flat in New York, confident he would be far enough away from the prying eyes of Chief Inspector William Warwick to return to his shady import and export business, a tax-free enterprise that yielded vast profits without being registered at Companies House. However, it wasn't long before he became homesick and wanted to return to England – unnoticed, he hoped. No such luck. A certain Agent James Buchanan of the FBI had been keeping a close eye on Faulkner in case he needed to report his activities back to Superintendent Warwick – someone he not only admired, but wanted to thank for all the good advice he'd given him when they'd first met on holiday while he was still at school. James was now in Washington working for the FBI, but he'd watched with admiration as his mentor had continued to climb through the ranks. He wondered if the superintendent would remember him.

Miles stepped out of the taxi and stood on the pavement for some time before he entered the hotel. During his self-imposed exile, not a day had passed when he hadn't thought about lunch at the Savoy. He could still recall a prison diet of cold, lumpy porridge, burnt toast and a hard-boiled egg. The prison chef had not been familiar with his favourite Savoy cabbage or Peach Melba.

A liveried doorman saluted and pulled open the front door of the hotel. Miles stepped inside and headed straight for the Grill.

'Good morning, Mr Faulkner,' said the maître d' as if he'd never been away. 'Your usual table?'

Miles nodded and Mario led him across a crowded dining room to an alcove table where he would not be overheard. He sat down in his usual seat and spent a few moments surveying a room that hadn't changed since he'd last dined there. He recognized several well-known personalities dotted around the room. The editor of the *Daily Mail* was lunching with a cabinet minister, whose name he could never remember, while in the next alcove sat an actor he could never forget. He'd watched every episode of *Poirot* while he was in prison, some more than once, to help him while away the unrelenting hours.

He began to think about his lunch guest. A man who was never late, but then he was paid by the hour. A man who always selected the sirloin steak and a vintage bottle of wine to be found near the bottom of the list.

During those forced years of emigration, Mr Booth Watson had been Miles's only contact back home. A weekly consultation with his lawyer to bring him up to date with his numerous business affairs, or to bid for a painting or sculpture he wanted to add to his collection. A judge and jury might have sent him down, but the value of his various properties and shares had continued to go up.

Following a successful appeal at the high court, Booth Watson had managed to get a year taken off Miles's original five-year sentence. A few weeks later Miles was transferred to Ford Open Prison, which felt like a holiday camp compared with Wormwood Scrubs.

After a few days at Ford, he had been moved to a single room – there are no cells in an open prison – and a month later he was taken off cleaning duties and appointed prison librarian, a position that had cost him three hundred pounds. One hundred for the old librarian to switch jobs and another two hundred for the prison officer in charge of job allocation. He would have paid three thousand but the PO made the wrong opening bid. Both payments were made in cash, which, although a punishable offence, is still the only acceptable currency in prison.

Not many inmates made their way to the library, and almost all those who did headed straight for the crime section in search of a well-thumbed paperback. *War and Peace* had gathered dust on the shelf for the past twenty years, serving its own life sentence.

Miles had taken advantage of being alone during those endless sixty-minute hours. He began his day by reading the *Financial Times*, which was delivered by an officer along with his morning coffee. After lunch in the canteen, he returned to the library to turn the pages of the latest novel he was reading. During those years of incarceration he'd read everything from Daphne du Maurier to Thomas Hardy, and by the time he was released, he could have taken an English degree at Oxford, which had turned him down thirty years before.

The governor dropped in for a chat from time to time, when they exchanged confidences over coffee and a plate of shortbread biscuits – his coffee and the governor's shortbread biscuits. It quickly became clear that Miles knew more about what was going on in the prison than the governor did. Inside information he traded, ensuring further supplies of biscuits during his coffee breaks.

But during all those exiled years in New York only one thing remained constantly on his mind. *When will it be safe for me to return to London and exact revenge on first Warwick, then Hogan, and finally the commander?*

CHAPTER 2

WILLIAM AND ROSS SAT ON the edge of their seats in the back of the Land Rover. They peered out of a side window as familiar landmarks shot by and, although the journey back to the palace wouldn't take more than fifteen minutes, they were both aware it was the one time something could go wrong. And if it did, then fifteen minutes of infamy would be the only thing they were remembered for.

Five police outriders from the Special Escort Group accompanied them across the middle drawbridge at a courtly pace, but once they'd passed under East Gate and were back on St Katharine's Way, any speed limit was ignored. At every red light, the traffic was held up by two of the outriders, while two more sped through to the next light, and carried out the same procedure, thus ensuring the convoy was never held up.

William looked out of the front window to admire the polished drill of his colleagues. While one motorcycle shot ahead to the next crossing where he would hold up the traffic with a sharp blast on his whistle, the second drove straight past him and continued until he'd reached the next intersection, where he would carry out the same drill. While that was happening, the two motorcycles hovering behind the convoy would take their place in front of the Lord Chamberlain's car, and once the lead pair had ensured a smooth passage for their VIP, the first bike would once again shoot ahead and repeat the exercise, while the pair who had been holding up the traffic would slip in behind the Land Rover in a seamless relay that made it possible for the convoy to maintain a speed of around forty mph, while the rest of London's traffic was averaging about eight, or if they were lucky, maybe nine miles an hour.

William and Ross continued to check in every direction as they sped through Blackfriars and onto the Embankment, touching speeds of sixty, occasionally seventy mph. They shot past the back of the Savoy Hotel, blissfully unaware that Miles Faulkner and Mr Booth Watson QC were about to order lunch in the Grill and humble pie wasn't on the menu.

• • •

Miles put down the menu when he spotted his lawyer waddling towards him. The lines on his forehead seemed more pronounced, and the pace was definitely slower. Booth Watson was dressed in a well-tailored double-breasted suit that attempted to hide his ample frame, a pale blue shirt and a creased Middle Temple tie. He was carrying a Gladstone bag that looked as if it was permanently attached to his hand.

'Welcome back, Miles,' he said as he leant over and shook hands with his most remunerative client, before slumping down into the chair opposite him. He placed the Gladstone bag on the floor by his side.

A few platitudes were exchanged, which neither of them believed, before a waiter appeared. Miles took his time perusing the contents of the large leather-bound menu, not sure where to start. Booth Watson, on the other hand, had selected both his courses and a wine he considered would complement them even before Miles had turned to the second page.

'I'll have the sirloin steak, rare,' said Booth Watson, handing the menu back to the waiter.

'And for you, sir?' asked the waiter, turning his attention to Miles.

'The smoked salmon.' Another dish that hadn't found its way to the Scrubs. 'Bring me up to date on what Hawksby, Warwick and Hogan have been up to in my absence,' he said once the waiter had departed.

'Commander Hawksby is still in overall charge of the Royalty Protection squad, while Superintendent Warwick remains his second-in-command.'

'And Hogan?' demanded Miles, not hiding the disdain in his voice.

'Inspector Hogan is no longer Princess Diana's personal protection officer as the authorities thought they were getting a little too close for comfort, so he's been transferred back to the Yard.'

'So what are they all up to?'

'Today, for example,' said Booth Watson, 'the Lord Chamberlain is being driven from Buckingham Palace to the Tower of London to pick up the Crown Jewels in preparation for tomorrow's State Opening of Parliament. Warwick and Hogan are part of the back-up team, and tomorrow they will escort the Crown Jewels back to the Tower, a responsibility they carry out once a year.'

'As you are clearly so well-informed,' said Miles, 'I assume Lamont is still on the payroll?'

'The retired superintendent is still part of my team, and I can assure you he feels the same way about Warwick and Hogan as you do, so will continue to keep me informed on what those two are up to.'

'Now I'm back, you can tell him to redouble his efforts. It remains a priority for me to see those two humiliated, and it would be a bonus if you could throw in Hawksby.'

'Now you've returned to London, Miles, don't you think it might be wise to put all that behind you and keep a low profile?'

'Not a chance. In fact I've thought of little else since Warwick had his say in court. Have you forgotten he was responsible for me ending up in jail? I won't be satisfied until I've repaid the compliment and he finds out what it's like to be deprived of his freedom. I don't give a damn what it costs – he and those who were responsible for that must be humiliated.'

'But I would have thought—'

'Then you can think again, BW, because I look forward to the day when the Lord Chamberlain escorts them both to the Tower and leaves them there.'

Booth Watson stared at his pay cheque and thought again about trying to change his client's mind. Then he remembered Faulkner's face as he'd stood in the dock and realized he wouldn't rest until he'd had his revenge on Warwick, Hogan, and Hawksby. Nothing Booth Watson could say would change that. He satisfied himself instead with sipping a rare Bordeaux he hadn't enjoyed for some time.

'Are there any other problems I should be considering?' Miles asked as a waiter appeared with their main courses.

The ever-reliable accomplice bent down, extracted a copy of yesterday's *New York Times* from his Gladstone bag and handed it to Miles. He waited for the volcano to erupt.

'Stop playing games, BW, and tell me what I'm meant to be looking for.'

'Page forty-three,' said Booth Watson as he tucked into his steak.

Miles flicked through the pages, not stopping until he reached page forty-three, which he studied for some time before saying, 'I'm none the wiser.'

'In the property section you'll find a luxury flat on East 61st Street is up for sale.'

'I'm well aware my Manhattan pad is on the market,' said Miles, 'but what you don't know is that I've recently purchased the penthouse in the same building, so no longer need the ninth-floor flat. So, unless you're thinking of buying it, BW, stop wasting my time.' He tossed the paper to one side before squeezing half a lemon over his smoked salmon.

'I suggest, Miles, that you take a closer look at the advertisement,' said Booth Watson, well aware he wasn't wasting his time.

Miles reluctantly picked the paper back up and studied the details of a five-bedroom luxury apartment in Manhattan, overlooking Central Park. Offer price, seven million dollars. After a second look at the accompanying photo, the volcano finally erupted. 'Who the hell allowed that to happen?' he said, loud enough for one of the diners on the next table to look around.

'I'm not your estate agent,' said Booth Watson calmly, 'just a humble QC who does his best to protect your backside.'

'Have that photograph removed immediately,' said Miles, almost as loudly.

'I already have,' said Booth Watson, a smile of satisfaction appearing on his face. 'I've also given instructions that that particular photograph is not to appear in any future sales material.'

Miles continued to stare at a photo of Rubens' *Christ's Descent from the Cross* that was hanging on the wall in the drawing room of his Manhattan apartment, for a million readers to admire.

'I feel sure I don't have to remind you, Miles, that the art world is under the illusion that that particular masterpiece is currently gracing the walls of the Fitzmolean Museum and not your New York apartment.'

'Should anyone ask,' murmured Miles, leaning across the table, 'make it clear that mine is a copy.'

'But if an interested party were by chance to come across the ad and decided to check—' began Booth Watson as the sommelier appeared by his side to refill his empty glass. Booth Watson waited for him to move on to another table before he continued. 'I don't have to remind you, Miles, that you gifted the original to the museum in exchange for a lesser sentence, and should the CPS find out—'

'That must never be allowed to happen,' snapped Miles, not touching his wine.

'It doesn't help,' added BW, 'that the director has recently announced his retirement, and I have it on good authority that Mrs Beth Warwick is the favourite to replace him.'

'Something else that must never be allowed to happen, because if she ever suspected her Christ was not the Saviour, the first person she'd inform would be her husband.' He paused before lowering his voice and saying, 'Is there anything we can do to prevent it?'

'Your ex-wife is still a member of the board and should

therefore be able to influence the outcome. She might just be persuaded . . .'

'I wouldn't trust that woman as far as I could throw her,' said Miles. 'Don't forget she's a close friend of Mrs Warwick and would be only too happy to double-cross me given the slightest opportunity.'

'Agreed,' said Booth Watson. 'However, as you well know, Christina's a little short of cash at the moment, so perhaps . . .'

'But I was the cause of that,' said Miles, 'just in case you've forgotten.'

'All the more reason to give her some back?' suggested Booth Watson, raising an eyebrow.

'Possibly,' said Miles as he devoured a sliver of smoked salmon while BW emptied his second glass of wine. 'First, find out if she's seen the ad in the *New York Times*, which seems unlikely. If she has, you can be sure she'll send Mrs Warwick a copy – open at the right page.'

'I'll need a reason for seeing her if I'm not going to make her suspicious.'

'Once you're confident she hasn't seen the article, you can tell her I don't want Superintendent Warwick's wife to be the next director of the Fitzmolean, and I will pay good money to make sure it doesn't happen. Christina won't find that hard to believe.'

Booth Watson dug into his steak and smiled as the blood began to run.

• • •

Danny sped past the Savoy, only slowing down when the Special Escort Group swung right into Northumberland

Avenue to see no other vehicle in sight. More bells and whistles allowed them to proceed across Trafalgar Square and into the Mall unimpeded before they continued on their way towards Buckingham Palace.

Startled tourists tried to take photographs as they shot by, wondering if it was a member of the Royal Family seated in the back of the car with blacked-out windows.

When they finally reached the huge gates at the entrance to the palace, no one stepped forward to demand, 'Halt, who goes there?' A sentry presented arms as the car entered the courtyard, went through an archway and disappeared into an inner sanctum, to find two young subalterns from the Irish Guards standing to attention waiting to collect 'the swag' as it was known in the officers' mess.

Phil Harris was first to leap out when the Jaguar came to a halt. Once he'd opened the back door for the Lord Chamberlain, he quickly unlocked the boot and stood aside to allow the two guardsmen to take over. One of them removed the box containing the Sword of State, while the other gently lifted the Imperial State Crown out of the boot as if it were his first born.

William watched as the three men turned their backs on him and marched away. The Lord Chamberlain would return at one o'clock tomorrow afternoon when they would escort him and the Crown Jewels back home after their night out.

'Let's get going,' said William once the two subalterns had disappeared into the palace.

Danny drove slowly out of the inner courtyard and on to Buckingham Gate, before heading back to Scotland Yard, not once breaking the speed limit.

'It's always puzzled me,' said Ross as they turned into Petty France, 'why they bother to deliver the crown to Buckingham

Palace, when we could always take it direct to the House of Lords.'

'I can think of two reasons,' said William. 'First, I wouldn't trust their Lordships with the Crown Jewels overnight – after all, there might well be a Colonel Blood among them. And second, don't forget, the Sword of State and the Imperial State Crown have their own carriage which precedes Her Majesty whenever she travels from Buckingham Palace to the House of Lords before delivering the Queen's Speech.'

Ross nodded before admitting, 'I couldn't sleep last night.'

'Why not?' said William, turning to face his friend.

'I always assume something will go wrong during the transfer and let's face it, it only needs to go wrong once!'

'Unlikely while they're so well protected and only we know the details of the transfer. In any case, the public never think about the Crown Jewels being out of the Tower for a couple of days. Why should they?'

Ross remained silent while he considered the possibility that . . .

When Danny pulled up outside Scotland Yard, William was the first to leap out. He walked quickly into the building and took the stairs to the second floor two at a time, before knocking on the door of the Hawk's office.

'Enter!' bellowed a voice.

William immediately informed the commander that the annual exercise had once again gone without a hitch.

'I will only relax,' said the Hawk, 'when the Resident Governor calls me to confirm the Imperial State Crown and the Sword of State have been returned to the Jewel House and are safely locked up for another year.'

So Ross wasn't the only one who thought that way, was William's immediate reaction. He sometimes forgot that if anything were to go wrong during those critical fifteen minutes, he wouldn't be the only person who would have to resign.

'Well, I'd better get back to the day job,' said William.

'Before you leave, Chief Superintendent, there's something else we need to discuss.' It took William a few moments for the news to sink in. 'The commissioner called earlier this morning to confirm your promotion. Many congratulations, William. Heaven knows, you've earned it.'

Unusually lost for words, William eventually managed to say, 'Thank you, sir.'

'I suggest, Chief Superintendent, you forget the day job for a change. Go home and spend some time with Beth and the children. Just make sure you're back at the palace in time to collect the State Crown and Sword before returning them to the Tower. Because if they're not safely back in place by this time tomorrow, it might become your permanent residence.'

• • •

'Why are you home so early, caveman?' asked Beth when William strolled into the kitchen. 'Have you been sacked?'

'No, promoted,' said William. He smiled as the expression on Beth's face changed when he told her his news but was taken by surprise by her response.

'Snap!'

'Snap?' queried William.

'The director of the Fitzmolean has resigned, and the chairman has just phoned to say he hoped I would apply for the position.'

'That's wonderful news,' said William, taking his wife in his arms. Although he'd never raised the subject since she'd resigned as deputy director, he'd always hoped Beth would return to the Fitz as the museum's director.

'I haven't got the job yet, Chief Superintendent.'

'The board won't make that mistake a second time,' said William confidently.

'To be honest, I still haven't decided if I really want the job,' said Beth.

'You must be joking!'

'Don't forget I'm earning almost twice as much as a dealer as I would if I returned to the Fitz as director.'

'Then it's a good thing I've been made up to Chief Superintendent.'

'And there's the Christina problem,' continued Beth. 'Now she and Faulkner are divorced, she relies on fifty per cent of our company's profits to keep up her present lifestyle.'

'Don't lose a moment's sleep over that woman,' said William, his tone changing. 'If your positions were reversed, she'd only do what was in her best interest.'

'You seem to forget, Chief Superintendent,' countered Beth, 'that when I was sacked from the Fitzmolean, Christina was the only person who was willing to back my fledgling company.'

'And very well she's done out of it!' William reminded her.

'No more than she deserved,' snapped Beth, 'which is why I consider her not just a partner but a close friend.'

'When it suits her. And if she's such a close friend,' suggested William, 'she'll be delighted to hear you could be the next director of the Fitzmolean. Don't forget she's on the board so will have a vote. Anyway, she knows only too well you've always wanted the job, so it will hardly come as a surprise. And I repeat, when push comes to shove, she'd happily shove you out of the way if it suited her purpose.'

'But—' began Beth as the kitchen door burst open and three hungry children came charging into the room. They took their seats at the table, mouths open like chicks in a nest expecting to be fed.

'You'll never believe what Peter and me have been chosen to do,' said Artemisia, bringing them both back down to earth.

'Peter and I,' said Beth.

'. . . we've been selected by our head teacher to represent the school in a national essay competition and—'

'. . . the winner,' continued Peter, 'will visit Disneyland in Paris and stay overnight at a hotel.'

'An hotel,' said Beth.

'And have tea with Donald Duck and Mickey Mouse,' proclaimed Artemisia.

'What subject have you chosen to write about?' asked William.

'We haven't decided yet,' admitted Artemisia.

'We were rather hoping, Dad,' continued Peter, 'that you might come up with some ideas. With all your experience of catching criminals—'

'Not a hope,' said William firmly. 'It's not me who's been chosen to represent the school. This has to be your work and yours alone, otherwise I might as well collect the prize.'

'I'll have to ask Uncle Ross,' Artemisia whispered to her brother. 'I once overheard Dad telling Mum there are no rules left for him to break.'

• • •

Once the children had been packed off to school the following morning, Beth began to open the mail. Bills, circulars, and one letter that needed to be read a second time.

'What are you doing this weekend?' she asked.

William put down his paper and thought for a moment. 'I'm on the duty rota. It's my one in four. Ross is taking the children to Legoland, it's the new rage,' he added as he buttered a second slice of toast. 'And you?'

'I was planning to visit the Fitz and see how much it's changed since I left. But I'm now thinking of driving to Buckingham and visiting an old lady I've never met before.'

'Sounds intriguing,' said William. 'So far the only clue is the envelope you're still clutching.'

'It's from a Mrs Eileen Lomax, the widow of Gordon Lomax, a West End art dealer who died last month,' said Beth. 'I sent her a letter of condolence and she's replied thanking me and asking if I could visit her as she needs some advice on a private matter.'

'I need more clues,' said William as Beth removed two eggs from a saucepan of boiling water and dropped them into the egg cups in front of him.

'Lomax owned one of the most successful galleries in the West End but, following the collapse of the market for Dutch landscapes, it's thought he wasn't doing much better than breaking even.'

'Death, debt and divorce, as you so often remind me,' said William, 'are the art dealer's best friends.'

'And two of those might well apply in Gordon Lomax's case. So I think I'll put off my planned visit to the Fitz and make the journey to Buckingham instead. Gordon was very kind to me when I first joined the art world so it's the least I can do.'

'And to think you could have gone to Legoland with Ross and the children,' teased William, picking up a teaspoon and cracking his egg.

'Perhaps I'll find a Rembrandt or a Vermeer gathering dust in her attic,' said Beth as William removed the top of his egg to find it was hard-boiled.

CHAPTER 3

The Irish State Coach, pulled by a team of four greys and escorted by a guard of honour, clip-clopped out of the palace gates and onto the Mall as Big Ben struck eleven.

Her Majesty the Queen, in lilac silk and wearing a diadem, sat on one side of the carriage, while the Duke of Edinburgh sat bolt upright opposite her, bedecked in the uniform of an Admiral of the Fleet, one hand resting on his sword. Ahead of them trundled Queen Alexandra's State Coach, carrying the royal regalia – the Imperial State Crown, the Sword of State and the Cap of Maintenance, accompanied by a dozen mounted officers from the Household Cavalry with the Blues and Royals acting as the Queen's ceremonial bodyguards.

Large crowds had gathered along the Mall to view the spectacle. Some had been waiting for hours to secure a place in the front row so they could cheer the monarch as she passed by. The familiar wave was accompanied by a smile as she switched her attention from one side of the road to the other. As they passed the Mall Galleries, the two state carriages swung right, and proceeded across Horse Guards and through the main archway onto Whitehall, a privilege afforded only to a reigning monarch.

An even larger crowd awaited them in Parliament Square and began to cheer long before the royal party had reached the Sovereign's Entrance to the House of Lords, where only moments before the Union Flag had been lowered, to be replaced by the Royal Standard.

As she climbed out of the carriage, the Queen was greeted by the Earl Marshal of England, the Lord Great Chamberlain and Black Rod. They bowed before leading her slowly up the wide blue and white carpeted staircase preceded by two Heralds, each bearing a mace declaring her authority. The royal party accompanied the monarch to the door of the Robing Room on the first floor, but no further.

Only a select few were permitted to join the sovereign in the Robing Room, where she disappeared behind two large red screens in the far corner of the room. The Queen removed the diadem she had worn during her journey in the State Coach to Westminster and placed it on the table by her side. Mrs Kelly, her dresser, assisted Her Majesty as she put on the long red robe and fixed the wide satin straps onto her shoulders, hooking them tightly on to their clasps to ensure the heavy garment remained in place.

Once the Queen was satisfied, Mrs Kelly opened the two red screens wide enough to allow the Lord Chamberlain to present the sovereign with the Imperial State Crown. She lifted the crown from its plush crimson cushion, placed it on her head and checked in the mirror, twisting it from side to side until it felt comfortable. She was once again reminded just how heavy the crown was.

Moments later, two pageboys stepped forward to join her. They picked up the satin handles on each side of the robe so the Queen could set off on her procession to join their Lordships in the Upper Chamber.

At 11.26 a.m., the Queen left the Robing Room on the arm of her consort. They entered the Royal Gallery to be greeted by two vast landscape paintings of Wellington at Waterloo on one side and Nelson at the Battle of Trafalgar on the other. When President de Gaulle had been invited to address both Houses, a detour was arranged so that he never saw the two conquering heroes. On each side of the Queen as she proceeded slowly along the red carpet were temporary fitted benches, occupied by ambassadors, high commissioners and foreign dignitaries, and the husbands and wives of peers.

The Queen left the Royal Gallery and crossed the Prince's Chamber, never breaking her stride as she passed the imposing figure of a young Queen Victoria before entering the House of Lords. Five hundred men and seventy women, bedecked in long ermine-trimmed red robes, rose to greet their sovereign before she sat on the throne as eleven thirty struck. The Duke of Edinburgh took his place on her right, while the seat on her left remained unoccupied.

She looked up at the far end of the chamber to see the Prime Minister and the Leader of the Opposition, along with ministers and their shadows, standing at the bar of the House. They would be entrusted to translate into acts of law the proposed bills the monarch was about to recite. John Major waited to hear the speech although he knew every word it contained.

The Lord Chancellor stepped forward, climbed the three steps to the throne and handed the Queen's Speech to the monarch, though in truth she hadn't been responsible for one word of its content. That task had been left to several seasoned mandarins dotted around Whitehall after being instructed by the Prime Minister and members of his recently appointed cabinet.

Her Majesty opened the red leather cover that bore her crest and glanced down at the opening line. '*My Lords and members of the House of Commons. My government will be making a priority of building more houses to accommodate an increasing population. My government will also be presenting statutes that ensure . . .*'

During the next twenty minutes, the Queen announced seven new bills her government would enact, but only she could finally sanction. Her Majesty ended with the words, '*Other orders and statutes will be placed before your Lordships in due course.*' The Queen looked up from the final paragraph before saying, '*God bless the Commonwealth.*'

The House rose again as Her Majesty made her way out of the Upper Chamber, accompanied by the Duke of Edinburgh. The Earl Marshal led the royal couple slowly back to the Robing Room where the Queen surrendered her crown, disrobed and, after a few words with the pageboys, walked back down the steps to the Sovereign's Entrance where the Irish State Coach awaited her.

Prince Philip climbed into the coach and waited for the Queen to join him before the four horses set off once again to take the monarch back to Buckingham Palace. The Imperial State Crown and Sword of State had already preceded them in their own carriage, while her dresser would follow later in a Rolls-Royce carrying all the surplus regalia in a large red bag to be stored away for another year – and possibly another Prime Minister?

• • •

Danny stood to attention when the Irish State Coach trundled through the archway and across the inner courtyard. The two footmen on the back of the carriage may have remained still, but their eyes were moving in every direction. He recognized one of them as a Royalty Protection officer, suitably dressed for the occasion.

William and Ross bowed when the Queen passed by while the four horses threw their heads in the air as they came to a halt outside the entrance door. An equerry and two footmen were waiting for Her Majesty as she got out of the carriage and made her way back into her townhouse.

Moments later, two Guards officers appeared carrying the black boxes that contained the Crown Jewels. The Lord Chamberlain followed a few paces behind. Phil Harris opened the boot of the Jaguar and waited for the treasures to be safely locked inside before taking his place behind the wheel, the sign that the outriders could set off on their journey back to the Tower of London. They took off immediately, clear roads and green lights making it possible for them to cross the middle drawbridge and enter the East Gate of the Tower thirteen minutes later, where they found the Resident Governor and the Chief Warder waiting for them outside the Jewel House.

William jumped out of the back of the Land Rover and watched the ancient ceremony being played out in reverse. The Lord Chamberlain and the Governor disappeared into the Jewel House, accompanied by the two Jewel House Warders carrying the treasures.

William relaxed only when the Lord Chamberlain reappeared empty-handed, got back into his car and set off on the return journey to the palace.

Danny would have followed him if the Governor hadn't

reappeared, headed straight for their car and tapped on the window. William jumped out, fearing something must have gone wrong.

'Chief Superintendent, you may not be aware that I will be retiring at the end of the year, so if you and the children would like a tour of the castle and the chance to see the Crown Jewels, I'd be only too happy to act as your guide.'

'How kind of you, general,' said William. 'May I also include Inspector Hogan's daughter, Jojo, who lives with us and whom we all look upon as a member of the family?'

'Of course,' responded the Governor. 'However, the invitation does not include the Inspector as I have a feeling that, given half a chance, Hogan might try to steal the Crown Jewels.'

William watched as the Governor hurried off, not altogether sure he was joking. But then William would have been the first to admit that Ross didn't always keep to the letter of the law and on more than one occasion had stepped over the line and had to face the consequences. His natural charm and good looks regularly got him off the hook with his female colleagues and, in truth, the Hawk cut him far more slack than he did with any other officer. However, William could only wonder when Ross would go one step too far and he would find there was nothing he could do to help him.

'Job done for another year,' said William as he climbed back into the car, tapped Danny on the shoulder and added, 'Back to the Yard.'

'What did the Governor want?' asked Ross as they drove over the middle drawbridge, out of the rear entrance of the Tower and onto St Katharine's Way, where they were held up at the first set of traffic lights.

'General Stanley told me he retires at the end of the year

and wondered if the children, including Jojo, would like to visit the Tower as his guests,' said William, not voicing any other sentiments the Resident Governor may have expressed.

'So what's next for us?'

'The commander assures me he has something a bit special to get our teeth into but refused to divulge any details until the Crown Jewels were safely back in the Tower.'

'Now that he's back in England,' said Ross, 'let's hope "special" includes going after Miles Faulkner again. I've still got a couple of scores to settle with that man.'

'Seems unlikely,' said William. 'After all, Faulkner hasn't appeared on our radar since he was released from Ford over four years ago. Although I find it hard to believe he's retired.'

'In case you've forgotten,' said Ross, with some feeling, 'that man was responsible for my wife's death.'

CHAPTER 4

Once William had left for the Yard on Saturday morning and Ross had picked up the children and taken them off to Legoland for the day, Beth set out for Buckingham, but not before she'd given Mark Poltimore a call at Sotheby's, as she needed his advice before she met Mrs Lomax.

'The Lomax Gallery has been around for three generations,' Mark reminded her. 'However, it's well-known that Gordon Lomax had been struggling for some time after the recession hit. What might also interest you is that a couple of years ago he asked us to value his stock for probate, so he must have known he didn't have long to live.'

'Can you give me a ballpark figure?' asked Beth hopefully.

'Not something I can reveal,' said Mark. 'But of course, Mrs Lomax might be willing to tell you.'

Armed with this information, Beth thanked Mark, put down the phone and began to leaf through her AA handbook. Once she'd settled on the most direct route, she set off for Buckingham. She would have made good time had it not been for the countless roundabouts she encountered between Buckingham and her destination that the AA guide had failed to mention.

As she stepped out of the car, the front door of the little ivy-clad cottage, which could have been painted by Helen Allingham, opened to reveal an elderly lady standing in the doorway, who had clearly been waiting for her. From her appearance, Mrs Lomax might also have been Victorian, attired as she was in a long faded floral dress that didn't allow you to see her ankles. Her thick grey hair was tied up in a bun with what looked like a knitting needle stuck through it. She wore no jewellery and, although it was a warm day, she had a thick shawl draped around her shoulders.

'It's so kind of you to come all this way, Mrs Warwick,' were her first words as Beth entered the house. Mrs Lomax closed the door and led her guest through to a lounge littered with old oak furniture and ancient bric-a-brac. A few Victorian watercolours adorned the walls, but none that would have excited even a provincial auction house.

No sooner had they sat down than a maid who might have come out of a Daphne du Maurier novel appeared, carrying a tray on which rested a teapot covered in a crocheted cosy, alongside a plate of chocolate digestive biscuits. Beth was reminded of her half-term visits to Kardomah Café in Piccadilly for afternoon tea with what her mother imagined were the gentry.

'Milk and sugar?' Mrs Lomax asked once the tray had been placed on the table between them.

'Milk, no sugar, thank you,' said Beth as she settled into the corner of a sofa already occupied by a large ginger cat who clearly had no intention of moving. After handing Beth a cup, her host offered her a biscuit which Beth placed on the chipped Wedgwood plate beside her.

'You must be wondering, Mrs Warwick, why I wanted to see you.'

Beth considered asking her to call her Beth but thought better of it. 'I was delighted to come,' she said. 'When I first entered the art world after leaving university, your husband was among the few people who welcomed me as if I were his equal. Something you don't forget when you're young.'

'Gordon thought very highly of you, my dear,' ventured Mrs Lomax, 'and made no secret of the fact he hoped you would eventually become director of the Fitzmolean, as he didn't have a lot of time for the present occupant. However, I read in *The Times* he'd recently resigned.'

Only just before he was sacked, Beth didn't add.

'Should I presume you are now the favourite to replace him? Because if you are, I can tell you nothing would have pleased my husband more.'

Beth felt guilty that she hadn't attended the funeral. 'Thank you,' she said. 'I'm on the shortlist, but there are three other candidates who are also well qualified for the job.'

'I'm sure you'll get it,' said Mrs Lomax with a confidence that lacked authority. 'But as I said, you must be wondering why I wanted to see you.'

'I assume it concerns the gallery,' replied Beth, 'and I'm only too delighted to help, if only to point you in the right direction.'

'Can I top you up?' asked Mrs Lomax, picking up the teapot.

'No, thank you,' said Beth, keen to find out the answer to the old lady's question.

'I do hope Oliver isn't bothering you, my dear.'

Beth looked at the cat, who hadn't stirred or purred, and said, 'Not at all.'

'We named him Oliver because we weren't quite sure who his parents were.'

Mrs Lomax sipped her tea before she continued. 'Gordon's grandfather, as you may know, founded the company in 1873 and, under his stewardship, it flourished for many years until his death in 1919, when Gordon's father, Bertie, became chairman following the Great War.'

Three words that dated an entire generation, thought Beth.

'When my husband took over,' Mrs Lomax continued with a sigh, 'Dutch landscapes were much sought after. However, that changed soon after the end of the Second World War, which coincided with Gordon taking over the reins. Although the gallery remained prosperous for several years, my husband's most loyal customers began dying off, and it quickly became clear that Dutch landscapes were no longer fashionable, especially among the young.' She paused and took another sip of tea. 'I confess it's been some years since the gallery has made a profit.' It was some time before she continued. 'Sadly, Gordon and I weren't able to have any children, so there's no one to leave the gallery to.'

Beth didn't interrupt the old lady as, so far, she hadn't revealed anything she didn't already know.

'But then a kind gentleman who I'd never come across before turned up at the funeral to pay his respects. During tea following the service, he rather took me by surprise when he asked if I had considered selling the gallery, and if so, he had a client who might be interested.'

Who, and how much, Beth wanted to ask, but kept her counsel, like a well-trained detective.

'Such a kind man,' Mrs Lomax repeated. 'You know, he gave the vicar a donation of a thousand pounds for the church restoration fund—' she paused again, 'in memory of Gordon.'

Beth was now desperate to find out who and how much but waited patiently for Mrs Lomax to tell her in her own good time.

'Sotheby's have recently valued the gallery's stock at around a million pounds, and the kind gentleman said his client would be willing to match that. I've never had a head for figures, so I just wanted to be sure I was doing the right thing and thought you were the obvious person to advise me.'

'Does the company have any assets other than the stock?' was Beth's first question.

'The gallery in Jermyn Street which I couldn't possibly afford to keep going. In fact, I've just received a rates bill for the next quarter of twenty-six thousand pounds which I can ill-afford. So, the quicker I get it off my hands, the better.'

'That's no more than the going rate for a gallery in the West End,' Beth assured her.

'I don't suppose you would have any interest in taking it over, Mrs Warwick?'

'I'm afraid not, Mrs Lomax,' said Beth firmly. 'I fear your husband was right. I'd be more suited to managing a public gallery than a private one.'

Mrs Lomax couldn't hide her disappointment.

'However,' added Beth, 'my father has spent his life working in the property market, so I could ask his opinion, if you'd like me to.'

'That would be most kind.'

'Why don't I give him a call while I'm with you,' said Beth, 'and find out his initial reaction.'

'Would you?' asked Mrs Lomax. 'I'd be most grateful.'

'I'd be delighted to,' said Beth. Without another word she took out her mobile phone and dialled her parents' home.

'What number in Jermyn Street?' she asked as the phone began to ring.

'12A,' Mrs Lomax replied as a voice came on the line.

'Dad,' Beth began, 'I need your advice on a property matter, to make sure I haven't missed something.'

Arthur Rainsford listened carefully as his daughter offered a précis of everything Mrs Lomax had told her.

'You haven't missed anything,' was her father's immediate response. 'Almost all the commercial properties in Mayfair are owned by the Crown or the Grosvenor Estate. And you can be pretty certain the gallery will be on a short-term lease. Twenty-five years at most, with five-year upward rent reviews. The going rate is around a hundred thousand a year, according to the square footage, so the rates will be the least of her problems.'

'So a million for the stock is beginning to sound like a fair deal?'

'That's your world, not mine,' said her father. 'But I'll make a couple of discreet enquiries and call you back just in case we've both missed something.'

'Thank you, Dad. We're all looking forward to visiting next weekend,' said Beth before she rang off.

'That's most helpful,' said Mrs Lomax, once Beth had passed on her father's opinion. 'The timing couldn't be better because the kind gentleman has sent me a contract to consider over the weekend and promised he would telephone on Monday to find out if I've made up my mind.'

Beth had another cup of tea before she left while Mrs Lomax told her how she'd watched the Queen's coronation on a black and white television in 1953 and had seen Dame Edith Evans playing the nurse in *Romeo and Juliet* at Stratford-upon-Avon in 1960 . . . or was it '61? However, her most abiding memory was . . .

'I ought to be leaving, Mrs Lomax . . .' Beth suggested for a third time.

'Won't you stay for lunch, my dear? Janet's fishcakes are considered quite exceptional.'

'I'm sure they are, Mrs Lomax, but I'd like to be back before the children return from their trip to Legoland.'

'Legoland?' queried Mrs Lomax, which meant it was another fifteen minutes, while Beth explained to the old lady, who only possessed oak furniture, what Lego was. She finally escaped after a third cup of tea.

Beth had reached the seventh roundabout when the phone in her car began to ring. She pulled into a layby and picked up the phone to hear a familiar voice.

'Where are you?' her father asked.

'Just about to join the A5. Should be back in London in about an hour.'

'I want you to turn around and go back to Buckingham immediately. Find a hotel, book a room for me and another for your father-in-law.'

'Dare I ask why?' said Beth.

'Because the kind man isn't quite as kind as Mrs Lomax thought he was, and as he'll be calling back on Monday morning, time isn't on our side.'

'Then I'll have to return and tell Mrs Lomax I'll be delighted to sample Janet's fishcakes.'

CHAPTER 5

BOOTH WATSON SAT ALONE IN chambers, well aware Mrs Faulkner would be late. She always imagined it would give her an advantage. But while her bank balance was consistently overdrawn, she was at a perpetual disadvantage.

Mrs Faulkner finally turned up at eighteen minutes past three without any suggestion of an apology. As she took the seat opposite him, BW once again admired how immaculately turned out she was, although he suspected it now took her a little longer to achieve. Her couture outfit reminded him why her suit wasn't the only thing in red.

'How nice to see you again,' Booth Watson said, 'and how well you're looking,' he added as she made herself comfortable.

'Cut the crap, BW. You only ever ask to see me when you want something. So what is it this time?'

Booth Watson couldn't fault her logic, but had his next line well prepared. 'Can I assume you and Mrs Warwick are still bosom pals?'

'As well as business partners,' Christina reminded him.

'An association that would end were she to become the next director of the Fitzmolean.'

'Don't remind me,' said Christina a little too quickly.

'Which, no doubt, would make a considerable dent in your income,' suggested Booth Watson.

Christina didn't immediately comment on Booth Watson's double-edged riposte. 'What's going on in that devious mind of yours, BW?' she finally asked.

'It might not come as a complete surprise that Miles, like you, wouldn't be disappointed if Mrs Warwick failed to become the new director of the Fitz.' He leant back and lit a cigarette, while he waited to find out how she would react. If she raised the subject of the fake Rubens hanging in the Fitzmolean, he accepted it was going to cost Miles a lot of money. But not a word. And he knew from past experience that if Christina had a trump card, she always played it a little too early, so she couldn't have seen the advertisement in the *New York Times*. Thanks to his diligence, the ad had appeared only once, so it looked as if Miles had got away with it.

'Why would Miles give a damn who gets the job?' Christina queried.

A question Booth Watson was ready for. 'My dear Mrs Faulkner,' he began as he blew a large plume of smoke into the air. 'No one knows better than you how vindictive Miles can be, and he doesn't have a short memory.'

A judgement Christina felt unable to disagree with. 'But it will be the museum's board who will appoint the new director and I'll be a lone voice.'

'Then you'll need to be very persuasive, won't you?'

'But there are eleven other board members besides me,' she pointed out.

'You'll have to play Judas,' said Booth Watson without any hint of irony.

'And look where that got him.'

'All you have to do is convince five of your fellow board members that one of the other candidates is better qualified for the position.'

Christina considered the proposition and all its implications before she said, 'How much is Miles willing to pay?'

Another question he'd anticipated. 'Fifty thousand,' said Booth Watson. 'But only if you're successful.'

Christina sat in silence for a little longer before she said, 'Five thousand in advance,' she paused, 'as an act of good faith.'

'You drive a hard bargain, Mrs Faulkner,' said Booth Watson, who'd thought she'd ask for ten. He returned to his desk, opened the top drawer and took out five cellophane packets each containing a thousand pounds, before handing them over to his new recruit. He didn't tell her he'd been instructed to give her fifty thousand up front if she'd mentioned the Rubens that was hanging in Miles's New York flat. She hadn't, so he quickly closed the drawer.

• • •

'Arthur Rainsford.'

'Ah, yes sir,' said the hotel receptionist. 'Your daughter booked a room for you earlier this afternoon. Is Sir Julian Warwick with you?'

'No, but I expect him to join us within the next hour.'

'Then I'll keep a lookout for him,' she said before handing over a key. 'You're in room eleven, sir, on the first floor. Dinner will be served from seven, last orders at nine thirty.'

'Thank you,' said Arthur before he made his way up the narrow staircase to the first floor. The last thing on his mind was dinner. Once he'd unpacked, he sat down at a little desk overlooking the back lawn and went through the notes he'd made during his conversation with a director from the Crown Estate office. He was trying to calculate a fair price for the company when there was a knock at the door. He pushed back his chair, walked across the room and opened it to find Beth and Julian standing in the corridor.

'Enter,' he said with a sweeping gesture of the hand. He kissed his daughter on the cheek before shaking hands with Sir Julian. 'Take a seat, because we don't have a moment to waste if we're going to be ready in time. First, Beth, were you able to get answers to those questions I suggested over the phone?'

'Every one of them,' said Beth as she perched on the corner of the bed. 'Though it meant having to suffer a second helping of Janet's "exceptional" fishcakes. I even have the contract the kind and generous gentleman sent to Mrs Lomax for her to consider before he calls back on Monday morning.' Beth opened her bag, pulled out a thick document and handed it over to her father who turned to the last page and checked the bottom line.

'And if you consider a million is a fair price, Father,' continued Beth, 'Mrs Lomax will be happy to take your advice and sign the agreement.'

'It's a derisory offer that she would have fallen for had she not sought your advice,' came back Arthur's immediate reply, before passing the contract over to Sir Julian for his legal opinion. 'It turns out,' continued Arthur, 'that Bertie Lomax, Gordon's father, purchased a 999-year lease on number 12A Jermyn Street in 1942 for the princely sum of ten thousand pounds.'

'That sounds ridiculously cheap,' suggested Beth.

'Not while the Germans were dropping bombs all over London, and it looked as if Adolf Hitler might be your next landlord. Don't forget that in 1941 Christie's was razed to the ground, and Jermyn Street is only a hundred yards away.'

Beth hadn't realized.

'Bertie Lomax took one hell of a risk, I grant you, but one that turned out to be a shrewd long-term investment. Because I estimate the present value of 12A to be somewhere between one and one and a half million. So if Sir Julian can draw up a contract before the "kind and generous" gentleman calls Mrs Lomax on Monday morning, I'd be willing to throw in another million for the lease, and even make a ten thousand pound donation towards the church's restoration fund.'

'Drawing up a new contract between you and Mrs Lomax shouldn't prove too difficult,' said Sir Julian, 'as most of the work has already been done by someone who's clearly a practised member of my profession.'

'Do you think it was a lawyer who turned up to Mr Lomax's funeral uninvited?' said Beth.

'I most certainly do,' said Julian, 'and a very sharp one. You'll both have heard of ambulance-chasing lawyers, but you might not be quite as familiar with a more select group known as funeral-attending lawyers. They select their prey carefully and turn up to funerals assuming that most wives won't know all the details of their husbands' business affairs. When they leave, they pay their respects to the widow, but not before delivering an oft-repeated homily along the lines, "If there's anything I can do to assist you, dear lady, don't hesitate to call on me." They then hand over their card. I wouldn't be surprised if they threw in the term "pro-bono" for good measure because, I can assure you, it isn't their goodwill that's on offer.'

'When are you expecting to see Mrs Lomax again?' Arthur asked his daughter.

'I promised to accompany her to Matins tomorrow morning,' said Beth. 'She wants me to meet the vicar and learn more about his plans to repair the church roof, which she tells me is leaking again.'

'Then you can hand over a cheque for two million and let her decide how much she leaves in the offertory plate,' he said as a gong sounded for dinner.

'And if you're both very good,' said Beth, 'I might even tell you the name of the funeral-attending lawyer.' She took his business card out of her bag before leading them out of the room.

• • •

'My text this morning is taken from One Corinthians, chapter thirteen, beginning at verse thirteen,' intoned the vicar. 'Faith, hope, and charity, these three, but the greatest of these is charity,' he emphasized as he looked down from the pulpit at Mrs Lomax, who appeared captivated by his every word.

Beth had joined the widow for breakfast and made her an offer that had stopped her talking for more than a minute. They both listened to the rest of the sermon, which seemed to be aimed at an audience of one. In fact, Mrs Lomax remained on her knees long after the vicar had delivered the final blessing.

After the last of his congregation had departed, the vicar invited Mrs Lomax and her guest to join him in the vestry.

'I wanted you to be the first to hear the good news, vicar,' said Mrs Lomax as she entered his private domain. 'Mrs Warwick's father has offered me two million pounds for my late husband's gallery, including the stock, and after listening to your sermon, I've decided to donate half of it to the church's restoration fund.'

Both of them were left speechless by the widow's mite, but the vicar was the first to recover. 'You have single-handedly solved all our problems, my dear Mrs Lomax, and be assured, you will remain constantly in my prayers.'

'And don't forget my father is also willing to donate a further ten thousand towards such a worthwhile enterprise,' threw in Beth.

'Amen to that,' said the vicar, offering Beth the sign of the cross. 'Between you and Mr Booth Watson, you will have contributed one million and eleven thousand to the cause. God bless all three of you.'

'Why don't you join us for tea around three o'clock, vicar,' suggested Mrs Lomax, 'when I'll be signing the contract.'

'The feeding of the five thousand,' said the vicar, while Mrs Lomax looked as if she had already entered the promised land.

• • •

Beth, her father and Sir Julian arrived at the little thatched cottage just after three o'clock to find the vicar already in attendance.

The tea ceremony would have been worthy of a Japanese geisha, and another hour passed while Mrs Lomax took them from Vera Lynn singing to the forces during the war, on to the wedding of Charles and Diana at Westminster Abbey, ending on the recent Queen's Speech to the House of Lords, before Beth felt it safe to raise the subject of the contract. Once Mrs Lomax had nodded her approval, Sir Julian produced a three-page document which he placed on the table in front of her along with his pen.

Mrs Lomax immediately turned to the last page, signed the agreement, and handed the pen to the vicar so he could witness her signature.

'No, no,' interjected Sir Julian firmly. 'As the church will be a major beneficiary, it is important that the vicar remains at arm's length.'

Mrs Lomax immediately rang a little bell by her side and, when her housekeeper reappeared, asked her to do the honours.

Once all three copies had been signed by both parties and returned to Sir Julian's briefcase, Arthur handed Mrs Lomax a cheque for two million pounds. The beneficiary studied the figures for some time before she asked, 'Haven't you forgotten something, Mr Rainsford?'

Arthur looked puzzled.

'The ten thousand you promised to donate to the church's restoration fund?'

Arthur's expression shifted to embarrassment. 'Yes, of course,' he said. He took out his cheque book and wrote out a second offering which he handed to the vicar.

'Bless you,' the priest responded, but it was still another hour before they finally departed, along with a further blessing.

As Beth drove off, Arthur looked out of the window and waved at the old lady. Once she was out of sight, he remarked, 'That woman is not quite as naïve as she would have you believe. I have a feeling, Beth, she knew exactly who she was seeking advice from when she got in touch with you.'

CHAPTER 6

Mr Booth Watson spent some considerable time preparing questions on a yellow pad in front of him, along with several arrows pointing in different directions depending on Mrs Lomax's responses.

He'd already decided that if she accepted his offer of a million pounds for the gallery along with its stock, he would raise the money privately and sell it on to Miles for a million and a half, guaranteeing them both a worthwhile return. If she pushed him beyond his limit, he still intended to offer the deal to Miles and charge him ten per cent for his services. Either way he would make a handsome profit. He decided not to call Mrs Lomax before eleven, as he didn't want to appear overenthusiastic.

He ran through the questions one more time before picking up the phone. It took several rings before his call was answered.

'Buckingham 2418.'

'Good morning, Mrs Lomax,' said Booth Watson warmly.

'I was calling to ask if you'd had time to consider my offer of a million pounds for your husband's company?'

'More than enough time,' replied Mrs Lomax without hesitation, 'and I've decided to turn it down.'

'I could possibly increase my offer,' said Booth Watson, following an arrow across the page, 'to, say, one and a half million. But I fear that would be my limit.'

'I'm afraid you're too late, Mr Booth Watson,' she said. 'I've already accepted an offer of two million from another party, with whom I think you're well acquainted.'

It took Booth Watson only moments to work out who that had to be.

'Along with a donation of ten thousand for the church's restoration fund,' she added for good measure.

Booth Watson slammed down the phone and quickly picked it back up again, while at the same time searching for a number on his Rolodex. He began to dial the new number which seemed to take forever to answer.

'Midland Bank,' said a voice.

'Craig, it's Booth Watson.'

'Good morning, sir, how can I assist you?'

'That cheque for a thousand pounds made out to Buckingham Parish Church. I'd like to put a stop order on it.'

A long silence followed before Craig said, 'I'm afraid that cheque was cleared earlier this morning.'

Booth Watson slammed the phone down a second time, opened the top drawer of his desk and stared down at the cellophane packets that Miles had supplied if Christina had spotted the advertisement in the *New York Times*, and more importantly, recognized the Rubens. Perhaps she had?

• • •

Beth was the first to arrive for their annual lunch at the Ritz. Although she and Christina met regularly, Beth would allow only one partners' meeting a year to be charged on expenses, especially when Christina chose the venue.

The maître d' guided his guest across the elegant belle époque dining room to a table by the window overlooking Green Park. Beth wasn't surprised Christina was late. For her, a watch was an accessory, not a timepiece. However, it gave Beth a little more time to think about how she would break the news to her friend.

'Champagne, madam?' asked a hovering waiter.

'No, thank you,' replied Beth. 'A glass of tap water will be fine.' The maître d' quickly left her to deal with customers who didn't consider tap water was for drinking. Beth studied the menu and had already decided which salad she would select by the time Christina appeared at the entrance wearing a tight-fitting bright orange dress that testified to how many hours she spent on the treadmill. Beth couldn't recall seeing the dress before, though in truth she'd never known her friend wear the same outfit twice and wondered just how many wardrobes there must be in her flat. She then noticed Christina's shoes. Imelda Marcos would have been proud of her.

When Christina spotted her seated by the window, she began to weave her way across the room as if it were her personal catwalk, which achieved its purpose as several male heads turned to take a second look, and some a third, long before she reached her destination. She bent down and kissed her friend on both cheeks, as a glass of champagne appeared by her side, without needing to be ordered.

'You're looking gorgeous, my darling,' gushed Christina, although Beth was well aware she was once again playing Amelia Sedley to her friend's Becky Sharp. 'I can't wait to find out how our little enterprise has flourished this year,' she added before taking a sip of champagne.

'Shall I start with the good news or the bad news?' Beth enquired.

'Let's begin with the good news,' responded Christina. 'As I have a feeling I already know the bad.'

'Up until about a month ago, we were showing a reasonable return on your investment, without a great deal for me to report,' began Beth. 'That was until a ripe apple fell from an unlikely tree right into my lap.' Christina put down her glass. 'An apple that not only produced an unexpectedly juicy return but had the added bonus of leaving our mutual friend, Mr Booth Watson QC, out of pocket.'

Christina sat up, suddenly more attentive.

'The Lomax Gallery in Jermyn Street,' continued Beth, 'has recently come on the market following the untimely death of its proprietor, Gordon Lomax. Sotheby's have valued the gallery's stock at around a million pounds, but the corner site turned out to be worth at least another million.'

'But we don't have that sort of capital at our disposal,' interrupted Christina.

'True,' admitted Beth, 'but my father does. However, as he had no interest in the gallery's stock, I sold the pictures to Agnews for a million as Dutch landscapes have never been my bag.'

'Where's the profit?'

'Patience,' said Beth. 'My father then sold the gallery's long lease back to the Crown Estate for one million two hundred thousand, making a profit of two hundred thousand, which he split with me.'

'So we made a profit of one hundred thousand!' said Christina, unable to hide her delight.

'And that doesn't include the seventy-four thousand the company made this year, giving you an overall return of eighty-seven thousand.' Beth opened her briefcase, pulled out a cheque and handed it over to her partner.

'Thank you, my darling,' said Christina, before adding, 'But where does Booth Watson fit in?'

'He tried to swindle an old widow out of her inheritance and ended up a thousand pounds out of pocket.'

'Do you think he was acting on Miles's behalf?'

'No, I suspect he forgot to brief Miles on this occasion.'

'He went behind his back?' queried Christina.

'Try not to sound too surprised. After all, you've done so on more than one occasion.'

'Touché,' came back Christina. 'So, what's the bad news?' she asked after she'd checked the noughts and deposited the cheque in her bag.

Beth took a sip of water before she continued. 'I've had a letter from Sir Nicholas Fenwick to let me know that the Fitz is looking for a new director and he hoped I'd apply for the post.'

'And will you?' asked Christina, trying to keep her tone casual.

'I haven't made up my mind yet,' admitted Beth. 'Not least because I'm no longer sure I want the job.'

'But you've wanted to run a major gallery for as long as I've known you,' said Christina, hoping to be contradicted.

'True, but that was before we set up our company. If I were to become the next director of the Fitz, it would mean taking a fifty per cent cut in salary while only occasionally having supper with my children and probably only seeing my husband at weekends.'

Christina tried not to think about the even bigger drop in

her income if their partnership was dissolved. She began to think carefully about how to play her cards, remembering BW's 'strings attached' offer.

'Though I confess,' continued Beth, 'I would enjoy the challenge of running one of the nation's most prestigious galleries – who wouldn't?'

I wouldn't, thought Christina, as her mind began working overtime before she played her first card. 'Whatever you decide,' she eventually managed, 'I'll back you to the hilt, and don't forget, I'm still on the board, so should be able to persuade any doubters.'

'That could make all the difference,' said Beth, 'because I'm told that one or two heavyweights have already applied for the position, so it's not exactly a done deal.'

'They won't get my vote,' promised Christina, who intended to find out who else was on the shortlist the moment she got home.

'That's very generous of you,' said Beth, 'remembering you have even more to lose than I do.'

'It's the least I can do after all you've done for me, Beth.' Christina was already wondering if she could arrange it so that Beth didn't even get onto the shortlist. A plan was beginning to form in her mind as the head waiter reappeared by their side.

'Louis,' Christina said as she handed him back the menu, 'I'm slimming, so I'll just have the Beluga caviar, followed by the Dover sole.'

'An excellent choice, madam,' he said before turning to Beth. 'And for you, madam?'

'I'll have a Caesar salad, Louis,' she said as the sommelier poured her partner a second glass of champagne.

CHAPTER 7

William watched Beth getting dressed and couldn't fail to notice how nervous she was. She must have tried on five or six different outfits before she settled on a navy blue suit with large white buttons and a cream silk blouse. She then took almost as long selecting a matching bag and a pair of high-heeled shoes that would complete the outfit.

When she'd finally settled on her choice, William decided not to mention it was the one he would have chosen in the first place.

'Why do you want this job, Dr Warwick?' he asked.

'I've always hoped to return to this great museum, having served as its keeper of pictures in the past, and after five years as a dealer, I now realize it's my long-term calling.'

'A bit over the top, perhaps?' suggested William.

'A day hasn't passed when I didn't wish I was back at the Fitz.'

'Better,' said William, before continuing his interrogation.

'I'd like to know a little more about your five years as a dealer. Did you learn anything during that period which could be of value to the Fitzmolean?'

'First and foremost, chairman, you quickly learn the value of money, especially when it's your own money you're spending, and not the funds of a public body or generous benefactors.'

'For example?'

'I recently purchased a Henry Moore maquette from his King and Queen series, on behalf of an American client who asked me to ship it to their home in Philadelphia. I put the order out to tender to five different shipping companies and discovered their prices ranged from twelve hundred pounds to four thousand seven hundred. This reminded me that the Fitzmolean used the same transport company, framers, insurance brokers, and even window cleaners, during the entire period I was working here. All publicly funded museums should behave like private galleries whenever they spend other people's money. The director should think like a barrow boy while behaving like a trustee.'

'Convincing,' said William. 'But if you were to become our director, Mrs Warwick, you do realize we couldn't hope to match the amount you've been earning as a dealer.'

'Which I hope, Mr Chairman, only proves how much I want the job.'

'Good line,' said William. 'But are you absolutely sure you do want the job?'

'They won't ask me that.'

'But I am,' said William, switching from interrogator to husband.

'I blow hot and cold,' admitted Beth as she once again looked at herself in the mirror and wondered if she should wear any jewellery. 'One minute I want the job, the next minute I'm not sure.'

'As the interview is in about an hour's time,' said William checking his watch, 'you'd better make up your mind fairly quickly.'

'What do *you* think?' she asked, turning to face her husband.

'I don't want to be director of the Fitzmolean,' said William.

'Behave yourself, caveman, and answer my question.'

'If you were financially independent, my darling, which job would you prefer?'

'Director of the Fitz, without a second thought.'

'Then you've answered your own question.'

'But you have to admit, the extra income does come in useful.'

'Make up your mind, Beth,' said William, trying not to sound exasperated. 'But for now, let's concentrate on more practical matters. How do you intend to get to Kensington Gardens?'

'Taxi there, bus back.'

'And if they offer you the job?'

'I'll always take the number fourteen both ways.'

'That's not what I meant,' said William grinning.

'I know exactly what you meant, Chief Superintendent,' responded Beth as she tried on a string of pearls her father had given her on her thirtieth birthday. 'But I still don't know the answer to your question.'

'Then I'll drive you there and you can mull it over.'

'But you'll be late for work.'

'I like the pearls,' said William.

• • •

Miles was cracking his second egg when Collins appeared carrying a letter on a silver tray. He didn't mask his surprise as the morning post was usually left in his study for him to consider after he'd finished breakfast.

He picked up the long cream envelope and studied it closely. It was addressed to Miles Faulkner Esq., 37 Cadogan Place, London SW1, but it wasn't until he turned the envelope over that he understood why Collins had made an exception to the rule. He gazed down at the embossed royal crest.

If it was a hoax, someone had gone to considerable trouble to attract his attention, as Miles was confident the envelope would not contain an invitation to join the Queen for one of her garden parties. It was the wrong-sized envelope for a start. Several alternatives ran through his mind before he picked up the butter knife, edged it into one corner of the envelope, and slowly slit it open. He carefully extracted a letter to see the words BUCKINGHAM PALACE embossed in blue at the top of the page. The only thing written on the paper in clear blue ink were eleven numbers which meant nothing to him. He assumed it must be a telephone number. But whose?

Miles rang the little bell on the breakfast table and moments later Collins reappeared.

'Who delivered this letter?' he asked, holding up the envelope.

'It came with the morning post, sir,' Collins replied.

Miles rose from the table, not letting go of the single sheet of paper. 'I'll be in my study. Make sure no one disturbs me.'

'As you wish, sir,' said Collins as Miles dropped his crumpled napkin on the table, left the room and disappeared into his office.

He sat down and placed the letter on the desk in front of him. He waited before picking up his phone and dialling the number slowly. It rang for some time before a voice said, 'Good morning, Mr Faulkner.'

'How did you know who was calling?' demanded Miles.

'You're the only person who has this number,' came back the immediate reply.

'Then you can start by telling me your name.'

'I have no intention of revealing my name,' said the voice with a pronounced cockney accent, 'until you agree to meet me.'

'Why would I want to do that?'

'Because for the past nine years someone inside Scotland Yard has been unwittingly feeding me with snippets of information that you would find most valuable.'

'Snippets of information that no doubt come at a price.'

'One million pounds,' said the voice calmly.

Faulkner burst out laughing. 'What could possibly be worth that much?'

'The public humiliation of Chief Superintendent William Warwick. Having Inspector Ross Hogan dismissed from the force for gross misconduct, while leaving Commander Hawksby with no choice but to resign.'

'How could that be possible?' asked Miles, suddenly interested.

'That's what's going to cost you one million pounds, Mr Faulkner,' said the voice. 'Because once you've pulled off my little coup, it won't take Warwick and his cronies that long to work out who supplied you with the information to make it all possible.'

'Let's meet,' said Faulkner, 'so I can find out if you're full of crap.'

'Not that easy,' said the voice, 'because if anyone spotted the two of us together, they might just put two and two together.'

Faulkner thought for a moment before saying, 'Do you know the Imperial War Museum?'

'I haven't visited it since I was a child, but I pass it on my way to work.'

'Which I assume has to be Buckingham Palace?' said Miles, but no reply was forthcoming. 'In common with several other museums, the Imperial is virtually empty first thing on a Monday morning.'

'First thing?'

'Their doors open at ten, so we could meet in the café on the ground floor. We're unlikely to be disturbed other than by the occasional school party or a Japanese tourist, and I'm confident they wouldn't recognize either of us.'

'You mean ten o'clock this morning?'

'I do,' came back the immediate reply.

There was a long silence before the voice said, 'I'll be there at ten.'

'But I won't be,' said Miles, 'unless you tell me your name.'

Another long silence followed, and Miles might have thought the anonymous man had hung up, if he hadn't still been able to hear him breathing.

'Phil Harris,' said the voice quietly.

• • •

Beth took the seat at the other end of the boardroom table and wondered if they could hear her heart thumping. Finally, she realized just how much she wanted the job.

She tried to settle as twelve faces stared back at her, and

began to relax only when she saw Christina giving her a warm smile. Unconsciously she straightened her skirt, trying not to reveal just how nervous she was.

'May I begin, Dr Warwick,' said the chairman of the board, 'by thanking you for your application to be the new director of the Fitzmolean. Perhaps you could start by telling us why you want the job.'

'I've never made any secret, chairman, of wanting to be part of the future of this great institution,' said Beth, 'having had the privilege of following Mark Cranston as the keeper of pictures, and then later becoming the museum's deputy director.'

'But you've been out of the public sector for over five years,' continued the chairman, 'and by all accounts, you've been having considerable success as a private dealer. So why would you want to return to the Fitz?'

'It's kind of you to say so, Sir Nicholas. But not a day passes when I don't miss the camaraderie of the museum world. I'm not a commercial animal by nature. I'm one of life's volunteers, so what more could one ask for than to be director of one of the nation's most prestigious galleries.'

Beth could hear William saying, 'Over the top, you're sounding desperate.'

'But you would have to accept, Dr Warwick,' the finance director chipped in, 'that we could not hope to match the amount you've been earning as a dealer.'

Beth wasn't in any doubt which member of the board had supplied them with that piece of information. 'Perhaps this shows just how much I want the job,' Beth responded as she looked across the table at Christina to see her head was bowed. Something else William had been right about. When would she ever learn?

'Is there anything else you would like to share with us, Dr Warwick,' asked the chairman after Beth had answered several more questions, none of which William hadn't anticipated, 'before we come to our decision?'

• • •

Miles was standing on the top step of the Imperial War Museum at one minute to ten, not surprised to find the doors opening on time. He marched straight in but couldn't resist pausing to admire the First World War field artillery and a Churchill tank before making his way to the café on the ground floor – a venue he often used when he didn't want to be recognised. The café was, as he'd predicted, empty. Even the kitchen staff hadn't yet made an appearance. He took a seat at a table in the far corner of the room, from where he had a clear view of the battlefield.

He didn't have long to wait before a stray infantryman appeared on the horizon. He looked around the empty room, revealing that he was on unfamiliar ground. Miles raised a hand.

The stranger walked across to join him but didn't sit down. He couldn't hide the fact he was nervous, his eyes continually darting around like a trapped animal's. Miles wouldn't have been surprised if he'd retreated without a shot being fired.

Miles studied his prey more carefully. Harris didn't look like a master criminal. He was about five foot nine, late fifties, wore a smart, if well-worn, suit and what he suspected was a regimental tie. His laced leather shoes shone as if he were on parade, which in effect he was. When he finally sat down, Miles broke the silence.

'As you seem to know so much about me,' was his opening salvo, 'while I know almost nothing about you, perhaps I can begin by asking a few questions?'

Harris nodded.

'I'm puzzled as to how you were able to lay your hands on a sheet of Buckingham Palace notepaper, which I confess certainly caught my attention.'

'I work at the palace,' Harris replied. 'Have done since I left the army just over eleven years ago.'

'In what capacity?'

'I'm the Lord Chamberlain's driver. A job I've done for the last three holders of that office.'

'But surely that doesn't entitle you to write a letter on Buckingham Palace stationery.'

'No, it doesn't,' admitted Harris. 'But it was simple enough to remove a single sheet of paper, an envelope and a stamp from his secretary's office, and later drop it into the night bag just before his mail was due to be collected.'

Miles accepted his explanation and moved on. 'How come you know so much about me, when I'm fairly certain we've never met? We don't exactly mix in the same circles.'

'We have a mutual acquaintance,' said Harris. 'One Constable Danny Ives.'

'Does he know you're here?' was Miles's immediate reaction. His turn to look around the room.

'Not a chance,' said Harris. 'If he did, he'd shop me without a second thought.'

'Perhaps you're old friends?' Miles pressed.

'He might like to think so,' came back Harris. 'Although we only meet twice a year when we're left hanging around waiting for our masters, but that's been more than enough time to find out all about you, while in return all I've let slip is which brand of tea Her Majesty prefers and the name of her latest corgi.'

'Why should I believe a word you're saying?'

'Because you'd only have to make one phone call to my boss at the palace and I'd get the sack just months before I'm due to retire.'

'I'll bear that in mind,' said Miles. 'But I'm bound to ask, what could you possibly have to offer that I might consider is worth a million pounds?'

'Danny suggested you'd do anything, short of murder, to bring down Chief Superintendent Warwick.'

'Even if that were true,' responded Miles, 'a million is a large sum of money.'

'What if I were to throw in Ross Hogan?'

'He's an accident waiting to happen. For him it can only be a matter of time before he shoots himself in the foot.'

'Along with Commander Hawksby . . . making it a full house?'

'He retires in just over a year, so he'll no longer be able to cause me any trouble.'

'When, I'm reliably informed,' said Harris, 'Warwick will take his place – which you could prevent.'

'How?'

It was some time before Harris responded, aware that what he was about to propose would be met with incredulity. He took a sip of water before saying, 'I can show you how to steal the Crown Jewels.'

Miles burst out laughing, stood up and was about to leave without another word, when Harris quickly added, 'At least allow me to tell you how, with my knowledge and your financial backing, we could pull it off.'

Miles sat back down and listened to an idea Harris had been working on for the past three years. He didn't make any notes but occasionally interrupted to ask a question to which Harris always had an answer. When he'd finally finished outlining his audacious idea, Miles understood why he'd been chosen to finance it. This wasn't a concept that could be shopped around town in the hope someone would eventually back it. Despite Miles having to admit it was a well-thought-out plan and might even succeed, he'd already made up his mind and didn't leave Harris in any doubt how he felt about the whole idea.

'The risk isn't worth the reward,' said Miles, dismissively waving a hand. 'Not least because the Jewel House is more closely guarded than Fort Knox.'

'Only for three hundred and sixty-four days a year,' repeated Harris, not flinching.

'And on the three hundred and sixty-fifth you expect them to meekly hand over the Crown Jewels?' said Miles, not attempting to disguise his contempt for the whole idea.

'They will if I'm there.'

'Well, I'll tell you one thing, Mr Harris. I won't be, so you'll have to look for someone else to finance your hare-brained scheme.'

'I can't risk telling anyone else,' admitted Harris. 'You were always going to be my first and last choice.'

'Then you'll have to learn to live off your pension,' said Miles. 'Because I can think of better ways of spending my money.'

Miles pushed his chair back and once again rose to leave, when Harris said, 'If you should change your mind, Mr Faulkner, you know where to find me.'

• • •

Once Beth had left the room at the end of her interview, the chairman called the meeting to order.

'Now that we've seen all three shortlisted candidates,' said Sir Nicholas, 'I would like to have an informal discussion giving all of you an opportunity to express your view.'

An hour later, everyone around the boardroom table had offered their opinion, some more than once, although it had quickly become clear that the majority were in favour of one particular candidate. However, one board member, who held a contrary view, continued to voice her opinion.

'Are we all convinced Dr Warwick is the right person to take on such a demanding responsibility?' she asked.

'Everyone else on the board seems to think so, Mrs Faulkner,' said the chairman. 'So I'm bound to ask what makes you feel otherwise?'

'I know that Dr Warwick is currently involved in several important art deals involving large sums of money, one of which is taking up a considerable amount of her time.'

'When that question was put to her,' said the board secretary, 'she could not have made her position clearer, and I quote from the minute I made at the time: "I can wrap up any outstanding commitments I have fairly quickly and would be available to take up the post at the board's convenience."'

'Despite the fact it would mean a considerable drop in her income,' the chairman added before Christina could respond.

'But can we be sure that when Dr Warwick represents the museum, she can be relied on not to be doing deals on the side?'

'That was unworthy of you, Mrs Faulkner,' retorted another member of the board, 'especially as you claimed earlier you were a close friend.'

'Perhaps I'm a closer friend of the museum,' said Christina, not backing down. 'And I shouldn't have to remind you we have two other outstanding candidates, worthy of our consideration. A recent director of the Edinburgh Festival, who has won countless awards, and the chief executive of the Courtauld, who also has a first-class reputation.' No one else offered an opinion, but as Christina looked around the table, she couldn't fail to notice hers was a lone voice.

Several heads nodded when the board secretary suggested the time had come to take a vote.

'Those in favour of Dr Warwick being appointed as director, please raise your hands.' Christina's was the only hand that didn't move. The chairman smiled. 'I am delighted to confirm that Dr Beth Warwick will be invited to join us as the new director of the Fitzmolean.'

'I can only hope you don't all live to regret your decision,' said Christina, playing her final card.

'I feel confident we won't, Mrs Faulkner, although I'm not sure I can say the same for you and wonder if, given the circumstances, you ought to consider your position as a member of the board.'

Several 'Hear, hears' could be heard around the table, and Christina remained silent, painfully aware she'd burnt her bridges both with Beth and the board, and what made it worse was she'd already spent the five thousand advance BW had bribed her with and had to accept that there wouldn't be any more coming from that particular source. She also feared that when the new director read the board minutes, she would quickly discover who'd been the only person to oppose her appointment. She would now not only have to forfeit the extra income Beth regularly supplied, but the respect of her closest friend – her only friend. By the time she'd left the meeting, she was already regretting her decision. It certainly hadn't been worth five thousand pounds.

• • •

'Congratulations,' said William when Beth told him her news.

'But I'm still not sure I want the job,' she admitted.

'How long have they given you to make up your mind?'

'A week – ten days at most,' she said as the phone in the hall began to ring.

William was annoyed to be interrupted as he had so many more questions he wanted to ask. He dashed out into the hall, grabbed the phone and said impatiently, 'Who is it?'

'Good evening, sir,' came back a voice he thought he recognized. 'It's James Buchanan.'

'Good to hear from the man who made it possible for me to put Miles Faulkner back behind bars,' said William, his tone softening. 'However, should I assume you made it to Harvard, and are now the Director of the FBI?'

'Not yet, sir, but I was appointed editor of the *Law Review* in my final year at Harvard and am now a junior field officer in Washington attached to the Director's office.'

'Why am I not surprised,' said William. 'So how can I help you, Agent Buchanan?'

'You can't sir, it's your wife I need to speak to.'

CHAPTER 8

Ross arrived a couple of minutes early to pick up his daughter from St Luke's, well aware he couldn't risk being late for Jojo; William occasionally, the Hawk rarely, but his daughter, never.

He found a space to park his Mini not far from the school gate. As he reversed into it, he saw Ms Clarke – Jojo's favourite teacher who was regularly mentioned in dispatches – conducting an animated conversation with a man Ross immediately recognized. It was the clenched fist that made him move so quickly. He switched off the engine, leapt out of the car and charged across the road, ignoring the screeching brakes and blasts of horns which caused the man to turn and spot the last person he wanted to see heading towards him.

The man unclenched his fist and let go of several small white pills that fell to the ground, most of them disappearing down a drain he'd been hovering over. He was about to take off when Ross grabbed his shoulder and yanked his arm half-way up his back.

'You're nicked,' he said before cautioning the man, although Ross suspected he was well familiar with the procedure.

Several parents stared on in disbelief as Ms Clarke gathered up the remaining pills that were still lying in the gutter. She placed them carefully in a handkerchief and handed them over to Ross. Moments later, Jojo came rushing out of the front gate to see her father marching someone she didn't know across the road.

'Where's Dad going with that man?' she asked Ms Clarke but didn't get a satisfactory reply as her father disappeared across the green.

Ross didn't let go of the suspect's arm until they'd reached the nearest police station on the far side of the green. He took him straight to the custody suite and told the sergeant that he'd caught Simpson in possession of a class A drug, while loitering on the pavement outside St Luke's playground. The sergeant authorized the prisoner's detention and advised him of his rights before preparing a custody record. He began filling in the details, starting with his name, Reg Simpson, or at least that was the name he'd gone by when he'd last appeared in front of the beak.

Simpson didn't respond to any of the questions put to him by the custody officer, including his date of birth, address or next of kin. When he finally did speak, it was only to say, 'I know my rights and demand to see my lawyer.'

One phone call and fifteen minutes later, a well-known local solicitor turned up, who represented most of the villains on the patch. Mr Danvers Meade, a dapper man in his early forties, was dressed in a three-piece suit, white shirt and striped tie, the picture of respectability, although Ross knew that whenever one of Meade's wealthier clients ended up in the dock, Mr Booth Watson QC would appear for the defence.

Meade gave Ross a curt nod and after reading the charge sheet made no attempt to hide his own brand of sarcasm. 'So he had three ecstasy tablets and a packet of Liquorice Allsorts on him? If that's the best you can come up with, I have a feeling the CPS won't be pressing charges.'

'Liquorice Allsorts won't get him off the hook. He'll still have to explain what he was doing there in the first place.'

'Should it ever get to court, Inspector, you'll find out exactly what my client was doing there.'

Ross clenched his fist but didn't respond, aware that any altercation would only help Simpson when he applied for bail. Meade knew every loophole in the book and had invented a few of his own.

'Simpson's got a record as long as his arm,' snapped Ross.

'Which I don't have to remind you, Inspector, cannot be revealed in court, unless of course you want the case thrown out before the judge puts on their wig.'

The two men continued to glare at each other like fighting cocks before the referee came between them.

'Lock him up,' said the custody officer, looking directly at the lawyer. 'His usual cell.' A burly young constable led Simpson away.

'Have to leave you, Sarge,' said Ross, once he'd finished filling in the arrest form and handed it in. 'My daughter's waiting for me.'

Ross quickly left the police station without another word and ran all the way back to St Luke's, relieved to find Ms Clarke still chatting to Jojo. A smile crossed his daughter's face when she first saw her father, to be replaced by a frown, reluctantly followed by the suggestion of a smile.

'Who was that man?' she demanded.

'Your father did a great service for the school this afternoon,

Jojo,' said Ms Clarke before Ross could respond, 'and we should all be very grateful.'

Ross thanked Ms Clarke as he took Jojo's hand and they walked slowly across the road together. He had for some time wanted to ask her teacher out for a drink, after meeting her at a parent teacher get-together when it quickly became clear that she knew Jojo better than he did. But as she was now certain to be a key witness for the prosecution when the case eventually came to court, he realized that would have to wait until after the jury had reached its verdict. However, that didn't stop him asking his daughter some fairly unsubtle questions as he drove her back home. Ross didn't know if Ms Clarke was married, had a boyfriend, or even had kids of her own. In fact, he didn't even know her first name.

'Her name is Alice,' said Jojo without further prompting. 'No boyfriend at the moment, although one or two of the other teachers have tried, and she's thirty-two.'

'How can you possibly know all that?' asked her father as they drew up outside William's home.

'I'm the daughter of a detective,' teased Jojo, tapping her nose with a forefinger as she'd seen her father do so often in the past. She paused before adding, 'You fancy her, don't you, Dad?' which silenced Ross in a way no criminal had ever managed.

Ross parked his Mini outside the house and pressed a pound coin in the meter. The front door was opened by Artemisia before they were half-way up the path. He got a hug from his second favourite girlfriend, and a more reluctant one from Peter.

'You're later than usual,' said William, checking his watch when Ross joined him in the front room.

'I caught Reg Simpson red-handed outside St Luke's with some ecstasy tablets. He'd got rid of most of them down the nearest drain before I could arrest him, but he still had enough to be charged with possession.'

'Given half a chance,' said William, 'I'd lock up every dealer along with their suppliers and throw away the key. Half the petty crimes on our patch are committed by desperate addicts in need of cash that ends up in Reg Simpson's back pocket.'

'Locking them up is far too good for them,' said Ross. 'I'd happily castrate them,' he said as Beth walked into the room. 'You look terrific,' he added without drawing breath.

'Thank you, Ross,' replied Beth. 'But who would you happily castrate this time?'

'Drug dealers. So where are you two off to this evening?' Ross asked, wanting to change the subject.

'I'm driving Beth to Heathrow but should be back in a couple of hours. Three at the most,' William added without further explanation.

'Please make sure the children are in bed by nine and have spent at least half an hour reading something worthwhile,' chipped in Beth, 'and I'm sure I don't have to remind you, Ross, Harold Robbins is not yet considered a classic, but maybe it's only a matter of time.'

'Will do, ma'am,' said Ross, giving Beth a mock salute.

'Now you know what I go through every day,' whispered William as they walked out into the hall and he helped Beth on with her coat. 'A commander in the office and another one at home.'

Lucky you, thought Ross, as he opened the front door and watched them walk down the path and get into their car, still wondering where Beth was going, because they hadn't given him a single clue. He closed the door and joined the children in the kitchen.

• • •

If you'd told Beth twenty-four hours earlier that she'd be boarding a plane to New York the following evening, she wouldn't have believed you. However, once James had called to tell her his news, she realized she didn't have much choice if she still hoped to take up the role as director of the Fitzmolean.

Beth sat at the back of a packed jumbo jet considering the consequences of James Buchanan's bombshell but decided not to jump to any conclusions before she'd seen the painting for herself. She hoped it would be a wasted journey.

At first, she hadn't told William the real reason her plans had been thrown into disarray, other than to hint that the trip might help her make up her mind whether she really wanted the job. William didn't question her, assuming she was involved in an important deal. But when Beth finally told him the truth, he agreed that she hadn't been left with a lot of choice.

'Say nothing to Ross,' said Beth when William dropped her off outside Departures. 'If he found out the truth, he'd probably end up killing Faulkner,' were her final words.

William couldn't disagree as he watched his wife disappear into the terminal before he set off back to Fulham. It was while he was heading back down the motorway that he worked out the consequences for both of them if her worst fears were realized. He knew Ross's antennae would be working overtime, even though he hadn't asked any questions.

• • •

Monday nights had a routine of their own that didn't always comply with Beth's strict instructions. Supper in the kitchen – four margherita pizzas (large) picked up from the local Italian by Peter, followed by a large dollop of chocolate ice cream taken out of the freezer by Artemisia five minutes after her parents had left.

Once supper had been devoured and the kitchen left as they had found it, with no clues as to what they'd been up to, they moved into the living room where Ross and Artemisia would play a game of Scrabble. She seemed to know a lot more words than he did, although he suspected one or two of them hadn't yet made it into the Shorter Oxford English Dictionary. Ross had long ago given up playing chess against Peter, as the word 'checkmate' had become more and more frequent with each encounter.

They would then take it in turn to read the current books Beth had selected, *Swallows and Amazons* and *A Tale of Two Cities* – both of them for the first time. On one occasion Ross had suggested to Beth they might add Ian Fleming to their reading list only to be greeted with a short, sharp shake of the head.

'One James Bond in the house is quite enough,' was her only comment on the subject. But which of them did she have in mind, Ross wondered.

After reading a couple of chapters from *The 39 Steps*, the twins began discussing once again what would be a suitable subject for their prize essay competition. Drugs, global warming and the future of the Royal Family all made the shortlist, without a final decision being made.

Getting the three of them to go to bed was Ross's final challenge of the day, often achieved only moments before Beth and William returned.

Ross was watching the *News at Ten* which was reporting on Britain's chances of staging the 2004 Olympics, when he heard the front door open. He switched off the TV and went out into the hall. He assured William, before he had a chance to ask, that the children had gone to bed over an hour ago. William didn't look convinced.

'How was *The 39 Steps*?' he asked.

'I enjoyed it,' admitted Ross. 'Although I would have arrested Hannay long before he set off for Scotland.'

'Of course you would,' said William, stifling a laugh. 'But I suggest you read a few more chapters because it's possible you would have ended up arresting the wrong man. Anyway, back to the real world. I'll go up and make sure the children are asleep.'

Ross had no doubt that even if the little monsters were wide awake, they would pretend to be fast asleep as they wouldn't want to get him into any trouble.

'I'd better get going,' said Ross as William left the room. 'I'm on the early shift tomorrow.'

'Thanks for not asking,' said William as Ross opened the front door, which only made him even more curious to find out where Beth had gone at that time of night.

On the drive home, Ross thought once again about how fortunate Jojo was to be a fully fledged member of the Warwick family, with Peter and Artemisia acting as her older brother and sister. Artemisia considered it nothing less than her duty to explain the ways of the world to her younger sister, while Peter feigned indifference, but was always the first to come to Jojo's defence whenever she got into any trouble . . . which she regularly did.

As a single parent, Ross had long ago accepted his way of life was not compatible with raising a young woman. He had to admit if only to himself that he was envious of Beth and William – but not jealous.

After he'd arrived home and closed his own front door, he went straight to bed. But he lay awake thinking about the only woman he'd ever really loved and wondering if he would be lucky enough to experience such happiness again.

Who would want a middle-aged cop set in his ways, who enjoyed nothing more than locking up hardened criminals and whose only recent experience of love had been one night stands with women he didn't want to wake up with? His thoughts turned to Alice Clarke and he began to wonder if it was possible . . .

CHAPTER 9

ON LANDING AT JFK, BETH moved slowly through passport control, but as she had only hand luggage she was among the first to emerge in Arrivals.

Ever-reliable James was waiting to greet her. Although he'd retained his boyish good looks, with those piercing blue eyes and tousled fair hair, he was now a couple of inches taller and clearly no longer a child. In fact, he looked every inch an FBI agent, dressed in a dark blue suit, white button-down collared shirt and what she assumed must be a Harvard tie.

After James had given Beth an American hug, he took her bag and guided her to a nearby car park. During the long walk they chatted about William and the children, not touching on the real reason she'd flown to New York at a moment's notice following his phone call. It was not until they set out on the bumper-to-bumper journey into the city that she finally asked James the burning question.

He replied, 'I would never have found out if I hadn't visited my dentist for an annual check-up and come across the ad while browsing through an old copy of the *New York Times*.'

'Were they surprised when a G-man asked to view such an exclusive property?'

'Why shouldn't James Buchanan, scion of the Buchanan shipping line, be looking for a luxury apartment on East 61st Street overlooking Central Park? After all, seven million should be well within his budget.'

'But not within the salary of an FBI agent,' teased Beth. 'More importantly, why did you bother to follow it up?'

'I wouldn't have, if I hadn't thought I'd seen the painting before, and then I remembered how much I'd admired the original in the Fitzmolean when I visited you a couple of years ago.'

'As Miles Faulkner is involved,' said Beth with some feeling, 'I can no longer be sure it is the original.'

'What will convince you otherwise?' asked James.

'If I can remove a tiny sliver of paint from Faulkner's picture, a lab will be able to test it and confirm when it was painted, fairly accurately to within ten or twenty years.' She opened her handbag and produced what looked like a small compact. 'Everything I require is in here, but I'll need a few minutes alone if I'm going to get a sample.'

'I've already told the realtor I'll be bringing my interior designer with me tomorrow morning, so I'll just have to take a little longer inspecting the master bedroom,' said James.

After they drew up outside the apartment block the following morning, James handed his car key and a five-dollar bill to the doorman, saying, 'I shouldn't be more than an hour.'

When they entered the apartment block he gave his name to the concierge on the front desk, who told him the realtor had already arrived and was waiting for them on the ninth floor. Indeed, when the lift doors opened, she was standing there waiting to greet them.

'Good morning, Mr Buchanan,' she said with a welcoming smile.

'Good morning,' said James, shaking her warmly by the hand. 'This is my interior designer—' he didn't offer a name '—so I hope you'll forgive her poking around while we discuss terms.'

The word 'terms' brought a smile to the realtor's face. She unlocked the front door to let them both in, before beginning on a tour of the apartment. Beth quickly learnt that adjectives were her speciality.

'This is the entrance hall, which you can see is spacious . . .' But it was not until they reached the 'magnificent', 'vast', 'superb' living room overlooking the park that Beth saw the painting for the first time.

It hung above an Adam-style fireplace and dominated the room. James ignored the picture and walked out onto a balcony that overlooked Central Park, which was indeed magnificent, vast and superb.

'I'll catch up with you,' Beth said, her eyes never leaving the painting of *Christ's Descent from the Cross.* She understood immediately why James had suggested it would be worth crossing an ocean to see it for herself.

James took his time admiring the view and pointing out several landmarks to the agent, while keeping his back to Beth.

The painting was certainly identical to the one on display in the Fitzmolean, which had been donated to the museum by none other than Miles Faulkner. William had hinted at the time of Faulkner's trial that such an act of selfless generosity might have persuaded the judge to settle on a more lenient sentence as it clearly showed remorse. But such was the quality of the work that Beth couldn't be sure which was the masterpiece and which a convincing counterfeit. Both bore the name Peter Paul Rubens painted in bold black lettering on the bottom of the frame.

Beth still wanted to believe the original was hanging in London, and this was nothing more than a superb copy, but her experience of Miles Faulkner over the years didn't fill her with confidence. Looking around to check the realtor was nowhere to be seen, she opened her handbag and extracted the little compact. Removing a scalpel no larger than a nail file, she carried out the delicate exercise of removing the tiniest sliver of paint from a dark corner of the canvas which she deposited carefully in the box before dropping it back in her bag. She could feel herself sweating as she replaced the compact with a pocket camera and took several photographs of the painting. The ornate gold frame clearly wasn't the original, but she couldn't be sure about the canvas.

She measured the frame, followed by the canvas itself, before finally joining James in the master bedroom where she pretended to take an interest in the soft pastel colour scheme. As they moved from room to room, she regularly stopped to admire the many magnificent – no exaggeration – works that hung on almost every wall. The realtor didn't mention a single one of them, but then they weren't part of the fixtures and fittings. Beth had to say one thing for Faulkner: he may have been a crook, but he was a crook with taste.

James didn't give the impression of being in any hurry as they moved on to the 'well-equipped' kitchen, followed by the 'well-appointed' study, before finally returning to the 'spacious' hallway.

'I'll be meeting with my broker later this afternoon,' he

assured the realtor, before once again shaking hands with her. 'Broker' was another word that always brought a smile to a realtor's lips.

'There's already been a great deal of interest in the apartment,' she claimed as she accompanied them back to the elevator.

'I'm sure there has,' said James.

'I look forward to hearing from you, Mr Buchanan,' said the realtor as he stepped into the elevator. James wondered if the permanent smile was etched on her face. 'And you only have to call me if you or your designer would like to have another viewing,' she gushed as the lift doors closed.

Beth was bursting to tell James her news but was prevented from doing so by an elderly lady chatting to her chihuahua about her latest investment in a company called Enron, so she remained silent until the elevator doors opened on the ground floor. James guided her to a nearby café on the edge of the park before he asked, 'A wasted journey?'

'Still not sure,' admitted Beth, 'and I won't be certain until I've had a chance to get the sample analysed for texture and date. But on behalf of the museum, James, thank you for an amazing, fantastic, superb piece of detective work.'

James burst out laughing before asking, 'What's your gut feeling?'

'I'm bound to admit, as Miles Faulkner's involved, I'm not optimistic.'

'What will it take to convince you that the Fitzmolean is in possession of the original and that was nothing more than an impressive copy?' he asked after ordering two coffees.

'Rubens' catalogue raisonné won't prevaricate on the subject. The exact size of the canvas will be the first clue, and whether it's in its original frame could well tip the balance.'

'But Faulkner's well capable of holding onto the masterpiece while leaving you with the original frame,' suggested James.

'Which is why the lab report will be the final arbiter,' said Beth, tapping her handbag. 'However, I'll also have to take a sample from our painting in London and have it tested before I can be sure who actually owns the original.'

'If I was a betting man . . .'

'With that in mind, James, I hope you'll forgive me if I catch the next available flight back to London so I can find out the truth as quickly as possible.'

'I'll drive you to the airport,' said James as he took out his wallet, extracted a couple of dollars and left them on the table.

'By the way,' said Beth as she climbed back into his car, 'do you have any idea why Faulkner's selling his apartment?'

'Sure do. The duplex on the top floor has become available, and he's moving up in the world.'

'Clearly the damn man flourishes.'

'It would seem so,' said James. 'Let's just hope it's not at your expense.'

CHAPTER 10

WILLIAM WAS SURPRISED TO FIND the Resident Governor standing by the public entrance to the Tower of London waiting to greet them. Fortunately, they were a couple of minutes early and, despite several protests from the children, all three of them were smartly dressed in their school uniforms.

'How nice to see you again, Chief Superintendent,' said the Governor. 'Will your wife be joining us?'

'No. I'm afraid not,' said William, glancing at his watch. 'But I'm rather hoping she'll be on her way back from New York by now.'

After the Governor had shaken hands with William, he bent down to welcome his special guests, Artemisia, Peter and Jojo, who then followed their distinguished guide into the grounds of the castle.

'I don't want what I have to say to sound like a history lesson,' the Governor began, 'but in truth, the Tower of London represents, in its own way, the whole pageant of

English history, from the Roman occupation right up to the present day. So, let's begin with William the Conqueror, who, having won the Battle of Hastings – in which year?' he asked, looking at the children.

'1066,' said Peter and Artemisia in unison, while Jojo nodded.

'. . . set about building the Tower. In those days, Londinium, as the Romans had known it, was a small town on the banks of the Thames with a population of just over ten thousand. A far cry from the seven million who now inhabit the capital. If you look to your right,' the Governor continued, 'you'll see the massive stone wall that surrounds the Tower which is twenty feet high and two miles long and was built to protect King William from his enemies.'

'Who were the King's enemies?' asked Peter.

'Pretty well everyone,' said the Governor, 'including the Germans, the French, the Italians and of course the Spanish, not to mention a few aldermen not so far away in the City of London, who were always causing trouble.'

'What's an alderman?' asked Artemisia.

'A member of the common council of the City of London, someone who hopes one day to become the Lord Mayor,' said the Governor, coming to a halt beside a vast stone building. 'This,' he announced, 'is the Great Tower, which we're fairly sure was built over nine hundred years ago, somewhere between 1075 and 1080. It has more recently come to be known as the White Tower. King William sadly didn't live to see his great project completed as he died in . . .?' The Governor paused, but the faces of all four of his guests remained blank.

'1087. Funny how everyone remembers when the Battle of Hastings took place, but not when William the Conqueror died.'

'Did you know that, Dad?' asked Peter.

'No,' admitted William, who was learning almost as much as the children.

'Something else you might not have been aware of,' continued the Governor, 'is that for some considerable time, the Tower was a zoo.' He turned to see all three children hanging on his every word. 'In 1235, the Holy Roman Emperor presented Henry III with three leopards, that historians now think were probably lions. The King became quite enthusiastic about his menagerie and, during his reign, added an elephant and a polar bear to the collection, turning the Tower into London's first tourist attraction. In fact, as late as 1597 a Czech visitor recorded in his diary that he had seen a porcupine in the Tower that just might have been the one Shakespeare alluded to in *Hamlet – And each particular hair to stand on end, Like quills upon the fretful porpentine.* By the early seventeenth century, the menagerie had expanded to include three more elephants, two more bears, a tiger and a jackal.'

'Where are they now?' demanded Jojo as she turned a complete circle, hoping to spot one.

'They're no longer with us,' admitted the Governor, 'because one of my predecessors, the Duke of Wellington, was determined to return the castle to its original purpose as a fortress, so gave orders that the one hundred and fifty animals should be transferred to the zoological gardens in Regent's Park, now better known as London Zoo.'

'My dad took me there once,' said Jojo. 'I even saw some snakes and vultures.'

'We don't have any snakes or vultures,' said the Governor. 'But keep a lookout for a particular breed of bird who've been in residence since 1624, and when you spot one, I'll tell you why I can't allow them to leave the castle, on pain of having my head chopped off.' Peter looked interested. 'They've even retained the axe and block as a gentle reminder.' Artemisia wanted to ask where they were. 'And what purpose do you think this particular building served in the past?' continued the Governor as he came to a halt by the outer tower wall.

'Torture chambers?' said Peter hopefully.

The Governor laughed. 'Not exactly. In 1279, this was known as Mint Street, and even housed the Royal Mint, as King Edward I, like so many monarchs, wanted to control the city's finances.'

'Isn't that the Chancellor of the Exchequer's job?' asked Artemisia.

'It is now, but it wasn't in the thirteenth century. Indeed, as late as 1696, Sir Isaac Newton, the renowned Cambridge mathematician, was appointed as warden of the Mint after he was able to prove to the King that the amount of silver in each coin had been diminishing over the years, causing the city bankers to lose confidence in their own currency. The first known example of devaluation.'

Peter ran on ahead when he spotted some stone steps that led down to a dark, cold, foreboding room, offering only a glimmer of light through the bars blocking the one small window. He shivered and began to feel nervous so quickly bolted back upstairs to rejoin the family.

'Don't go down there, Jojo,' he said, 'it's not very nice.'

'It's not meant to be,' said the Governor. 'Don't forget that over the years the Tower also served as a prison, incarcerating both heroes and villains, according to your point of view. Can you name any of them?'

'Guy Fawkes,' said Artemisia confidently.

'And what was his crime?'

'The Gunpowder Plot, when he and four of his conspirators tried to blow up the House of Lords—'

'—During the State Opening of Parliament in 1605,' said Peter, completing his sister's sentence.

'What about a hero?' asked the Governor.

'Sir Thomas More,' said Artemisia. 'Henry VIII's Chancellor, who refused to condone the King's marriage to Anne Boleyn and was later beheaded for his convictions.'

'Anne Boleyn also ended up in the Tower,' said the Governor, 'where she spent several months before she too was executed, unlike Sir Walter Raleigh who had his own set of rooms and was even allowed to entertain visitors until he was finally released in 1616. But then he had been a favourite of Queen Elizabeth I,' he added as they joined a long queue of visitors waiting outside a building where several alert Beefeaters were keeping a close eye on them.

One of the Beefeaters stepped forward the moment he saw Sir David and unhitched a red rope to allow his little party to enter the Jewel House. The Governor escorted them into a darkened room lit only by tiny spotlights that were focused on a display of glass cabinets. The children were spellbound as they stood silently admiring a row of ornately jewelled crowns on display in front of them.

'In 1660,' began the Governor, breaking the silence, 'King Charles II ordered the Crown Jewellers to make him a new set of regalia to replace the old jewels that had been melted down by Oliver Cromwell, a man who didn't approve of any outward trappings. But if you look at the crown in the centre of the display, you'll see the Tower's greatest attraction: the Imperial State Crown which Queen Elizabeth II wore at her coronation. Unique and irreplaceable, although it wasn't crafted by Garrard, the royal jewellers, until her father's coronation in 1937. King?'

The children looked unsure.

'King George VI,' the Governor reminded them.

'Were you alive then?' asked Jojo.

'Not quite,' said the Governor, stifling a laugh. 'But I did see the Queen being crowned on television when I was about your age.'

'How much is the crown worth?' demanded Peter. William scowled.

'That's the most common question I'm asked,' admitted the Governor, 'and I always reply by saying it's priceless.'

William didn't admit he was also seeing the Imperial State Crown for the first time. He wanted to ask a question about the two black boxes that were nowhere to be seen but remained silent.

'Any other questions?' asked the Governor.

'Yes, sir,' said Peter. 'Has anyone ever tried to steal the Crown Jewels?'

'Yes, in 1671, an attempt was made by an audacious rogue called Colonel Blood, but fortunately he didn't succeed, and no one has attempted to steal them since.'

'Was he beheaded?' asked Peter.

'No. He was pardoned by the King and released from the Tower after only a month, which has puzzled historians ever since.'

Artemisia looked across at her brother, and he nodded.

'Of course,' continued the Governor, who'd missed the exchange, 'the Jewel House also contains several other treasures, including the orb and sceptre, a solid gold christening font, and enough gold plates to serve a royal banquet. However, they are only ever brought out for state occasions, but can always be viewed by the public, which is why the Tower remains one of the nation's most popular tourist attractions.'

'Can I have an ice cream, please?' asked Jojo.

'You most certainly can,' said the Governor before William could respond. 'Because the Tower now has its own ice cream parlour, even though William the Conqueror wouldn't have known what an ice cream was!'

Without another word, he led his guests out of the Jewel House and took them to a little shop discreetly hidden behind the Great Tower, where Peter took more interest in a couple of large black birds that were perched on a ledge above them.

'The ravens,' said Peter in triumph, 'who mustn't be allowed to escape, or you'll be beheaded.'

'Despite the Duke of Wellington's orders,' said Artemisia.

'You're both right,' said the Governor, 'I quite forgot to tell you about the ravens who have been in situ since the seventeenth century, so play their own unique role in the history of the Tower.'

The two ravens looked studiously down at their Governor, almost as if they knew he was talking about them.

'Who takes care of them?' asked Jojo.

'A ravenmaster,' said the Governor. 'A post that dates back to Charles II, who believed if there weren't at least six ravens in the Tower at any one time, his kingdom would be overthrown.'

'How many are there now?' asked Artemisia.

'Eight,' came back the immediate reply. 'Safety in numbers, as I have no desire to be beheaded.'

'Why don't they fly away?' asked Jojo.

'I have to admit,' responded the Governor, 'that their flight feathers have been trimmed, and the ravenmaster feeds them only the choicest leftovers from Smithfield Market. That didn't stop one of them flying off last year and ending up outside a well-known local pub! But as they didn't have any choicest leftovers on the menu, he returned to the Tower the following morning,' said the Governor as they arrived back at the public entrance.

'Thank you, sir,' said Peter, giving his host a slight bow, while Artemisia began to clap and Jojo continued to eat her ice cream.

'You've been most generous with your time, general,' said William. 'And you can see how much the children have enjoyed the experience.'

'I enjoyed it every bit as much as they did,' confessed the Governor who handed Artemisia a short history of the Tower – 'Just in case there's something I forgot to tell you' – before adding, 'I'll miss this place when I retire at the end of the year. But let's hope we'll meet again.'

'Perhaps I could show you around the Black Museum,' suggested William, 'and tell you about the history of some of our more recent rogues, most of whom should have ended up in the Tower?'

'That would be fun,' he said, winking at the children before he shook hands once again with William.

On their way back to Tower Hill tube station, William asked what they would most remember about their visit.

'The ravens,' said Jojo, 'and I'll always leave something on my plate each night in case one of them comes to Fulham.'

'And you, Artemisia?'

'The 1937 Imperial State Crown,' she said. 'The Governor told us it was unique and irreplaceable.'

'What does unique mean?' asked Jojo.

'There's only one in the whole world,' replied Artemisia.

'And what about you, Peter?' asked his father as they jogged down the steps to the tube station. 'What did you learn from the experience?'

'That we've found our subject for the prize essay competition,' Peter said triumphantly.

'Dare I ask?' said William.

'Colonel Blood,' said Artemisia. 'Hero or villain?'

CHAPTER 11

Private & Confidential

The Fitzmolean Museum
Kensington Gardens
London W8

Dear Mrs Faulkner,

As you know, the board have appointed Dr Elizabeth Warwick to be the next director of the Fitzmolean Museum and will be issuing a press statement to that effect later in the week.

As you were the only member of the board who opposed Dr Warwick's appointment, I would understand if you felt unable to continue serving as a board member.

Perhaps you would be kind enough to let me know your decision as soon as it's convenient.

Yours sincerely,

Nicholas Fenwick

Sir Nicholas Fenwick, Chairman
cc. Dr Elizabeth Warwick PhD MA

CHRISTINA HADN'T OPENED THE LETTER until after lunch on Sunday. After all, it had been a long night, and she hadn't got home until well after midnight.

She became even more anxious after she'd read the letter a second time. Christina was aware the chairman didn't like her, but she had no intention of resigning, confident that her annual donation would prevent him from attempting to remove her. But she would still have to see Beth before she read the letter so she could tell her side of the story. Time wasn't on her side.

• • •

The first thing Beth did as the prospective Director of the Fitzmolean was to take a tiny scraping from the museum's painting of *Christ's Descent from the Cross*, before sending both samples to the Hamilton Kerr Institute in Whittlesford for testing.

A week later, a letter came back marked private and confidential, confirming that one of the works contained a pigment that had not been invented until 1916, while the other was unquestionably painted early in the seventeenth century.

Beth stared up at a painting that had fooled the art world for several years and had to admit that part of Miles Faulkner's genius – as James had pointed out – was that while the museum was in possession of the original frame, Miles still owned the masterpiece.

Beth blamed herself for not checking the provenance more carefully, but at the time she hadn't looked a gift horse in the mouth. They had all been so overwhelmed by the generosity of the benefactor, no one gave it a second thought. As keeper of pictures, she should have given it a third thought. If the museum had been buying the work from an established dealer, the painting would have gone through a series of rigorous checks before they handed over any money. But they didn't have to hand over any money, which was all part of Faulkner's plan to make sure they ended up with the wrong picture. William had once told her that it's easy to be conned if you want to believe the conman.

Beth took a step back, admired the copy, and wondered if the best course of action was to say nothing. But she feared it could only be a matter of time before the truth came out and Christina reminded the board that she'd been keeper of pictures at the time.

She called James in Washington to tell him the news. He was sympathetic but didn't sound surprised. However, she was shocked when he said, 'I know exactly what I'd do in the circumstances.'

• • •

'There's something I haven't told you,' said William, after Beth had revealed the results of the paint analysis.

'Don't tell me you knew all along we weren't in possession of the original Rubens?'

'I had my suspicions,' he admitted.

'Then why didn't you tell me?' demanded Beth, sounding exasperated.

'I didn't have any proof other than that Miles Faulkner was involved.'

'But there must have been something else that caused you to have doubts.'

'Yes, there was,' William confessed. 'On the evening Princess Anne unveiled the painting, Faulkner crept up behind me and said, "If you're ever in New York, do come and visit my apartment, and then you'll be able to see the original."'

'And you didn't tell me!' said Beth, spitting out the words.

'I assumed it was nothing more than a bluff.'

'Well, now we know it wasn't, and it's too late to do anything about it.'

'Is it?' said William calmly.

'What do you mean?'

'I agree with James. You're now the one person who *can* do something about it and if you don't, you certainly can't consider taking up the post as director.'

'But you're talking about breaking the law?'

'Am I? The Fitzmolean is in possession of a legal document signed by Miles Faulkner and witnessed by Booth Watson, confirming that he gifted the original Rubens to the museum. So he's the one who's broken the law.'

'It would be one hell of a risk—'

'James seems willing to take that risk, and I'll bet Ross would also be only too happy to play along, so perhaps I—'

'But it's against every principle you've spent your whole life upholding,' Beth reminded him.

'While allowing Faulkner to get away with blue murder again and again.' He paused before adding, 'Perhaps just this once, I ought to—' but the door burst open, and Artemisia came hurtling in with Peter not far behind.

'You'll never believe what we've found out about Colonel Blood,' she announced.

'Brilliant timing,' said Beth.

• • •

James Buchanan flew into Heathrow on Friday evening and turned up an hour later at William's home. Three men and one woman sat down for supper in the kitchen soon after the children had gone to bed. Although the meeting was unofficial, there wasn't any doubt who was in charge.

Several different cheeses, biscuits and pickles had been laid out on a board in the centre of the table along with a bottle of Fleurie and half a dozen cans of lager, all chilled. This was clearly going to be a working supper.

Beth opened the meeting by thanking all three of them for attending. She seemed to have forgotten that one of them was her husband and lived there. 'And my particular thanks go to James for coming all the way from Washington at such short notice.'

'Simply returning the compliment,' said James. 'And in any case, one can never find a decent cheddar in DC.'

The laughter that followed helped ease the tension that permeated the atmosphere.

'It's somewhat ironic,' said Beth, 'that my first meeting as director of the Fitzmolean should be without the board's knowledge or approval.'

'But undoubtedly in their best interests,' suggested William.

'However, should I make the wrong decision,' continued Beth, 'I could be resigning before the doors open next Tuesday, having been director for the shortest period of time in the museum's history.'

'And if you make the right decision?' said Ross.

'The board must never find out what we did in their name. So, let's begin with what we know,' said Beth as William poured her a glass of wine. 'Let's start by admitting we've been living under the illusion for the past decade that our picture of *Christ's Descent from the Cross* was painted by the master, whereas in fact it's a copy executed by an extremely gifted forger who fooled us all, including the leading art critics.'

No one demurred, so Beth continued. 'We also know, thanks to James's initiative, the original of that masterpiece is presently hanging in an apartment on East 61st Street that just happens to be owned by Miles Faulkner.'

'Presently,' repeated Ross as he thumped a clenched fist on the table, causing several biscuits to have a life of their own.

'Despite the fact we have an indisputable legal claim to the original,' continued Beth, 'we mustn't forget possession is nine-tenths of the law, to use one of Ross's favourite expressions, which was never truer than in this case. So we must accept we have about a ten per cent chance of success.'

'I've backed horses with far longer odds than that,' said Ross, 'and won.'

'And a darn sight more who've lost,' William reminded him.

'The museum could always launch a legal challenge,' suggested James, trying to bring them back to the matter in hand, 'claiming they're the legitimate owners of the painting and have all the paperwork to prove it, including an agreement drawn up by Mr Booth Watson QC signed by Miles Faulkner and witnessed by Christina Faulkner, his ex-wife, who just happens to be a member of the museum's board.'

'Not for much longer,' said Beth without explanation.

'If the dispute ever came to court,' said William, 'it could take years to settle, and if Faulkner looked like losing the case, he'd have more than enough time to replace the original with yet another brilliant copy and then claim he'd also been cheated.'

'And by then,' chipped in Beth, 'the legal costs alone could bankrupt the museum. I don't have to remind you we are currently living on a shoestring and the board won't want to hand over any of our hard-earned donations to lawyers.'

'While that would only make a small dent in Faulkner's fortune,' threw in James.

'But we do have a second choice,' said Ross, looking directly at Beth. 'You could take back what is unquestionably yours.'

'Easier said than done,' said Beth, 'and I shouldn't have to remind you, Ross, that as a serving police officer you'd be breaking the law.'

'Not for the first time,' muttered William.

'Or would I?' said Ross, ignoring the barb. 'Is taking back something you already own technically a crime? And if it is, what would be the charge?'

'You read law at Harvard, James,' said Beth, 'so what's the definition of theft in your country, remembering that's where the exchange would take place?'

'Theft is the taking of another person's personal property with the intent of depriving that person of the use of their property.'

'Faulkner can always visit the Fitzmolean and see the Rubens during opening hours,' suggested Ross. 'Then we won't have deprived him of it.'

'And the English definition of theft?' asked Beth, turning to William.

'Doesn't differ greatly from the States, but I suspect if we were caught, we'd win the argument in the court of public opinion but lose in a court of law.'

'A fine point which once again the lawyers could debate for months on end. So, what we must decide,' said Beth, 'is whether it's worth risking our careers to rescue a dead Flemish gentleman from Faulkner's apartment in New York and bring him back to hang in London?'

'While at the same time getting the better of Miles Faulkner,' chipped in Ross. 'Which not a lot of people have done in the past and would tip the balance for me.'

'Before we do anything we might later regret,' said Beth, returning to the real world, 'let's focus on the facts and whether it's even possible to retrieve the painting.' The rest of the team remained silent while Beth checked her notes. 'The Fitz will be closed from five o'clock on Sunday afternoon to ten on Tuesday morning. Forty-one hours may sound like a long time, but if we decide to go ahead with our plan, we're going to need every minute.'

'The museum might be closed during that time,' interrupted William, 'but there would still be security guards on duty who would witness everything we're doing.'

'True,' said Beth. 'However, the museum can only afford a couple of guards over the weekend, and the present father and son duo who cover that particular shift are among the first people I'll be letting go in the near future. The father has a drink problem, while I'm not altogether sure the son owns a watch. So if we can handle the removal of the painting while they're on duty, chances are they won't even realize what we're up to.

'Although I'll have to teach you and William how to pack and unpack a large oil painting in the shortest possible time,' continued Beth, 'so you can carry out the switch just as quickly once you're inside Faulkner's apartment.'

'In less than thirty minutes would be my bet,' said James. 'While I try to keep the realtor occupied.'

'Professional handlers usually take over an hour to pack a painting of this importance,' said Beth, 'but I'll try and show you how to speed up the whole process. The good news is that in common with most other museums, we never throw anything away, so the large packing crate the painting came in is still sitting in our warehouse at Wroughton, and I can retrieve it at a moment's notice.'

'And you'll only have a moment's notice,' William reminded her.

'One other piece of good news,' continued Beth, looking back down at her notes, 'is that Art Logistics have confirmed they can fly the painting to New York as part of their regular Sunday evening manifest, and it should arrive at Newark in the early hours of the following morning. They've also guaranteed that the crate will be delivered to East 61st Street no later than eleven o'clock that morning. However, that doesn't come cheap.'

'What about customs?' said William. 'They can hold things up forever.'

'They've assured me as the work is valued at less than ten thousand dollars, that shouldn't be a problem.'

'When does the painting have to be back in Newark for us to have any chance of keeping to such a tight timetable?' asked James.

'The last flight out of Newark on a Monday evening is at seven fifty,' said Beth, checking her schedule, 'and lands at Heathrow at six the following morning. Which means Art Logistics would have to pick up the painting from East 61st Street before four o'clock at the latest if we hope to get the Rubens back on display before the museum opens to the public at ten on Tuesday morning.'

'And don't forget customs,' William reminded his fellow conspirators. 'Because on the way back they'll be carrying a masterpiece worth several million.'

'Ironically,' said Beth, 'because it will be returning in the same packing case with the same paperwork, the painting will still be listed as valued at less than ten thousand. And as long as they don't open the crate, they'll be none the wiser.'

'We've been none the wiser for the past ten years,' William reminded them. 'So frankly it will be timing at the New York end that remains our biggest problem.'

'That will be my responsibility,' said James as he emptied his glass of wine but didn't refill it. 'I've already made an appointment to view Faulkner's apartment again at eleven o'clock on Monday morning, by which time the painting should have arrived. I've warned the realtor I'll be bringing my lawyer and a mortgage broker with me, before I can make a final decision. That should give William and Ross more than enough time to switch the paintings while I check carefully over every clause of the contract.'

'Worst-case scenario,' said Ross, 'we fail to retrieve the painting, and James ends up with a luxury apartment in Manhattan.'

Laughter once again helped settle their nerves.

'I'm still hoping it will be the other way around,' said James. 'But even if I'm able to keep the realtor fully occupied while you switch the paintings, we still have to get the crate back downstairs and out of the building.' He took a sip of water before adding, 'And I can't see a vigilant concierge simply opening the front door and saying, "Your carriage awaits."'

Another long silence followed before Beth said, 'Decision time.'

CHAPTER 12

CHRISTINA THOUGHT CAREFULLY ABOUT WHAT she would wear for the encounter: a simple dress, sensible shoes and no jewellery. For once she must appear as if she were going to church, not a nightclub. She checked her outfit in the hall mirror before she left the flat. The perfect look for the task in hand.

She picked up her car keys and took the lift to the basement but sat in her car for some time going over a few well-prepared lines before setting off for Fulham.

When it came to the vote, I abstained so no one could suggest I was simply supporting a close friend.

I convinced one or two members of the board who were wavering to back you just before the final vote.

I found out something about your rivals that they wouldn't have wanted the board to know. But I made sure they did by the time the chairman called for the vote. By the way, he wasn't on your side.

If she caught Beth at home, she might still be able to

convince the new director she'd done everything in her best interests. She just had to hope the chairman had sent a copy of the damning letter to the museum and Beth hadn't yet read the minutes.

Christina parked on a double-yellow line outside the house, assuming any parking restrictions wouldn't apply on a Sunday afternoon. Not that she cared, as a fine would be the least of her problems. She got out of the car and nervously rehearsed her opening line as she walked slowly up the path, hesitating for a moment before she knocked on the front door. She dreaded it being opened by William, who would automatically assume the worst.

It seemed an age before it was finally opened, when she was greeted with a warm smile. 'Hello, Mrs Faulkner,' said Artemisia. 'If you were hoping to catch Mum, she's not at home.'

'Do you know where she is by any chance?' asked Christina, returning her smile.

'They all went off to the museum just after lunch.'

'They?' repeated Christina casually.

'Mum, Dad, Ross and a G-man from Washington who's been staying with us. He's a swell guy,' said Artemisia, trying out her American accent.

Christina turned and left without another word. It wasn't that she forgot to thank Artemisia, it just hadn't crossed her mind. After all, you don't thank children. She got back in her car and drove slowly off to the museum, fearing that Beth must surely have read the letter by now, and therefore any hope of a reconciliation was doomed. She abandoned her old script while attempting to prepare a new one.

Her thoughts turned to why William, Ross and an FBI agent from Washington had accompanied Beth to the museum on a Sunday afternoon. But by the time she turned into Kensington Gardens, she was none the wiser, and her script was far from polished.

She found a parking spot a hundred yards from the Fitzmolean and was about to get out of her car when the museum door swung open. She didn't move as three men dressed in brown overalls emerged. Two of them were carrying a large crate while the third went ahead of them to open the rear door of an Art Logistics van. He then jumped inside and helped his colleagues lift the crate into the van before strapping it firmly in place. After double-checking it was secure, he climbed back out and locked the door. He then returned to his place behind the steering wheel and she continued to watch as the van drove slowly off.

Christina didn't give a second thought as to why the museum was moving a large crate on a Sunday afternoon, as it wasn't part of her script. She finally got out and walked slowly up the steps to the main entrance, not sure if Beth would even agree to see her. She was greeted with the word CLOSED, so pressed the bell on the wall. It was some time before the door swung open to reveal a scruffily dressed security guard who looked as if he'd been interrupted.

'Good afternoon, Mrs Faulkner,' he said, touching his forehead with a finger. 'How can I help you?'

'I was hoping to see Mrs Warwick.'

'Of course, come on in and I'll let the director know you're here.'

In normal circumstances, Christina would have gone straight to Beth's office unannounced, but she hesitated, fearing that by now she must have read the letter and, worse, so would William, whom she suspected must be with her.

Christina began to pace up and down the hall while she

waited for the guard to return. She didn't notice the large empty frame propped up against the wall the first time she passed it, or even the second, but on the third perambulation, she stopped to take a closer look. The name Peter Paul Rubens adorned the bottom of an empty frame that was usually occupied by his painting of *Christ's Descent from the Cross*. She then recalled the Art Logistics van driving away with a large crate on board. Did two plus two make four?

As the minutes passed and the guard failed to return, Christina continued thinking about the empty frame and even began to wonder if . . . it would certainly explain why Miles would have been willing to part with fifty thousand pounds to prevent Beth becoming director.

'I'm sorry, madam,' said a voice as she continued to stare at the empty frame, 'but Mrs Warwick left about half an hour ago.'

She must have read the letter, was Christina's first thought, and wasn't willing to see her. 'Do tell the director I'll drop in again on Tuesday morning.'

'Will do,' said the security guard, giving away the fact she was still there. He shuffled across, opened the front door, and gave her another mock salute.

Christina walked slowly down the steps and back to her car, deep in thought. Could it be possible? Once she was behind the wheel, she sat there considering the implications, and wondered what she should do next. The decision was made for her when the entrance door opened once again, and this time four figures appeared. Three of them she recognized immediately. She assumed the fourth had to be the 'swell guy' from America who'd been staying with them.

Christina continued to watch as they got into William's Audi and disappeared off in the direction she had recently come from.

She had almost reached home before she'd worked out the common thread that linked all four of them. One of them must have discovered that the gallery's Rubens was a copy, while the original was in her ex-husband's apartment in Manhattan. She suspected it had to be the American, otherwise what was he doing in London? Up until now, only three people knew the truth as to where the original was hanging, and she'd signed a non-disclosure document, agreeing never even to hint at the fact that the Fitzmolean's version was a fake, otherwise Booth Watson had threatened to come after her for every penny she had – and worse.

She made an instant decision, drove three-quarters of the way around the next roundabout and headed in the direction of Knightsbridge. She now had information her ex would want to know about as quickly as possible, and she might even get her hands on the rest of that fifty grand.

By the time she'd parked her car for a third time that day, she'd come up with a plan.

Collins answered the door of Miles's townhouse, and the usually taciturn butler didn't attempt to hide his surprise.

'I need to speak to Miles urgently,' Christina said, quickly stepping inside before he could close the door.

'I'll see if he's available,' said Collins not sounding at all hopeful.

'Just mention the word "Rubens",' she said to the disappearing back, aware she now had something to trade. This time she wasn't kept waiting because Collins reappeared moments later and ushered her through to the boss's study. Miles remained seated behind his desk when his ex-wife entered the room.

'This had better be good,' he snarled as she took the seat on the other side of his desk uninvited.

'I think it's bad,' Christina responded, and proceeded to tell him everything she'd witnessed after turning up at the Fitzmolean earlier that afternoon.

Miles's initial reaction was very much in character. 'Are you sure it wasn't you who told her I have the original, and she's now aware you're here?'

'Think about it, Miles. There's nothing in it for me to go down that particular road.'

'I wouldn't put it past you to play both sides against the middle,' was Miles's immediate response. 'But let me first make sure I know all the details.'

Christina sat back and relaxed for the first time.

'You say you saw three men dressed in overalls coming out of the Fitzmolean carrying a large crate which they placed in the back of an Art Logistics van?'

'Yes.'

'And while you were in the main gallery, you spotted an empty Rubens frame propped up against the wall?'

'Yes,' she repeated.

'And despite asking to see Mrs Warwick, the security guard claimed she wasn't there when clearly she was.'

Christina nodded. 'I can see you've been paying attention.'

'While there's thirty million at stake, you bet I have.'

Christina smelt money.

'Describe the American,' said Miles.

'Mid-twenties, six foot, slim, fair-haired and, in different circumstances, dishy. And I think he may be a G-man,' said Christina, playing her trump card.

'I think I know who that might be, and it will only take one phone call to confirm my suspicions. But what I don't know, is how he found out I was in possession of the . . .' Miles had worked out the answer to his own question, even before he'd finished the sentence. 'Are you sure it was Art Logistics?'

'Certain.'

He spun a Rolodex on his desk, found the mobile number he was looking for and began to dial. The call was answered almost immediately.

'Good afternoon, Mr Faulkner, it's Ken Forbes,' who didn't point out to one of his most valued customers that it was Sunday afternoon and he was watching a movie with his son. All Forbes said while keeping an eye on the screen was, 'How can I help you, sir?'

'I'm calling to see if you're about to send a large package to one of my homes.'

'Let me check,' the man said as he turned off the television.

Miles could hear a short conversation going on in the background, followed by several expletives.

'Nothing coming up in your name, sir. However, one of our regular customers has just dispatched a package to be delivered to your flat in Manhattan, with an ETA of sometime between ten and eleven o'clock tomorrow morning.'

'Value?' asked Miles.

'They've insured the package for ten thousand dollars.'

They got that right, thought Miles, but only offered, 'Just as I thought. Please forget I called, as I wouldn't want to embarrass them.'

'You can be sure of my discretion, sir. Can I just confirm it's going to the right address? Number three East 61st Street, New York?'

'That's correct,' said Miles. 'Let me know the moment you've delivered it.'

'Will do, sir,' said Forbes.

Miles replaced the receiver only moments before the television was switched back on. Christina watched as her ex put the phone down and immediately picked it up again. She didn't need to ask who would be on the other end of the line as she was about to find out.

'Good afternoon, Tom, it's Miles Faulkner. Just checking to see if anyone's made an appointment to view my apartment on Monday?'

'Give me a moment, sir, while I check the diary.' It was a few moments before the concierge came back on the line. 'Yes, sir, a Mr Buchanan will be visiting your apartment for the third time at eleven a.m. on Monday morning.'

'A large crate is being delivered around that time, Tom. Make sure it's sent straight up to my flat.'

'Will do, sir.'

'And don't let either party know I called.'

'Understood, sir.'

Christina waited for him to replace the handset before she said, 'If the painting is still in England, why not have it sent straight back to the museum which would certainly embarrass the new director?'

'Because Mrs Warwick would then know I know that she knows it's a copy, and I can't afford to take that risk. No, we're going to have to play them at their own game, and you, Christina, will act as the go-between.'

'Are go-betweens well paid?' she asked.

'You have a one-track mind, Christina. But the answer on this occasion is yes. However, the amount as always will depend on results. Fifty thousand if the Rubens is still on the wall of my apartment by the time they leave on Monday afternoon, and a further fifty when their copy is returned to the Fitzmolean.'

'But if the picture is already on its way to your apartment in New York,' Christina reminded him, 'I suspect three avenging angels won't be far behind.'

'Which is why you'll be catching Concorde later this evening. That way you'll land in New York well ahead of them and be able to prepare the ground for their arrival.'

Christina listened carefully to what Miles expected her to do for one hundred thousand, and she could only admire the simplicity of his plan, which would not only ensure he kept the masterpiece but the copy was returned to London at their expense.

Miles opened his desk drawer, took out ten thousand pounds in cash and handed it across to Christina. 'Your expenses,' he explained. 'When you check in at the Concorde desk at Heathrow, you'll find a return ticket waiting for you in your name. A car will pick you up at Kennedy and drive you to the Waldorf, which, if I remember correctly, is your favourite hotel.'

'And the first fifty thousand?' pressed Christina.

'Will be deposited in your account when the bank opens on Monday morning.'

'And the other half?'

'Will follow once the copy of the Rubens has been returned to the Fitzmolean, and if Mrs Warwick feels she has to resign, I'll throw in another twenty.'

Christina was pleased that Beth had felt unable to see her.

CHAPTER 13

TIME WASN'T ON CHRISTINA'S SIDE so when she left Miles's flat on Cadogan Place, she immediately drove home, hastily packed an overnight case and only just remembered her passport. She was back on the street thirty minutes later and hailed a taxi.

'Where to, miss?' asked the cabbie.

'Heathrow,' she told him.

'Which terminal?'

'Concorde,' said Christina, which elicited a large grin as it almost always meant a larger tip.

During the journey, Christina went over in her mind what Miles expected in return for his hundred thousand pounds, confident she'd struck a good deal. She tried not to think about how Beth would react when she discovered she'd sent the museum's copy of Rubens' *Christ's Descent from the Cross* all the way to the States only for it to be returned to the Fitzmolean forty-one hours later at the gallery's expense.

She would make sure a board member asked Beth why she had authorized such an unnecessary expense, aware she couldn't afford to tell them the truth. Because if she did, she'd be left with no choice but to resign. It even crossed her mind that she might take over as chairman. After all, she'd been the only one who hadn't voted for Beth.

When the taxi drew up outside Terminal 3, Christina handed over one of Miles's fifty-pound notes to see the cabbie's grin return. She entered the terminal and made her way quickly across to the dedicated Concorde ticket desk.

'Your passport please, madam,' said a smartly dressed assistant with silver Cs embroidered on the lapels of her navy jacket. She checked the monitor. 'Ah yes, Mrs Faulkner, your husband called earlier and provisionally booked you on the flight. I'll print up your ticket. Do you have any bags?'

'Only hand luggage,' said Christina, having already decided to purchase a new outfit while she was in New York. And thanks to Miles, she had enough cash to drop into several stores on Fifth Avenue before taking the flight back to London.

'That will be four thousand, six hundred pounds, madam.'

'But I thought—'

'Your husband said you would be paying.'

'He's not my—' but she didn't bother to finish the sentence. She took one of the cellophane packets out of her bag and removed a large number of notes, before the assistant handed her a boarding pass. But she could hardly complain, because by the time she returned, her bank account would have been credited with a hundred thousand pounds. Not bad for a couple of days' work.

'Would all passengers travelling to New York's JFK on flight number 001, please make your way to gate ten as the plane is now ready to board.'

• • •

William, James and Ross all arrived at Heathrow with a couple of hours to spare.

This was not a flight they could afford to be late for. William didn't let them know that the cost of a return ticket and DHL charges had been enough to ensure his bank account was no longer in credit. However, if he came back accompanied by *Christ's Descent from the Cross*, it would have been worth every penny.

The three of them sat in a corner of the departure lounge, each trying to pick flaws in their master plan, which didn't prove too difficult as they were reminded just how much could go wrong even before they reached Faulkner's apartment. And if they did, would they be able to switch the two paintings, then somehow get the crate out of the flat and, even trickier, out of the building and on its way back to London so the painting would be hanging on the wall of the Fitzmolean before their doors opened to the public at ten o'clock on Tuesday morning?

William tried not to think about the consequences of failure, both for himself and, more importantly, for Beth. The worst possible outcome would be having to return to London with the copy, in which case he realized Beth would feel she had no choice but to resign.

'Would all passengers booked on United Airlines 7626 to New York please make their way to gate number twenty-three as your plane is ready for boarding.'

They were the first in line.

• • •

Christina was surprised how narrow Concorde was compared to a normal aircraft. More of a cigarette than a cigar.

She liked the idea of breaking the sound barrier and being able to arrive in New York in less than three and a half hours, making it possible for her to spend the night at the Waldorf rather than being sardined into the back of a jumbo with a snorer on one side and a man who read with his light on on the other.

She would wake in the morning refreshed and ready for the day's work ahead of her, while her three rivals would be tossing and turning at thirty thousand feet, trying to snatch the occasional moment of sleep, and it wouldn't be just the discomfort that was keeping them awake.

She was about to take her seat when she spotted an attractive young man a couple of rows back who was sitting on his own. She gave him a warm smile, but he didn't return it.

'This is your captain speaking. Please fasten your seatbelts as we're about to take off. If this is your first trip on Concorde . . .'

• • •

Ken Forbes called DHL just before he went to bed to make sure the package addressed to Mr Faulkner was safely on board. His night manager confirmed that although the aircraft had been delayed by forty minutes, they expected it to make up any lost time during the flight across the Atlantic. He said he'd call back first thing in the morning and give him an update.

• • •

Miles was as good as his word.

A driver was waiting for Christina in the arrival's hall. She told him she'd never experienced anything like it. 'Concorde passengers are treated like royalty,' she gushed. 'They have their own passport control as well as a separate carousel for their luggage. It was like getting off a train in the middle of the day.'

It wasn't so much how the other half lived, more like the other 0.001 per cent, because she still couldn't believe that only a few hours before she'd been in London wondering what she would do next.

• • •

William, Ross and James found their seats at the back of a crowded aircraft that didn't hint at a peaceful night. Several passengers were opening miniatures, while several miniatures were crying in their mothers' arms.

Following a long delay, the 747 finally took off after waiting for a passenger who failed to show, so his luggage had to be removed from the hold.

'It's not a problem,' William kept repeating. 'We'll have more than enough time to spare once we touch down. It's on the way back we must pray for no hold-ups.'

'Yuk,' was the only opinion Ross voiced when he saw what United described as dinner. He lowered his seat and closed his eyes, but didn't sleep.

• • •

Christina checked into her suite at the Waldorf fifty minutes later. She luxuriated in a warm, bubble-filled Jacuzzi before slipping into bed and resting her head on a soft feather pillow. She fell asleep within minutes.

• • •

The United Airlines carrier circled JFK several times before it was allocated a landing slot.

The long queue at immigration control meant that James was left waiting in customs for over an hour. Once the Brits had finally escaped, they joined an equally long taxi queue only to experience bumper-to-bumper traffic accompanied by the noise of blaring horns as they made their way across the Queensboro Bridge into Manhattan. By the time they pulled up outside The Pierre, they were exhausted, but couldn't afford to rest for long.

• • •

The DHL carrier touched down at Newark a few minutes later and a red priority sticker attached to the Art Logistics crate ensured that the painting was among the first packages to reach the customs hall.

Beth was proved right. Because the contents were valued at less than ten thousand pounds, the crate cleared customs within a couple of hours and was dispatched to East 61st on the first available truck. She couldn't have known it was Miles Faulkner who was greasing the wheels.

• • •

James had booked a room on the second floor of The Pierre, overlooking East 61st Street. His last-minute request had been easy to grant. After all, most customers who stayed at the hotel preferred a suite on one of the upper floors with a view of Central Park. James also confirmed they would be vacating the room by midday at the latest. A dream customer.

Once they'd checked in and had a brief nap, they took it in turns to eat breakfast, have a shower or keep an eye on who was entering or leaving the apartment block on the other side of the street.

James was hoping the crate would arrive long before his realtor was due to turn up at eleven, otherwise they could be booking in for the night. Not part of the plan. When William took his turn at the window, James had a shower and quickly discovered there weren't enough towels for three men.

• • •

Christina made her way down to the hotel's shops on the lower ground floor; hotels in America don't have 'basements'. She took her time selecting a smart new outfit with matching accessories. What else was a girl meant to do before going to work? She added a Le Blanc handbag that she just couldn't resist.

'Charge it to my room,' she told the assistant.

She returned to her suite, ordered breakfast, and took her time turning the pages in the entertainment section of the *New York Times*. She spotted several shows she would have liked to see but not this time. Once she was dressed in her new ensemble, only a glance in the long hall mirror convinced her that she was more than ready for the challenge ahead.

Breakfast arrived and was served by an attractive young man with an Italian accent. Christina only wished she had more time on her hands.

She was enjoying an eggs Benedict when Miles phoned to check up on her. Did the damn man ever let go?

The crate had arrived at Newark on time, he informed her, was already on its way to East 61st Street, and should be dropped off around ten. James Buchanan had an appointment to view the apartment at eleven o'clock, so she would have at least an hour to switch the paintings. Two experienced hangers from the Schwartz Gallery would be there to assist her, but she must make sure to leave the apartment before eleven o'clock, so the 'three Musketeers' would have enough time to switch the painting back, ensuring that their copy of the Rubens was returned to London while the original remained in his apartment where it belonged.

Christina felt a twinge of guilt when she thought about Beth sitting in her office in London, hoping against hope that the transfer would take place without a hitch. However, Miles assured her he'd already transferred the first fifty thousand to her account, and a further fifty would follow as soon as the copy of the painting was back on the Fitzmolean's wall, which helped to assuage any lingering doubts.

After breakfast had been cleared by another equally attractive young man – Irish this time – she once again checked her appearance in the long mirror, confident she was ready to carry out the deception. She left the room and made her way slowly downstairs, feigning not to notice several women's admiring glances when they spotted her outfit. She strolled across to the reception desk and handed in her room key. She was just about to leave when the receptionist enquired, 'How will you be paying your bill, madam?'

'But I thought—' she began, only to be reminded once again that the ten thousand was to cover necessary expenses that clearly didn't include unnecessary accessories.

Christina checked the bill and wished she hadn't bought the handbag. When they exchanged her pounds for dollars, she was made painfully aware that the hotel operated its own exchange rate.

She left the Waldorf having emptied the first cellophane packet of fifties and didn't want to check how much was left in the second. The doorman hailed a cab for her but he didn't get a tip.

'Three East 61st Street,' she said, before climbing into the back.

• • •

It was William's turn to read the *New York Times* while Ross was given the chance to finish what was left of breakfast, and James kept a close eye on the comings and goings across the street.

Two men dressed in brown overalls and carrying a couple of small stepladders were the only people of any interest to enter the front door during James's shift, but as the building had over a hundred apartments, he made a note but didn't give it a third thought. A few moments later a taxi drew up outside the block and a smartly dressed woman stepped out onto the sidewalk. She strolled into the building as if it wasn't her first visit. James, who was coming to the end of his shift, made a detailed description, even though he could only see her back. However, as the doorman saluted her, he assumed she had to be a resident. William took his place a few minutes later.

Long before Christina reached the front desk it became clear she was expected. The concierge jumped up to greet her as if she was still Mrs Miles Faulkner. She may as well have been.

'Mr Faulkner has already been in touch,' he said, 'and

instructed me to take you straight up to his apartment on the ninth floor. Two gentlemen from the Schwartz Gallery have already arrived and are waiting for you.'

Without another word he came from behind the desk and accompanied Christina across to the elevator. When they reached the ninth floor, he opened the door to the apartment with his pass key for the second time that morning.

The first thing Christina noticed as she entered the lounge was that the Rubens was no longer hanging on the wall but had been placed face up on the floor waiting to be put into the crate.

The concierge left them and took the elevator back down to the ground floor. He once again phoned Mr Faulkner, who was reading the *Evening News* over afternoon tea in London, and brought him up to date.

• • •

'An Art Logistics van has just arrived,' said Ross, barely able to contain his excitement.

William and James leapt up and rushed across to the window. They all watched as a man opened the rear door of the van and, along with two colleagues, gently lifted a large crate out onto the sidewalk before placing it on a dolly. Both front doors of the apartment block were held open, and six eyes never left the crate as it was wheeled slowly into the building, before disappearing out of sight.

James checked his watch. 'It shouldn't be too long before we're going through those doors, by which time the crate should have been delivered to the ninth floor. I'll stay on lookout duty, as I'm the only one who'll recognize the realtor, who should be arriving . . .' he checked his watch again, 'in about twenty minutes' time. Be ready to move at a moment's notice,' he added, leaving them in no doubt who'd taken over command.

• • •

When the crate was delivered to the ninth floor, the chief hanger nodded and said, 'Let's get on with it.'

Christina watched in admiration as the two professionals went about their work. First, they removed the twenty-eight screws that kept the lid firmly in place, before lifting the false Christ out of the box and propping him up against the wall. Next, after wrapping the real masterpiece in acid-free tissue and a layer of polythene, they lowered it gently into its bespoke foam-lined box. A perfect fit. The lid was replaced, and the process reversed as each of the screws were slowly twisted back into place. A lengthy process, and once they'd completed the task, they took a cigarette break.

Don't you realize we're on a tight schedule, Christina wanted to remind them, as she pointedly kept staring at her watch. At last, the chief hanger stubbed out his cigarette and they both went back to work.

First, they lifted the museum's copy of the Rubens off the floor, and climbed their little ladders, pausing on each step before moving on to the next one in unison. Their co-ordination would have impressed an Olympic gymnast. When they reached the top step, they slowly lowered the Fitzmolean's fake onto the hooks where a few minutes before the masterpiece had hung. They stood back for a moment to admire their work. The whole process had taken about forty minutes.

Christina found herself clapping as the chief packer looked

up at the copy on the wall and remarked, 'Not sure I can tell the difference.'

'That's the point,' said Christina, but didn't tell him there was a thirty-million-pound difference.

'Time for us to leave,' said the chief packer after checking his watch. 'We had strict instructions to be out of here before eleven.'

Christina handed the chief packer a hundred-dollar bill and regretted it even before he'd pocketed the money.

Once they'd left, she phoned Miles on his mobile. 'Your original is now in the crate as instructed,' she assured him, 'and their copy is hanging on the wall, so I've played my part.'

'Good timing,' said Miles, 'because any minute now our three keystone cops will turn up and switch the paintings back, assuming they've got their hands on my original. However, if they were to bump into you, our cover would be blown. So you've only got a few more minutes to get out of there.' The line went dead.

Christina had reached the elevator and was about to press the down arrow when she decided just to check. She dialled a number on her mobile and waited.

In answer to her enquiry, Mr Stewart replied, 'No money has been deposited in your account, Mrs Faulkner, and as it's almost five o'clock in London, there will be no further transactions carried out today.'

• • •

'The realtor has just entered the building,' said James, 'so we'd better get moving.'

'She's early,' said Ross as the three of them quickly left the room and hurried down the wide staircase to the hotel lobby.

'Thank you,' shouted James as he handed his key to the receptionist while still on the move. They didn't stop running until they were out on the pavement.

Despite the heavy traffic, they nipped across the busy road, dodging in and out of screeching vehicles accompanied by a cacophony of blasting horns and loud expletives, mainly expressed by drivers in yellow cabs. New Yorkers continued to stride along the sidewalk, oblivious to what would have raised eyebrows in any other city.

James was the first through the door and marched straight up to the front desk. He shook hands with the realtor before introducing his out-of-breath lawyer and mortgage broker, who also shook hands but didn't speak as their accents would have betrayed them.

'Now we're all here,' said the realtor, 'shall we go up to the apartment?'

'There's someone already up there,' said the concierge. 'So you'll have to wait for a few more minutes.'

'I did warn you, Mr Buchanan, that you're not the only person interested in the property.'

While they all hung around in the lobby waiting impatiently to get on with the job, the concierge turned his back on them, picked up the phone on his desk and dialled an internal number.

Christina had made her way back to the apartment and collapsed into a chair. It hadn't crossed her mind that once again Miles would double-cross her despite a long history of doing just that. She was staring up at the copy of the Rubens hanging on the wall when the phone by her side began to ring. She picked it up, unaware of how much time had passed.

'Just to let you know, Mrs Faulkner,' whispered the

concierge, 'a realtor has arrived with a Mr Buchanan. Can I send them up?'

'Are there three of them?' she asked.

'Yes,' replied the concierge, sounding surprised.

'Then I'll need some help moving the crate before they come up.'

'Not a problem, madam. I'll send up a couple of my guys who can take you and the crate up to the penthouse.'

The concierge instructed two of his front desk assistants to go up immediately to the ninth floor and assist Mrs Faulkner. He allowed a few more minutes to pass before accompanying the four visitors up in the elevator. As they stepped out on the ninth floor, the doors of the adjoining elevator closed before continuing up to the penthouse.

If Christina had considered the apartment on the ninth floor luxurious, the penthouse was in a different class. It quickly became clear Miles still had money to burn, if not on her bonfire. She sat alone with a crate that now contained the original masterpiece and thought carefully about her next move.

• • •

The first thing William and Ross did the moment they entered Faulkner's apartment on the ninth floor was to go in search of the crate, while James kept the hapless realtor occupied with a series of well-prepared questions concerning rates, service charges, fixtures and fittings, and when it would be possible for him to move in.

When William saw the painting hanging on the wall in the living room, he assumed the crate had to be nearby, but despite searching through every room in the apartment, under tables, sofas and beds, there was no sign of it. As they had all witnessed the crate being carried into the building, and hadn't seen it come back out, surely it couldn't be far away.

William grabbed the phone, dialled the front desk and shouted, 'Where the hell is it?' when the concierge eventually came on the line.

'If you're referring to the crate that was addressed to Mr Faulkner,' replied the concierge calmly. 'It's been sent up to the penthouse.'

'But it should have been delivered to the ninth floor,' shouted William, no longer able to control himself.

'Then you'll have to have a word with Mr Faulkner, because the package was addressed to him, not you, Mr . . .' William didn't respond. 'And I have the paperwork to prove it.'

'How did he find out?' said James, not under his breath.

'Once again he's a yard ahead of us, because he's not only kept the original,' said Ross, looking up at the picture on the wall, 'but he's also got our copy, and there's nothing we can do about it.'

The three men stood looking at each other, while the realtor, who hadn't understood a word they were talking about, asked innocently, 'Are you ready to sign the contract, Mr Buchanan?'

'Fuck the contract,' said William, shocking Ross and James who had never heard the choirboy swear. They led their friend back out into the corridor before he did something he might later regret. James shoved him gently into the elevator and pressed the button for the ground floor. The doors slowly closed.

• • •

Christina picked up the ringing phone in the penthouse to hear the concierge's voice.

'DHL have just arrived to pick up a crate, Mrs Faulkner. What shall I tell them?'

'Where are the three men who came up to view the ninth-floor apartment?'

'They left about twenty minutes ago, and I don't think we'll be seeing them again.'

Christina continued to stare at the crate that now contained the original Rubens of *Christ's Descent from the Cross*. She hesitated for a moment before saying, 'Send them up.'

• • •

'It's the fact we can't do anything about it that pisses me off,' said William as the three of them sat in a yellow cab heading back to JFK.

'Except kill Faulkner,' suggested Ross, sounding as if he meant it.

'Then we'd all end up with life sentences,' said William.

'Rather than the twelve years we're likely to get for attempting to steal a painting worth thirty million pounds,' suggested James.

'Twelve?' repeated William. 'But I thought you told me six was the maximum possible sentence?'

'Mea culpa,' said James. 'I forgot to mention the difference between theft and grand larceny, and I think you'll find thirty million qualifies as "grand".'

'But Faulkner still has the Rubens and we don't even have our copy,' protested Ross.

'The police don't know that,' said William, 'and one thing's for sure, Faulkner won't be enlightening them.'

'Can it get any worse?' asked James.

'Oh yes,' said William. 'Faulkner will take his time sending our copy back to the Fitzmolean but not before Beth has been sacked and I've had to resign,' he added as the cab drew up outside International Departures.

William dashed into the terminal and quickly scanned the departure board. 'If we can catch the six fifteen,' he said, 'we could still be back in London before Beth leaves for the museum.'

'Wouldn't it be better to call her now?' suggested James. 'So she can prepare herself before having to face the chairman . . .?'

'. . . and offer her resignation,' said William. 'No, I'm not going to wake her in the middle of the night and try to explain why I don't even have the copy of the Rubens, let alone the original. I'd rather do it in person and then at least I can accompany her to the Fitz and warn her all she's got for her trouble is the hope that Faulkner will eventually return the copy. I just wish there was some way of getting back to London more quickly.'

'Would all passengers travelling to Heathrow on Concorde please make their way to the departure gate?'

• • •

Christina felt good about how it had all worked out, though if Miles were to discover she had been responsible for exchanging his masterpiece for a worthless copy, she could be looking over her shoulder for the rest of her life.

She joined a small queue at the Concorde ticket desk and, when she reached the front, cancelled her booking, as she no longer had enough cash to pay for the ticket. 'Can you get me on your six fifteen overnight flight to Heathrow?' she asked.

The assistant tapped away on her computer. 'I have one first-class seat still available on that flight, madam.'

'What about economy?'

More tapping followed before the assistant enquired, 'Window or aisle?'

• • •

It was Ross who spotted her as she took her seat a few rows in front of them. He nudged William and pointed. He didn't seem that surprised, but then he didn't believe in coincidences.

'Do you think it's possible Christina knew exactly what we were up to?' asked Ross.

'It would certainly explain why Faulkner was always one step ahead of us.'

'But I thought she was a close friend of Beth?'

'Christina's a close friend of anyone who will pick up her next meal ticket.'

• • •

Christina was among the first off the plane when it landed at Heathrow. She would have taken a taxi to her flat in Mayfair, but didn't have enough cash to cover the fare, so she climbed aboard a coach showing 'Victoria Station'. Another first.

'That'll be four pounds ninety,' said the ticket collector as she climbed aboard. She handed over her last five-pound note and waited for the change.

William and Ross took the next tube to arrive and slowly learnt just how many stops there were on the journey into

London. William finally reached home at 8.33 a.m., only to discover Beth had already left.

'Mum wanted to be early for her first day at work, so she took your car,' explained Artemisia. 'By the way, Dad, where have you been?'

'New York,' said William.

'Nice one, Dad,' Peter responded as William ran back out of the house in search of a taxi, still hoping to get to the Fitz in time to brief Beth before the chairman turned up.

When Christina finally got off the bus, she decided to go directly to the museum so she could tell Beth what she'd done. It began to rain.

'Why can't you ever find a cab when you want one,' muttered a frustrated William to an audience of one. He gave up and began jogging towards Knightsbridge.

• • •

Miles called the concierge desk at his New York apartment building even before he'd sat down for breakfast.

'Did the shippers pick up the crate?' he demanded without announcing his name.

'I'll check the logbook, Mr Faulkner,' said the night porter, and a moment later reported, 'Yes, sir. DHL signed for one crate at three forty-two yesterday afternoon to be delivered to the Fitzmolean Museum in London.'

'Couldn't be better,' said Miles, before he put down the phone and said to Collins, 'I think I'll have a glass of champagne with my breakfast.'

• • •

Beth was among the first to arrive at the museum that morning.

She walked briskly up the sweeping staircase to the first floor and paused for a moment in front of a door marked DIRECTOR. She nearly knocked, before she opened the door and walked into her office. A vase of fresh flowers was on her desk along with a welcome back card from the chairman of the board. Beth wondered if she would be replaced before the flowers had shed their petals. Her thoughts were interrupted by a knock on the door.

'Come in,' she said, fearing it might be Sir Nicholas enquiring why an empty frame was propped up against the wall in the main gallery. But it was a young lad who poked his head around the door. A face she didn't recognize.

'Sorry to bother you, director' – *for how much longer?* she wondered – 'but a large crate has just been delivered to reception and they won't release it without your signature.'

Beth began to pray as she leapt up from behind her desk and charged out of the room, almost knocking the young man over. She slipped off her high heels and ran down the stairs two at a time before reaching the entrance hall. She recognized the crate immediately, and could only assume that, as William hadn't rung, the trip had been unsuccessful, not least because the manifest was labelled RETURN TO SENDER. After letting out a deep sigh, Beth accepted she needed to get the painting back on the wall in the main gallery before the doors were opened to the public at ten o'clock, even if it was a fake.

The courier handed over a release form along with a chewed Biro. 'Sign here, here and here, miss,' he said, pointing to three dotted lines. She scoured the small print for a clue, but was none the wiser. The value of the contents was recorded as less than ten thousand pounds, along with her signature.

After Beth had signed the form, she asked the doorman and the young lad to carry the crate into the main gallery, where the old frame was still propped up against the wall.

'Is Fred still the works manager?' Beth asked the doorman.

'Sure is, miss,' he said.

'Please tell him I need his help with hanging a picture and pronto.' The lad immediately scampered off. Beth stood there, staring at the empty frame, and didn't stop praying while she waited for the works manager to appear. Fred joined her a few minutes later, tool bag in hand with an assistant in tow carrying two small stepladders.

Fred and his assistant fell on their knees and set about extracting each screw from the crate one by one while Beth looked on, becoming more and more frustrated as she wondered if they could take any longer.

When the last screw had been removed, she quickly stepped forward to assist in yanking the lid off the crate but was once again held up as he and his assistant took their time removing first the polythene and then the acid-free tissue wrappings from around the canvas that had protected it from any mishaps during its long journey.

When the last acid-free layer had been removed, Beth stared down at the painting, still unsure if it was a masterpiece or an old friend returning home after a weekend abroad. It took the three of them to slowly, very slowly, lift the painting out of the box and ease it gently back into its frame. It was then the turn of the two hangers to step forward and mount the four steps of the ladder one by one before slowly lowering the chain back on its hooks. Beth stared up at the central figure that dominated the canvas, still unsure if he was the saviour or an imposter.

As ten o'clock struck on the long case clock in the hall, the front door was opened to allow the public to enter. The first person to come rushing in was a drenched and bedraggled Christina, taking Beth by surprise. They stood and stared at each other for some time, not a word passing between them until Beth finally demanded, 'Which one is it?'

'You've got the original,' said Christina, 'and Miles now has your copy hanging in his apartment. But promise me you'll never let on,' she whispered, 'because if Miles found out . . .' It was the last sentence that convinced Beth that Christ had risen from the dead.

She threw her arms around her old friend and said, 'How can I begin to thank you,' just as William came charging through the door.

'I'm so sorry,' were William's first words as he looked up at the painting, 'but he saw us coming,' he added, staring accusingly at Christina.

'You couldn't have done any more,' said Beth as Christina's mobile began to ring.

'Good morning, Mrs Faulkner,' said a cheerful voice. 'It's Craig Walker at Midland Bank. Just wanted to let you know that the first transfer of fifty thousand pounds arrived after close of business on Saturday, and a second one for the same amount has just been deposited with us. So your personal account has been credited with one hundred thousand pounds.'

• • •

Miles took a long-distance call from the manager of the Schwartz Gallery in New York after he'd returned home from a celebration lunch with Booth Watson at the Savoy. He'd had a little too much to drink.

'Thought I ought to let you know, Mr Faulkner, that the

painting you asked me to switch on Sunday didn't quite fit the frame. Just a few millimetres too large, and I wondered if you wanted me to make the necessary adjustment?'

'That won't be necessary,' said Miles. 'It was switched back after you'd left.'

'I don't think so, sir,' said the manager. 'Because when I dropped into your apartment earlier this morning to double-check everything had gone to plan, I found the copy you commissioned from us some years ago was now hanging on the wall.'

'So where's the original?' demanded Miles.

'When I last saw it, sir,' said the manager, 'it was in a crate due to be shipped back to London. And as it's no longer here, I can only assume . . .'

Miles hurled the phone from one end of the room to the other.

BOOK II

'Stirred up with envy and revenge.'

John Milton,
Paradise Lost

CHAPTER 14

FAULKNER SAT AT HIS DESK and began to write out two lists of names. The first was those who'd been responsible for stealing his Rubens, and the second was the team that would assist him in exacting revenge.

For	Against
Phil Harris	William Warwick
Bruce Lamont	Beth Warwick
Booth Watson	Ross Hogan
Tulip	James Buchanan
Collins	Christina Faulkner

Miles knew he couldn't make the next move unless Phil Harris was still on board, and they hadn't exactly parted on good terms. However, he hadn't been left with a lot of choice, because he couldn't hope to pull off such an audacious coup unless Harris was sitting in the front seat of the Lord Chamberlain's car when the exchange took place.

He opened the bottom drawer of his desk and delved through some papers until he came across a single sheet of Buckingham Palace stationery with nothing more than a mobile telephone number neatly written on it that he hadn't thought he would be calling a second time.

Miles picked up the phone and dialled the number slowly. It was answered on the third ring.

'Good morning, Mr Faulkner,' said a voice that didn't introduce himself.

'Good morning,' responded Miles, who wasted no time. 'Is the proposition you put to me when we first met a few weeks ago still on the table?'

'If I recall your exact words,' countered Harris, 'you considered the whole idea a ridiculous waste of your time and money?'

'I've had time to think it over,' said Miles, having anticipated the rebuke. 'Perhaps I was a little hasty.'

'I've also had time to think it over and the entry fee has changed.'

'If you're hoping to get more than a million,' snapped Miles, 'you can forget it.'

'A million was always a fair price,' came back Harris, 'and I won't go back on my word. But just to make sure you don't change your mind again, I want a hundred thousand upfront.'

'But you don't have anywhere else to go,' Miles reminded him.

'Neither do you,' parried Harris. 'Otherwise, I don't suppose you would have rung a second time.'

Miles began to wonder if Harris even knew about the Rubens or if he was just becoming paranoid. One thing Miles did accept was he would never have a better opportunity to bring down Warwick and Hogan, and possibly even Hawksby all at the same time.

'Why don't you join me around six at my place?' said Miles, 'and let's see if we can take this to the next stage. I'm assuming I don't have to tell you my address?'

'Not possible, I'm afraid, Mr Faulkner. This evening I have to drive my boss to Mansion House for a dinner with the Lord Mayor, but as he won't be out before ten, you could join me.'

'Where?'

'In the back of the Lord Chamberlain's car. The one place you can be sure no one will overhear us. And by the way, bring the hundred grand with you if you're hoping for a third meeting.'

Miles put down the phone and placed an expansive tick against Harris's name. He took his time considering the second person on the list. He was well aware the ex-copper hadn't been overwhelmed with offers since leaving the Met, with neither friends nor reputation to fall back on. He dialled his number.

'Lamont,' said a voice after only one ring.

'Bruce, it's Miles Faulkner. I wondered if we could meet? I have a proposition I'd like to discuss with you.'

'Any time that suits you,' responded Lamont.

'Tomorrow morning at my flat, ten o'clock.'

'I'll be there,' said Lamont.

'And be sure no one else knows you're coming to see me,' said Miles before he put the phone down and placed a second tick on his list.

Miles looked at the third name for some considerable time, and even wondered if he was on the right list. The damn man had gone behind his back so many times in the past. However, for the moment, he required his counsel, though if he put a foot wrong, Miles wouldn't hesitate to shift him from one list to the other.

Miles dialled a private number he knew went straight through to his desk in chambers.

'Booth Watson.'

'Miles Faulkner, BW. I'd like to seek your advice on an unusual enterprise I'm considering, and wondered if we could meet?' He waited for his response.

'Always available for you, Miles,' came back the immediate reply, revealing that clients weren't exactly rushing in and out of BW's chambers seeking his learned advice.

'Can we meet at our usual rendezvous around midday tomorrow?' asked Miles. 'I don't need anyone other than the royal swans to overhear our conversation.'

'I'll be there,' said Booth Watson, not even checking his diary.

Desperate, thought Miles, as he added another tick to his list, although he knew BW wouldn't come cheap. He couldn't phone the next person on the list as he'd have to book a prison visit if he wanted to see him. He made an entry in his diary for Saturday afternoon between three and five p.m., the only time Tulip would be available.

The only other member of the team who would play a vital role in the success of the operation was also the one person he trusted without question. He pressed the buzzer under his desk and Collins appeared a moment later.

• • •

William arrived home before Beth, aware that would be happening more often now she had taken up her position at the museum and would have to attend evening events fairly frequently. He made a noble effort to prepare the children's supper but warming up a pizza in the microwave wasn't going to earn him a Michelin star.

'How's your Colonel Blood project coming along?' William asked as he joined the children at the kitchen table.

'We're going to win the prize essay competition,' said Peter with a confidence that didn't entertain doubts.

'That goes without saying,' said William, 'but wasn't what I asked.'

'All will be revealed as soon as Mum gets home,' said Artemisia, 'when we're going to read you the first chapter of *Colonel Blood: Hero or Villain?*'

'That might depend on which side of the fence you're sitting,' said William just as Beth came bustling into the room.

'How was your day?' asked William, even before she'd taken off her coat.

'Exhausting,' Beth replied as she joined them at the table and grabbed a large slice of pizza before adding, 'Didn't even have time for lunch.'

'You can tell me all about it later,' said William, giving Beth a wink, 'but the twins are just about to read the opening chapter of their prize-winning essay.'

'They haven't won the prize yet,' Beth reminded them.

'Oh, ye of little faith,' said William, as he poured her a glass of wine.

'I've already heard it,' piped up Jojo, 'and it's certain to win.'

'Can't wait,' said Beth between mouthfuls.

Artemisia pushed her plate aside, bent down and extracted a couple of sheets of lined paper from her satchel and placed them on the table. She cleared her throat before she began.

'Thomas Blood was born in Sarney, County Meath in 1617—'

'Or possibly 1618,' chipped in Peter. 'We can't be certain as there weren't any birth certificates in those days.'

'His father, Neptune,' continued Artemisia, 'owned a prosperous ironworks as well as a fair portion of land. He was also mentioned in published accounts as *serious, honest and of no inferior credit.*'

'His son, Thomas,' continued Peter, 'left school at an early age to join the army and fight for the royalist cause in the Civil War. He became a lieutenant, then as the years passed styled himself as Captain Blood and later Major Blood, finally ending up as Colonel Blood.'

'At some time in the 1650s,' Artemisia said, taking over the story, 'Blood abandoned the royalist cause and joined up with Oliver Cromwell, the newly appointed Lord Protector of the Commonwealth. We can't be sure why he deserted his former comrades in favour of Cromwell but, over the next few years, he regularly switched sides whenever it suited his purpose.'

'He sounds like one of your friends,' said William, looking directly at Beth.

'If only you knew the . . .' began Beth, but she stopped mid-sentence.

'Blood next turns up in Lancashire in 1651,' continued Peter, ignoring his parents' exchange, 'and in 1654 he married a Miss Mary Holcroft, the daughter of Colonel Holcroft of Holcroft Hall, so he was what you might call today upwardly mobile.'

'Can't use those words,' said Artemisia firmly. 'Too modern.'

'How about ambitious, and clearly moving up in the world?' suggested Peter. Artemisia nodded, allowing Peter to continue.

'At some point in the 1650s, Blood returned to Ireland, possibly following the death of his father. He took over the ironworks and managing the estates that at the time yielded him around a hundred pounds a year, and he remained a respected citizen and a loyal supporter of Cromwell, which ensured that he prospered, acquiring further estates. He was even appointed a Justice of the Peace.

'In fact,' suggested Peter, 'Blood may not have troubled us again if Cromwell hadn't died in 1658, ushering in a period known as the Restoration, when in 1660 Charles II and the House of Stuart returned to the English throne. From that moment, Blood's comfortable existence began to falter and, within a couple of years, his lands had been confiscated by the King's representative, the Duke of Ormond, which resulted in him being deprived of his income. It is perhaps easy to understand why Blood once again decided to switch sides and become a rebel, which led to him being involved in a dastardly plot to take over Dublin Castle . . .'

'Dastardly?' said Artemisia. 'Too melodramatic.'

Peter put a line through the word and replaced it with 'outrageous', '. . . and kidnap the Duke of Ormond, who he considered was the cause of all his troubles.'

'Who can blame him,' said Beth.

'And that's as far as we've got,' said Artemisia, closing her notebook. 'Miss Elton, our history teacher, told us we'll have to do a lot more research before we can tell you the outcome of Blood's raid on Dublin Castle.'

'Well, I, for one, can't wait to find out what happens to Colonel Blood when he raids Dublin Castle,' said Beth as she began to clear away the plates.

'And on that note,' said William, looking across at the children, 'I think it's time for bed.'

Peter grabbed the last chocolate biscuit as his sister and Jojo got up from the table and left the room.

'One quick question before I come back down,' said William, before he reached the door. 'Are you still the director of the Fitzmolean?'

'I am,' replied Beth. 'But only thanks to Christina.'

'Sounds every bit as unlikely as Colonel Blood attempting to take over Dublin Castle and capture the Duke of Ormond with a handful of rebels,' said William, 'and I have a feeling that book will also have several more chapters before the ending is revealed.'

Beth said nothing.

• • •

Collins parked the Mercedes about a hundred yards from Mansion House and switched off the engine. He pointed to a grey Jaguar on the corner of Walbrook.

Miles, briefcase in hand, got out of the car and made his way slowly across the road. He remained in the shadows until he recognized a familiar figure seated behind the wheel of the Jaguar. Miles opened the back door, slipped inside and crouched down in the far corner.

'What if someone should ask who I am?' were his opening words.

'If you put on my cap, they'll assume you're just another driver waiting for his boss.'

'That would be a first.'

'One of many, I suspect,' suggested Harris, 'if we're going to end up working together. Forgive me for asking, Mr Faulkner, but what made you change your mind?'

'Let's just say it's personal and leave it at that. Though I'm puzzled why you're willing to take such a risk when if you were caught, you could end up spending the rest of your life in jail.'

'Or worse.'

'What could possibly be worse?'

'It's treason even to attempt to steal the Crown Jewels and remains one of the few crimes left on the statute books you can still be hanged for.'

'Then I repeat, why take the risk?'

'A million pounds is incentive enough when the alternative is eking out an existence on a pension of eleven thousand four hundred pounds a year for the rest of my life. Something you wouldn't begin to understand.'

'But your family?'

'I'm divorced, no kids. But I still have alimony payments hanging around my neck along with a stack of unopened brown envelopes on my desk, and an overdraft limit I reached some time ago, not to mention I've got a bookie who's threatening to break an arm and a leg if I haven't settled my account by the end of the month. Frankly, it's a far bigger risk for you.'

This wasn't the time to let Harris know he had no intention of stealing the Crown Jewels, only of ending the careers of three men and one woman who'd crossed him once too often.

'So what will you do with your million?' asked Miles. 'Because one thing's for certain, you won't be able to settle down in the country and enjoy a long and well-earned retirement.'

'I will be flying to Mexico on the same day while leaving all my debts behind. And don't forget that Mexico is a country that doesn't bother with extradition treaties, but they do have a police force who are happy to supplement their income with bribes. However, I'll also need a new identity and a new passport, which Danny tells me is one of your specialities.'

'That's the easy part, assuming you make it to the airport,' said Miles, leaving an implied threat hanging in the air.

'If I don't, they will already have caught you.' Miles was beginning to realize he couldn't afford to underestimate Harris. 'Before you leave,' said the chauffeur, not looking around, 'don't forget my hundred grand.'

Miles placed the briefcase on the front seat. 'I'll be in touch,' he said as he got out of the car. 'I don't know what else Danny told you, but be warned, I'm a mean loser.'

CHAPTER 15

BRUCE LAMONT REFLECTED FOR A moment on the conversation he'd had the previous day with his new boss, whom he'd first met after he'd arrested him for fraud. However, since then he'd had to leave the force in what might be described as unfortunate circumstances. Faulkner had quickly taken advantage of those circumstances, and become his paymaster on an ad hoc basis. Cash, no tax, no prospects and no pension. What one might describe as 'role reversal'.

The fact that he'd called him Bruce when he phoned, and not Lamont, rather suggested how much he needed his particular skills for his latest questionable project, whatever that might be. He knew the words 'be sure no one else knows you're coming to see me' referred to Mr Booth Watson QC and his boss's ex-wife Christina, both of whom he had worked for in the past. And he suspected they'd be off-limits for the foreseeable future.

After he'd gone for an early morning run, taken a shower and shaved, he selected a double-breasted, dark grey flannel suit, blue shirt and a navy silk tie for the meeting. He then polished his shoes a second time as this was clearly going to be a job interview.

He'd left himself more than enough time to make the journey from Hammersmith to Chelsea, and was just about to leave when his wife said, 'Where are you off to at this time in the morning?'

'To see my bank manager,' he replied, hoping he sounded convincing.

The raised eyebrow rather suggested she didn't believe him. He'd closed the front door before she could ask any more questions.

Lamont didn't head for the nearest tube station, but hailed a cab, an unusual expense, but he couldn't afford to arrive not looking at his best for this appointment. He was dropped outside Faulkner's home on Cadogan Place with twenty minutes to spare, so he walked slowly around the block, looking in shop windows at goods he couldn't afford. He was back outside the front door at three minutes to ten.

'Good to see you, Bruce,' said Miles, after Collins had shown his guest through to the study. The two men shook hands as if they were old friends, although neither considered the other more than an acquaintance who from time to time served a purpose.

'It's good to see you again too, sir,' said Lamont as Miles ushered him into a comfortable chair by the fire. Another first.

'Sorry about the short notice,' said Miles, 'but something has come up that I think can only be described as a once-in-a-lifetime opportunity. However, I wouldn't consider going ahead with such a demanding challenge, without your particular expertise.'

'I'm flattered,' said Lamont, which was exactly what Miles had intended, 'and will be only too happy to assist if I possibly can.'

'Of course, there's an element of risk involved,' continued Miles. 'But I'm confident I've found a way of minimizing that, and if we can get the timing right, completely eliminating it.'

'I'm intrigued.'

'What I'm about to tell you, Bruce, is highly confidential, so much so that I will only be sharing the finer details with two other close associates, both of whom you've already had dealings with in the past.'

Lamont suspected he knew who they were.

'There will, however, be a large cast of extras involved in the final performance, who will play a vital role before the curtain rises. But like any audience, they will not know the ending until the curtain comes down. With that in mind, there will have to be several dress rehearsals.' The ex-Chief Superintendent didn't interrupt. 'Yesterday,' began Miles, 'I had a second meeting with a Mr Phil Harris, who is currently . . .'

Lamont remained on the edge of his seat and didn't interrupt the boss for the next twenty minutes.

• • •

Ross had been looking forward to the Reg Simpson case, because he despised anyone who tried to tempt children with drugs, knowing they would then have a helpless customer under their control. He hoped he would be called early, as he needed to get to St Luke's before four o'clock. He'd promised Jojo he'd be there in time to see the class's end of term art exhibition. Jojo thought she just might win a prize.

And there was also another reason he wanted to be there . . .

The first thing Ross did on arrival at Southwark Crown Court was to check with the clerk when he thought he might be called.

'There are two witnesses before you, Inspector,' the clerk said, looking at his list, 'so you should be called before lunch. Latest two o'clock.'

More than enough time, thought Ross, as he sat down in a draughty soulless corridor waiting for proceedings to begin. He kept checking his watch during the next two hours, but he wasn't called. And what made it worse, he couldn't enter the court and find out how the case was proceeding.

The lunch break came and went and, despite the clerk's prediction, he still hadn't been called. When the clerk stepped out into the corridor at the start of the afternoon session, Ross leapt up.

'Mr Ken Simpson,' he pronounced for all to hear. Ross sank back down as the defendant's brother made his way into the court, disappointed that he now wouldn't make Jojo's art show, let alone have a chance to invite Ms Clarke out to dinner.

Another forty minutes passed before he was eventually called. When he entered the witness box, he took the Bible in his right hand and didn't have to read the oath from the card being held up by the clerk of the court. Once the oath had been administered, Ross turned to face prosecuting counsel, who greeted him with a warm smile.

'Please state your name and rank for the record.'

'Ross Hogan. I'm a Detective Inspector attached to the Royalty Protection squad,' he said, before looking directly at the jury.

'And were you, until recently, Princess Diana's personal protection officer?'

'I had that privilege,' replied Ross.

A woman seated in the front row of the jury box sat up and took a closer look at Ross.

'Can I also confirm that you have twice been awarded the Queen's Gallantry Medal and, during your distinguished career, have received no fewer than six police commendations?'

'I think, Sir Julian,' interrupted the judge, 'you have established the witness's commendable record as a police officer, so perhaps it's time to move on.'

'Or have you?' murmured Booth Watson, loud enough for both the judge and jury to hear.

'I'm glad you feel that's the case, m'Lud,' suggested Sir Julian, ignoring his learned friend, before turning back to face the witness. 'Inspector, perhaps you would take us through what happened on the afternoon of Monday 4th November when you went to St Luke's School in Fulham to pick up your daughter.'

'I arrived a few minutes early, and while I was reversing into a parking space, I saw the defendant was involved in a heated conversation with one of the teachers.'

'Did you recognize the teacher in question?'

'Yes, it was a Ms Clarke, Jojo's class teacher.'

'So what happened next?'

'I jumped out of my car, ran across the road and stepped in between them.'

Booth Watson made a note on his yellow pad – *stepped in between them?*

'Did you notice anything else as you crossed the road, Inspector?'

'Leading,' said Booth Watson from a sedentary position.

'The defendant opened his clenched fist and dropped some pills down a nearby drain,' said Ross, ignoring the sotto voce remark.

'What did you do next?' asked Sir Julian.

'I immediately arrested him on suspicion of being in possession of and dealing in drugs.'

'And was he in possession of drugs?'

'No, sir. But three of the pills ended up in the gutter and, while I was holding onto the suspect, Ms Clarke gathered them up, wrapped them in her handkerchief and handed them to me.'

Booth Watson made a note, *only three?*

'And what did those pills turn out to be, Inspector?'

'Methamphetamine, more commonly known as ecstasy.'

'Methamphetamine is, correct me if I'm wrong Inspector, a class A drug, as defined under section four of the 1971 Misuse of Drugs Act.'

'That is correct,' said Ross.

'And at the time of the arrest, the defendant was loitering outside a school playground.'

'My Lord,' protested Booth Watson, heaving himself up.

'I agree,' responded the judge. 'Sir Julian, you will in future refrain from asking and answering your own questions.'

'I do apologize, m'Lud,' said Sir Julian, but only needed to glance in the direction of the jury to confirm that his point had been made. He suppressed a smile before saying, 'No more questions, m'Lud.'

'Mr Booth Watson,' enquired the judge, looking down from on high, 'do you wish to cross-examine this witness?'

'I most certainly do, m'Lud,' replied Booth Watson, even before he had risen from his place. He looked long and hard at the witness and certainly didn't offer him a warm smile before posing his first question. 'Inspector, can I begin by congratulating you on your commendable record as a police officer, although I fear we only heard your side of the story.' He paused, hoping for a response, but none was forthcoming, so he continued. 'Is it not also the case that you have, during that same period, been suspended on two occasions for conduct unworthy of a police officer?' Ross still didn't respond so Booth Watson pressed on. 'And have you also been placed on disciplinary reports on no less than five separate occasions?'

Ross continued to return Booth Watson's stare but still said nothing.

'Should I assume from your silence, Inspector, that you are not denying your past indiscretions?' Still nothing. 'Would it therefore be fair to suggest you are from time to time a good cop, while at other times, perhaps not quite so good?'

'Move on, Mr Booth Watson. I think you've made your point.'

Booth Watson bowed to the judge, leant down and extracted a single sheet of paper from his original notes. 'This, Inspector,' he said, holding it up for all to see, 'is your incident report following the arrest of my client, so let me ask you, when did you hand it in?'

'The following morning,' admitted Ross.

'Not at the time of the arrest?'

'No. Once the custody record had been completed by the sergeant, I returned to St Luke's to collect my daughter.'

'Despite the fact that she was in the safe hands of Ms Clarke.'

'Yes,' said Ross. 'But I still had to take her home.'

'So you ended up writing your report the following day,

giving you more than enough time to go over your story with Ms Clarke.'

'Mr Booth Watson!' said the judge.

'I apologize, m'Lud. I should have said had enough time to think it over.'

'Equally damning, I would suggest,' said Sir Julian, rising to his feet.

'Then allow me to withdraw the question altogether and simply ask the witness to confirm that he wrote his report some twenty-four hours after the arrest had taken place.'

'More like eighteen hours.'

'Once you'd slept on it.'

Ross nodded reluctantly.

'With that in mind, Inspector, can I confirm that despite having some considerable time to consider the contents of your hindsight report, you decided to omit one vital piece of evidence that would have undoubtedly helped my client's defence and possibly made the CPS think twice about pressing drug-dealing charges?'

'Like what?' said Ross, unable to remain calm any longer.

'Correct me if I'm wrong, Inspector, but when you searched Mr Simpson on arriving at the police station, all you found on him was a packet of Bassetts Liquorice Allsorts, which I don't think you'll find are classified as a class A drug in the 1971 Misuse of Drugs Act.'

One or two members of the jury smiled, and not at Ross.

'Along with three methamphetamine pills,' Ross reminded him.

'Well, let's also be clear on that point, Inspector,' came back Booth Watson, 'you did not find my client in possession of those three pills, because it was Ms Clarke who confirmed, during my cross-examination of her yesterday, that she picked them up from the gutter, wrapped them in her handkerchief and handed them to you.'

'That's correct,' said Ross.

'So you have absolutely no proof those pills ever belonged to my client?'

'As I've said, and also wrote in my report,' countered Ross, 'I witnessed Simpson dropping several more pills down a drain that was conveniently nearby.'

'You did indeed, Inspector, but are you familiar with the case law set out in the Crown v Turnbull?'

'Yes, I am.'

'Then you won't be surprised when I ask you how far away you were when you witnessed the incident you have described, remembering you were crossing an extremely busy road during rush hour?' Before Ross could respond, Booth Watson added, 'Because I am bound to ask if you are seriously suggesting to the court that you had a clear and unobstructed view of my client at all times?'

'I saw what I saw.'

'Or perhaps what you wanted to see, Inspector. So allow me to move on and ask an obvious question. Why didn't you lift up the drain and retrieve the pills you thought you saw?'

'At the time,' replied Ross defiantly, 'my immediate concern was Ms Clarke's safety, as well as my daughter's.'

'But your daughter wasn't there at the time and didn't appear until after you'd arrested my client and marched him off to the nearest police station.'

'She came out of school a few moments later.'

'How can you possibly know that, Inspector, when you'd already left? Perhaps you have eyes in the back of your head which would explain your twenty-twenty vision.' Booth Watson extracted another sheet of paper from his file before he continued.

'Inspector, would you describe yourself as a seeker after the truth when it comes to writing a report—' he paused '—the following day?' Ross didn't respond, despite Booth Watson waiting for some considerable time. 'Did you by any chance,' he continued, 'ask my client why he was outside the school at that time of day?'

'I didn't need to. That's the time when the kids come out of the school and are most vulnerable to being approached by a stranger.'

'And being offered a Liquorice Allsort?' Booth Watson suggested. Ross scowled but couldn't come up with a suitable reply. 'So you didn't realize at the time, that my client was waiting to pick up his nephew, Kevin, when he came out of St Luke's so they would walk home together?'

Ross would like to have told the jury that Simpson's nephew was the son of a local drug dealer, and undoubtedly his contact in the playground, but that wasn't something he could refer to in his report.

After it became clear Ross wasn't going to respond, Booth Watson looked directly at the witness and said, 'Of the eleven questions I've put to you, Inspector, you've only managed to answer five. So I think it shouldn't be too difficult for the jury to decide whether on this occasion you were playing the role of a good cop, or,' he paused, 'a not so good cop. No more questions, my Lord,' he declared, his eyes never leaving the jury as he slumped back down in his place.

Mr Justice Roberts turned his attention back to prosecuting counsel and asked, 'Do you wish to re-examine this witness, Sir Julian?'

'Just a couple of questions, m'Lud,' he said as he rose from his place. 'Inspector, may I ask how old your daughter is?'

'Jojo is eight, sir.'

'And do you, by any chance, know how old the defendant's nephew Kevin is?'

'Yes, I was able to confirm that Mr Simpson has a nephew at St Luke's who is sixteen.'

'And as a seeker after the truth, which my learned friend seems so concerned about,' said Sir Julian, turning to face the judge, 'I should point out that Kevin Simpson will be seventeen in two weeks' time.'

'Is this leading anywhere, Sir Julian?' enquired the judge.

'Not directly, I must admit,' conceded Sir Julian. 'However, I don't know many seventeen-year-old boys who need to be picked up from school by an uncle before being taken home.'

A little laughter broke out in the court and Sir Julian was pleased to see one or two members of the jury had got the message.

'That was uncalled for, Sir Julian,' remonstrated the judge, who, turning to the jury, said, 'you must dismiss that suggestion from your minds and not allow it to influence you when you retire to consider your verdict in this case.'

But will they dismiss it, wondered Sir Julian before adding, 'No more questions, m'Lud.'

The judge turned his attention back to Inspector Hogan and said, 'Inspector, you can leave the witness box.' He looked at his watch and, turning to the jury, pronounced, 'I think that will be enough for today.'

He finally reminded them not to discuss the case with anyone other than their fellow jury members and that included their families. 'I look forward to seeing you all again in the morning,' he added, giving the five men and seven women a beneficent smile.

'All rise!' bellowed the clerk at the top of his voice.

Everyone obeyed the order and bowed as the judge left the court. When Ross stepped out of the witness box, the same juror caught his eye and smiled. He didn't acknowledge her. Sir Julian apologized for how long he'd had to hang around before being called, and thanked him for his contribution.

Once he was back on the street, Ross headed for the nearest tube station and was taken by surprise when the persistent juror reappeared by his side.

'Hi Ross,' she said, almost running along beside him. 'Am I allowed to speak to you?'

'No,' he replied, not stopping. 'At least not until after a verdict has been reached.'

'It's just that I wanted to find out more about what it was like being Princess Di's personal bodyguard?'

'Protection officer,' said Ross, who didn't stop walking. 'And as I made clear, not until the trial is over.'

'Can I give you my telephone number?' she asked.

Ross gave her a second look.

• • •

'Its simplicity is its genius,' said Lamont once Miles had come to the end of his monologue. 'I've never known a crime where the victim willingly hands over the "swag" without being threatened.'

'But only because they'll think they're handing over the "swag" to a member of their own team.'

'But it's still one hell of a risk you'd be taking, when you consider the consequences.'

'You'll be taking it,' said Miles. 'But if you can get your timing right, everything else should fall into place with the added bonus it will be Warwick who ends up in the dock. Any recent updates on what he's been up to?'

'You'll already know he's been promoted to Chief Superintendent, but you may not be aware that he's being strongly tipped as a future commissioner.'

'He'll be lucky to end up as the commissionaire of his local Odeon, with his sidekick selling the ice creams by the time I've finished with them.'

'And what role would I be expected to play?' asked Lamont.

'You'll be my second-in-command,' said Miles. 'Because I want everything run like a military operation. However, your immediate task will be to assemble a team of foot soldiers, men and women, who can be trusted and will remain schtum long after the event has taken place. You can recruit them from those officers who had to leave the force rather suddenly following Warwick's recent inquiry into police corruption, along with any first-time offenders who are no longer on probation. It's essential they don't know the end game, only that they'll be well paid for their trouble, with the added bonus they'll be responsible for finally bringing down Warwick, Hogan and possibly even the commander himself.'

'For some of my former colleagues, that will be more than enough; there's one in particular who had to take early retirement because Warwick doesn't know how to turn a blind eye.'

'Are there any other ex-coppers who fall into that category?' Faulkner asked.

'Half a dozen, possibly more, but do any of them need to be specialists?'

Miles opened a file that had been growing by the hour and turned a couple of pages before saying, 'First and foremost,

I'll need three elite motorcycle riders along with their SEG motorbikes.'

'That shouldn't be a problem,' said Lamont. 'I know exactly where they end up before being scrapped.'

'I'll also need a Jaguar and a Land Rover, both grey, two garage mechanics who can switch a number plate in seconds, along with four taxi drivers and their cabs, a uniformed constable, preferably an ex-copper, half a dozen women and a couple of prams, but no children.' He removed a duplicate list from his file and handed it across to Lamont, who realised he was going to have to do a lot of preparatory work that couldn't be witnessed by his wife.

'How long have I got?' he asked.

'A month, six weeks at the most, before we begin rehearsals. But don't rush, because we only need one person to look out of place and the whole operation will be compromised long before you reach the East Gate. However,' said Miles, 'your biggest challenge remains who will take the Lord Chancellor's place.'

'I've already got someone in mind,' said Lamont, but didn't elaborate. Miles simply nodded. Lamont now felt confident enough to ask the one question that had been on the tip of his tongue since Faulkner had phoned. 'How much will I be paid?'

'Let me assure you, Bruce, your reward won't be in heaven. If the operation is successful, you'll earn a quarter of a million pounds, as well as having all your expenses covered, which will more than make up for the pension Warwick deprived you of.'

Lamont remained silent as he weighed in the balance £250,000 and, on the other side of the scales, the possibility of spending the next ten years in jail.

Miles interrupted his thoughts. 'You'll get fifty grand today,' he continued, 'another fifty when your team is in place, fifty more once the two crowns have been switched, and the final hundred as long as the Queen has delivered her speech to their Lordships in the Upper House and returned to the palace empty-handed.'

Miles unlocked the middle drawer of his desk and took out ten cellophane packets each containing five thousand pounds and pushed them across the table. The scales fell to one side.

'In future, you will call me on my mobile at eight every morning, before my secretary arrives, and again at six in the evening, after she's left. So, when the police question her, as they undoubtedly will, her lack of knowledge will be convincing.'

'Plausible deniability,' said Lamont, 'which on this occasion will have the virtue of being true. And may I make another suggestion?' Miles nodded. 'Change your mobile regularly and make sure the old one can never be traced. That's the first thing the police will look for should you be arrested.'

'Where's the one place they never look?' asked Miles.

'The bottom of the Thames, where there are more mobile phones than fish.'

Miles laughed for the first time. 'One more thing before you go, Bruce. If Hogan was absent on the day of the operation, it would make our job a whole lot easier, and I'd be willing to pay another twenty grand if you were able to pull that off.'

'Hogan can't be bribed,' said Lamont.

'Then find another way,' said Miles, 'and the twenty grand will be yours.'

Lamont thought for a moment. He was sufficiently obsessed with getting some sort of payback against Hogan and Warwick that various mates still working inside the system kept an eye on them for him. There was probably something one of them could tell him which would give him leverage. He gathered up the cellophane packets, rose from his place and gave Mr Faulkner a slight bow before departing. Once he'd closed the door, Miles put a tick by his name. He waited for a moment before picking up a phone and dialling a number he no longer needed to look up. When it was answered, all he said was 'Game on,' before putting the phone down.

He closed one file marked 'Traitors Gate' and opened another headed simply, 'Christina'.

CHAPTER 16

'DO YOU THINK MILES HAS worked it out by now?' asked Beth.

'Can't have done, otherwise I'd be toast,' replied Christina. 'With a bit of luck, you're still the only other person who knows the Fitz have the original Christ, while the fake Messiah is hanging in my ex's New York penthouse.'

'I'm still curious to know,' said Beth, 'if you'd received the hundred thousand before William, Ross and James turned up at Miles's apartment, would the Fitzmolean still have the fake and Miles the original?'

'How can you even suggest such a thing,' chided Christina, as Beth poured her another cup of coffee.

Beth didn't want to admit that it was William who'd made the suggestion after she'd told him the truth. In fact, he'd gone one step further and recommended she check another paint sample before he would be convinced. A week later, when the test result came back, he reluctantly gave Christina the benefit of the doubt.

'You've done wonders with this café,' said Christina, deliberately changing the subject. 'It may be the Fitz and not the Ritz, but a great improvement on the last time I was here.'

'It's kind of you to say so,' said Beth. 'We even have visitors who come to the café without going into the museum, which increases our footfall, and the numbers help towards our government grant.'

'Admit it, Beth, you're every bit as devious as I am.'

'But only when it's in aid of a good cause,' responded Beth, which caused Christina to change the subject once again.

'How are the twins?'

'They're both spending every spare moment working on their prize essay about a seventeenth-century rogue called Colonel Blood, who's looking more like your ex-husband every day.'

'And Jojo?'

'She's already drawing her own greeting cards, which Peter sells at a profit.'

'Perhaps they should join—'

'I'm sorry to bother you,' interrupted a man sitting at the next table, 'but could I steal one of your sugar lumps?'

'Of course,' said Christina, handing over the bowl. She turned back and whispered, 'Perhaps you should have a sugar bowl on every table.'

'We do,' said Beth. 'I think he's more interested in you than the sugar lumps.' Christina gave him a second look. 'Mind you,' continued Beth, 'he's not in your usual age bracket.'

'He's older than me!' protested Christina.

'That's what I meant.'

'Aren't we sharp today,' said Christina, giving the man a third look.

'Must dash,' said Beth, after she'd drained her coffee. 'We're making preparations for an exciting new exhibition.'

'Any clues?'

'Not yet. So much depends on whether the Prado will play ball.'

'Then it has to be Goya or Velasquez.'

'Not bad. I'll tell you more when I get back from Madrid, along with the latest episode of Colonel Blood,' Beth promised as she leant over and kissed Christina on both cheeks before she left.

'Thank you,' said the man sitting at the next table, as he passed back the sugar bowl.

Christina gave him a fourth look. Beth was right. He must have been around forty-five, perhaps fifty, with a handsome rugged face and strands of grey appearing at the edges of his dark wavy hair. But it was his solemn grey eyes that made her look more closely. She also clocked the Patek Philippe watch and the gold cufflinks.

'Do you come here often?' he teased.

'Yes,' replied Christina, rather pompously. 'I'm on the board of the Fitz.'

'It's one of my favourite galleries,' said the stranger, sounding serious. 'The Rubens, Vermeer, Rembrandt and Frans Hals are all quite exceptional.'

'Do you have a favourite among them?'

'Probably Rubens' *Christ's Descent from the Cross*,' he replied. 'A genuine masterpiece.'

Christina smiled. 'I convinced my ex-husband to donate that particular work to the museum.'

'I'm surprised he was willing to part with it,' he paused, 'or you.'

'Reluctantly,' said Christina, ignoring the flattery. 'But I finally convinced him.'

'Then it's you who I should thank,' he said, raising his coffee cup as if it were a wine glass.

'Are you a collector by any chance?' ventured Christina.

'No, but my father was, so I grew up surrounded by beautiful things.'

'And are you still surrounded by them?'

'Sadly not. When he died, death duties, inheritance tax and a wicked stepfather who was more interested in selling than buying meant there wasn't much left over for the prodigal son. But I'm not complaining, as I still ended up with enough to ensure I don't have to rely on my wits to survive.'

'So you don't own a painting that in the fullness of time you might consider gifting to the Fitz?' asked Christina, delivering a sentence she'd heard Beth repeat many times without even blushing.

'I'm afraid not,' he said as he moved across and took the seat opposite her. 'I fear my stepfather put a stop to that.'

'You know my name, but I—'

'Percy. Percy Singleton,' he said.

'You're not by any chance related to the distinguished art critic, Sir Peregrine Singleton?'

'My late father, God bless him.' He raised his coffee cup once again.

'But you hinted he left you other things,' said Christina, still hopeful.

'Yes, but nothing that would interest the Fitzmolean. A stamp collection that regular visits to Stanley Gibbons over the years have helped keep the wolf from the door, and a few coins that should make it possible for me not to have to rely on a state pension.'

'I had no idea coins could be that valuable.'

'Oh, yes,' said Percy. 'A 1343 Edward III florin, for example, recently sold at Sotheby's Parke-Bernet for four hundred and eighty thousand pounds, while a rare 1794 Flowing Hair silver dollar, thought to be among the first struck by the US Mint, was bought by a private collector for over ten million dollars. Despite the Mint striking one thousand eight hundred of them, it's thought fewer than a hundred still survive.'

'Do you own one?'

'I wish. No, but I recently sold my George V 1917 sovereign for just over eight thousand pounds. But I'm afraid all I have left are the old man's two-pence silver coins.'

'But I thought two-pence coins were made of bronze?'

'A bronze-coloured metal base,' explained Percy. 'Truth is, that for the past five hundred years, our coinage has been quite literally debased. However, the rare exception is the 1971 two-pence coin, of which about a thousand were accidentally minted with the wrong base – in this case, silver – which is hardly surprising remembering the Royal Mint manufactures around three to four million coins a day. So make sure you always check your change, because you might just get lucky and discover you have an example of one of the rare silver coins that can fetch over a thousand pounds on the open market.'

'And do you have one?' asked Christina.

'A hundred and forty-four, to be precise. My father got hold of what's called a rack, which consists of twelve shelves, each containing a dozen coins. The Royal Mint took their time coming to terms with decimalization.'

'That should take care of your pension problems.'

'It certainly would have done if my father hadn't listed them in his will, which means I can only risk selling one or two at a time if I don't want to alert the taxman. Inheritance tax is bad enough, but when they add capital gains tax, it's a killer.'

'Would I know one when I saw it?'

'Only if you were looking for it,' said Percy, taking a silver coin out of his pocket and placing it on the table in front of her.

Christina picked up the two-pence piece, turned it over, and studied it for some time before saying, 'And you're telling me this is worth a thousand pounds?'

'Probably more.'

'So remembering your tax problem, would you be willing to sell it to me for, say, five hundred?'

'No way,' said Percy, slipping the coin back into his pocket. 'They're currently trading on the black market at around seven hundred and fifty, and you'd be lucky to pick one up in Spink's for less than twelve hundred.'

'I'd be willing to risk seven-fifty,' said Christina as she took a cheque book out of her handbag.

'I don't do cheques,' said Percy. 'All too easy for the taxman to trace.'

'Then let's meet again after I've picked up some cash from my bank.'

'Fine by me,' said Percy as he handed Christina his card, 'especially if it means I get to see you again.'

'Sir Percy Singleton Bart, no less,' said Christina, sounding impressed.

'Just something else I inherited from my father,' said Percy. 'It guarantees you a table in a packed restaurant, but what's the point if you can't afford to pay the bill?'

'Same time tomorrow suit you?' asked Christina.

'Fine. But why don't you take this one and have it checked

out by a dealer. After all, I could be a con man preying on an impressionable young woman.'

'That's a risk you'd be willing to take?' asked Christina as he took the coin back out of his pocket and handed it to her.

'Why not? I know where to find you. That's assuming you really are on the board of the Fitzmolean. But as you were having coffee with the director, I'll take my chances.'

'Thank you,' said Christina as she slipped the coin into her handbag and called for the bill.

A waiter appeared moments later. Percy handed him a ten-pound note and said, 'Keep the change.'

• • •

The two men met outside the Churchill War Rooms but didn't join the queue.

Booth Watson had arrived on time and was already waiting for his client, which didn't surprise Miles as he was paid by the hour.

The two men crossed the road and joined one of the many winding paths that criss-cross St James's Park, with only tourists, dog walkers and women pushing prams joining them.

'There are a couple of urgent problems I need your advice on, BW,' said Miles as they began to stroll around a lake with Buckingham Palace in the background. 'I have reason to believe,' he continued, 'that Christina, aided and abetted by Warwick and Hogan, recently took a trip to New York, when they managed to switch my Rubens for the Fitzmolean's worthless copy.'

'How can that be possible?' asked Booth Watson. 'Houdini wouldn't have been able to break into your apartment.'

'He could have done if he'd read the *New York Times*

property section. As you know, it's currently on the market and one of the interested parties was an FBI agent called James Buchanan. But more important, he turns out to be a close friend of the Warwicks.'

'How do you know that?'

'It's a long story, but all that matters is that the Fitzmolean are now in possession of my Rubens, while I've ended up with the counterfeit I commissioned several years ago because Christina double-crossed me at the last minute.' Booth Watson didn't comment. 'What I want to know is if there is anything I can do about it.'

Booth Watson continued walking for some time before he passed judgement. 'Not a thing, I'm afraid. When you gifted the painting to the Fitzmolean some years ago, you not only assured them it was the original but presented the director with the provenance and paperwork to prove it. I don't have to remind you, Miles, your singular act of generosity, if I recall the judge's exact words, unquestionably influenced His Lordship's decision to give you a suspended sentence. Remorse was the word he kept repeating during his summing up.'

'So you're telling me there's no way I can get my painting back?' said Miles, unable to hide his frustration.

'No way,' Booth Watson repeated. 'Short of stealing it, which I wouldn't recommend unless of course you want to go back to prison for an even longer spell.'

'Not a chance,' said Miles with some feeling. 'However, I have come up with a plan that will not only prevent Warwick from eventually taking Commander Hawksby's place but could well see him back on the beat.'

'Amen to that,' said Booth Watson. 'But what about Christina?'

'She's just about to get her two pennies' worth.'

'Should I presume that's the other reason you wanted to see me?'

'No,' said Miles as they lingered by the side of the lake and watched two ducks scrabble over a piece of bread. 'I need to ask you a couple of personal questions before we discuss the real reason I wanted to see you.' Booth Watson nodded and was once again wrong-footed. 'How's business been lately?'

'Up and down, like Tower Bridge. Why do you ask?'

'Have you considered retiring?'

'Often,' admitted Booth Watson. 'But I simply can't afford to.'

'What if I could make that possible?'

'No doubt by involving me in something that could get me disbarred or worse.'

'Far worse, because if they could prove I was responsible for the Crown Jewels being stolen, I would be hung, drawn and quartered.'

'I feel sure I could get you off the drawing and the quartering,' said Booth Watson, trying to lighten the mood.

'Not if it could be proved that I had been responsible for stealing the Crown Jewels,' said Miles as he set off again.

'But every schoolboy knows that's impossible,' said Booth Watson once he'd caught up with his client. 'Unless of course you've found a way to get everyone who works at the Tower to take a holiday on the same day, while the Governor hands you the keys to the Jewel House.'

'Not me, because I don't plan to be there when the exchange takes place, although the whole operation won't come cheap.' Miles slowed down to allow a couple of tourists to overtake them before he began to outline his plan in great detail.

By the time the two of them had returned to the Churchill Rooms, Booth Watson made no attempt to disguise his lack of enthusiasm for the whole project, although he accepted that Harris had come up with a genuinely original idea that had never been considered before, and, without question, Miles was the one person he knew who just might pull it off – even though it would cost him a vast sum of money. However, he didn't hesitate to offer his expensive advice.

'I'm against the whole idea,' was Booth Watson's immediate response.

'Why?' demanded Miles.

'For a start, the odds are stacked against you.'

'Wrong again,' said Miles, 'because I won't be taking any risks. I'll be leaving that to others, so the only people who will end up with the odds stacked against them will be Warwick, Hogan and their precious boss.'

'What about your own team, who could all end up in jail?'

'I don't give a damn about them. They know the risks they're taking, and will be well-rewarded if they succeed.'

'But if they fail,' said Booth Watson, 'we're discussing treason, and the least of my problems will be being disbarred.'

'Not if you're in court on that day and shocked when you discover I've been arrested by Chief Superintendent Warwick while in possession of a crown, and need a lawyer to defend me.'

'But think about the expense Miles, and for what?'

'Complete and total revenge on three people who thought they'd got the better of me.'

Booth Watson knew when he was beaten and began to think about the lucrative fee he would earn when he represented five clients for treason. Someone had to.

'Then all I need to know is the date, time and place,' he said.

'I'll be outside the House of Lords sometime between three and four o'clock that afternoon – assuming everything goes to plan.'

'And the date?'

'I'll know that once the result of the upcoming general election has been declared and the new PM, whoever that might be, has kissed hands with the monarch, appointed his government and selected the date for the Queen's Speech, which is usually held on a Wednesday two weeks after the election has taken place.'

'What if it's a hung parliament?'

'At least I won't be hanged because I'll have to call off the whole operation.'

'But why, when there will be another Queen's Speech in a year's time?'

'Because, by then, the two main participants will have been replaced. So frankly it's now or never, and I can assure you, BW, I won't be given a second chance.'

'I think the result of the election will be a thumping majority for Tony Blair and the Labour Party,' Booth Watson predicted, 'so the Queen's Speech is almost certain to be sometime in May.'

'Then it's game on,' said Miles as they continued to circle the lake.

'Forgive me for mentioning this, Miles,' said Booth Watson after they'd walked in silence for some time. 'Even if you succeeded in stealing the crown, you wouldn't be able to sell it, and if you broke it up, no one would be willing to buy the Cullinan II Diamond or the Black Prince's Ruby, not to mention the St Edward's Sapphire, even on the black market.'

'It's not my intention to sell the crown,' said Miles, 'or even to break it up. On the contrary, I intend to return it to the palace at the earliest possible opportunity, but not before Warwick has resigned, Hogan has been dismissed, and Commander Hawksby feels he has no choice but to take early retirement.' He paused, stared at Booth Watson and said, 'So, are you willing to be my defence counsel, as they are bound to ask you if you knew about the plan before I was arrested?'

'You're the only client I have who consults me before they commit a crime,' Booth Watson assured him. 'What have I got to lose?'

'If I fail, it could be your last job.'

'And if you succeed?'

'You'll be able to retire on a pension that would make a high court judge weep.'

The expression on Booth Watson's face allowed Miles to put another metaphorical tick on his list.

• • •

Beth was preparing a cheese and tomato salad while the twins were impatiently waiting to read the next chapter.

'You may recall,' began Artemisia, opening her notebook, 'that Captain Blood was planning to take revenge on the Duke of Ormond for confiscating his land by storming Dublin Castle and kidnapping His Lordship.'

'Yes, but what happened next?' demanded Jojo, who'd already heard the story but couldn't wait to hear it a second time.

'Several of the rebels, disguised as "handicraft men", entered the castle gates waving petitions that the Duke of Ormond was accustomed to hearing in the morning. At the same time, a local baker, who was in on the plot, arrived pushing a cart laden with bread, which he tipped over just as he passed the guard house.'

'That was the signal,' interrupted Peter, 'for about eighty rebels who were led by Blood to storm the castle, armed with cudgels and pistols. And the plan was that while the guards were helping themselves to the bread, Blood would take over.'

'A well-planned diversion,' suggested William.

'Yes,' said Peter, 'but it didn't work. Because the Duke had been forewarned of the plot by one of Blood's closest allies, who turned out to be a government informer. So the Duke doubled the guard that morning and instructed them to arrest everyone they could lay their hands on.'

'Blood somehow managed to escape unharmed,' said Artemisia, turning a page, 'but his brother-in-law, James Lackie, was arrested, thrown in jail and later hanged.'

'How do you know all this?' asked Beth.

'It's all recorded in the pages of John Evelyn's diary, who made Blood even more notorious.'

'The Miles Faulkner of his time,' mused William with a smile.

'However,' said Peter, determined to return to the script, 'after Blood escaped, he somehow managed to make his way across to England, disguised as a priest. He even had the gall to roam around the countryside disguised as a priest, openly preaching while no one realized he was in fact on the run.'

'You've got to admire his nerve,' said Beth.

'He had one or two things going for him,' suggested Peter.

'Like what?' demanded William.

'The authorities were quite preoccupied at the time with the plague which killed twenty thousand people in London alone, followed by the Fire of London.'

'And don't forget,' said Artemisia, 'that in 1667, London didn't even have a police force. So Blood happily settled in Romford, a small village in Essex. However, he was still determined to seek revenge on the Duke of Ormond, who was now Lord High Steward of His Majesty's household and living at Clarence House in the centre of London.'

'Blood bided his time,' Peter said, taking over the story once again, 'until one night when the Lord Mayor was hosting a dinner at the Guildhall in honour of the Prince of Orange who was visiting London at the time. Among his guests was the Duke of Ormond, and as he was on his way home after the banquet, out of the darkness sprang six men who held up his carriage and dragged him out onto the road.'

'It had been Blood's intention,' said Artemisia, 'to take Ormond to Tyburn and hang him as if he were a common criminal, but to Blood's surprise, the elderly peer put up a fight and, when they attempted to lift him onto a waiting horse, he dragged them both back onto the ground. Blood decided to kill the Duke there and then, and even took a shot at him, but missed.' Artemisia looked up and Peter took over.

'A Mr James Clarke was among those passing at the time,' said Peter, 'and he spotted the glistening Order of the Garter on the gentleman's coat. Clarke immediately went to the Duke's aid, picked him up and carried him back to his home at Clarence House, where he found a dozen servants standing outside waiting for their master's carriage to return from the banquet. Two of them carried him up to his bed while another ran off to fetch a doctor. To everyone's surprise, within a few days the Duke had fully recovered.'

'However, the House of Lords later formed a special committee to investigate the incident,' Artemisia picked up the story again, 'and offered a thousand guineas' reward for the capture of Blood, dead or alive. The proclamation caused Blood and his co-conspirators to go underground again, and not one of them was captured. In fact, Blood's whereabouts for the next few years remains a mystery. Though we do know that during that time he was planning an even bigger coup.'

'What was that?' asked Jojo.

The twins looked at each other before they said in unison, 'To steal the Crown Jewels from the Tower of London!'

'But that's not possible,' said Jojo, 'because we know how well they are guarded.'

'Not in 1670 they weren't,' said Peter. 'In fact, at that time, anyone could stroll into the Tower and, for the price of a penny handed over to the Jewel House keeper, they were able to view all the state treasures, including the crown.'

'Turn the page,' said William.

Peter did, but it was blank.

'How long will we have to wait to find out if Blood succeeded in stealing the Crown Jewels?' asked Beth as she placed four plates on the table.

'Another week,' said Peter, 'by which time our contact should have supplied us with all the relevant details.'

'Your contact?' said William, as if questioning a suspect.

'Idiot,' hissed Artemisia at her brother.

'And who is this contact?' pressed William.

'The Governor of the Tower,' admitted Peter, sheepishly.

'Sir David?'

'Well, to be more accurate,' said Artemisia, 'he's the former Governor, as he's just retired. But he still phones us once a week – before you get home.'

'That's impressive,' said Beth, 'but I thought Miss Elton said you were not to have any outside assistance.'

'He only recommends books we can find in the library and occasionally answers our questions.'

'This must stop,' said William. 'The poor man has far more important—'

'Then why don't you call the Governor yourself, Dad,' suggested Peter. 'I think you'll find he's enjoying the whole exercise every bit as much as we are.'

Both parents were rendered speechless.

CHAPTER 17

When the phone rang at eight o'clock that morning, Miles picked it up, knowing who would be on the other end of the line.

'I thought you'd want to know that Hogan has recently been giving evidence in a drugs case at Southwark Crown Court,' was Lamont's opening line.

'So what?' said Faulkner.

'A court official, a mate of mine, left the building at the same time as he did.'

'So what?' repeated Faulkner.

'He saw Hogan talking to a member of the jury and took a photo of him with the woman.'

'And how's that going to help?' said Faulkner, beginning to sound exasperated.

'The trial was still in progress,' said Lamont, who paused for a moment before he added, 'and under the 1994 Criminal Justice & Public Order Act, that could amount to evidence of jury tampering, or possibly the even more serious offence of attempting to bribe a juror. And what's more, although the dealer was convicted, it was a close-run thing – just the kind of case where a quiet intervention could have swung the whole verdict.'

'What would be the likely sentence if Hogan was found guilty of attempting to influence an impressionable juror?' asked Faulkner, suddenly more interested.

'Two years minimum. But as he's a police officer, it could be a lot longer.'

'How much longer?' pressed Miles.

'Six years, possibly even ten.'

'Ten would be satisfactory. But what do we know about the juror?' was Miles's next question.

'A Mrs Kay Dawson. She's a shop assistant at M and S, and appears to enjoy the good things in life. Unfortunately, her husband's just been laid off so he won't be able to provide them.'

'Then I'll leave it to you, Bruce, to make sure she continues to enjoy the good things in life, and I'll add a little incentive.'

'What did you have in mind?' asked Lamont, licking his lips.

'How about an extra ten grand for every year Hogan gets?'

• • •

A taxi dropped Christina outside Spink & Son in Bloomsbury, founded 1666. A quaint, old-fashioned bell tinkled above her as she opened the door.

An elderly man was standing behind the counter, looking more like a retired schoolmaster than a shop assistant. 'How may I assist you, madam?' he asked, sounding like a retired schoolmaster.

'I wonder if you'd be able to tell me if this coin is authentic?' asked Christina, handing him the 1971 silver two-pence piece Percy had given her.

The dealer picked up his loupe and studied the coin for some time before he offered an opinion.

'An error coin, as we describe it in the trade,' he said, 'and much sought after by serious collectors.'

'And how much would you be willing to pay for it?'

The dealer studied the coin more closely. 'A thousand pounds would be my best offer,' he eventually managed. 'And be assured, madam, you won't get a better price from any other dealer.'

'Cash?' queried Christina, leaving the coin on the counter.

The dealer peered at the customer over his half-moon spectacles. 'I'll need to check how much I have in the safe.' He left her and disappeared into a back room, returning a few minutes later with £935 in used notes. He opened the till and extracted another £47, before finally emptying his wallet but he was still two pounds shy. He searched his pockets, but they were empty.

'Not a problem,' said Christina, placing the cash in her handbag. 'But before I go, can I ask you if you've heard of the Singleton Rack?'

'Of course, madam. One hundred and forty-four error coins mounted on a dozen shelves of twelve that were part of the late Sir Peregrine Singleton's private collection.'

'And if that rack were to come on the market, would you be able to put a price on it?'

The old man took even longer to consider this question, but finally responded. 'It would be in excess of two hundred thousand pounds, as several of the world's leading numismatists would want to add such a unique rack to their collections.

However,' said the dealer, after pushing his spectacles further up his nose, 'for such a large transaction, we would not be able to pay cash.'

'A cheque would suffice,' said Christina as she left the shop, the little bell above the door tinkling again.

• • •

Ross was deep in thought about Jojo's birthday present when his phone began to ring. UNKNOWN CALLER flashed up on his screen.

'Hi, Ross,' said a voice he didn't recognize. 'It's Kay Dawson, remember me? We met when I was on jury service at Southwark and you gave evidence on behalf of the Crown.'

'Kay, hi,' said Ross, vaguely recalling the woman who'd stopped him in the street and wanted to know more about Princess Diana. He tried to concentrate on what Mrs Dawson was telling him, but was distracted by Jojo trying to get in touch with him on the other line.

'We convicted that drug dealer you caught hanging around outside your daughter's school playground,' she said, only telling him something he already knew.

When she finally rang off, Ross still wasn't quite sure why she'd called, other than to let him know how much she admired Princess Diana and how very sad she was when she and Prince Charles had announced their divorce, although she was clearly fishing to be invited out on a date, which he studiously avoided. By the time he got off the line, Jojo had given up on him.

He called his daughter back immediately, but she didn't respond. It was later, after he'd mulled over Kay's words, that he couldn't help thinking something about the conversation didn't ring true. However, one good thing did come out of it. He could at last get in touch with the other woman he hadn't been allowed to contact until the trial was over. He looked up her number.

• • •

'Did you get everything you needed?' asked Kay after she'd put the phone down.

'Once we've doctored the tape,' said Lamont as he rewound the spool, 'it should prove more than enough.'

'So what's next?'

'Time for you to meet Mr Booth Watson, so he can take you carefully through your lines.'

'Is he a director?' asked Kay.

'Something like that,' said Lamont as he handed the woman another brown envelope.

• • •

'Hi, Alice, it's Ross Hogan. Jojo's father.'

'You didn't come to the end-of-term art exhibition last week, Mr Hogan, and your daughter won first prize,' said Ms Clarke, taking Ross by surprise.

'I'm sorry, but I was giving evidence in the Reg Simpson case, and it went on far longer than I had expected.'

'Was he convicted?'

'Yes. Got two years. No more than he deserved. But that wasn't the reason I was calling.'

'Were you hoping I would help you solve another major crime, Inspector?'

'No. But I was hoping you'd let me take you out for dinner.'

It was Ms Clarke's turn to be surprised. 'When and where did you have in mind, Ross?' she eventually managed.

'Le Barca, next Thursday. Eight o'clock suit you?'

'Suits me fine, Inspector. But what chance is there of you turning up on time?'

'They'd have to steal the Crown Jewels to prevent me being there.'

• • •

'How can I help you, sir?' asked a second-hand car salesman, who shook him by the hand as if they were old friends.

'I'm looking for a Jaguar XJ8,' said Lamont.

'Then you've come to the right place, sir. We have all the latest models, straight off the production line.'

'I'm actually looking for one of last year's models,' said Lamont.

'Let me find out what we have in stock,' the salesman said, masking his disappointment. He disappeared into a back office and began rummaging through an overstuffed filing cabinet. A smile returned to his face and he hurried back to join his customer. 'I think we have exactly what you're looking for, sir. In fact, we can even give you a choice as we have a recent demonstration model as well as a second-hand car with only eight thousand miles on the clock. One careful driver.'

Lamont could only admire the way he was able to deliver the words with a straight face. 'Is either of them grey?' he asked.

'Yes sir,' replied the salesman, 'our demonstration models are always grey, and come with a five-year warranty.'

'The price?'

'Twelve thousand, four hundred.'

'Twelve, and you have a deal,' said Lamont. 'That's assuming I like the car.'

'I can promise you, sir, it's exactly what you're looking for. If you come to my office, I'll prepare the paperwork.'

Once Lamont had signed on the bottom line and put down a deposit of £1,200 in cash, he told the salesman he would return and pick up the car in a few days' time. Following the inevitable shaking of hands, Lamont left the Mayfair showroom and made his way across to Park Lane, where he shook hands with another second-hand car salesman.

'I'm looking for a Land Rover, preferably last year's model, with a few thousand miles on the clock.'

'I have half a dozen cars that fall into that category, sir,' said the salesman. 'Were you looking for any particular colour?'

'Grey,' said Lamont.

• • •

'How much do I have in my current account?' asked Christina.

'If you'll give me a moment, madam, I'll check,' said the accounts manager.

Christina paced around the room with the phone attached to her ear as she waited for him to come back on the line.

'At close of business last night, madam, you were one hundred and thirty-four thousand, seven hundred and twelve pounds in credit.'

'I'll be dropping by tomorrow morning and making a withdrawal of one hundred and thirty thousand pounds, in cash,' she warned him.

There was a long pause before the account manager said, 'As you wish, madam.'

Christina put the phone down and checked the number on his card, before she began to dial the eleven digits.

'Percy Singleton,' said a voice.

'Percy, it's Christina. How much would you be willing to sell the Singleton Rack for?'

'Wow, Christina, you don't hang about. But I have to warn you I've had several offers in the past north of two hundred thousand.'

'But none of them in cash, would be my bet. So I repeat, how much?'

'A hundred and fifty thousand?'

'One hundred and twenty,' countered Christina.

'Let's say one forty, shall we?'

'A hundred and thirty thousand is my final offer.'

'And a hundred and thirty-five is mine,' said Percy.

'Done,' Christina heard herself saying, aware it would leave her account overdrawn for the first time in years. But not for long. 'Shall we meet in the museum café tomorrow morning at, say, eleven?' she added. 'And don't forget to bring the rack.'

'I most certainly won't,' replied Percy. 'Any hope of taking you to lunch at my club afterwards, to celebrate?'

'No, but I could join you for dinner at the Ritz.'

CHAPTER 18

'I've just had a heads-up from a well-placed colleague that a serious allegation against Inspector Hogan is working its way through the system,' said the commander even before William had closed the door.

'Who's he pissed off this time?' asked William, taking a seat opposite the Hawk.

'I'm afraid it's more serious than that,' said the Hawk. 'A young woman has come forward and made a statement claiming she was a juror in the Simpson drugs case where he gave evidence on behalf of the Crown, and he asked her out for a drink.'

'That's foolish, but not an offence.'

'Unless he contacted her while the trial was still in progress.'

'Never in a hundred years,' said William. 'Ross isn't that stupid. Even if he fancied the woman he would have waited until the trial was over.'

'She's also claiming they slept together the night before the jury reached its verdict, when he tried to influence her decision.'

'I don't believe it,' said William.

'I don't want to believe it either,' said the Hawk. 'But, as we both know, it wouldn't be the first time he's stepped out of line.'

'He may well have slept with her,' said William, 'but I can't believe it was before the verdict had been reached. And there's no way he'd ever try to influence a juror. I'd stake my reputation on that.'

'So would I,' said the Hawk. 'But unfortunately, there's enough circumstantial evidence, including a tape recording and photographs to support the allegation. CIB3 have yet to interview Ross, but if the woman sticks to her story, they'll have no choice but to charge him. And if he's found guilty, suspension will be the least of his problems.'

'But he hasn't even raised the subject with me.'

'That's because CIB3 haven't contacted him yet, so we've got some time to decide what our tactics should be.'

'Then the least I can do is warn Ross,' said William.

It was some time before the Hawk responded. 'Tread carefully, William. However, while he hasn't been charged, I can see no harm in you alerting him as to what he might be up against. But I repeat, tread carefully.'

'And if he's charged?'

'You must stand back, as you don't need to be named as an accessory in a criminal case, which could end your career as well as his. I can just about afford to lose Ross, but I'm not willing to sacrifice you on the same altar while the commissioner is considering you as my successor.'

'But he's like a brother,' protested William.

'More like Cain than Abel, I fear.'

'There must be something I can do to help,' said William, unable to hide his frustration.

'There is. If the case ends up in court, you could ask your father to represent him.'

• • •

Lamont called Miles at eight o'clock the following morning to let him know he'd found both the cars they were looking for, and they were identical to those used by the Lord Chamberlain and Warwick on their journey to the Tower the previous year. He couldn't get himself to say Chief Superintendent Warwick.

'Good start,' said Miles. 'Once you've picked them up, Harris and Collins will need to do several dry runs, half a dozen in fact, so they can familiarize themselves with all the possible routes.'

'Is it too early to be thinking about the three police motorcycles?'

'Yes, we won't need them until the last moment. Don't want to attract any unnecessary attention and cause someone to become suspicious.'

'Understood,' said Lamont.

'Have you begun putting your team together?' asked Miles, moving on.

'Sure have. I caught up with Jerry Summers yesterday evening. We had a long chat in an empty tube carriage on the circle line. He's on side.'

'Summers? Remind me.'

'He got four years for taking kickbacks from a local drugs boss in Romford. Warwick was the arresting officer despite the fact they were at police college together, so he'll be only too happy to return the compliment. He also knows several other former officers who fall into the same category of having lost their jobs, and would be grateful for some ready cash. But I'll double-check each one of them before I sign anyone up.'

'Triple-check,' said Miles. 'We can't afford to have a weak link in the chain. Can I assume that Summers doesn't know what we're really up to?'

'Not a clue. All he was interested in was how much he'll be paid and when.'

'Let's keep it that way. The fewer people who know what the end game is the better.'

'Agreed,' said Lamont.

'And finally, Bruce, are you any nearer to finding the right person to be sitting next to Harris when he drives the Lord Chamberlain's Jaguar across the middle bridge and into the Tower?'

'Yes, sir, but he still has one more test to pass before I'm willing to sign him up.'

'Time isn't exactly on our side,' said Miles.

There was only one way Lamont ever knew a call had ended, and that was when there was no longer a voice on the other end of the line.

Miles added three more ticks to his growing list before closing a file that was becoming thicker by the day. He put it back in the safe and twiddled the dial back and forth, content that no one else knew the combination.

• • •

Christina was sitting at her usual table in the museum's café when Percy appeared in the doorway. He was carrying a large Tesco shopping bag, which brought a smile to her face as she suspected it wasn't full of groceries. He strolled across to join her.

Once Percy had sat down and ordered a coffee, Christina handed him a thick brown envelope containing twenty-eight packets stuffed with £50 notes, which included £998 she'd been paid by Spink for the first error coin he'd given her.

Percy tore open one of the packets and began to count the notes slowly, while Christina pulled out each of the twelve trays containing a dozen silver two-pence coins, to find all a hundred and forty-three were in place. Both satisfied, they sat in companionable silence enjoying a cup of coffee. If anyone was in a hurry to leave, it appeared to be Christina.

'Are we still on for dinner tonight?' Percy asked as he dropped the cash into his Tesco bag.

'Yes, of course,' said Christina. 'The Ritz?'

'No,' replied Percy. 'Harry's Bar.'

'Are you a member?' asked Christina.

'Something else my father left me,' said Percy. 'Eight o'clock suit you?'

'See you there,' said Christina, getting up to leave. 'But it's my treat.'

'No way,' said Percy. 'I would never allow a woman to pay the bill.'

Christina picked up the wooden box, surprised by how heavy it was. She made her way slowly out of the café and up the staircase to the front entrance, not looking back. Once out on the pavement, she hailed a taxi and climbed into the back, still clutching onto the box.

'Where to, miss?' asked the cabbie.

'Spink's, Southampton Row,' she replied.

The cabbie began to weave his way through the afternoon traffic before finally circling Russell Square and driving into Southampton Row where he dropped his fare outside Spink & Son.

When Christina entered the shop for a second time – the same old reliable bell tinkling above her – she placed the wooden box on the counter in front of the same old reliable man, without saying a word. He couldn't take his eyes off the treasure trove, as if it were the Holy Grail.

Christina settled down in the shop's only chair, accepting that the numismatist would want to take his time examining such a rare find. He pulled open the top tray and, with his loupe, studied each of the eleven coins one by one. A look of respect, almost awe, on his face.

That changed when he pulled open the second tray to be introduced to a dozen coins of a different parentage, when the look of respect was replaced with one of disappointment, and by the time he'd reached the bottom tray had turned to silent despair.

Christina was sitting on the edge of her seat when the old man let out a long sigh of resignation. 'What's wrong?' she asked anxiously.

Like a doctor having to impart bad news to a terminal patient, the old man appeared to be searching for the right words before he delivered his prognosis. He slowly removed his half-moon spectacles, ran a hand over his bald head and, looking directly at his customer, pronounced in an authoritative voice, 'The top tray, madam, contains eleven error coins, each worth a thousand pounds. However, despite the other eleven trays containing a dozen two-pence coins, they have all been dipped in a silver liquid that might well deceive a casual observer, but not, I fear, an X-ray fluorescent spectrometer. You are welcome to join me in my lab should you doubt my word.'

'So what are they worth?' asked Christina, beginning to sound desperate.

'We would be happy to offer you eleven thousand pounds for the eleven remaining error coins on the top shelf. The other one hundred and thirty-two are worth no more than the figure engraved on their surface, making a total of two pounds and sixty-four pence, while not forgetting the two pounds we owe you from our last transaction,' said the manager, before checking his calculator. 'So all I can offer you in the circumstances, madam, is eleven thousand and four pounds, sixty-four pence.'

The old man suddenly felt sorry for the lady, who had sunk back into the chair and visibly aged in front of him.

'May I be permitted to ask you a question?'

He only just heard her murmur, 'Yes.'

'From whom did you acquire these coins?'

'Sir Peregrine Singleton's son, Percy.'

'The late Sir Peregrine was a respected customer of this establishment, and I can tell you to my certain knowledge, madam, that he didn't have a son, but two daughters, Eleanor and Victoria, who were the only beneficiaries of his will.'

• • •

Three men met up in the saloon bar of the St Pancras hotel. It wasn't rush hour, so they didn't need to look for a quiet corner. The bar was always empty at that time of day.

One of them handed Faulkner a Tesco shopping bag containing £135,000. Miles double-checked the contents. Satisfied, he handed over ten thousand in cash to a man whose name he didn't know, and didn't want to know. The man rose from his place and thanked him.

'Before you leave,' said Lamont, raising a hand, 'keep your diary clear. It's possible I may have something even bigger for you soon. I'll be in touch.'

'I look forward to hearing from you,' said the nameless man, who slipped out of the bar without another word. He made his way quickly to platform 14 where he boarded a train to Potters Bar so he could be home in time to have supper with his wife. Pity, he thought. He would have enjoyed having dinner with Christina at Harry's Bar.

'Does he have a name?' Miles asked once the anonymous man had departed.

'It's never the same for two days in a row,' replied Lamont. 'He's known in the trade as "The Understudy".'

'How did you come across him?' pressed Miles.

'I arrested him for impersonating the Lord Lieutenant of Gloucestershire,' said Lamont, 'and if I hadn't nicked him he would have ripped off a local cancer charity for twelve grand.' He took a sip of his drink before he added, 'He specialises in bishops and Lord Mayors, and even convinced a security guard at Buckingham Palace that he had an invitation to the royal garden party. And after his superlative performance as Sir Percy Singleton,' continued Lamont, 'I think he's ready to take on the more challenging role of Lord Chamberlain.'

Miles raised an eyebrow.

'He's about the same age and height as the present Lord Chamberlain – and if he can get himself into Buckingham Palace, perhaps he can pull off the same trick at the Tower.'

'The Tower of London will be a far more demanding stage than a garden party at Buckingham Palace,' suggested Miles. 'And the Resident Governor somewhat more of a challenge than my ex-wife. Although, I confess, he made it possible for me to tick her off my list.'

'In normal circumstances I would agree but, as you yourself pointed out, the new Resident Governor will be meeting the

Lord Chamberlain for the first time, which gives our man a built-in advantage.'

'Let's hope you're right, because if anything goes wrong, it will be you who ends up in jail, and you needn't bother to put me on your visitors' list,' Miles said as he downed his whisky in one gulp.

Lamont didn't need to be reminded that their relationship was based solely on risk reward, and that neither of them liked or trusted the other. However, Lamont had one more ace up his sleeve. He waited, because he knew Miles wouldn't let him go before . . .

'Have you been able to prevent Inspector Hogan being around on the day of the switch?' asked Miles, coming in bang on cue.

'One of my old contacts tells me that Hogan is currently under investigation for perverting the course of justice, and it shouldn't be too long before a hand is placed on his shoulder. And even if he's out on bail, he won't be sitting next to Warwick when he sets off for the Tower.'

'I wish I could be there when the judge passes sentence, but I'll have to be satisfied with you giving me the details. And don't forget, you'll receive ten thousand for every year Hogan goes down.'

'It can't be soon enough for me,' said Lamont. 'In fact, I'm looking forward to watching him squirm in the witness box when the damning tape is played.'

Miles removed another ten thousand from the Tesco bag and handed it across to Lamont, who quickly pocketed his latest bonus for the role he played in bankrupting Christina.

They both raised their glasses.

'Now that Christina has been dealt with, and Hogan is about to go down, who's next on your list?' asked Lamont.

'The biggest prize of all,' said Miles. 'Chief Superintendent William Warwick. So perhaps the time has come to hold a board meeting and make sure we're ready to carry out a hostile takeover.'

• • •

As the door began to open, the Hawk barked, 'I thought I'd made it clear I was not to be disturbed under any circumstances?' But the door continued to open and moments later two smartly dressed men walked in, who could only have been police officers. They'd caught everyone's attention.

'I'm Detective Superintendent Ian Ferguson, sir. I'm in command of CIB3, the Anti-Corruption Command. I apologize for interrupting you, but I am here to arrest Inspector Hogan.'

'On what charge?' demanded the Hawk, who knew only too well.

'Suspicion of corruption and attempting to pervert the course of justice in that he tried to influence a juror while a trial was still in progress.'

Ross leapt up and said, 'Is this some kind of joke?'

'I'm afraid not, Inspector,' said King. 'I must therefore warn you that you do not have to say anything, but it may harm your defence if you do not mention when questioned something which you later rely on in court. Anything you do say may be given in evidence.'

Ross was used to delivering those words, not receiving them.

William was already on his feet. 'Don't say anything, Ross, until I've spoken to my father – and I mean anything,' he repeated even more firmly. Ross nodded in his direction almost as if it were an order. No one spoke as Ross was led silently out of the room.

'And that also applies to the rest of you,' said the Hawk once the door was closed. 'Don't forget, if the case were to come to trial, you may well be called on to provide evidence as to character, and you won't want to be reminded in the witness box of something you wish you hadn't said.'

'Ross is incapable of trying to influence a juror,' said DC Rebecca Pankhurst without hesitation. 'He sets standards the rest of us try to live up to.'

'And, unfortunately, one or two you don't,' said the Hawk.

'Does that mean you think he's guilty?' asked DS Paul Adaja.

'Never,' said the Hawk. 'However, I know no one more likely to get himself into trouble because of his own stupidity.'

'And no one more adept at finding a way out,' added William.

'But he may need a little help from his friends this time,' said the Hawk, looking around the table. 'I intend to make sure I'm called as a witness, and I won't hesitate to let the jury know that Inspector Hogan is one of the finest officers I've ever had the privilege of working with. The moment he's cleared, I'll welcome him back so he can continue doing what he's best at.'

The team erupted, showing their support as if their colleague was a boxer who'd been temporarily felled but would surely get back up and knock out his opponent. Not that they were altogether sure who that opponent was. The Hawk wasn't in any doubt.

• • •

'Alice, I'm so sorry,' said Ross. 'But I have to postpone our dinner date.'

'Ah, so someone has stolen the Crown Jewels,' came back the immediate reply.

'No, I've been arrested, and as you're likely to be a key witness, I won't be able to contact you again until after the trial.'

'Arrested?' said Alice, sounding genuinely concerned.

'A juror in Simpson's trial is claiming I tried to influence her before a verdict was reached.'

'How could anyone possibly believe that?'

'Perhaps they don't,' said Ross, 'and someone has a motive to make sure the real criminal is released from prison and I end up taking his place.'

'Can anyone be that evil?' asked Alice.

'Oh yes,' said Ross, 'and he's not someone who takes no for an answer.'

'I'm so sorry,' she said quietly. 'Is there anything I can do to help?'

'That's the irony,' said Ross. 'You mustn't do a thing except agree on a rain check and then not until after the trial is over. That's assuming I get off.'

'And if you don't?'

'It will be tea and biscuits on a Saturday afternoon in Wormwood Scrubs for heaven knows how long,' said Ross, trying to make light of it.

'It wouldn't be my first visit to Wormwood Scrubs,' said Alice quietly.

• • •

William travelled down to Kent to see his parents at the weekend and, while Beth and the children went for a walk with their grandmother, William headed straight to his father's study.

He knocked on the door, and entered to find 'the old man'

reading the Sunday papers. As he looked up, William waited for a moment before saying, 'I need your advice on a personal matter.'

'Of course, dear boy,' replied Julian, putting down his paper. He gave his son a smile and said, 'The clock is ticking.' William didn't laugh.

'My friend and colleague, Ross Hogan, has got himself into a spot of trouble with a woman.'

'Hardly a new experience, I would have thought.'

'Agreed,' said William, 'except this time he could end up in prison and there isn't a lot I can do to help.'

'Details,' demanded Julian, leaning back in his chair and closing his eyes as he always did when considering a new case.

'He's been accused of trying to influence a member of the jury during a case at which he was giving evidence on behalf of the Crown.'

'A serious offence,' said Julian, 'and as a serving officer, if he were found guilty, the judge wouldn't be lenient, and neither should they be.' Julian's eyes remained firmly closed before he added, 'A young woman, no doubt?'

'Middle-aged. But Ross is adamant they only met once and he never slept with her.'

'But the witness claims otherwise?'

'Yes, and she's made a written statement claiming the casual affair began before the trial ended, and worse, he tried to influence her the night before the verdict was reached.'

'A woman scorned, perhaps? In which case it will all depend on the dates and who the jury believe.'

'I would normally agree with you, Father, but on this occasion I don't think it's quite as simple as that. I read her statement and believe it could only have been written by a leading criminal QC.'

'There's nothing unusual about that,' said Julian. 'After all, that's how we make a living.'

'I understand that,' said William, 'but it turns out the QC in question is none other than Mr Booth Watson.'

Sir Julian's eyes opened, alert and suddenly more interested. He was about to offer an opinion when Jojo came rushing into the room, grabbed him by the arm and said, 'Granny needs you to do the carving.'

'It seems Granny isn't the only one,' said Sir Julian, as Jojo took his hand and led him out of the study and into the dining room. She handed him the carving knife.

• • •

'In 1671,' began Artemisia once everyone had settled, a couple of weeks later. 'Colonel Thomas Blood visited the Tower of London disguised as a clergyman. He was accompanied by an actress pretending to be his wife, while his real wife was in Lincolnshire, unaware of what he was up to.

'At that time, you could visit the Tower of London and see the Crown Jewels if you paid a Mr Talbot Edwards, the jewel keeper, one penny. So Colonel Blood handed over the entrance fee to Mr Edwards, who dutifully showed him the Crown Jewels, but Blood's sole interest was finding out how well the Jewel House was guarded, which he quickly discovered was poor.'

'We've got to come up with a better word than poor,' interrupted Peter.

'A few days later, Colonel Blood returned to the Tower,' continued Artemisia, 'with the sole purpose of deceiving Mr Edwards into believing they could be friends despite the difference in their station. On this occasion, his wife, the actress, pretended to fall ill, and Edwards's wife took her up to their rooms in the Martin Tower so she could rest. But this was only a ploy to get Edwards alone,' said Peter, looking up.

William and Beth said nothing.

'A few days later, Blood returned to the Tower, this time with a pair of white gloves, a thank-you gift for Mrs Edwards for her kindness, which was all part of his plan.'

'We can't be sure,' continued Peter, taking over from his sister, 'how many more times Blood visited the Tower to cement the friendship with Edwards and his wife, before he carried out his plan.'

'We shouldn't use the same word twice,' said Artemisia. She crossed out the word 'plan' and was replacing it with 'crime' when the doorbell rang.

Jojo jumped up, rushed out of the room and opened the front door to see her father standing on the doorstep. 'We're in the middle of Arte and Peter telling us all about Colonel Blood and how he stole the Crown Jewels! But you're just in time for the next bit,' she said as she grabbed her father by the hand and led him through to the kitchen.

Once Beth had poured Ross a drink and Artemisia was satisfied they were all paying attention, she cleared her throat and carried on.

'A few days later, Blood returned to the Tower, but on this occasion, he was accompanied by his nephew, George. Blood had already suggested to Edwards over a drink in his rooms that his nephew, who had an income of over two hundred pounds a year, might be an eligible . . .' – she tried to pronounce the word three times – 'husband for their unmarried daughter.'

'We also know,' said Peter, once again taking over, 'that Blood's nephew presented Edwards with a pair of silver-mounted pistols to cement the agreement. Edwards fell for this deception and invited Blood and his nephew George to supper in his rooms at the top of the Martin Tower.'

'What's happened to Blood's wife?' asked Beth. 'Wasn't she invited to supper?'

Peter and Artemisia looked at each other and spoke as one, 'Don't know, Mum.'

'What we do know,' countered Artemisia, 'was that Blood promised Mr Edwards that he would bring his nephew to the Tower on the morning of the ninth of May 1671, so they could both sign the marriage contract.

'And that's as far as we've got,' said Artemisia. 'But we're off to see Colonel Blood before we begin the next chapter.'

'And Guy Fawkes,' added Peter.

'In a play or a film?' asked Ross.

'Neither,' responded Peter. 'They're both on display at Madame Tussauds, which we're visiting on a school trip next month.'

'But I'm not allowed to go,' said Jojo, 'unless accompanied by a parent.'

'Which day next month?' asked William, checking his diary.

'Wednesday May fourteenth.'

'I'm afraid I've got a board meeting that day,' said Beth, 'which I can't get out of. So one of you will have to accompany the children.'

'We'll have to hope that's not the day of the Queen's Speech,' replied William. 'I don't think Her Majesty would be amused if I failed to turn up for work because my daughter wanted me to visit Madame Tussauds.'

'Then it has to be you, Daddy,' said Jojo, turning to her father. 'Please say yes!'

William glanced across at his friend, well aware that by May 14th Ross's case could have already opened, and if the verdict didn't go in his favour he wouldn't be taking Jojo anywhere. Both of them knew it could only be a matter of time before he had to let his daughter know . . . He waited for Beth to go upstairs and put the children to bed before he decided to confront the elephant in the room. He'd already discussed the problem with the Hawk, who'd recommended that such a sensitive subject should be discussed only in the privacy of William's home and not back at the Yard where even the walls had ears.

William had gone over the questions endlessly, even the order he would take them in, while accepting that Ross would almost certainly take him by surprise.

• • •

Once Beth had taken the children up to bed, William poured his friend a large glass of Jameson's and handed it to him as he sat down. William took a deep breath before delivering his first well-prepared sentence.

'We have to talk about your future at some point,' he said, 'and assume the worst.'

'Spell it out,' said Ross as he took a large gulp of whisky.

William stood up and began pacing around the room before he stopped in front of him. 'If you're found guilty of trying to influence a juror, you could be sent down for two years, possibly longer as a serving police officer.'

'But I'm innocent,' protested Ross, 'as you well know, and surely any jury—'

'Will go on the evidence presented to them in court, which is looking pretty bleak at the moment, so for Jojo's sake, if for no other reason, perhaps it's time for you to consider every eventuality.'

Ross remained silent for some time before he responded. 'I know there's still some time to go before the trial, but don't think I haven't given it a lot of thought. I've already made out a standing order for Jojo's school fees, as well as a monthly payment to Beth which should be more than enough to cover any extra costs.'

'So you have given it some thought,' said William, sounding relieved.

Ross looked up at his friend, put down his whisky and admitted, 'Little else for the past month.'

William hesitated again before he ventured, 'Have you also decided if Jojo will be allowed to visit you in prison?'

'Never,' said Ross firmly. 'I don't want her to see her father in jail surrounded by a bunch of criminals, some of whom are there because of me and will be only too happy to taunt the poor girl given the slightest opportunity. I don't want that to be the abiding image of her father that remains in her mind. Never,' Ross repeated.

'But she could be a young woman by the time you come out,' said William.

'So be it,' said Ross with a finality that brooked no discussion.

'Does that also apply to me and Beth?'

'No. I can just about tolerate seeing you two from time to time,' he said, trying to lighten the mood.

William would have laughed but he hadn't come to the end of his inventory. 'You'll also need to have a bag packed and ready with all the essentials they allow in prison.'

'An overnight bag,' said Ross quietly. 'But I fear not for overnight.'

'And who should tell Jojo if the worst comes to the worst?'

'Beth would be the obvious person to let her know,' said Ross without hesitation.

'And what do you want Beth to tell her?'

'I've been sent abroad on an important assignment and I'll be away for some time.'

'That won't wash, Ross, and you know it. Someone in her class, and not necessarily a friend, will find pleasure in telling her the truth, and that shouldn't be the way she finds out.'

'You're right of course, so Ms Clarke will also need to be briefed, although I'm sure she'll allow Jojo to stay at home while the trial is in progress.' Ross emptied his glass in one gulp, sank back and covered his eyes. 'I sometimes forget how lucky Jojo and I are to be part of your family,' he whispered.

'Let's hope we're just taking all the necessary precautions for an accident that isn't going to happen.'

'That just about sums me up,' said Ross.

CHAPTER 19

IT WAS THAT TIME OF year when one can't decide if it's the end of winter or the beginning of spring. The six conspirators boarded Miles's yacht at different piers on the Thames, and they all ended up sitting around the same dining table on the lower deck, not that any of them had been invited to lunch.

Booth Watson was the last to join them and, once he'd taken his seat at the boardroom table, Miles assumed the role of chairman. Lamont, as his second-in-command, sat on his right, with Booth Watson on his left. Phil Harris, Collins and The Understudy occupied the three remaining places.

There was no agenda as they couldn't afford to put anything down on paper. All the details would remain minuted in their minds.

'On your left, you can see the Tower of London, built by William the Conqueror in 1075 . . .' could be heard coming from the loudspeaker of a passing tourist boat. A more up-to-date commentary about the future history of the Tower was taking place around a large circular table on the lower deck of Miles Faulkner's private yacht.

'As we are coming to the end of a five-year parliament, a general election is likely to be called in the near future,' said Miles, opening the meeting, 'and therefore it shouldn't prove too difficult to predict the day of the Queen's Speech, which is always on a Wednesday, two weeks after a new government has been formed. That means we've only got a couple of months at most to make sure everything is in place. With that in mind, I'll ask Bruce to bring us up to date.'

Lamont unrolled a large map of London and spread it out across the centre of the table, using four ashtrays to hold down the edges. Six alternative routes from Scotland Yard had been marked with different-coloured felt-tip pens, all ending up at Traitor's Gate.

'We won't know which route the official party will be taking until the last minute,' said Lamont. 'So, every member of the team has to be ready to move at a moment's notice.'

'Our primary objective must be to hold up the Lord Chamberlain's car for long enough to ensure you can take his place,' said Miles, 'and equally important, you must have left the Tower with the Crown Jewels before he turns up.'

'To that end, I'll have three "not for hire" taxis stationed here, here, and here,' said Lamont, placing three sugar lumps at different road junctions on the map. 'Once we know which route Warwick has chosen, our taxis will drive their non-paying passengers to the chosen locations and drop them off. However, it's imperative we remain the only people aware of what we are really up to, and it's kept to this inner circle.'

'Imperative,' repeated Miles, looking around the table. 'Any loose talk and I won't hesitate to call off the whole operation.

Let's start from the moment Warwick leaves Scotland Yard in the back-up Land Rover and heads for Buckingham Palace. I want to be sure we always remain one step ahead of him. Bruce?'

'There will be an ex-copper secreted inside St James's Park tube station opposite Scotland Yard,' said Lamont, placing a salt cellar on the map, 'and the moment Warwick appears he will make a note of the number plate on his Land Rover. Our man will then pass that information on to a local garage in the East End who can make up false plates in a matter of minutes. They should be attached to our Land Rover before Warwick leaves Buckingham Palace about forty minutes later, when he'll be accompanying the real Lord Chamberlain.'

'Thanks to Phil Harris,' said Miles, 'we know the number plates of the Lord Chamberlain's Jaguar, and those duplicates have already been made up and will be attached to our identical Jaguar the night before.'

'By the time the two official cars leave Buckingham Palace,' continued Lamont, 'we will be waiting in the underground car park of the Tower Hotel, just a couple of minutes from the rear entrance to the Tower, ready to move.'

'At some point during the journey,' chipped in Harris, 'Warwick always calls the Tower to let them know he's on his way. After that, he maintains radio silence until his arrival at the East Gate.'

'Unless he spots something that doesn't ring true,' said Lamont. 'In which case he will abort the whole operation.'

'And we won't be given a second chance,' said Miles. 'So make sure it's not one of you who's responsible for any cock-up,' he added with a cutting edge to his voice.

'But if everyone else plays their role on the day,' said Lamont, 'we should have around ten to twelve extra minutes before the real party arrives. But think of it as seven hundred and twenty seconds.'

'We do have a couple of things going for us,' Miles reminded them. 'A driver who will be immediately recognized by the guards manning the East Gate, and more importantly a Chief Yeoman who has known Phil for several years. Add to that the fact we have a new Resident Governor of the Tower who Phil has confirmed will be meeting the Lord Chamberlain for the first time.'

'But there's still the problem of the password,' Booth Watson reminded them. 'Which even Warwick won't know until the dice are thrown.'

Once again Harris was prepared. 'They never told me the password until the last possible moment. However, one person who's always among the first to be let in on the secret is the Resident Governor's wife, because every morning she drives her two young children to the City of London school which is less than a mile away, and she wouldn't be able to get back into the grounds if she didn't know the password.'

'That doesn't solve the problem of how we find out what it is,' said Miles.

'For the past month,' said Lamont, 'one of my team has been working as a ticket collector on the main gate, so when the Governor's wife leaves for the school run that morning, she'll ask her if she knows what the password is. Thirty seconds later it will appear on my mobile.'

'That's hardly foolproof,' said Miles. 'Make sure we have a back-up plan in case something goes wrong on the day.'

'Like what?' asked Lamont.

'The Governor's wife just says yes when asked if she knows the password.'

Lamont accepted the rebuke and made a mental note that

he would have to speak to the girl again and make sure she had a back-up plan should that fail.

'Who will be taking Inspector Hogan's place as Warwick's partner?' asked Booth Watson, moving on. 'Because it won't be Hogan as, I can assure you, he'll be otherwise engaged.'

'Sergeant Paul Adaja would be my bet,' said Lamont. 'And don't forget, it will also be his first outing. But I'll get our man at St James's Park station to brief me on who it is sitting next to Warwick the moment the police Land Rover leaves the Yard.'

'Are all the other specialists now fully briefed and on board?' was Faulkner's next question.

'Summers, Atkins and Ellwood, who all had to resign because of Warwick, were only too happy to act as our elite police outriders.'

'How will they get hold of the three SEG motorbikes?' asked Booth Watson.

'I've arranged for them to go missing from a police depot in Wandsworth that morning. They'll be returned the same afternoon,' said Lamont. 'The daily rental didn't come cheap.'

'Do they know why we need them?' asked Booth Watson.

'They didn't ask.'

'What about mothers and their prams?' asked Miles.

'Strollers, chief, are the latest thing. We'll have three of them in place with mothers waiting to discover which route the Lord Chamberlain is taking, even though only one of them will be required on the day.'

'And remember, no children; a breed we can't control.'

'Agreed,' said Lamont.

'Will we have a uniformed constable ready and waiting for Warwick when he's about a mile away from the Tower?'

'Already covered. I've hired an actor who thinks he's

auditioning for a commercial. I watched him performing his part the other day and he was word-perfect. What's more, he only expects to be paid Equity rates.'

'Make sure he doesn't overact,' said The Understudy, speaking for the first time.

'May I ask why you have a Scottish accent?' asked Miles.

'The current Lord Chamberlain is the thirteenth Earl of Airlie, an hereditary Scottish peer with a distinctive Edinburgh twang. I've been working on it for the past month.'

Miles gave the man – whose real name he still didn't know – a nod, the nearest he ever got to showing respect for anyone. He switched his attention back to Lamont. 'Outriders, mechanics, number plates, strollers, taxi drivers and a lone uniformed constable. What have I missed?'

'Pedestrians,' said Lamont, 'who will be standing at every crossing along the chosen route waiting to move.'

'And what's the point of them?'

'Half a dozen members of my team will be posted at every zebra crossing along the way. The moment the Lord Chamberlain's car comes into sight, they will take their time crossing the road. When we did a dry run last week, it gave us an extra four minutes and twenty-two seconds while they held up the traffic.'

'They also serve who only stand and wait,' remarked Booth Watson.

'Time to move on to our individual roles on the day,' said Miles as Collins topped up his whisky. 'Let's begin with you, Phil.'

'When we arrive at the Tower, I'll give the password to the duty warder. The barrier will be raised and the East Gate opened.'

'How will you be dressed, Phil?' asked The Understudy.

'The Lord Chamberlain never calls me Phil. You must get used to calling me Harris, if you don't want the Tower staff to become suspicious.'

'How will you be dressed, Harris?'

'In the chauffeur's uniform I always wear for the occasion,' he replied.

'And you?' Miles asked, staring at the nameless man.

'The Lord Chamberlain has his suits made at Gieves and Hawkes. He's slightly thinner than me, so I've had to lose a few pounds and have my trousers taken in a couple of inches.'

'And what about you, Bruce?' Miles asked, turning to Lamont.

'I'll be wearing the uniform of a superintendent, which I held onto after leaving the force. I've had to add a star to both epaulettes, so I'll be the same rank as Warwick. I'll also be wearing a peaked cap with silver braiding, making it difficult to see my face.'

'Don't forget it will be the first time the Governor has taken part in the ceremony,' Harris reminded them, 'so he'll also be on unfamiliar ground.'

'And you, Collins? Where will you be while all this is going on?'

'Sitting behind the wheel of the Land Rover, looking innocent.'

Laughter broke out for the first time.

'It's not a laughing matter,' said Miles sharply. 'We all have to look not only innocent, but as if we're meant to be there. So what happens after you've parked the Jaguar outside the Jewel House?'

'The Resident Governor will take the Lord Chamberlain inside to collect the two boxes containing the Imperial State Crown and the Sword of State.'

'And when they come back out?'

'They'll be accompanied by two Jewel House keepers who will put the two boxes in the boot of the Jag,' said Harris. 'I must warn you that the Resident Governor and Lord Chamberlain usually chat for a few moments before he gets back into the car.'

'Not this time they won't,' said Miles. 'Seconds wasted. His Lordship will shake hands with the Governor and suggest they have lunch at his club some time, old chap – no more!'

'What's the name of the Lord Chamberlain's club?' asked Lamont.

'White's,' came back the nameless man. 'It's at the top of St James's.'

Miles did like dealing with professionals. 'What happens next?' he asked, moving on.

'Once I'm back behind the wheel,' said Harris, 'the elite motorcyclists will move off. The whole exercise usually takes around fourteen to fifteen minutes.'

'It's going to be tight,' suggested Miles.

'Not if my team play their parts properly,' said Lamont.

'When they take off,' continued Harris, 'I'll drive slowly out of the Tower, across the middle drawbridge along the Embankment and back through the East Gate. The moment we're on the main road, we would normally return to the palace by the quickest possible route.'

'But not on this occasion?' said Miles.

'No. I'll continue on past the front of the Tower as if heading back towards Westminster, but after about a hundred yards, I'll swing left into All Hallows by the Tower. A local church that has four parking spaces.'

'But if there's space for only four cars,' began Booth Watson, 'isn't it possible—'

'I've had someone watching that church for the past week,' said Lamont. 'They're only ever full for Matins on a Sunday morning. Even the Reverend Pascoe arrives by tube.'

Booth Watson nodded; he had to admire Lamont's unfailing attention to detail.

'Once you've parked,' said Miles, 'the next two or three minutes could prove crucial, before you all go your separate ways. Bruce?'

'After leaving the Tower,' said Lamont, 'and before reaching All Hallows, I'll have changed out of my police uniform and back into mufti, so when I get out of the car no one will give me a second look. I've rehearsed the whole exercise several times, and I have it down to one minute forty seconds. Unlacing and lacing brogues is the only thing that might hold me up.'

'You could wear slip-ons,' suggested Miles.

'Warwick never wears slip-ons while on duty,' said Lamont.

Miles proffered another slight bow. 'And you, Harris?'

'Once both cars have been parked inside the church yard, I will unlock the boot, take out the smaller of the two boxes, the one containing the crown, and put it into a Tower of London shopping bag.'

'Nice touch,' said Booth Watson.

'Then, I will hand the bag to Collins, close the boot, but not lock it, while leaving the Sword of State behind.'

'And finally . . .' said Miles.

'I will cross the road and take a taxi to City airport, where I will board the first available flight out of the country.'

'Regardless of where it's going?' queried Booth Watson.

'Regardless,' repeated Harris. 'I'm not going to hang about when airports will be the first place the police are checking, and by then I'll be the one person they'll be looking for.'

'What's your final destination?' asked Booth Watson.

'Only Mr Faulkner knows that, and I intend to keep it that way.'

'However,' chipped in Lamont, 'the rest of us need to remember that the hour following any crime is known as the golden hour and is a copper's best chance of catching any criminal. Don't forget that during that time, forty-two thousand eyes will be on the lookout for us . . .'

'Whereas I'll be the one person who will be making sure everyone knows exactly where I am while you're all in the Tower collecting the Crown Jewels,' said Miles.

No one asked the obvious question, and Miles made no attempt to enlighten them. Booth Watson smiled at the thought that Sir Julian Warwick would be the main witness to exactly where his client was that morning, giving him no choice but to confirm his well-planned alibi.

'Any other business?' asked Miles as the yacht tied up at the Tate Gallery pier.

CHAPTER 20

'THERE ARE SEVERAL MATTERS WE need to discuss,' said the Hawk once the team had settled, 'beginning with some good news and congratulating Detective Sergeant Adaja on his promotion to Detective Inspector.'

Loud banging on the table followed, and Paul tried to look suitably modest. He failed.

'My next piece of news is not so good,' continued the Hawk in a more sombre tone. 'The CPS has decided, in their wisdom, to press ahead with charges against Inspector Hogan, and his case will come up at the Old Bailey in the not-too-distant future. As you know, he's currently suspended and I must advise you, once again, not to get in touch with him until the trial is over. Is that clear?'

The stony silence and frozen looks that followed rather suggested it was, although William didn't admit he'd already ignored that particular piece of advice on several occasions.

'Let's move on to our immediate responsibilities,' continued the Hawk. 'Now the Prime Minister has called a general election for May the first, it becomes our responsibility to protect both Mr Major and Mr Blair during the run-up to polling day.

'We will be assisted by our colleagues from Diplomatic Protection as during any election campaign the Royal Family goes into hibernation to ensure they don't become involved in any political disputes.

'Chief Superintendent Warwick,' he said, turning to William. 'You will take command of the PM's detail, while Inspector Adaja will be responsible for the Leader of the Opposition. If the polls are anything to go by, Paul, Mr Blair will be our next Prime Minister, and should be treated as such, because we must never, I repeat never, show any political bias.'

It amused William that he'd voted for all three parties during his lifetime, and still hadn't made up his mind which one to support this time.

'Jackie,' continued the Hawk, turning to DS Jackie Roycroft, 'you will take charge of the Home Secretary's detail, while you, Rebecca, will head up the Chancellor of the Exchequer's team. Diplomatic Protection will cover the Foreign Secretary's engagements as well as those of the Northern Ireland Secretary. But should anything go wrong during the next few weeks, there are no prizes for guessing who will shoulder the blame. With that in mind, I would advise you all to draw a line through your diaries up until May second. Don't even think of going to bed before your Secretary of State and be sure to be up before their alarm goes off in the morning. And finally, remember only the funerals of close relatives can be attended. Any questions?'

It was almost an hour before the Hawk moved on to the final item on his agenda. 'If Ross were to be convicted . . .'

• • •

A general election is always a demanding time for any police protection officer because they have to let their ministers off the leash and allow them to visit marginal constituencies and help prospective candidates go in search of votes.

Cabinet ministers and shadow front bench ministers will walk slowly down an unfamiliar high street, listening intently to the views of the local people.

'Of course, you're right, sir,' one will say.

'I'll bear that in mind, madam,' another will promise.

'I'll pass your views on to the Prime Minister when I next see him,' a third will offer. But they always end with the words, 'I do hope I can count on your vote on . . .' The date of the general election would be mentioned only if the minister concerned was confident the constituent was likely to support their candidate.

William decided to use the run-up to the election to watch his top ministerial protection officers in action. He began with the Leader of the Opposition, Tony Blair (*what's the first thing you'll do if/when you become Prime Minister?*). Jackie, who was covering the Home Secretary (*several tough questions about immigration*), followed by the Chancellor, Rebecca's responsibility (*Britain should never have joined the European Exchange Rate Mechanism*), and ending on the most sensitive of all, the Northern Ireland Secretary, who rarely left the safety of his car.

His final brief was the Prime Minister, who could be found listening intently to the same sentiments being expressed again and again without ever sounding bored. John Major made several visits to marginal seats during the campaign, in the hope it would tip the balance in his party's favour.

William remained quietly in the background, watching his officers going about their business. He regularly reported back to the commander to let him know what a professional job they were doing, often under considerable pressure. He called home most nights to speak to Beth and the children, but didn't admit to the Hawk that he was still in regular touch with Ross as the date of his trial, like that of the general election, drew inexorably closer. He was sure of one result, but not the other.

William often reflected that if Ross had remained Princess Diana's protection officer, none of the problems he was now facing would have arisen. When he shared those thoughts with Beth, all she said was, 'And if he had, he might be facing an even bigger problem.'

With just a couple of days to go before the general election, the Prime Minister returned to his constituency in Huntingdon, while Tony Blair travelled up to Durham.

When the sun rose on May 1st to allow the public to cast their votes, William had finally made up his mind which party he would support.

• • •

By four o'clock the following morning, it was clear that New Labour had won by a landslide, sending the Tories into opposition for the first time in eighteen years.

Once Mr Blair had visited the Queen at Buckingham Palace and kissed hands, he announced from the steps of Number 10 that Her Majesty had agreed the Queen's Speech would be delivered to the House of Lords on Wednesday 14th May, just as Booth Watson had predicted.

Artemisia and Peter began working on the final chapter of their essay on Colonel Blood, not allowing the election to interfere with their chances of winning the prize essay competition.

William returned to Scotland Yard having had – not unlike the public – more than enough of general elections. He was relieved there wouldn't be another one for at least four years. He'd voted Labour.

Ross spent election day having a long consultation with Sir Julian Warwick in preparation for the opening day of his trial. He didn't vote.

Miles held a team meeting on his yacht on the morning of the election to wrap up the finer details of Operation Queen's Ransom. He'd voted Conservative.

Booth Watson became so involved in preparing his opening statement for the Crown v Hogan, he forgot to vote.

Miles Faulkner, Ross Hogan, William Warwick, Booth Watson and the twins were all expecting to win. But all of them had other things on their mind.

CHAPTER 21

THE CENTRAL CRIMINAL COURT, BETTER known as the Old Bailey, resembles a theatre on the opening night.

Although the doors to its courts are not opened until thirty minutes before the curtain rises, business is already taking place backstage. The actors – the judge, barristers and solicitors – are all rehearsing their lines. The critics – the jury who have their own box in the front row – are waiting to consider their verdict on the play and the individual performances. The two leads – Inspector Ross Hogan and Mrs Kay Dawson – are standing in the wings and experiencing first-night nerves as one waits to enter the dock and the other the witness box. Both have everything to lose.

Already on stage is the clerk of the court. His job is to make sure all the props are in place before the curtain rises. Next to appear will be the court stenographer, who will record every word of proceedings of a yet unwritten script.

Once the doors are opened, members of the public will take their places in the dress circle overlooking the stage. As with any West End performance, it's only ever packed for a hit.

They will be followed in the stalls by the press, who have reserved seats, usually unoccupied, but not on this occasion because the case offers their readers the ingredients they most enjoy over breakfast: sex, police corruption and money. The one great difference between the Old Bailey and the West End is that no one can be sure of the ending.

By 9.50 a.m. almost all the actors are in place except for the judge, the Honourable Mrs Justice Stephens. Meanwhile, Mr Booth Watson QC, representing the Crown, is going over his opening lines, while Sir Julian Warwick QC, for the defence, is chatting to his junior, Ms Grace Warwick, and their instructing solicitor, Ms Clare Sutton, none of whom will deliver a line until the curtain rises for the second act.

Inspector Hogan will be the next to appear, stage left. He will be accompanied by two security guards and take his place in the dock moments before proceedings begin.

When the clock strikes ten, Mrs Justice Stephens makes her entrance and everyone in the stalls rises. She bows and the compliment is returned before she takes her place centre stage, in a high-backed chair on a raised platform above them.

She adjusts her gown, opens the red leather notebook in front of her, removes the top from her fountain pen, leans back and nods to the clerk of the court. Everyone remains silent as the seven men and five women file in and take their places in the jury box, which has a commanding view of the stage. Once they are settled, the clerk looks up at the defendant from behind his desk and says, 'Will the defendant please rise.'

Inspector Ross Hogan, dressed in a dark grey suit, white shirt and Metropolitan Police tie, stands and looks directly at the judge who is staring down at him.

'Inspector Hogan,' the clerk says in a clear crisp voice. 'You are charged with attempting to pervert the course of justice. How do you plead?'

'Not guilty,' replied Ross, looking directly at the judge.

Once the clerk sat down, this was the cue for the judge to deliver her opening lines.

'Mr Booth Watson,' she said, looking down at counsel's bench, 'are you ready to deliver your opening statement?'

'I most certainly am, m'Lady,' said Booth Watson, giving her a slight bow before he cleared his throat. 'M'Lady, I think you and the jury will find this is a simple case of police corruption where an experienced officer took advantage of a naïve and innocent woman.' Once Booth Watson had fired his opening salvo he went on to outline the case for the prosecution, and forty minutes later, having described Inspector Hogan as louche, duplicitous and corrupt, bordering on evil, he sat back down, a satisfied look on his face. If the jury had been called on to deliver a verdict at that moment, Ross would have been hung, drawn and quartered.

The judge, who'd seen it all before, was not quite so ready to assume guilt, and after prosecuting council had delivered his opening statement, she looked down at Mr Booth Watson and said, 'You may call your first witness.'

Booth Watson rose from his place once again and said, 'I call Mrs Kay Dawson.'

'Call Mrs Kay Dawson,' could be heard echoing around the corridor. A few moments later a middle-aged woman entered the court and made her way slowly across to the witness box without even glancing at the defendant in the dock. She was wearing a smart white suit, a white blouse buttoned to the neck, with a simple marcasite brooch and little make-up. She'd dressed for the jury.

Once Mrs Dawson had taken her place in the witness box, the clerk handed her a copy of the King James Bible which she held in her right hand before reading out the oath from a card held up by the clerk.

'I swear that the evidence I shall give will be the truth, the whole truth, and nothing but the truth. So help me God,' she added, which was not on the proffered card.

Mr Booth Watson looked across at the witness and in a gentle and soothing voice asked, 'Will you please state your name and occupation for the record?'

'My name is Kay Dawson, and I am a senior sales assistant at Marks and Spencer's in Bromley.'

'Will you please tell the court how you first came into contact with the defendant?'

'I was serving on a jury at Southwark Crown Court, where Inspector Hogan was giving evidence on behalf of the Crown in a drugs case.'

'Did anything surprise you when he gave his evidence?'

'Leading,' muttered Sir Julian.

'Yes. He kept staring at me, and when he left the witness box, he winked.'

'He winked?' repeated Booth Watson in disbelief. 'And when did you next come across Inspector Hogan?'

'Later that afternoon. I had left the court at the end of the day and was on my way home when he passed me in the street. I thought nothing more of it until he stopped, turned around and said hi.'

'How did you respond?' asked Booth Watson.

'I hesitated, because I was fairly sure I wasn't allowed to speak to a witness during the trial. However, he assured me that was not the case, as he'd finished giving his evidence.'

'What happened next?'

'He asked me if I'd like to join him for coffee, which I agreed to, but now realize was a mistake.'

'While you were having coffee together, did he raise the subject of the trial?'

'No, he did not. That came later.'

'How much later?'

'He called me the following morning and invited me back to his place that night for a drink.'

Sir Julian made a note on his yellow pad.

'Was the trial still in progress?'

'Yes, it was. It had been going for a couple of days, and although it was drawing to a close he still didn't raise the subject that night.'

Sir Julian wrote down the words 'DATES/TIME/PLACE' on a yellow sticky note which he passed back to Clare, who immediately began tapping away on her laptop.

'I'm sorry to have to ask you this, Mrs Dawson, but during this time did you sleep with the defendant?'

Every eye in the court was now fixed on Mrs Dawson.

The witness hesitated for the first time and, in what looked to Sir Julian like a well-rehearsed gesture, bowed her head and said quietly, 'Yes, I did.' She paused again. 'At the time I was going through a rough patch in my marriage, which I'm pleased to say is now behind us.'

'I'm happy to hear that,' said Booth Watson.

'Tread carefully, Mr Booth Watson,' said the judge sharply, while Sir Julian was already on his feet.

Booth Watson bowed, but the look on his face didn't suggest contrition. 'And did you see the defendant again after spending Friday evening with him?'

'Yes, I did. I joined him again on Sunday evening.'

'The night before the verdict was reached?'

'Yes,' said Mrs Dawson, bowing her head.

'And was it then that he tried to influence your decision?'

'Not directly, but he did tell me something about the defendant that I now realize caused me to change my mind before I reached a final decision the following morning.'

'And what was that?'

'He told me that the defendant was a known criminal and had a record as long as his arm.'

Booth Watson waited for the raised whispers to subside before he moved on to his next question. 'For the record, Mrs Dawson, what was the jury's verdict?'

Mrs Dawson looked up at the judge and said, 'Guilty.'

'She's remembered her lines well,' said Julian, loud enough for Booth Watson to hear.

'Did you say something, Sir Julian?' enquired the judge.

'Simply complimenting my learned friend on how well he's conducting his case,' said Sir Julian, barely rising from his place.

'In future, Sir Julian, you will keep your opinions to yourself. Please continue, Mr Booth Watson.'

'Thank you, m'Lady. Can I ask you, Mrs Dawson, how you would have cast your vote, if you had not been made aware that the defendant had a record as long as his arm?' said Booth Watson, his eyes never leaving the jury.

'He's at it again,' said Sir Julian, barely able to control himself.

'Sir Julian, you're beginning to try my patience.'

Julian half rose again but barely managed a bow.

'Don't allow my learned friend to prevent you telling us what happened while the trial was still taking place, Mrs Dawson,' purred Booth Watson as he turned back to face the witness, giving her another reassuring smile.

'To tell the truth,' said Mrs Dawson, 'up until that moment I hadn't made up my mind which way I would vote, but I confess I did allow Inspector Hogan's words to influence me.'

'Word-perfect,' whispered Julian under his breath, but the accompanying background noise meant the judge failed to pick up the remark.

'And after the trial was over,' said Booth Watson once a semblance of order had been restored, 'did you continue to have a relationship with the defendant?'

'For a short time, yes, but it didn't last much longer. It quickly became clear that I'd served my purpose, and he was ready to move on.'

Booth Watson switched his attention to the jury, delighted to see every eye was fixed on his client, and one or two of them looked sympathetic.

'And what made you come forward and make a statement to the police?' asked Booth Watson.

'I finally admitted to my husband I'd had an affair, and he advised me that telling the police was nothing less than my duty. Not least because he—' she said, looking at Hogan for the first time, 'might well be preying on other women, and who knows how many more there have been in the past?'

'M'Lady,' said Sir Julian, no longer able to control his feelings. 'Is this witness going to be allowed to be both judge and jury?'

'I agree,' said Mrs Justice Stephens, and turning her attention to the jury instructed, 'You will ignore the witness's last statement. It was both hearsay and prejudicial and will therefore be ruled inadmissible. Final warning, Mr Booth Watson.'

'Mea culpa, m'Lady,' said Booth Watson, well aware it might be ruled inadmissible but not erased from the jurors' minds. 'Allow me to end with something that is neither prejudicial nor hearsay,' he continued, looking directly up at the judge. 'Mrs Dawson made a recording of her final conversation with Inspector Hogan, which has only just come to light, and with your permission . . .'

'Only just come to light?' said Sir Julian. 'I doubt that . . .'

'I was under the illusion, Sir Julian, that I was the judge in this case, and it may surprise you to know I would like to hear the tape.'

'But it wasn't presented in the pre-trial bundle of evidence, m'Lady, so I haven't had a chance to consider—'

'And neither have I,' admitted the judge. 'So it will be of interest to us both, and when it comes to cross-examining this witness, Sir Julian, be assured I will give you considerable latitude.'

Sir Julian could barely control himself as Booth Watson nodded to his junior, who was sitting behind him. He touched the play button on his Grundig tape recorder, while everyone waited in anticipation.

'We convicted him, Ross, but I wouldn't have been able to convince the jury of his guilt if you hadn't told me he had a record as long as your arm.'

'I'm glad you felt that was helpful.'

'I kept my word and didn't tell anyone on the jury that we'd had a private conversation the night before the jury reached its verdict.'

'Better to keep it that way.'

'The last few days have been among the happiest of my life, Ross, and now the trial is over, I'm looking forward to getting to know you even better.'

'Me too.'

'Can I come to your place this evening?'

'I'll look forward to that.'

'Then I'll see you at eight. Goodnight, my darling.'

'Goodnight, Kay.'

Ross began furiously scribbling a note which he handed to an usher who took it across to defence counsel. After Sir Julian had read it, he was not at all surprised to learn that although his client's words were exactly what he'd said, Mrs Dawson's must have been inserted sometime later. He sent a sticker back to Ross in the dock asking if he'd also recorded the conversation and, when he turned around, was disappointed to see his client shaking his head. He began to wonder just how far BW would go to secure a conviction and who his paymaster was.

Having scored an open goal, Booth Watson moved on to his next question. 'Mrs Dawson,' he continued, sounding even more confident. 'Did the defendant ever contact you again?'

'No, not once,' replied the witness, almost in a whisper, a tear running down her cheek.

'Bang on cue,' whispered Sir Julian.

'Thank you, Mrs Dawson, for your brave and honest contribution, which I am sure the jury will appreciate.' Booth Watson sank back onto the counsel's bench before the judge could rebuke him.

Mrs Justice Stephens closed her red book, put the top back on her fountain pen and said, 'Perhaps this would be a good time to take a short break.' She then asked everyone involved in the case to be back in their places in twenty minutes when defence counsel would begin his cross-examination of the witness. Without seeking a second opinion, she rose from her place and left the courtroom, with loud chattering and several opinions following in her wake.

Grace was among the first to offer an opinion. 'The tape didn't help our cause.'

'Even though it was clearly doctored,' said Sir Julian, quietly seething like a volcano about to erupt.

'You can be fairly sure BW will have anticipated most of your questions,' said Clare, trying to keep them both on track. 'So don't be surprised if Mrs Dawson already has all her answers off-pat.'

'Has no one ever told BW it's against the law to rehearse your client until they're word-perfect?' said Sir Julian, unable to hide his anger.

'Losing your temper won't help,' said Grace.

'Is this my junior speaking, or my daughter?'

'Both,' said Grace firmly.

'Have you noticed,' said Clare, 'that former Superintendent Lamont is seated at the back of the court making notes?'

'Which only confirms who's paying Booth Watson's exorbitant fees,' said Grace.

'Why am I not surprised,' said Sir Julian as the judge re-entered the court and everyone fell silent, rose and bowed.

She returned the compliment. 'Are you ready to begin your cross-examination of this witness, Sir Julian?'

'I most certainly am, m'Lady,' said defence counsel as he waited for Mrs Dawson to return to the witness box.

Sir Julian adjusted his wig, tugged at the lapels of his gown and stared across at the witness before asking his first question. 'Mrs Dawson, you told the court you met Inspector Hogan while you were a member of the jury at a trial where he was giving evidence.'

'That is correct,' said Mrs Dawson confidently.

'But that trial only lasted for three days,' said Sir Julian, checking Grace's notes.

'Three days in court, but that doesn't include the weekend

– Friday night, Saturday, and Sunday, before we reached our verdict on the Monday morning.'

'I would suggest you met for the first and last time on the day Inspector Hogan gave evidence.'

'I'm sure you would, Sir Julian. But how could you possibly know when you weren't there?' This produced the odd snigger from an attentive audience.

Grace placed an X against the first question she had prepared for her leader the night before.

'You also told the court,' continued Sir Julian, trying to recover, 'that my client only discussed the case with you on one occasion.'

'That is also correct.'

'I would suggest that discussion was instigated by you, and didn't take place until the trial was over, and lasted for less than a minute.'

'You can suggest what you like, Sir Julian. But when Ross delivered the sentence I'm not allowed to repeat, I can assure you it was the night before the jury retired to consider their verdict. What you might call "pillow talk", but he knew exactly what he was saying and how vulnerable I was at the time.'

Grace took one look at the jury and placed another X against that question.

'Where did this liaison take place?' asked Sir Julian.

'At his flat,' came back her immediate reply.

'Which is where, exactly?'

'St Catherine's Mews, SW3 2PX.'

'You even know the postcode?' said Sir Julian, not attempting to hide the sarcasm.

'You did say "exactly", Sir Julian,' the witness reminded him.

While others laughed, Booth Watson allowed himself a smirk.

Sir Julian changed tack. 'Would it be fair to describe you as a woman scorned,' he paused, 'who is now seeking revenge?'

'Not revenge, Sir Julian, justice.'

Uproar broke out in the court, including a smattering of applause led below the bench by Booth Watson, which clearly took Sir Julian by surprise and didn't please the judge, who frowned.

Grace placed another X against that particular question.

Sir Julian glanced down at his list of prepared questions and selected one he didn't think she could possibly have been prepared for. He looked up at the witness and said, 'Take your time before you answer my next question, Mrs Dawson.'

The witness gripped the railing to steady herself, a bead of sweat appearing on her forehead.

'Are you aware that it's a criminal offence to speak to the prosecuting counsel before a trial begins?'

'Yes, I am,' said Mrs Dawson, not wavering.

'So when did you first meet Mr Booth Watson?' asked Sir Julian.

'I've never met him,' came back the immediate reply. 'I saw him for the first time when I came into the court this morning.'

'Do you expect us to believe that, Mrs Dawson?' said Sir Julian, his eyes never leaving the witness.

'Yes, I do,' said Mrs Dawson defiantly, 'because it's the truth.'

'She was even prepared for that question,' murmured Clare, who put another cross on her prepared list and assumed Sir Julian would move on.

'So you haven't been coached on how to answer my questions,' he paused, 'by a professional?'

If Grace was surprised, the judge made no attempt to hide

her displeasure. 'Sir Julian,' she said firmly, 'that was uncalled for.'

'Was it, m'Lady? Don't you find it remarkable that a sales assistant never hesitates even for a moment before answering any of my questions?'

'M'Lady,' said Booth Watson before the judge could respond, 'could it be possible that my learned friend has underestimated Mrs Dawson?'

'No, it isn't,' snapped Sir Julian. 'But once again, I've underestimated how far my learned friend will go to win a case.'

Grace covered her eyes as she waited for the outburst.

'Sir Julian,' said the judge, leaning forward in her chair. 'That was unworthy of you. I'm going to take a short break so you can reconsider your last statement that questions the veracity of a senior colleague. Do I make myself clear?'

Sir Julian just about managed, 'You do, m'Lady.'

'We will resume again in twenty minutes,' said the judge. She left the court without another word, while Sir Julian slumped down in the corner of the bench, aware he'd made a bad error of judgement.

'What came over you, Father?' asked Grace once the judge had left the court. 'I've never known you to behave so unprofessionally.'

'I admit,' said Sir Julian with a deep sigh, 'BW has continued to rile me over the years with his duplicity and half-truths, but this time he went too far. We all know Mrs Dawson's a fully paid-up member of the prosecution team, that it was BW who wrote her statement, why she has an answer to every one of my questions, and even who Lamont is reporting back to at the end of the day.'

'I don't disagree with you, Father, but that's no reason to risk a client's chances of a fair trial.'

'You're quite right of course,' said Sir Julian, 'and I'll apologize to the judge when the court resumes, and refrain from asking this witness any more questions.'

'Which will be playing into Booth Watson's hands,' said Grace, 'but I can't see any alternative. I'll prepare an appropriate statement for you to deliver before the judge returns.'

'I can think of one alternative,' said Sir Julian, 'but I'm not sure the judge would approve.'

'Sorry to interrupt you, Sir Julian,' said Clare, leaning forward. 'But I think I may have spotted something we've missed.'

Both counsel turned their backs on Booth Watson, bent down and listened intently to what Clare had to say.

'It could be a fake,' was Grace's immediate reaction.

'There's only one way we're going to find out,' said Sir Julian as the judge returned and resumed her place on her bench. 'But it's still one hell of a risk,' said senior counsel. 'And perhaps I've already used up my share of those.'

'Phone Cartier and find out if they can supply us with any worthwhile ammunition,' whispered Grace, ignoring her father's advice. Clare quietly left the court as Grace handed her father the final draft of her prepared statement.

He read it quickly and said, 'It's a surrender document. Do you really expect me to—'

'Yes,' was all Grace had to say.

'Are you ready to continue, Sir Julian?' prompted the judge.

'I am, m'Lady,' said Sir Julian sounding reluctant as he once again glanced down at his daughter's statement, which he began reading word for word.

'M'Lady, I wish to offer an abject and unreserved apology both to you and my learned friend Mr Booth Watson. I hope you will consider my unacceptable behaviour nothing more than a temporary lapse of judgement, which I can assure you will not happen again.'

Booth Watson rose slowly from his place and said, 'I accept my learned friend's apology in the spirit with which it was offered, m'Lady, and consider the matter closed.' A Buddha-like expression appeared on his face as he sat back down.

The jury smiled their approval.

Sir Julian remained standing. 'M'Lady, given the circumstances, I wondered if you would consider allowing my junior to complete the cross-examination of this witness, which I can assure you is drawing to a close.'

If anyone was more surprised than the judge, it was Grace.

'I have no objection,' said the judge. 'However, Mr Booth Watson may . . .'

'I certainly have no objection, m'Lady,' said Booth Watson, rising from his place. 'In fact, I welcome it.'

Sir Julian sat down and whispered to his daughter, 'Lull her into a false sense of security. It's our only chance. She won't realize you know the details of this case every bit as well as I do, or that you're now in possession of a vital piece of evidence she can't have been prepped for.'

Grace rose slowly from her place, emboldened by her father's confidence in her, and although she had only prepared a couple more questions for this witness, she felt she had the measure of Mrs Kay Dawson.

The judge turned her attention to the witness and said, 'I'm sure you realize, Mrs Dawson, that you are still under oath, but you will no longer be questioned on behalf of the defence by Sir Julian, but by his junior, Ms Grace Warwick.'

The witness couldn't resist a smile as she turned to face Grace, looking more than ready for Sir Julian's replacement.

Grace adjusted her wig, tugged the lapels of her long black

gown and returned the witness's smile. Like father, like daughter, thought Sir Julian.

'I'd like to return to the tape recording of the conversation between you and my client.' The witness nodded. 'Is it just possible the tape you were so keen for the jury to hear had been doctored,' suggested Grace, 'in order to show my client in a bad light?'

'I'm sure the jury can decide which one of us is more experienced at doctoring tapes, Ms Warwick,' came back Kay Dawson's immediate response. 'An M and S senior sales assistant or an Inspector in the Metropolitan Police force who has been reprimanded on two separate occasions in the past for unprofessional conduct. One of which ended up with him being suspended for six months.'

Uproar once again broke out in the court and Grace waited patiently for calm to return before she asked her next question. 'From whom did you find out that particular piece of information?' she asked, turning to face Booth Watson, who remained head bowed in the corner ignoring her.

'Ross, of course.'

'Of course,' said Grace. 'And did Ross also tell you he'd won nine police commendations, not to mention twice being awarded the Queen's Gallantry Medal for bravery, during his long and distinguished career?'

Mrs Dawson stared at her counsel, but he didn't stir. 'No. I don't remember him mentioning that,' she finally managed.

'How unlike a man who you claim had seduced you to only tell you about his failures.' A ripple of laughter followed and even the judge allowed herself a smile. 'Let us return to the tape, Mrs Dawson, because I'm puzzled why you made it in the first place. Did you tell the Inspector you were recording the conversation?'

'Yes, of course I did, and I wouldn't have started the tape if he hadn't agreed.'

Grace was delighted to see the witness had switched from cautious back to confident as she needed Mrs Dawson to win one or two more points before she delivered a question Booth Watson couldn't have prepared her for.

'Remind me, was it you who rang my client?' said Grace, pretending to refer to her notes.

'Yes, it was, Ms Warwick. But I was returning his call.'

'And that's when you told him you'd be recording the conversation?'

'Yes, it was,' said the witness defiantly.

'Can you explain to the court, Mrs Dawson, how that request wasn't part of the recording?'

'I only switched on the tape recorder after Ross had agreed to my request.'

The murmurs that followed rather suggested Mrs Dawson had scored another point.

Grace turned the page and wondered if, even with the help of Booth Watson, the witness would have an equally convincing response to her next question.

She paused for a moment as she first looked at the judge, then the jury, before finally returning to the witness. 'Mrs Dawson, do you really expect the court to believe that a police officer with twenty years' experience, having been warned he was being recorded, would then have delivered a statement that could later be played back in court and would undoubtedly condemn him to a lengthy prison sentence?'

For the first time, Mrs Dawson didn't have a prepared reply; she simply stared at her counsel.

Sir Julian felt the looks on the jurors' faces rather suggested that doubt was entering their minds for the first time, but although Grace knew she had scored a point, she wasn't convinced it was enough to win the battle. However, the questions she had prepared so meticulously for her father had come to an end, and she was about to say, 'No more questions, m'Lady' and sit down, when Clare came rushing back into the court, clearly anxious to share her latest news.

'I wonder, m'Lady, if I might be allowed a moment to consult my instructing solicitor?'

'Of course,' said the judge, before Booth Watson could object.

Both Sir Julian and Grace listened carefully to what Clare had to say before leading counsel offered his opinion.

'I repeat, it's one hell of a risk,' whispered Sir Julian, 'and if it were to backfire it will give our opponents an advantage from which we may not recover.'

'The sort of risk Booth Watson would be willing to take?' suggested Grace.

'Yes, but I wouldn't,' said Sir Julian, looking at the jury, 'not while I'm ahead on points.'

'I think I can knock her out,' said Grace as she got back on her feet and, facing the judge, said, 'I'm ready to continue my cross-examination of this witness, m'Lady.'

'Are you also ready, Mrs Dawson?' enquired the judge.

'Yes,' she said, not sounding quite as confident.

'Can I ask you, Mrs Dawson, how much a senior sales assistant at M and S earns? A rough figure will suffice.'

'Around eighteen thousand pounds a year.'

'A decent enough wage, but I think you'd agree, Mrs Dawson, one that would keep you on a fairly tight budget, unless—'

'Is this leading anywhere that's vaguely associated with this case, Ms Warwick?' asked the judge.

Patience, m'Lady, Grace wanted to say, but satisfied herself with 'I am rather hoping so, m'Lady.'

'Sooner rather than later, I would suggest.'

Grace took one more look at Clare's notes before she turned her attention back to the witness. 'Mrs Dawson, what time is it?'

If anyone was more surprised by the question than the judge, it was Sir Julian.

'Eleven forty-three,' said Mrs Dawson, glancing at her watch.

'What is the make of the watch you are wearing?'

The witness looked unsure and the judge puzzled, while Booth Watson's Buddha-like expression evaporated.

'It's a Cartier Tank watch,' said Mrs Dawson.

Grace hesitated for a moment while she had second thoughts about taking the risk. Booth Watson would have . . . but not her father. She checked Clare's notes once again.

'I'm bound to ask, Mrs Dawson, how a sales assistant, on eighteen thousand a year, can possibly afford to pay four thousand one hundred pounds for a Cartier watch, unless of course she has a rich lover, or perhaps an even richer backer?'

'Neither,' said the witness, the smile returning. 'It's a fake. I picked it up for ten lira in a Turkish bazaar while on holiday last summer.'

One or two sniggers followed, suggesting Sir Julian's replacement was not up to the job. Booth Watson closed his eyes and looked as if he had fallen asleep.

'Would you be kind enough to take the watch off, Mrs Dawson.'

'M'Lady,' said Booth Watson, rising unusually quickly from his place. 'I must object. Can I remind the court it is not my client who is on trial, but the defendant.'

'I agree with you,' said the judge. 'But when you asked for a tape to be played that neither I nor Sir Julian were aware of, I gave you considerable latitude, so I think I'll allow the request. Please take off your watch, Mrs Dawson.'

The witness obeyed the judge's command, while even Sir Julian wasn't sure what his daughter's next question would be. Grace hesitated as she recalled her father's words: *if it were to backfire it will give our opponents an advantage from which we may not recover*. But it was too late now to turn back. 'May I ask if there's a serial number engraved on the back of your watch?'

Everyone's eyes were now fixed on the witness as she turned the watch over and it was a few moments, the longest few moments in Grace's life, before she replied, 'Yes.'

'Please read out those numbers.'

'One two zero two one nine eight six.'

Booth Watson was back on his feet. 'Sit down, Mr Booth Watson,' said the judge firmly. 'I want to hear Mrs Dawson's response.'

'Perhaps you were unaware, Mrs Dawson,' continued Grace, 'that Cartier engraves each of their watches with a serial number so they can retain the names of their most frequent customers and keep in touch with them.'

Mrs Dawson stared helplessly across at her silk, but Booth Watson could only sit there, head bowed, unable to supply his client with the answer to that question, although he knew exactly what her reply should be and hoped she'd worked it out.

'Please think carefully before you answer my next question, Mrs Dawson, remembering the judge reminded you when you returned to the witness box, that you are still under oath.'

The witness gripped the sides of the witness box, the confident look no longer on display.

'Will it be your name recorded on Cartier's files as one of their most frequent customers, or was it, as you suggested, purchased for ten lira from a bazaar in Turkey while you were on holiday?'

Grace pointedly took a blank sheet of paper out of her file and pretended to study it – a trick she'd seen Booth Watson perform in the past. More than once. She looked up to see the witness was trembling uncontrollably.

'I'm not a frequent customer,' she said quietly. 'It was just the once.'

Grace placed the blank sheet of paper back in the file as someone seated behind her jumped up and quickly headed for the exit. Mrs Dawson leant forward and pointed at a man who was opening the courtroom door. Everyone turned around to see Lamont's back as he slipped out of the court and disappeared from sight.

Mrs Dawson began to sob uncontrollably, but the judge showed no sympathy, and with a nod of the head, indicated that Grace could continue with her cross-examination.

'Allow me to once again return to the tape, Mrs Dawson, and the conversation you recorded with my client that you claim met with his approval.' No response from the witness was forthcoming so, after a short pause, Grace continued, 'Can I presume that you have no objection to an independent expert examining the tape for any signs of tampering?'

Booth Watson was quickly back on his feet and about to speak when the judge said, 'I presume, Mr Booth Watson, you're not about to object to Ms Warwick's reasonable request?'

Prosecuting counsel fell into his seat to hear a voice say, very quietly, 'They made me do it.'

'Wouldn't it be more accurate to say they paid you to do

it?' came back Grace. 'Which would explain how a sales assistant on eighteen thousand pounds a year was able to buy an expensive Cartier watch.'

The witness bowed her head and made no attempt to answer the question. Grace milked the moment for as long as she could.

'Who did you mean when you said *they*, Mrs Dawson?'

The witness looked up and stared across at her counsel, and, when she saw the look on Booth Watson's face, settled for the greater of two evils and remained silent. Grace had come to the end of her questions and was about to sit down when the judge, glaring from on high, said, 'Mr Booth Watson, in view of what I've just heard, or not heard, I am bound to ask if it is still your intention to proceed with this case.'

Booth Watson didn't rise and didn't speak, just shook his head.

'Then it is my intention,' said the judge, 'to direct the jury to retire and return a verdict of not guilty.'

Booth Watson made no attempt to appeal. The clerk immediately rose and led the jury silently out of the court and back to the jury room.

Sir Julian sat back and basked in his daughter's triumph. But once the jury had retired, he couldn't resist leaning across and asking, 'What was the risk that Booth Watson would have taken, and I wouldn't?'

'One two zero two one nine eight six,' said Grace. Sir Julian waited for his daughter to enlighten him. 'It's simply the date and year the watch was made.' She paused and smiled at her father. 'Booth Watson worked it out immediately, but the judge, who'd also worked it out, didn't allow him to come to his client's rescue.'

'You were right,' he said. 'It was a risk I wouldn't have

taken.' Sir Julian was about to ask another question when the jury returned and took their places in the box.

The judge nodded to the clerk who rose and said, 'Will the foreman please rise.'

The only jury member dressed in a suit stood and looked up at the judge.

'Have you reached a verdict?'

'We have, m'Lady.'

'Do you find the prisoner at the bar guilty or not guilty?' asked the clerk.

'Not guilty,' said the foreman without hesitation.

Mrs Justice Stephens looked down from the bench and, addressing Booth Watson directly, pronounced, 'I intend to send the case papers to the DPP. No doubt you will inform your client of the seriousness of my decision.'

Booth Watson rose slowly from his place. He bowed meekly and said, 'I will indeed, m'Lady, but be assured, I had no idea—'

'Of course you didn't,' said Sir Julian, loud enough for the judge to hear, but this time no admonition was forthcoming.

The judge then turned her attention to the dock and declared with finality, 'Inspector Hogan, you are free to leave the court and I wish you well.' The jury all smiled for the first time.

The judge made no attempt to stop the applause that followed, even though she hadn't left the court. The journalists were the first out of the door, already on their mobiles, not needing to demand, 'Hold the front page.'

The two security guards were the first to shake hands with Ross before he stepped out of the dock to join his colleagues. William gave him an uncharacteristic hug and said, 'Welcome back, old friend.'

Ross walked across to join Sir Julian, shook hands with him and said, 'Thank you, sir.'

'It's not me you should thank,' responded Sir Julian, 'but my clever daughter who saved the day.'

Grace didn't suffer from her father's inhibitions and hugged her client as if he were a football player who'd just scored the winning goal.

Ross continued to shake hands with several well-wishers, some of whom he didn't even know, while his eyes went on searching for the one person he wanted to hug, but there was no sign of her.

The Hawk and William accompanied the victor out of court, down the wide sweeping staircase and back out onto the street, leaving the Old Bailey behind them. William was just about to suggest they go and celebrate when Ross spotted her standing on the other side of the road. He left them and walked slowly across to join Alice.

'There must be easier ways to pick up a girl,' she said.

'I must remember to thank Reg Simpson when I next see him,' said Ross as he took her in his arms. 'About the only good thing he's ever done in his life.'

The Hawk looked across at the two of them as they walked away hand in hand. 'I do believe one of our problems may have been solved.'

'I'll miss Jojo,' was all William had to say on the subject.

CHAPTER 22

JOJO KEPT LOOKING TOWARDS THE door, hoping her father would appear, but there was still no sign of him. Artemisia unfolded a copy of the 1597 map of the Tower of London and laid it out on the kitchen table in front of them. Five pairs of eyes peered down.

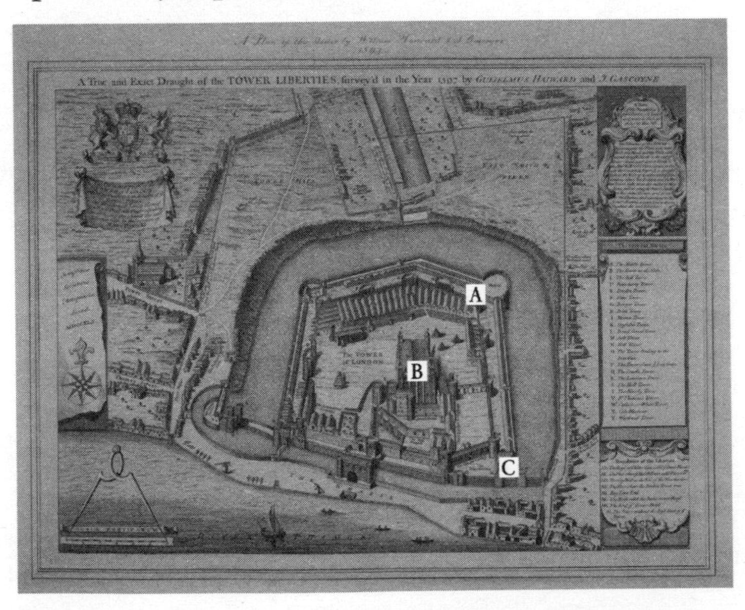

'First, you need to know where the Martin Tower is,' began Jojo, pointing to an A on the map, 'because that was where the Crown Jewels were stored in 1671. Not as they are today in a modern fortified Jewel House.'

'Also keep an eye on the East Gate,' said Peter, 'little C, as it shows where Blood and his three conspirators entered the grounds unobserved.'

'And later left in a hurry by the same route,' prompted Artemisia.

'With or without the Crown Jewels?' asked William.

'To use one of Mum's favourite expressions, Dad,' she said with an exaggerated sigh, 'patience is a virtue.'

Beth burst out laughing.

'At around seven o'clock on the morning of the ninth of May 1671,' continued Artemisia before her father could respond, 'Colonel Blood arrived at the Tower accompanied by three conspirators – his son Thomas, Robert Perot and Richard Halliwell, while a fourth conspirator, William Smith, remained by the outer gate with four horses so they could make a quick get-away.'

'All three of them were known to have previous, as Dad would describe it,' chipped in Peter.

'Each of them,' continued Artemisia, ignoring the interruption, 'was armed with a sword stick, a dagger and a pair of pistols, as well as a sack.

'After visiting Edwards that morning in the Martin Tower' – a small finger returned to the map – 'Blood asked if his three compatriots might be allowed to see the Crown Jewels and assured the jewel keeper that they would all be happy to pay a penny for the privilege.

'Edwards took the four of them down to the jewel room and, once he'd unlocked the door, young Blood immediately overpowered him while Perot shoved a plug of wood in his mouth. Halliwell threw a cloak over his head as the Colonel snatched his keys. Edwards, however, was a courageous man, and although he was alone, he put up a fight, so he ended up having to be bound and gagged while one of the thieves knifed him in the chest until he finally collapsed on the ground.

'Blood then grabbed the State Crown and secreted it under his cloak, while Perot stuffed the orb in his breeches and the younger Blood cut the sceptre and cross in half before dropping the separate pieces into the sack. They locked the door behind them and left Edwards lying in a pool of blood while they made off with the Crown Jewels.

'We even found an old engraving recording the incident,' said Artemisia, proudly producing a sepia picture which she placed on the kitchen table beside the map. Beth and William began to applaud as they studied the picture.

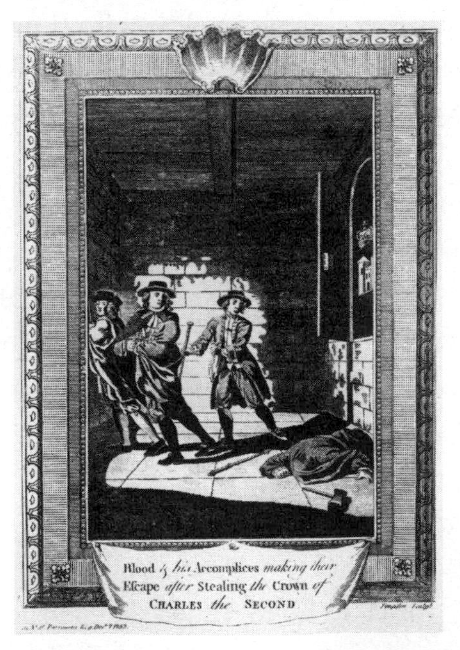

Robert Perot, Colonel Blood, Richard Halliwell and Edwards, circa May 1671.

'At the very moment they were making their escape,' said Peter, 'Edwards' son Wythe, an army officer who had been serving in Flanders, arrived home on leave.'

'And you expect us to believe that?' said William.

'Yes,' said Artemisia. 'Why wouldn't you?'

'Because you couldn't get away with a coincidence like that in a novel!'

'But this isn't fiction, Dad,' said Peter. 'It's fact.'

'So what happened next?' asked Beth, wanting to turn the page.

'Blood and his fellow conspirators panicked, dropped the sack and fled to the East Gate, where they had left their horses, but they were pursued by Edwards' son shouting, "Stop, thief! Stop, thief!"'

'A Captain Minton Betham,' continued Peter, 'who was passing by at the time, took up the chase and quickly overpowered Blood, even though Halliwell fired two shots at him. The other two assailants didn't get much further before they too were apprehended and later locked up in the White Tower, little B,' said Artemisia, placing a finger on a building in the centre of the map.

'I presume that Blood was hung, drawn and quartered?' said William with some relish.

'No, that's the strange thing,' said Peter. 'He wasn't. In fact, he was set free. However, there's one final twist in this tale that neither of you are going to believe.'

'The King made him Resident Governor of the Tower,' suggested William, 'and gave him a knighthood?'

'Stop being silly, Daddy,' said Artemisia firmly.

'Then why wasn't Colonel Blood hanged for stealing the Crown Jewels, not to mention knifing the Jewel House keeper?' their father demanded. 'Because he certainly deserved to be.'

'No one can be sure,' said Artemisia. 'All we know for certain is that immediately after Colonel Blood had been locked up in the White Tower, he requested a private audience with the King, and to the Lord Chamberlain's surprise and dismay, his request was granted.'

'Mine too,' admitted William.

'It's not certain what took place at that meeting,' chipped in Peter, 'because only the King and Blood were present and nothing was written down. What we do know is the King had made several enemies during his reign and Blood may have offered his services as a spy, because over the years he'd served both sides without fear or favour.'

'He certainly would have known where the bodies were buried,' chipped in Artemisia, using another of her father's favourite expressions.

'What we also know,' continued Peter, 'is a few days after that meeting took place, Blood and his compatriots were not only released from the Tower, but the rank of Colonel was restored to Blood, along with all his properties in Ireland, yielding him an annual income of five hundred pounds a year.'

'He's sounding more like Faulkner every moment,' said William.

'So what happened to Edwards?' asked Beth, trying to get them back on track. 'After all, he is the real hero of your story.'

'He sadly died three years later in 1674 from the injuries he'd sustained when taking on Blood and his thugs. His son Wythe took his place as Keeper of the Jewels and no one has attempted to steal the Crown Jewels since.'

'But why did the King pardon such a scoundrel in the first place,' asked William, 'after he'd committed so many crimes?'

'We can't be sure,' said Peter. 'But one report, probably

put about by Blood himself, suggests he told the King he had planned to kill him while he was swimming in the river at Battersea. He claimed he raised the pistol and took aim, but when he set eyes on the monarch, he couldn't pull the trigger.'

'He fell for that?' said William.

'At the same time he warned the King that, if he were to be hanged, a hundred of his faithful followers would not rest until they had sought revenge.'

'The King,' said William, 'should have packed Blood off to the Tower after such a blatant display of false flattery followed by an idle threat.'

'Historians think it more likely,' said Artemisia, turning the page, 'that Blood offered to act as the King's spy and name all the rebels who were plotting against him.'

'Just the sort of friend one can rely on,' said William.

'And not long after his release,' continued Peter, 'several militants were arrested, among them three of Cromwell's captains, who did end up on spikes on London Bridge.'

'Blood also convinced several of his own followers,' added Artemisia, 'to give themselves up, including the four rogues who assisted him when he attempted to steal the Crown Jewels.'

'What happened to them?' asked William.

'They were also pardoned.'

'Why?'

'Perhaps the merry monarch considered a pardon the lesser of two evils,' suggested Beth.

'But Blood certainly wasn't the lesser of two evils,' said William. 'Or perhaps the King was more fearful of his own life and Blood's silver tongue convinced him it wasn't a risk worth taking.'

'Possibly,' said Peter, 'but as both men took the secret to

their graves, we'll never know. However, "an unknown Londoner" reported in his diary in August of that year that he had seen Blood strolling down the Strand in a new smock coat and periwig, only two weeks after he'd been released. He described him as a rough-honed man with a pock-ridden face and sunken blue eyes.'

'So did Blood return to Ireland and die of old age?' asked Beth.

'No. He remained in London,' said Peter, 'and not many years after his release, he fell ill and died at his home in Bowling Green Alley. Several well-known people attended his funeral to watch the coffin being lowered into the ground. But even that wasn't enough for the Duke of Ormond's son, who had the body disinterred to check that one thumb was twice the size of the other, a peculiarity that had betrayed Blood on more than one occasion when he was on the run from the law.'

'Several citizens are said to have slept more easily once they were convinced he could no longer betray them,' said Artemisia. 'And although he died with few friends to mourn him, one poet wrote:

At last our famous hero Colonel Blood
Seeing his prospects all will do no good
And that success was still to him denied
Fell sick with grief, broke his heart and died.'

Artemisia and Peter closed their notebooks, looked up and said in unison, 'The end!'

They were greeted with as warm applause as one could hope for from an audience of three.

'Do you think we'll win the prize?' asked Peter once the applause had died down.

'If you don't,' said William, 'I'll want to read the essay that does.'

'Very diplomatic,' said Beth as the door opened and Ross came rushing in.

'I'm afraid you missed the final episode of the Colonel Blood story,' said William as Jojo threw her arms around her father and said, 'Where have you been?'

Ross was about to reply, when Artemisia said, 'I'd be quite happy to read the whole story again.'

'Yes, please!' said Jojo, jumping up and down.

'First you need to know where the Martin Tower is . . .' began Artemisia, pointing to the letter A on the map.

• • •

The last time Ross had visited San Lorenzo, he was still Princess Diana's protection officer. In those days, he would stand a discreet distance away while she had lunch with someone he didn't always approve of.

He'd arrived a few minutes early and been welcomed by Lucio as if he'd never been away. Ross was flattered when the head waiter took him to Diana's old table. He sat waiting for Alice to appear, occasionally glancing at a menu he was familiar with. He couldn't help remembering that San Lorenzo was where he'd taken Josephine on their first date.

When Alice walked in, he had to take a second look to be sure it was her. She was wearing a black and red dress, a black silk scarf, and carrying a fashionable leather handbag that he suspected no one at St Luke's had ever seen. Was this the same young woman who rang the school bell at five to nine every morning to make sure her charges were sitting behind their desks on time? He stood up, greeted her with a kiss on both cheeks and held back her chair so she could sit down. *Wow*, he wanted to say, but remained speechless as Lucio reappeared by her side.

'Can I get you a drink, madam?'

'No, thank you,' she said. 'Just a glass of water.'

'Still or sparkling, madam?'

'Sparkling please.'

Something else she had in common with Princess Diana, who'd once told him if a girl asks for a glass of champagne on their first date, don't go shopping with her.

Alice studied the menu for a little while before saying, 'Should I assume you're claiming this on expenses, Inspector, or have you won the lottery?'

Ross smiled. 'Neither,' he replied. 'But when Josephine died, she left me everything, which turned out to be far more than I'd expected. In fact—'

'I'm so sorry,' said Alice, looking embarrassed. 'I didn't mean to imply . . .' she began as Lucio reappeared by her side.

'Madam, have you decided what you would like to order?'

'I'll have the endive salad followed by the monkfish, please,' she said, handing him back the menu.

'No wonder you're so slim,' said Ross. He flushed, wondering if he could have delivered a cornier line, although she still rewarded him with the same warm smile.

'And for you, sir?' said Lucio, turning to Ross.

'I'll have the same. I need to lose a few pounds,' he added, compounding his error.

'Do you know—' she said.

'Can I ask—' he said.

'You first, Ross,' she insisted.

'When I spoke to you on the phone before the trial and

warned you if I was convicted you'd have to visit me in Wormwood Scrubs, you told me it wouldn't be the first time.'

Alice sipped her water before she responded. 'My father spent ten months in the Scrubs. And before you ask, for shoplifting.'

'How tactless of me,' said Ross. 'I'm so sorry.'

'No, I wanted to tell you,' admitted Alice, taking another sip of water. 'It was his first and last offence, and I suspect it didn't help that he was Caribbean and out of work. However, as that was thirty years ago, let's hope things have finally moved on in "Cool Britannia".'

'Not in the Met, they haven't,' said Ross. 'I have a colleague, Paul Adaja, who's Ghanaian by birth, and another, Rebecca Pankhurst, a remarkably able woman, both of whom ought to reach the highest ranks, but it will still be some time before less qualified men don't assume they'll be promoted before an immigrant or a woman, however bright.'

'And you don't have any prejudices, Inspector?' teased Alice, raising an eyebrow.

'Can't afford to when you're Irish and have been married to a French woman.'

'My mother's Irish,' said Alice, taking him by surprise.

'That would explain—'

'Explain what, Inspector?'

'Why you're so beautiful.'

'And to think the Irish are universally known for their love of literature, subtle wit and persuasive charm. The nation that produced Yeats, Wilde and James Joyce,' she paused, 'not to mention Ross Hogan?'

Ross was rescued by Lucio returning with their first course.

'It can't have been easy for you,' said Ross as he stared at his endive salad. 'I mean, when you first went to school, as a—' immediately wondering if he could dig a deeper hole for himself.

'And it wasn't helped by young men assuming I'd be available after a first date. When they discovered I wasn't, they'd spread rumours I was a lesbian, which suited me at the time while I was trying to get a place at university.'

'Just like Josephine.'

'Who must have been very successful in her chosen career to have . . .' Ross remained silent. Her turn to be embarrassed. 'Oh hell,' said Alice, 'I haven't been on a first date for so long, I've forgotten how to—'

'My problem,' said Ross, 'is that I haven't been on a second date since Josephine died.'

'Don't worry, I won't be surprised if—'

Ross took her hand. 'Shall we start again, Alice?'

She smiled and nodded. 'Did you always want to be a policeman?'

'Yes. I couldn't wait to leave school and join the Met. Did you always want to teach?'

'Yes, although most of my contemporaries at the LSE joined the Socialist Workers Party and burnt effigies of Margaret Thatcher.'

'A great Prime Minister,' said Ross.

'Well, to be fair, most of them ended up in the City, got married, had two children, and I'm pretty sure now vote Conservative.'

'And you?'

'I've never kissed a Conservative,' admitted Alice.

Ross leant across the table and kissed her gently on the lips. 'Help, do we have anything in common?' he asked as he broke away.

'Jojo,' said Alice. 'I confess the little minx is one of my favourites, and it's clear she also has you wound round her little finger.'

'Do you have any children?' Ross asked, regretting his words even before he'd finished the sentence.

'Twenty-eight,' she replied, 'and they all give me up and move on a year later to be replaced by another equally demanding bunch who want to play football for England or become an air hostess or a vet.'

'Which category does Jojo fall into, as I can't see her playing football for England?'

'Her favourite subject is art, which she has a natural aptitude for.'

'Thanks to Beth, her surrogate mother.'

'Not to mention your friend, William.'

'Who might well end up sitting behind the commissioner's desk in the not-too-distant future, while I'm more likely to be back on the beat.'

'Not if Commander Hawksby has anything to do with it.'

'How can you possibly know that?'

'Jojo keeps me well-informed of what you two are up to. She listens to every word you say and picks up information you wouldn't dream of revealing in front of a criminal and then discusses it with Artemisia before passing it on to me.'

'I'll have to be more careful in future,' said Ross, 'remembering just how bright Artemisia is.'

'Not as bright as her brother,' said Alice, 'who doesn't like to be second in any subject.'

'I thought Arte was hoping to be head girl?' said Ross.

'She is, but that requires a different set of skills that

Artemisia has in abundance. Mind you, I'm not sure if St Luke's is ready to appoint a girl as head prefect, but if anyone can make it happen, she will.'

'Not unlike her mother.'

'The ideal role model. But Beth must have played a skilful hand to become chair of the Fitzmolean, while so many men already had their feet on the same ladder.'

'Not unlike you,' said Ross, taking Alice by surprise.

'I'm not sure I understand,' she said, trying to look innocent. 'I'm just a simple primary school teacher.'

'Who's recently been offered the chance to become a head-mistress.'

'How do you know that?'

'You obviously don't realize that Jojo is a double-agent and I'm her handler.'

'What has she told you?' asked Alice, putting down her knife and fork.

'She said you've been offered the chance to become head-mistress of a girls' school in Doncaster. Not bad for one so—' he hesitated '—young.'

'I'm thirty-seven,' came back Alice, 'and perhaps I'm ready to move on.'

'Jojo would miss you.'

'Only Jojo?'

'And Artemisia and Peter, both of whom you taught before they moved on.'

'Anyone else?'

Ross tried to think of a suitable reply which wouldn't get him into even more trouble. 'What else did Mata Hari tell you?' he asked, looking down at his untouched salad.

'That if I didn't go to Doncaster, she'd invite me to supper on a Thursday evening and share her pizza with me,' mused Alice. 'A different kind of second date.'

'I can't wait to introduce you to my mother,' said Ross.

'A Caribbean woman,' queried Alice, 'who isn't a Roman Catholic?'

'I'll start by telling her about your Irish mother.'

'Who is a Roman Catholic,' said Alice.

BOOK III

'Before you embark on a journey
of revenge, dig two graves.'

Confucius (circa 481 BC)

CHAPTER 23

THE COMMANDER TOOK TWO DICE out of the bottom drawer of his desk and tossed them onto the table. He waited for them to settle before he said, 'Snake eyes.'

William didn't need to be told which route they would be taking to the Tower that morning or the password that would guarantee the East Gate would be opened so they could once again collect the Sword of State and the Imperial State Crown before delivering them to Buckingham Palace.

'Try not to let it go to your head,' said the commander, but neither officer laughed at the Hawk's annual joke.

'We'd better get going, sir,' said William as he turned to leave. 'Can't afford to keep the Lord Chamberlain waiting.'

The Hawk nodded as William left the room, joined Paul, and jogged down the stairs and across the foyer to find Danny waiting behind the wheel of a grey Land Rover that was brought out only for special occasions. The Hawk had decided not to replace Paul at the last moment, as Ross hadn't been involved in the preparation work, and the trial had ended sooner than he'd anticipated.

'Good morning, sir,' said Danny, looking in the rear-view mirror when he heard the back door slam. He drove out of the Yard, swung left and headed in the direction of the palace.

A lone figure tucked behind a pillar inside St James's Park tube station wrote down the number plate of the Land Rover. He waited until the car was out of sight before he touched the green button on his mobile. It was answered after one ring.

'Papa seven one, whisky tango delta,' he pronounced slowly.

The voice repeated the sequence and rang off after he said, 'Got it.'

The second call the St James's plant made was to the team leader to confirm the Land Rover had left Scotland Yard, was on its way to the palace and Inspector Hogan had been replaced by Inspector Adaja.

'Did anyone spot you?' asked Lamont anxiously.

'Not even an old classmate from Peel House days,' came back the reply.

'And the number plates?'

'I passed on the details to the mechanic immediately.'

Lamont cut him off without another word, aware there were no seconds to be wasted. The man had served his purpose. In a few minutes' time, the number plates on his Land Rover would be the same as those on the police car that had just left Scotland Yard. Another phone began to ring.

Danny drove under Admiralty Arch and along the Mall to see a group of tourists taking photos of the palace. One of them was an ex-copper he recognized from his days on the beat. He assumed he must have taken a job as a tour guide after leaving the force. Then he remembered he'd had to take early retirement. He would have briefed the Super, but his thoughts were interrupted when he came to a halt outside the palace gates.

'Warrant card, please,' insisted a sentry.

Danny handed his over and was ticked off and waved through. He couldn't miss the familiar grey Jaguar parked on the far side of the courtyard.

Danny jumped out and introduced himself to Richard Mason, the Lord Chamberlain's new driver. He would miss catching up with Phil Harris, who Mason confirmed had recently retired.

'I was surprised not to see you at Phil's farewell party,' remarked Mason. 'Quite a bash. Held at the palace, and even Princess Anne dropped in. I spoke to her!'

Danny didn't admit he hadn't been invited and was disappointed not to have been, as he'd thought he and Phil were mates.

'So which route are we taking?' asked Mason as he opened the back door of the Jaguar and waited for his boss to appear.

'Number one,' said Danny.

'And the password?'

'Also number one.'

Mason checked both numbers in his notebook. Not something Phil would have had to do. When the Lord Chamberlain appeared, Danny nipped back to the Land Rover, jumped behind the wheel and waited as the Queen's Chief of Staff marched across the parade ground and gave William a warm smile and a wave, before getting into the back of his car. A man William considered wouldn't have displayed any nerves if the enemy had been marching up Whitehall, bayonets fixed.

• • •

It had been several years since Miles Faulkner had visited the Old Bailey, but he accepted Booth Watson's judgement that it was necessary if his alibi was to be believed without question.

Miles pitched up outside the Bailey in a taxi, but then his driver was occupied elsewhere. Booth Watson, dressed in his court garb, was standing on the pavement waiting for him, although he was not due to appear in any of the eighteen courts that morning.

Booth Watson accompanied his client up the sweeping marble staircase to the second floor, where they perched on a bench outside court number 8.

'He's due to appear in a GBH case first thing this morning,' said Booth Watson, 'so it would be difficult for him to miss us.'

Miles's mobile began to ring. He answered it and listened for less than a minute, only saying, 'Understood,' before he switched it off.

'Is everything going to plan?'

'Warwick has just left Buckingham Palace and is on his way to the Tower, so now there's no turning back.'

'What can go wrong?' asked Booth Watson.

'Everything depends on the timing as they will have no more than ten to twelve minutes at most to pull it off, and should they get it wrong by even a few seconds, the whole operation will go belly up.'

'But should that happen,' said Booth Watson, 'after what we've planned for this morning, no one will have any reason to believe you were in any way involved.'

'Let's hope you're right.'

'Time to move,' interrupted Booth Watson. 'I've just seen your alibi heading towards us.' He got up and began walking towards the exit with Miles a pace behind. Booth Watson feigned surprise when he saw Sir Julian Warwick, his junior and his instructing solicitor heading towards them.

'Good morning, Julian,' said Booth Watson, while his rival was still a few paces away. 'What a pleasant surprise. I think you both know my client, Mr Miles Faulkner.'

Sir Julian stopped and offered a cursory nod but didn't shake hands with either of them.

'Good morning, Ms Warwick,' said Booth Watson, giving Grace a perfunctory bow. 'Allow me to congratulate you on your recent victory, but be assured, young lady, I shall not underestimate you a second time.'

Grace couldn't hide her disapproval, but somehow managed, 'Kind of you to say so, Mr Booth Watson.'

'Well, I won't hold you up. Good luck, Julian, in whatever case it is you're prosecuting,' he added, before he and Miles left them standing there.

'What was that performance about?' said Julian as they continued on their way to court number 8.

'No idea,' admitted Grace, 'except that, like my brother, I don't believe in coincidences.'

'With that in mind,' said Julian, turning to his instructing solicitor, 'perhaps I could ask you, Clare, to find out if Booth Watson had any scheduled cases in the Bailey this morning. Because I suspect those two are up to something.'

Clare made a note while Julian opened the door to court number 8 and stood aside to allow his two colleagues to enter.

• • •

'So that's your alibi sorted out,' said Booth Watson as the two of them stepped out into the street. 'But I recommend you still carry out the second part of your plan just to make sure no one can be in any doubt that you couldn't possibly have been anywhere near the Tower at the time.'

Miles nodded and this time he did shake hands with his QC before he left him and headed off towards the Strand. He'd only gone a few yards when his mobile began to ring.

• • •

One of Lamont's three mobiles began to ring. He grabbed it, assuming something must have gone wrong. This was not a day to be a glass-half-full man.

'The Lord Chamberlain's car has just left the palace and it's now on its way to the Tower,' confided another voice. 'Warwick and an officer I didn't recognize were seated in the back of the Land Rover and both cars are heading up the Mall towards Trafalgar Square,' said a man who had broken away from the group of tourists to carry out his far better paid job.

'Then it has to be one, four or five,' said Lamont, who knew all six routes as well as any taxi driver. 'Move everyone working on two, three and six to their new locations sharpish,' he said before cutting the voice off.

He was becoming more nervous by the minute.

• • •

As the two cars swept around Trafalgar Square into Northumberland Avenue and headed towards the Embankment, William picked up the phone in his armrest.

'Yes?' said a voice.

'We're on our way, sir,' said William. 'Should be with you in about fifteen minutes.'

'What's the password?' he asked.

'Number one, sir.'

'I look forward to meeting you, Chief Superintendent.'

William replaced the receiver. In the unlikely event of someone overhearing the call, he had given nothing away. Despite this, he realized he couldn't afford to relax until the Imperial State Crown and the Sword of State had been delivered safely to the palace.

• • •

The Resident Governor of the Tower put down his morning paper as his wife entered the drawing room.

'Just off to take the children to school,' she announced. 'What's the password?'

'Colonel Blood,' replied the Governor.

'I'm glad to see someone's got a sense of humour,' his wife replied before going off in search of the children.

• • •

'Good morning, Mario, I'd like to book my usual table for lunch tomorrow.'

'Of course, Mr Faulkner,' Mario replied, before placing an entry in his appointments book. 'For two?'

'Yes, just me and Mr Booth Watson. Would you place a bottle of champagne on ice half an hour before we arrive?'

'Of course, sir,' Mario replied.

Miles turned to leave, hesitated for a moment, checked his watch and said, 'What time do you make it?'

'Twenty-two minutes past eight,' said Mario.

'As I thought, my watch is running a couple of minutes late.' He pretended to adjust it before leaving. On his way out of the hotel he said good morning to the manager and told the doorman he wouldn't be needing a taxi. He began to walk slowly along the Strand as he made his way towards Westminster, his alibi now firmly established.

• • •

Lamont pressed the green button on his third phone before it had a chance to ring a second time.

'They've just passed the Playhouse Theatre and are turning left onto the Embankment, so it can't be route four,' said yet another anonymous voice. 'I've informed the group leader that it has to be one or five, and he's already moving any surplus bodies to both those locations.' The phone went dead just as another began to ring.

'The new number plates are on their way. Should be with you in about five minutes.'

'Make it three and you'll get a bonus,' promised Lamont as the Lord Chamberlain's car came to a halt at the traffic lights outside Somerset House.

• • •

Paul watched as a young woman pushing a stroller crossed the road, followed moments later by a blind man with a guide dog. Paul could have sworn he'd seen the man somewhere before but couldn't place him. William became distracted by three taxis that slipped out of a side road and joined the traffic in front of the Lord Chamberlain's car. The light turned green, but one of them pulled over to pick up a passenger so they were held up once again. William considered telling Danny to use the bus lane and then he remembered the commander's advice. Never use the bus lane unless it's an emergency. It only attracts unnecessary attention.

Three taxis couldn't be described as an emergency, and he wasn't worried about the occasional hold-up on the way to the Tower. It was on the way back to the palace with the crown and sword on board when any hold-up would set alarm bells ringing.

No sooner were they on the move again than the second taxi slowed down at the next roundabout and made no attempt to slip into the oncoming stream of traffic until the road was clear. William accepted they were going to be a few minutes late, but his orders were clear: never call the Governor a second time, unless it's an emergency.

• • •

The Governor's wife came to a halt at the West Gate and waited for the barrier to rise. The helpful young woman who'd recently joined the ticketing staff walked across and tapped politely on the window.

'Just checking you know the password, ma'am.'

'Colonel Blood,' said one of the children from the back seat.

'Correct!' said the young woman, who until that moment had no idea what the password was, and was relieved she hadn't had to move on to Plan B. As the Governor's wife drove out of the Tower, she made her way to the nearest bathroom. Thirty seconds later COLONEL BLOOD flashed up on the screen of Lamont's second mobile. He immediately got out of the Land Rover, walked quickly across to the Jag and informed Harris, who was seated behind the wheel waiting impatiently for the off.

'Number one,' said Lamont, who returned to the Land Rover to see two men heading towards him. Neither of them even glanced in his direction. One went to the back of the 4x4 while the other knelt down by the front mudguard. He checked both ways to make sure no one was watching them. No one was. Lamont's eyes continued to dart in every direction looking out for someone, anyone, who wasn't a blot on the landscape. No blot appeared. Two minutes later the mechanics had completed their assignment. The back window of the Land Rover slid down and Lamont handed over two cellophane packets. Bonus earned.

Once the two men had disappeared, Collins switched on the ignition and palmed the gear lever into first.

'Not yet,' said Lamont firmly. 'Too soon will be just as fatal as too late.'

Collins switched off the engine as another phone began to ring.

'They've taken a left at the underpass, so it has to be route one.'

'Get those hanging around at the far end of the underpass to move across to Walbrook sharpish. I need to know the moment they reach Mansion House, because that's when we'll have to move.'

• • •

William watched as a young policeman stepped out into the middle of the road, raised an arm and stopped an articulated lorry. He walked slowly across to the driver's side and indicated that he should pull over, holding up the traffic once again.

Something worried Paul about the young constable, but he didn't realize what it was until later. Much later. It began to rain.

• • •

Lamont's third phone began vibrating with a message to warn him the Lord Chamberlain's party was approaching the Mansion House and were no more than ten minutes away.

'I need a couple more minutes,' said Lamont.

'I'm on it,' came back the reply as three police motorcycles appeared out of nowhere, took up their place at the front of the little motorcade and waited. Harris responded the moment Lamont raised his hand, knowing the journey to the East Gate of the Tower would take two minutes and eighteen seconds. Lamont next called Faulkner, who was just walking past Charing Cross station.

'We're on our way,' was all he said.

'Good hunting,' replied Miles, slowing his pace. He didn't want to reach Westminster tube station before the package was due to arrive.

Miles pressed his stopwatch. From now on, everything would be about timing.

Harris switched on the engine and headed for the nearest exit of the car park to find the barrier was already raised so there wouldn't be any hold-ups. Another member of the team who'd done their job for the day.

When they drove out onto St Katharine's Way, the little motorcade swung right under Tower Bridge and quickly covered the short distance to the rear entrance of the Tower, where they came to a halt in front of two enormous wooden gates that reminded them it had once been a prison.

Two Yeomen emerged from the sentry box, clearly expecting them. One checked the number plates of both vehicles while the other one went to the front of the Jaguar and asked the driver for the password.

'Colonel Blood,' Harris said.

'Hope you're keeping well, Phil,' said the guard before he swung round and gave the order, 'Open the gates.'

As the gates swung open, adrenaline took over. From that moment, Lamont knew there was no turning back and not for the first time he wondered if he'd made the right decision. Even though his financial reward was astronomical compared to a police officer's pension, the alternative was several years in jail. But he accepted he was past the point of no return. He checked his stopwatch, aware he had at most another eight minutes before the real Lord Chamberlain would drive up to the same gates.

• • •

Another zebra crossing caused the two official cars to be held up once again. Some of those crossing the road didn't appear to be in any hurry, including another woman pushing a stroller who looked strangely incongruous among the thrusting young City whiz-kids who were dashing in every direction. William picked up the phone in his armrest, but when the crossing cleared, put it back in place.

• • •

Once they'd passed through the East Gate, Harris drove slowly beside the Thames before turning right and crossing the middle drawbridge. He continued on up the slope, coming to a halt outside the Jewel House to find six Yeomen standing in line waiting for them. He leapt out and opened the back door, counting on the fact that the recently appointed Governor hadn't met the Lord Chamberlain before.

Dressed in a bowler hat and long black overcoat with a

scarf covering his lower face, The Understudy stepped out of the car and out onto the stage. He put up his umbrella to protect himself from the rain and any prying eyes.

'Good morning, Governor,' he said as the two men shook hands. 'Shocking weather for this time of year.'

'It is indeed, my Lord,' responded the Governor as six Yeoman Warders sprang to attention and presented arms. The Understudy doffed his hat in acknowledgement – another little detail supplied by Harris.

'Let's go inside before we get soaked,' suggested the Governor, and The Understudy didn't need any encouragement to speed up the whole process.

While the two men disappeared inside the Jewel House, Harris strolled across to Haskins, the Chief Warder, and said, 'I see the Gunners lost three-two at home to Spurs on Saturday.' He assumed that would get Walter climbing onto his hobby horse, but the Chief Warder's response wasn't part of his well-rehearsed script.

'I thought you'd retired, Phil,' said the senior warder, taking Harris by surprise.

'Couple of weeks' time,' said Harris, trying to recover. 'In fact, this will be my last outing. You and the missus must come to my leaving do at the palace.' Back on script.

'That's very generous of you,' said Walter, a puzzled expression appearing on his face. 'I'll look forward to that.'

'I'll put an invitation in the post,' said Harris. 'But for now, better turn the car around before his nibs comes back out.'

'Good thinking,' said Walter.

Harris climbed back into the car but was shaking uncontrollably. He had to grip the steering wheel firmly. He began to turn a half circle with the Land Rover following close behind, but when his eyes weren't on the Jewel House they were on the entrance, fearing the real party might appear at any moment. When he came to a halt, he thought he was going to throw up. Something he hadn't anticipated.

• • •

'Damn,' said William as the Lord Chamberlain's car got stuck behind a Corporation of London road sweeper, its brushes whirring around, filling the air with dust. A service that William had previously thought were like owls, who only came out at night.

He checked his watch again. They were running well over time. He thought about making a second call to the Governor, but didn't. An inconvenience that could hardly be described as an emergency.

• • •

When The Understudy entered the Jewel House, the Governor introduced him to the Chief Exhibitor, whose responsibility it was to hand over the crown and sword to the Resident Governor. They didn't shake hands because the Chief Exhibitor was wearing a pair of spotless white gloves. The Understudy watched anxiously as the man lowered the crown gently into a black leather box with EIIR etched in gold letters on one side. A perfect fit. He closed the lid, locked it and handed the tiny key to the Governor.

The whole process was repeated by the senior Jewel House Warder as the Sword of State was placed in a far larger box, but equally well bedded down. A second key was passed to the Governor, while the Chief Exhibitor and the senior Jewel House Warder each picked up their own box and followed their masters slowly out of the Jewel House as if they were part of a funeral cortège. But whose funeral, The Understudy wondered, as they couldn't have gone much slower.

When the Governor reappeared with the two Jewel House Warders carrying their black boxes, Harris remained by the back of the car and watched as both boxes were placed in the boot. He slammed the boot closed and locked it while his passenger and the Resident Governor continued to chat. Harris had to admit The Understudy was a real pro.

'Would you care to join me for lunch at my club, old chap?' said The Understudy, sticking to his script. 'White's suit you?'

'How kind of you,' said the Governor as his guest almost fell into the back of his car.

'I'll be in touch,' he promised as Harris closed the door and quickly took his place behind the wheel.

They were just about to move off when the Governor stepped forward and tapped firmly on the window. The Understudy wound the window down, a bead of sweat appearing on his forehead. This wasn't part of his script.

'You nearly forgot these,' he said, passing over two small keys. 'Otherwise, you might have had to come back.'

'And we wouldn't have wanted that,' said The Understudy, smiling before he'd wound the window back up. He put the keys in his pocket and tapped Harris firmly on the shoulder.

The moment Harris switched on the engine the three outriders immediately took off. Harris gave the Chief Warder a final wave and said under his breath, 'Sorry you won't be coming to my leaving party, Walter, unless you're planning to visit Mexico.'

'Or Pentonville,' suggested The Understudy, which helped Harris to concentrate. He kept a steady pace as he drove across the middle drawbridge, along the river and through the open gate, receiving several salutes along the way. Once they were back on St Katharine's Way, Harris continued up the slope towards a traffic light that wasn't conveniently green. When would his heartbeat return to normal? Not until the wheels of his plane had left the ground, he suspected, and perhaps not even then.

When the lights changed, the three outriders swung left, disappeared over Tower Bridge and headed for Wandsworth while the Jaguar and Land Rover went in the opposite direction.

'Don't break the speed limit,' Lamont barked. 'Because if you do, we'll end up with more than a fine.'

• • •

'At last,' said William, when the Westminster road sweeper finally turned left, allowing them to take off once again.

'Don't worry, guv,' said Danny. 'I'll have you there in no time.'

Paul glanced across the road to see two cars with blacked-out windows passing them on the other side of the road. He swung round and looked out of the back window. Same year, P, same colour, grey, but he wasn't able to get the number plate because Danny had already accelerated across the road, as he tried to keep up with the Jaguar as it sped down St Katharine's Way.

The Lord Chamberlain's party came to a halt outside the East Gate. William took out his warrant card so they wouldn't be held up any longer. But what happened next certainly wasn't in standing orders. The door of the Gate House swung open and out piled half a dozen guardsmen who didn't present arms.

Could it be possible, thought William as they surrounded both cars.

• • •

'That was a close-run thing,' said Lamont as he looked across the road to see the official party heading towards the Tower less than a couple of minutes away. 'All hell is about to break loose, so we can't afford to hang about.'

Harris swung into All Hallows by the Tower, relieved to see there were no other cars in the church's little back yard.

He was the first out and had opened the boot of the Jaguar before Lamont and Collins could join him. Harris unlocked both boxes, lifted the crown out of the smaller one, and lowered it gently into his Tower of London shopping bag, which he then handed to Lamont.

Harris slammed down the boot but didn't lock it.

'My guess,' said Lamont, looking back towards the Tower, 'is that we've only got a few minutes before every copper in the Met will be looking for us. So let's get moving.'

Harris didn't need any encouragement. 'Nothing personal,' he said, 'but I hope I never see any of you again.' He nipped across the road and hailed a taxi going in the opposite direction while Lamont and Collins headed for Tower Hill station. Nine stops on the Circle line. Average time, seventeen minutes.

Lamont felt Harris had earned his vast fee, but wondered would he ever get to spend it.

Neither of them noticed the fourth member of the team slip out of the Jaguar, the Old Harrovian tie discarded, to be replaced with a dog collar and black shirt. He walked to St Paul's, entered the cathedral by the West Door, fell on his knees and began to pray.

CHAPTER 24

THE GOLDEN HOUR

WILLIAM AND PAUL HAD WORKED it out within moments of comparing notes.

A woman pushing a stroller slowly across the road with no sign of a child. The Constable who was too young to be wearing a Falklands Medal Ribbon. The road sweeper that shouldn't have been cleaning the streets at that time of day. A taxi driver who hung back for a little too long when he came to a roundabout, and, most telling of all, a grey Jaguar followed by a Land Rover both with blacked-out windows and number plates bearing the letter P.

William quickly produced his warrant card and ordered the Yeoman to open the gates immediately and warn the Governor it was a red alert. The Yeoman guard ran back to his sentry box and called the Governor on his private line. Something he'd never done before.

William phoned the commander back at the Yard to be

told by his secretary he was in a meeting and not to be disturbed.

'Get him out now, Angela!' said William as he watched the Lord Chamberlain climbing out of his car and heading towards him.

58 MINUTES

'City airport,' said Harris as he pulled the taxi door closed. He slipped into the far corner so the cabbie couldn't see him in his rear-view mirror. Two police cars, sirens blaring, shot past them on the other side of the road. He turned away.

'What's their problem?' said the cabbie.

'No idea,' said Harris, fervently hoping it wasn't about to become his problem.

57 MINUTES

William didn't waste any words when he called the commander and told him what had happened. He wasn't surprised by the Hawk's immediate response.

'No one, and I mean no one, must be allowed to leave the Tower, under any circumstances,' said the commander. 'And don't allow anyone else to enter the grounds without my permission.'

'But the horse has already bolted, sir,' Paul reminded him. 'Shouldn't we be looking for the rider?'

'Someone on the inside might well have been responsible for opening the stable door,' snapped the Hawk. 'William, you start by interviewing everyone who works at the Tower, from the Resident Governor to the ravens. I'll have a dozen officers, including Rebecca and Jackie, to assist you within minutes. Begin with those working in the Jewel House. I'll order a full background check on every one of them. Do any of them have previous or are currently experiencing financial difficulties? Look under every stone and remember Locard's principle – every contact leaves a trace. If we don't find the crown, and quickly, this outrage will embarrass not only the Royal Family but also the new government, while humiliating the Metropolitan Police who will certainly be held responsible, and rightly so.'

'I'm sorry to interrupt you, sir,' said Paul. 'But if we do that, I think it will only cause even more problems.'

'Like what?'

'If we start interrogating everyone in sight, the whole world will soon know why the Tower is swarming with police.'

'Fair point,' admitted the commander. 'Any ideas?'

'Yes, sir,' said William. 'I'll suggest someone on the staff has run off with yesterday's takings, which I suspect will be quite a large sum of money. That lot are old-school, very proud, and wouldn't want it to get out that one of them is a thief.'

'Brief the home team accordingly,' said the Hawk. 'Meanwhile, Paul, you can start by looking for the duplicate Jaguar and Land Rover; identical number plates would be my bet. They've probably dumped them both within a mile of the Tower. Whoever is responsible for this outrage will know only too well that's the first thing we'll be looking for. Start by checking every car park within a three-mile radius. You can begin with the Tower Hotel,' he said, poring over a detailed map of the City that Angela had placed on the desk in front of him.

'We won't find the cars there,' said Paul.

'Why not?' demanded the Hawk.

'I realize now I saw them pass me on the other side of the road a few minutes before we turned up at the Tower.'

'Then they will almost certainly have seen you and have ditched both cars by now.' He didn't add, *if only Inspector Hogan had been in the passenger seat*, suddenly aware that it must have been part of their plan to make sure Ross was well out of the way for the operation. 'I'll get details of both duplicate vehicles circulated immediately. So don't waste a minute of the golden hour.'

He slammed down one phone and picked up another. 'Find Inspector Hogan,' he barked at his secretary.

54 MINUTES

'Paul,' said William, 'you heard what the boss said. So go back to the exact spot where you saw those two identical cars passing you on the other side of the road and start looking for the nearest car park.'

Danny switched on the engine.

'And the moment you've found them, report straight back to me, not that I expect you to find anything, even fingerprints. On your way,' said William as he got out of the car to face the Lord Chamberlain.

'Do I think what's happened has happened, Chief Superintendent?' he asked even before he'd reached him.

'I'm afraid so, sir.'

'And what do you expect me to do in the circumstances?' asked a man who was more used to giving orders than taking them.

'I'd like you to return to the palace—'

'Empty-handed?'

'Yes, sir. But my team's already working on it.'

'Then I won't delay you any longer, Chief Superintendent, but be sure to keep me informed.'

'I will, sir. But it would help . . .'

'If I kept my mouth shut,' said the keeper of the Queen's secrets.

'Yes, sir.'

'I'm willing to do that, Chief Superintendent, but must warn you there's a time limit. Because when the Queen enters their Lordships' house tomorrow morning at eleven thirty, if she is not preceded by the Sword of State and wearing the Imperial State Crown, she will have been stripped of her authority as monarch, and I wouldn't want to be the person who has to explain to her how that was allowed to happen.'

Without another word, the Lord Chamberlain turned on his heel and strode back to his car, just as the great doors of the East Gate opened and William spotted his next problem running towards him.

53 MINUTES

Satisfied that he'd played his role, Booth Watson headed slowly back to his chambers in Middle Temple, where he would wait for his client to call. It could only be a matter of time.

51 MINUTES

'How can that be possible?' asked the Governor as he and William ran across the middle drawbridge and on up the steep slope towards the Jewel House.

'A set of circumstances that could only occur very rarely,' said William. 'What you might call a perfect storm.'

'But I didn't even spot any threatening clouds,' admitted the Governor.

'That's hardly surprising,' said William. 'You've only been in the post as Resident Governor for less than two months, and clearly never came across the Lord Chamberlain or his driver during that time.'

'But there's the rub,' puffed an out-of-breath Governor. 'I was invited to a drinks party at the palace last week by the Duke of Edinburgh, but unfortunately the Lord Chamberlain was accompanying the Queen to another event so I didn't get to meet him.'

'And you were convinced by the man who took his place this morning?'

'Completely taken in,' admitted the Governor. 'He was every inch a Lord Chamberlain. Gilbert and Sullivan couldn't have cast him better.'

'Can you describe him?' asked William, still on the move.

'About six one, sixtyish, well-built like a former athlete. He was wearing a black velvet-collared overcoat, grey scarf and a bowler hat, and as it was raining at the time, he put up his umbrella as he got out of the car.'

'But once you were inside the building?'

'You must remember, Superintendent, once you've entered the Jewel House, it's almost pitch black. The only lights are directed on to the cases containing the Crown Jewels. In fact, now I remember, while the sword and crown were being transferred into their boxes, he stood some way back.'

'No doubt to avoid being picked up by any CCTV cameras. It's clear now that everything had been planned down to the finest detail. You've got to hand it to him,' said William.

'We did,' said the Governor, with some feeling.

'What about his voice, accent, demeanour, didn't anything cause you to think twice?'

'On the contrary,' came back the Governor. 'He was to the manner born, even wore an Old Harrovian tie, which I knew was the Lord Chamberlain's alma mater.'

A thought crossed William's mind, but he quickly dismissed it.

'And when Haskins immediately recognized his driver, I assumed . . .'

'Haskins?'

'The Chief Yeoman.'

'I need to speak to him immediately,' said William as they reached the Jewel House. 'Immediately.'

49 MINUTES

Danny screeched to a halt when he reached the spot where Paul had seen the two cars driving away in the opposite direction. Paul leapt out of the car and turned a slow circle as he scanned the landscape. To his left, the Tower, behind him Tower Hill tube station, while in front of him was a fine example of early English architecture, next to which was a large blue sign with an arrow pointing to the nearest NCP car park.

'That has to be where they've dumped the two cars,' said Danny, his eye following the direction the arrow indicated. He was about to take off when Paul said, 'I don't think so.'

He was staring at the church noticeboard on the other side of the road. All Hallows by the Tower. He started to run across the zebra crossing with Danny following in his wake.

48 MINUTES

The Governor introduced William to the Chief Yeoman, and even before he had a chance to ask his first question, the old soldier said, 'I should never have allowed this to happen on my watch.'

'I don't think anyone will blame you, Haskins,' said the Governor. 'After all—'

'Alarm bells should have rung the moment I first saw Harris driving the Lord Chamberlain's car.'

'Why?' said William. 'It was the usual car with the correct number plates, so why should you have been at all suspicious?'

'Because Phil Harris invited me to a farewell party that had already taken place.'

'How do you know that?' asked William.

'Because one of my mates attended the bash and hasn't stopped telling everyone since. Held at Buck House with . . .'

'So you've known Harris for some time?' said William as an out-of-breath Jackie appeared by his side, a bulky file under one arm.

'For the past eleven years, so I didn't need much convincing.'

'But what about the Lord Chamberlain?'

'They change from time to time,' said the Yeoman, 'and in any case, I don't exactly move in those circles. Mind you, he played the part to perfection. Didn't put a foot wrong, but then he'd had Harris to tutor him.'

'And where was Harris when the Governor went into the Jewel House?' asked Jackie.

'He turned the car around, opened the boot and waited as he has done for the past eleven years.'

'And when they came back out?' pressed William.

'He was still standing by the back of the Jag, waiting for the Chief Jeweller to appear and supervise locking the two boxes in the boot.'

Jackie produced a photo from one of her files. 'Is this Harris?' she asked.

'Sure is,' said Haskins, 'and if I ever set eyes on him again . . .'

'His mugshot has already been circulated to every police station in the Met,' confirmed Jackie, 'as well as an All Ports Alert being issued to every major transport hub within fifty miles.'

William nodded. 'One last thing,' he said, turning back to Haskins. 'Not a word to anyone, is that understood?'

'Goes with the territory,' said the Chief Yeoman of the Guard.

46 MINUTES

When Paul and Danny reached the pavement on the other side of the road, they both paused to stare at two cars, which couldn't have been parked much closer to the Tower.

Danny began searching the Land Rover, surprised to find all the doors were open and even more surprised to find one vital piece of evidence. Paul went straight to the boot of the Jaguar, assuming it had to be locked. Wrong again. He opened it and stared down in disbelief at two large black leather boxes with the letters EIIR painted in gold on one side.

Paul held his breath as he slowly lifted the lid of the larger box, expecting to find it empty, but there in front of him was the Sword of State, resting in all its glory. Tentatively, he lifted the lid of the second box hoping to find the crown equally resplendent, but nothing.

'The bastard,' said Paul, loud enough to cause Danny to quickly join him, clutching the discarded tie.

When he saw the Sword of State, he said, 'They must have panicked and bolted . . .'

'More likely they saw us coming,' said Paul as he stared at

a navy and silver striped Old Harrovian tie. He took a phone out of an inside pocket and dialled William's mobile. It was engaged.

46 MINUTES

Lamont and Collins got off the tube at Baker Street. When they emerged from underground, they were greeted by a famous detective who stood in front of them, familiar pipe in hand. Lamont bent down and touched the well-rubbed shoe of Sherlock Holmes for luck. They headed off towards a building just a block away which they had both visited several times during the past month, but never at the same time.

They went straight to the front of the queue and handed over their pre-booked tickets, before entering the building. Anything that would save time had been built into the master plan.

43 MINUTES

The commander picked up the phone to find William on the other end of the line.

'We've had an early breakthrough, sir,' he said. 'The senior Jewel House Warder, a Mr Walter Haskins, who's worked at the Tower for the past twenty years, told me a man called Phil Harris was driving the Jaguar when the first group turned up this morning.'

'Why's that important?' asked the Hawk.

'Harris has been the Lord Chamberlain's driver for the past eleven years. It seems that until today he had an unblemished record. Haskins was under the impression he'd recently retired, and when he raised the subject with him, Harris told him he was leaving in a couple of weeks' time, even had the nerve to invite him and his wife to his farewell party at the palace – a party that had already taken place.'

'Then we need to track down Harris before he gets clean away, as he's obviously their inside man. I need a photograph of him sharpish so I can distribute it to all the relevant agencies.'

'Jackie's already done that,' said William.

'And Paul?'

'Has gone in search of the two cars.'

'Let me know the moment he finds them,' said the Hawk, 'while I give you as much back-up as possible.' His other phone began to ring.

42 MINUTES

The taxi driver dropped his passenger outside City airport. Harris paid in cash, giving the cabbie a decent enough tip but not one that would be remembered.

The first thing the ticketless passenger did on entering the terminal was to check the departure board. Brussels was his best chance of a quick escape, but he'd have to move quickly. He headed for the BA desk to be told by the woman behind the counter that the gate for that flight was about to close. Mr Robinson explained that he didn't have any luggage, not even a cabin bag. What he didn't tell her was that he'd left everything behind, even his name. What's in a name when you have a million pounds deposited in a bank just a few hours away. She issued him with a business-class ticket but told him he'd have to hurry.

The last thing he'd done before he went to bed was to check the money had been deposited in Mr Robinson's account at the National Bank of Mexico. If it hadn't, he wouldn't have turned up at the Tower Hotel that morning, which would have left Faulkner and the rest of the team sitting in a basement car park with no choice but to abort the whole operation, aware that no one could take his place.

He checked once again to make sure his passport and business-class ticket were in the inside pocket of his jacket as he'd done countless times during the past few minutes. He waited for his flight to be called, unaware that no announcements are made at City airport, unless it's an emergency. Only for those looking for him was it an emergency. He glanced at his watch once again. Eighteen minutes of the golden hour had gone. But how long before . . .

41 MINUTES

The commander grabbed a phone that wouldn't stop ringing. 'Hawksby.'

'I've found the two cars,' Paul said. 'You were right, sir. They dumped them in a local churchyard only a couple of hundred yards from the Tower. But more important, they left the Sword of State in the boot of the Jag.'

'And the crown?'

'Just an empty box, sir.'

'Any clues?'

'Someone discarded an Old Harrovian tie on the front seat of the Jag.'

'It wasn't discarded,' said the Hawk. 'Someone we both know was presenting his calling card.'

'You can't be serious?' said Paul.

'Who's the one Old Harrovian who would do anything to humiliate your boss?'

'Miles Faulkner,' said Paul without hesitation.

'In one,' said the Hawk. 'But for now, stay put and I'll send a couple of squad cars over to pick up the Sword of State and take it to the palace. By the way, Paul, well done. But we still need to find the crown if your promotion isn't going to be temporary.'

'Track down Faulkner, sir,' said Paul, 'and I've no doubt we'll find the crown.'

40 MINUTES

Miles stepped back onto the pavement to allow a police car to fly by. As he crossed the road, a couple of policemen came rushing towards him, but quickly shot past without giving him a second look. He continued down Whitehall, Big Ben looming up in front of him; his final destination in sight.

39 MINUTES

Three police motorcycles were returned to a pound in Wandsworth long before the golden hour had passed. Six hundred pounds changed hands.

38 MINUTES

Harris was at the check-in desk by the time Miles was walking down Whitehall, and Lamont had set the museum's alarm off. Harris moved quickly through security, only stopping to check the gate number on the departure board. Brussels. Gate number 12.

36 MINUTES

Collins and Lamont emerged from the gallery shop at the rear of the museum, job done. Lamont jumped in an unlicensed minicab, not risking a black cab. He kept his head down as they headed for Hammersmith, where he would join his wife. They could now afford the postponed holiday he'd promised her.

Collins returned to Baker Street tube station – his turn to touch Holmes's foot – before disappearing underground. This time he headed for the Jubilee line, aware that if all had gone to plan, Mr Faulkner would be waiting for him when he arrived at Westminster. If he wasn't, the boss would already have been arrested, which wasn't part of the plan.

33 MINUTES

A grey Audi drew up outside the rear entrance of the Tower and a Yeoman Warder approached the car as the Governor's wife wound down her window and said, 'Colonel Blood.'

'I'm sorry, ma'am,' said the Yeoman looking embarrassed. 'No one's allowed to enter or leave the Tower without the Governor's permission.'

'But I'm his wife.'

'I know, ma'am, but them's my orders.'

28 MINUTES

When Harris reached the front of the queue, he handed his passport to the flight attendant, who seemed to take forever checking the photograph; or was he overreacting?

'Thank you, Mr Robinson,' she said after scanning his

boarding pass. He wondered how long it would take him to get used to his new name.

He headed down the stairs and out onto the tarmac. Another flight attendant was standing at the top of the aircraft steps, checking passengers' boarding passes. Was that normal?

22 MINUTES

Collins got off the tube at Westminster, made his way up the escalator and out of the station to see Mr Faulkner standing below Big Ben. He crossed the road and handed over the Tower of London carrier bag to his boss in a seamless relay without a word passing between them. He then began walking towards Knightsbridge, keeping only to side roads, on his way back to Cadogan Place. An escape route he'd honed to perfection during the past week.

21 MINUTES

Booth Watson sat behind his desk, attempting to read a brief while waiting for the phone to ring, expecting Miles to confirm he'd been arrested. Minutes seemed to take longer than sixty seconds as his third coffee went cold.

Even if Miles had succeeded in stealing the crown, he'd already warned him that if he was arrested, it would be almost impossible to get him out on bail.

'I don't want to get out on bail,' Miles had explained, without explaining.

20 MINUTES

'I'm grateful to you for agreeing to assist us with our inquiries, Lady Faber,' said William as he sat down next to Jackie, 'and am sorry you were held up at the gate.'

'That turns out to be the least of my husband's problems,' the Governor's wife responded.

'May I begin by asking you when you left the Tower this morning?'

'It must have been around twenty past eight,' she replied. 'I was driving the children to school as they have to be in assembly by eight forty-five.'

'Did you know the password?' asked Jackie.

'Yes, my husband told me just before I left. If he hadn't, I wouldn't have been able to return to the lodgings.'

'Did you tell anyone else the password?'

'Certainly not. But as I was leaving the Tower, the young woman on the entrance gate asked me if I knew it.'

'And did you tell her?'

'No I did not, but my youngest blurted out "Colonel Blood",' said Lady Faber. 'I'm so sorry. I should never have . . .'

'Don't blame yourself, ma'am,' said William. 'I was given a dozen clues but chose to ignore every one of them even though they were staring me in the face.'

'Do you know the name of the young woman, by any chance?' asked Jackie.

'Penny, but I don't know her surname.'

William jumped up and headed for the door.

'Is my husband going to lose his job?' she asked, trying not to sound desperate.

'If he does,' said Jackie, 'he'll be joining a large club.'

18 MINUTES

'Name?' said Rebecca.

'Penny, Penny Cummins,' replied a young woman who was dressed in the Tower's distinctive navy blue uniform with little red castles on the lapels, black stockings and black shoes – well polished.

'How long have you worked at the Tower?' asked Rebecca as William came in and sat down beside her.

'Just over six months, but I haven't done anythin' wrong.'

'No one's suggesting you have,' said Rebecca. 'But a large sum of money has gone missing.'

'I would never steal nothin'.'

'Were you on duty around twenty past eight when the Governor's wife left the Tower with her children?' asked William, cutting to the chase.

'Perhaps I was,' said Penny defensively. William couldn't miss the defiant shrug of the shoulders and slight reddening of the cheeks. Not a criminal, but he suspected someone who had something to hide.

'Did you ask the Governor's wife if she knew the password?'

'Might have,' she said, bowing her head. 'So what?'

'Because you didn't know what the password was at that time, did you?' said William a little more sharply. No reply was forthcoming.

'We'll need to check your mobile phone,' said Rebecca.

'Don't have one,' said Cummins.

William took her bag and tipped it upside down, spilling all the contents onto the table, which included a phone. Rebecca grabbed it and a few seconds later the words COLONEL BLOOD flashed up on the screen.

'Who were you sending this message to?' demanded William.

'Don't know,' Penny replied, shaking uncontrollably. 'It was all done over the phone.'

'Does the name Phil Harris mean anything to you?' asked William, moving on.

'No, never heard of him, I swear.'

William would have liked to continue questioning her but suspected she had nothing more to offer, while the sand in the golden hourglass was continuing to slip away. He quickly left the room with the feeling Ms Cummins was just another pawn on life's chess board, while the pieces were being moved by a grandmaster.

12 MINUTES

Once the minicab had dropped him off about a mile from his house, Lamont made his way quickly across the common until he reached the front door of his home, without looking back. Once inside, he went straight to the kitchen to find his wife was preparing lunch.

'Has anyone called in the last hour?' were his first anxious words.

'Only my mother,' she replied.

'What time was that?'

'About half an hour ago.'

'Did she ask where I was?'

'No. But where were you?'

'At a business meeting,' he said. 'And as far as you're concerned, I never left the house all morning, that's assuming you're still hoping to go on that shopping trip to Milan.'

'And was the business meeting successful?'

'I can't be sure yet,' he replied, now fearful of a knock on the front door or the sound of a phone ringing. 'What's for lunch?' he asked, although he wasn't hungry.

'Crown roast,' she replied.

11 MINUTES

Chris Robinson resisted the urge to look back as he climbed the aircraft steps. Well, not more than once.

Once on board, he quickly located his seat and fastened his seatbelt. He checked his watch: forty-nine minutes had already passed since he left the Tower. Would the next person to get on the plane be a police officer, checking every passenger against a recent photograph?

'This is your captain speaking. I'm sorry that we're running a few minutes late, but as we'll have a following wind, we can expect to make up the time before we land in Brussels.'

To hell with the following wind, thought Harris, just get moving.

'As soon as everyone's on board, we'll be taking off.'

Chris Robinson may have boarded the plane, but would Phil Harris be leaving by the same door, accompanied by the police officer, even before the plane took off?

9 MINUTES

As Lamont poured himself a whisky – one that even a Scot would have considered stiff – his wife noticed his hand was trembling. She didn't comment. Though as each minute passed, he felt more confident. He wondered if Faulkner had already been arrested, or was he standing outside the Palace of Westminster waiting to be caught red-handed? His thoughts were interrupted by his wife.

'Are we still going on holiday tomorrow?' Jenny asked as she removed the bottle of whisky from the table.

'Let's hope so,' he responded as if in another world.

'It's just that I've already started packing and even booked our flights.'

'Business class?'

'Yes, as well as a four-star hotel,' she said as a siren could be heard in the distance.

9 MINUTES

Miles crossed the road and began to walk slowly along a crowded pavement towards the Palace of Westminster. He passed the House of Commons and the statue of Oliver Cromwell, but didn't stop until he'd reached the Sovereign's Entrance to the House of Lords. He stood there, waiting patiently for the first copper to appear. He wondered how long it would be before they spotted him and demanded to see what was in his Tower of London shopping bag. He once again checked his stopwatch. Nine minutes of the golden hour still to go.

8 MINUTES

Lamont opened the front door to find Inspector Adaja and Sergeant Roycroft standing on the doorstep.

'Good morning, Paul,' he said, feigning surprise. 'To what do I owe this pleasure?'

'May we come inside, sir?' asked Paul formally.

'Of course,' said Lamont, who stood aside to allow them to enter. 'Let's go into the front room,' he suggested as his wife came bustling out of the kitchen.

'You know Jenny, of course. Paul and Jackie have just dropped round for a chat. Could you rustle up some coffee?'

'Not for me, thank you, Mrs Lamont,' said Paul.

'Nor me,' said Jackie.

'In fact,' said Paul, 'we would like to have a word with you later, Mrs Lamont, once we've finished questioning your husband.' She retreated back into the kitchen.

'That didn't sound very friendly,' said Lamont as he led them into the front room and offered them a seat.

'I won't bother cautioning you, sir,' said Paul who remained standing, 'but we are here to question you on a matter of national importance.'

The same surprised look returned to Lamont's face as he took the seat opposite them. Paul assumed Lamont would have anticipated every one of his questions and would have well-prepared answers.

'Let me begin by asking you where you were at eight thirty this morning?'

'That's easy,' said Lamont, sitting back. 'Right here. In fact, I haven't left the house all morning. After breakfast I read the newspapers before checking over my tax returns.' He swung round and pointed to a desk that was littered with official-looking documents alongside a couple of brown envelopes. Even the props had been prepared.

'And is your wife the only person who can confirm that you never left the house?' asked Jackie.

'I was interrupted once during the morning by a call from Jenny's mother,' said Lamont. 'Can't be sure of the exact time, but it must have been around quarter to nine.'

'Did you speak to your mother-in-law?' asked Jackie.

'No. Not if I can avoid it,' he said, laughing.

'I will be asking your wife to confirm that she did receive

a call from her mother, and that you were present at the time.'

'Isn't my word good enough?' demanded Lamont.

Paul didn't respond to his question. 'I think you know only too well why we're here. But like the consummate professional you are, you'll have covered your tracks. But then you've had twenty years of dealing with criminals.'

'Tread carefully, Adaja,' said Lamont, sounding defiant for the first time. 'Otherwise—'

'Otherwise?' queried Paul.

'My next call will be to my lawyer.'

'Mr Booth Watson, no doubt.'

'I always said we shouldn't have allowed your sort into the force,' snapped Lamont.

'My sort?'

'You know exactly what I'm getting at, sambo. So perhaps it's time for you to leave.'

'Not before I ask your wife what time you left the house this morning, and, more important, when you returned.'

'As I said, I never left the house.'

'And what was she doing during that time?'

'Packing for a holiday we've planned for several weeks.'

'Then she can start unpacking, because neither of you will be leaving until I've completed my inquiries.'

'What inquiries?' he repeated more sharply.

'I want to know who was sitting in the back of the Land Rover when you turned up at the Tower this morning.'

'I told you, I've been here all morning,' he said, his voice rising.

'And who it was in the back of the Jaguar?' pressed Paul. 'Because it certainly wasn't the Lord Chamberlain.'

'I don't know what you're talking about.'

'Does the name Phil Harris mean anything to you?'

'Never heard of him,' said Lamont, a little too quickly.

'Should have done,' came back Paul, 'because he was in the driving seat when you both turned up at the Tower this morning. He's just been arrested, and yours was the first name he gave us.'

If Jackie was surprised she didn't show it.

'It's definitely time for you to leave,' said Lamont, leaning forward in his chair, 'before you say something you'll later regret.'

'Like what?' replied Paul calmly. 'Because if the crown hasn't been returned to the Tower by this evening, I'll spend the rest of my days making sure you and your criminal friends end up in jail for the rest of your lives.'

'If the crown hasn't been returned to the Tower by this evening,' said Lamont, getting up from his chair, 'I suspect you won't even have the authority to issue a parking ticket. So I suggest you both bugger off.'

Paul didn't budge as Lamont clenched a fist and began to walk slowly towards him. Suddenly the door opened and Lamont's wife walked in carrying a tray of coffee and biscuits which she placed on the table between them.

'Just in case either of you change your mind,' she said, giving them both a warm smile.

7 MINUTES

'Mr Collins?' enquired William when the door was eventually opened, having travelled from the Tower to Knightsbridge in record time with the help of a police siren. Collins nodded. 'My name is Chief Superintendent Warwick and this is my colleague, Sergeant Pankhurst.'

'I know who you are,' said Collins, just as it began to rain.

'We'd like to have a private word with you, sir. May we come in?'

'No, you may not,' said Collins, 'unless of course you have a search warrant?'

'So you were expecting us,' said William. This time Collins didn't nod. 'We simply wanted to know where you were this morning?'

'I was polishing the silver, which I do every Tuesday morning.'

'And where was Mr Faulkner at the time?' asked Rebecca.

'He had an appointment with his lawyer at the Old Bailey. Mr Booth Watson, as I'm sure you know.'

'And after that?' said William. 'The Tower of London by any chance?'

'No. I think you'll find that after speaking to your father, he set off in the opposite direction. If I had to guess, he should have reached the Palace of Westminster by now. If you hurry, Chief Superintendent, you might just catch him.'

Before William could ask anything else, Collins slammed the door in his face.

'I could always arrest him, sir,' said Rebecca. 'Take him down to the station and interview him on tape?'

'A waste of time,' said William, 'because that's exactly what he wants us to do. Faulkner's thought this whole operation through to the last minute. I can even tell you where he is right now.'

'Where?' asked Rebecca, genuinely puzzled.

'Standing outside the Sovereign's Entrance to the House of Lords waiting for us.'

'How can you be so sure?'

'Because I'm his intended victim. It was never about the crown. It was always about me.' William took a mobile phone out of his pocket and dialled the Met's main control room.

Rebecca was none the wiser.

6 MINUTES

A flight attendant pulled the heavy aircraft door closed, but Harris still didn't feel in the clear.

'The cabin crew will now demonstrate the safety measures on this aircraft,' said the captain, 'and I would ask all passengers to pay careful attention to the instructions, even if you are a frequent flyer.'

Harris didn't pay attention but continued to stare out of the cabin window. Would a police car suddenly appear on the tarmac, race past them, order the plane to stop and return to its stand?

5 MINUTES

Miles stood outside the Sovereign's Entrance of the House of Lords waiting impatiently. Every time a police car shot by, he was tempted to wave, but surely it couldn't be much longer before they spotted him. After all, he was carrying a Tower of London shopping bag displaying a picture of the crown. What more could they want?

4 MINUTES

'Cabin crew, prepare for take-off.'

Harris turned to watch as the two flight attendants took their seats at the front of the aircraft and fastened their seatbelts. He looked back out of the cabin window to see the engines turning slowly, and then a little faster until the plane eased forward before gradually accelerating along the runway. Finally, the front wheels lifted off the ground and the plane took off.

Mr Robinson leant back and wanted to cheer.

3 MINUTES

Faulkner smiled when he heard a police siren in the distance. He remained standing outside the Sovereign's Entrance, hoping the Hawk would appreciate the irony.

Three squad cars screeched to a halt and half a dozen uniformed officers leapt out and came charging towards him. Perfect timing, he thought as he pressed his stopwatch for the final time. He handed over the Tower of London shopping bag to the sergeant while a PC thrust his arms behind his back and handcuffed him. A third officer arrested and cautioned him, before he was frogmarched to a waiting car and bundled roughly onto the back seat.

The sergeant looked inside the shopping bag and couldn't believe his luck. A broad grin appeared on his face.

'Magnificent, isn't it,' said Miles.

'Button your lip, Faulkner. You're going straight back where you belong, and this time they'll throw away the key.'

'I don't think so,' said Miles as the officer continued to cling onto the bag as if he were a goalkeeper who'd just saved a penalty.

'Call the Yard,' he ordered his driver, 'and get Commander Hawksby on the line.'

The Hawk listened carefully while an excited sergeant gave his report. When he came to the end, all the Hawk said was, 'It's all been too easy.'

60 SECONDS

Booth Watson picked up the private phone on his desk, not at all surprised to find who was on the other end of the line. After all, every prisoner is allowed to make one call.

'It's Miles Faulkner, BW. Just to let you know I've been arrested.'

'For what offence?' asked Booth Watson innocently, well aware that every word was being recorded and would be played back again and again, and later endlessly analysed by Commander Hawksby and his inner team.

'Theft,' replied Miles, sounding rather pleased with himself.

'And what have you been accused of stealing?'

'The 1937 Imperial State Crown along with the Sword of State from the Tower of London.'

'Where are you now?' asked Booth Watson.

'In custody at Canon Row police station. I think they're about to lock me up.'

'And the crown and sword, dare I ask?'

'They should both be on their way to Buckingham Palace by now.'

'Then you can sleep easy. Because I'll have you out first thing in the morning.'

'But make sure it's not before Her Majesty has delivered the Queen's Speech to the House of Lords,' Miles reminded him.

• • •

The team sat around the long table in the commander's office and listened to the tape once again.

'What's he up to?' said William.

'What makes you think he's up to anything?' asked the Hawk.

'The only words that matter on that tape are *but make sure it's not before Her Majesty has delivered the Queen's Speech to the House of Lords.*'

'Which will be at eleven thirty tomorrow,' Jackie reminded them.

'I still think he's got another surprise in store for us,' said Paul.

'I agree,' said William, 'because so far, he's always been a step ahead of us. Why did he give us back the Sword of State, but not the crown?'

'Where is the crown now?' asked the Hawk.

'Paul and I delivered it to Buckingham Palace about an hour ago,' said William. 'I was met by the Lord Chamberlain who was standing in the courtyard waiting in the rain. I've never seen such a look of relief.'

'Did he check inside the bag?'

'He certainly did,' said Paul, 'and as he allowed us to leave, I can only assume he was satisfied.'

'Or has Faulkner got away with it,' mused William, 'while we've walked straight into his latest trap?'

'But we've got the crown and the sword back, and arrested Faulkner,' said Jackie. 'What more could we ask for?'

'I don't know,' said William, 'but I have to wonder why he would give us back the sword but keep the crown, and then allow himself to be caught with the crown, knowing he would end up in custody. As you taught me when I was a young detective, sir, only three things matter in any crime.'

'Motive, motive and motive,' said Rebecca, speaking for the first time.

'Money, money and money?' suggested Paul. 'The crown must be worth millions.'

'Over a billion,' said Jackie, 'if the internet is to be believed.'

'Or nothing,' said William. 'Don't forget no professional criminal would touch the crown for fear that every police force on earth would want to take credit for apprehending the thief. So I don't believe that was ever Faulkner's *raison d'être*.'

'Unless he planned to break up the crown and sell the stones individually?' suggested Jackie.

'Something else he couldn't risk,' said William. 'The moment anyone saw the Cullinan II Diamond, they'd panic. It's the second largest diamond in the world and the size of a golf ball. So would be pretty hard to miss. As would the St Edward's Sapphire or the Black Prince's Ruby that any jeweller worth his salt would recognize immediately. No, if it had been Faulkner's intention to sell off the jewels individually,' continued William, 'it would have been a lot easier to have stripped the sword of its stones as they are not as well-known as those in the crown, but are still worth a fortune.'

'Then if it isn't money,' said the Hawk, 'what is it?'

'I suppose he could ransom it,' said Rebecca.

'For what?' said Paul.

'Me,' said William.

This silenced even the Hawk as they all waited for an explanation.

'Can you imagine how much publicity this story would create if it became known that someone had nicked the Crown Jewels from right under our noses? Not just in Britain, but across the world. While at the same time everyone around this table would have to resign and spend the rest of their lives being remembered for only one thing.' A long silence followed before William finally said, 'The press would hail Faulkner as the new Raffles, while I would be cast as Inspector Clouseau.'

No one laughed.

'But Faulkner would still end up spending the rest of his life in jail,' Jackie reminded them.

'Not if he tells the world's press he never intended to steal the jewels in the first place. He simply wanted to expose how inefficient the Royalty Protection squad is, and then remind everyone he left the State Sword in the back of a car a couple of hundred yards from the Tower with his old school tie discarded on the front seat to prove his point. He will then go on to tell them that he stood outside the Sovereign's Entrance of the Lords carrying the crown in a Tower of London shopping bag, waiting to be arrested. I know whose side I'd be on if I was a Fleet Street editor.'

'Or a member of the jury,' said Rebecca.

'But revenge implies that someone else has to be the target,' suggested the Hawk.

'Me,' repeated William. 'I should have worked that out after he'd bankrupted his ex-wife and almost destroyed Ross.'

'What are you not telling us?' demanded the Hawk.

'With the help of Christina and Ross, I took something every bit as precious to him as the Crown Jewels are to us, so I shouldn't have been surprised that after he'd taken his revenge on Christina and Ross, I'd be next in line, and should expect something even more outrageous.'

'Enlighten me.'

'Faulkner is seeking revenge because I was responsible for taking his Rubens, *Christ's Descent from the Cross*, off the wall of his apartment in Manhattan and replacing it with a fake worth only a few thousand dollars, while the original masterpiece can now be seen hanging in the Fitzmolean.'

'But I always thought the museum owned the original?' said Rebecca, unable to believe what she was hearing.

'They do now,' said William. 'But only because Christina helped us switch them when Faulkner put his East 61st Street apartment on the market last year.'

'It's not a crime to take back something that belongs to you,' the Hawk reminded him.

'It is if Faulkner considers it belonged to him in the first place.'

'But don't forget,' said Jackie, 'Faulkner's in custody while we're in possession of the Sword of State and the Imperial State Crown.'

'So what has he still got up his sleeve?' demanded the Hawk.

'I've no idea,' admitted William. 'But I have a feeling we'll find out when Her Majesty delivers the Queen's Speech to their Lordships tomorrow.'

'Perhaps he plans to steal the speech,' said Paul, trying to lighten the mood.

'I doubt it,' said William, 'there will be several copies of the speech.'

'Oh my God,' said the Hawk. 'You don't think he could have . . .'

CHAPTER 25

THE INNER TEAM WERE SEATED around a table in the commander's office, notepads open, Biros in hand, staring up at a large television screen at the far end of the room.

'What are we looking for?' asked Jackie.

'I don't know,' admitted William, 'and I suspect only Faulkner does.'

'Could we be overreacting?' asked the Hawk, playing devil's advocate. 'After all, we've got the crown and the sword back while Faulkner's been locked up overnight in the Scrubs.'

'I wish I knew,' said William as the letters BBC appeared on the screen, followed moments later by the caption, *The State Opening of Parliament*.

David Dimbleby's familiar voice reminded the audience that Tony Blair had won the general election with a hundred-and-seventy-nine-seat majority and would be the first Labour Prime Minister to hold that office since James Callaghan some eighteen years before.

'And now over to our political editor, Robin Oakley, who

will tell us what we can expect to hear in the Queen's Speech.'

'Frankly, David, there are unlikely to be too many shocks,' said Oakley. 'During the campaign, Tony Blair made it clear his priority was education, education and education. But there are always one or two surprises in any Queen's Speech, as no Prime Minister likes to be thought of as predictable.'

'And possibly one or two surprises that even the Prime Minister isn't aware of,' suggested William as he stared up at the screen.

A long-lens camera zoomed in on Buckingham Palace to pick up the Mall lined with expectant onlookers who'd travelled from all parts of the globe to witness the spectacle, along with millions more watching on television. Among them was Booth Watson, who'd stayed at home to watch the ceremony, and Miles Faulkner, who was sitting in the canteen at Wormwood Scrubs, having forgotten just how foul prison coffee was.

'Never thought of you as a royalist,' said Tulip as he sat down beside him.

'I'm not,' said Miles. 'Just interested to see who works it out first. I have a feeling it might even be the Queen,' which left Tulip even more puzzled.

'The first coach you'll see coming out of the palace,' said Dimbleby, 'is Queen Alexandra's State Carriage, which transports the Cap of Maintenance and the Sword of State, which will be carried in front of the Queen as she processes into the Lords—'

'At least that much is true,' said Miles.

'—Along with the Imperial State Crown, which King George VI first wore at his coronation in 1937 and will be worn today by Her Majesty when she delivers her speech.'

'I'm afraid not,' said Miles.

A loud cheer erupted as the second carriage made its way out of the palace and onto the Mall, with the Queen and Prince Philip returning the waves of a cheering crowd.

'The Irish State Carriage,' continued Dimbleby as the royal couple clip-clopped down the Mall towards Horse Guards, 'is accompanied by a mounted guard from a division of the Household Cavalry, who will escort the monarch to the Palace of Westminster.'

As William hadn't written a single note on his pad, he was beginning to wonder if . . .

The only thing Miles wondered was when Warwick would be called for and summarily dismissed. He would like to have been a fly on the wall at that particular meeting, but you can't have everything. He continued to watch the ceremony while Tulip fetched him another coffee.

Booth Watson poured himself a double gin, a little early perhaps, but then it was going to be a long day. He watched as the State Coach entered Parliament Square, and the Union Flag on the Queen's Tower was lowered, to be replaced by the Royal Standard, which fluttered in the breeze. The carriage came to a halt outside the Sovereign's Entrance as a guard of honour presented arms and the Band of the Grenadier Guards played the national anthem.

'Her Majesty is never late,' remarked Dimbleby as Big Ben struck the quarter hour.

The Queen stepped out of the carriage to be met by the Duke of Norfolk, the Marquess of Cholmondeley and Black Rod, who bowed before four royal ushers accompanied Her Majesty into the building, where she disappeared out of sight.

'At eleven twenty-seven,' declared Dimbleby with the confidence of history, 'the Queen will progress from the Robing

Room on the first floor to the chamber, where she will deliver her speech to both Houses.'

'She'll have worked it out by then,' said Miles, 'even if Warwick hasn't.'

Tulip was puzzled, but knew when to remain silent.

Her Majesty entered the Robing Room at 11.19 a.m. and disappeared behind two red screens to find her dresser awaiting her. Mrs Kelly curtsied and stepped forward to help Her Majesty on with the heavy red and gold robe of state. When the dresser had completed her task, the Queen double-checked her image in a long mirror, made a tiny adjustment and nodded. The sign for Mrs Kelly to pull open the red screens where the Lord Chamberlain would be waiting dutifully, holding a plush red cushion on which rested a crown.

When the Queen picked up the crown, a flicker of surprise appeared on her face, but she didn't comment. She placed the crown on her head and adjusted it until it was comfortable. She then joined the long procession line and took the arm of her liege, but not master.

The state trumpeters announced the arrival of the royal party, and the procession set off at an orderly pace, making its way slowly through the Royal Gallery and across the Prince's Chamber before finally entering the Upper Chamber. Their Lordships rose as one to greet their monarch and remained standing until she had climbed the three steps and taken her place on the throne. Prince Philip took the seat on her right, while Field Marshal Lord Bramall stood a step below on her left, bearing the Sword of State, to remind all those present of her authority as sovereign. Miles smiled. At least that was the real thing.

Their Lordships, wearing long red robes trimmed with white ermine, resumed their places on the red leather benches. The Lord Chancellor stepped forward, bowed and handed the Queen her speech, before retreating backwards.

The Queen opened the folder of a speech she was acquainted with, as she'd read it twice the previous evening in the privacy of her study.

She looked up to see the Law Lords perched around the Woolsack in front of her, the bishops in ecclesiastical dress seated in their reverend places, while the remainder of the red benches were filled with the ancient and the modern, from the hereditary fifteenth Duke of Hamilton to a recently ennobled life peer from Weston-super-Mare. Her gaze moved on to the bar of the House at the far end of the chamber and settled on Tony Blair, her tenth Prime Minister, who was standing next to the Leader of the Opposition, John Major, who looked as if he hadn't been invited to this party.

The Queen put on her glasses and looked down at the first sentence of the speech.

'My Lords and members of the House of Commons, my government intends to govern for the benefit of the whole nation. The education of young people will be my government's first priority.'

Miles looked closely at the Queen and assumed by now she must know the truth, and possibly they were still the only two who did. However, others would have to share their secret before darkness fell, including Commander Hawksby and Chief Superintendent Warwick, who surely would have both resigned before the day was out.

'. . . other measures will be laid before you. My Lords and members of the Commons, I pray that the blessing of Almighty God may rest upon your councils.'

The Queen closed the red folder that bore her crest and the Lord Chancellor stepped forward to retrieve it. When she rose from the throne and took the arm of her consort, their Lordships stood again and remained standing until the royal party had left the chamber and processed back to the Robing Room.

Only a select few witnessed the shedding of the royal robes along with the nation's treasures. The Sword of State was laid to rest in its box before being locked up for another year. The Lord Chamberlain hovered in front of the Queen as she lifted the crown from her head and placed it gently back onto its royal cushion. He was taken by surprise when the Queen whispered, 'I presume there's a simple explanation?'

• • •

Faulkner told Tulip to turn off the television before saying to a passing officer, 'I need to call my lawyer.'

• • •

Commander Hawksby switched off the television, turned to William and said, 'As the crown and sword are now on their way back to the palace, you'd better get moving if you're still hoping to play your part. Though I confess I won't totally relax until you're able to confirm they're both safely locked back up in the Tower for another year.'

'Agreed,' said William. 'And I'd be the first to admit I may have overreacted, but only because Miles Faulkner was involved.'

'Quite understandably,' said the Hawk. 'Now you'd better get going. Can't afford to keep his nibs waiting.'

William and Paul left the Hawk's office and quickly made their way downstairs to find Danny already seated behind the wheel of a familiar Land Rover, its engine running.

'Your next problem,' said Paul as he joined William in the back of the car, 'is what you're going to do about Faulkner.'

'Nothing before the Crown Jewels have been returned to the Tower, and only then will I give him a second thought.'

'I'd happily chop off his head for high treason and other misdemeanours,' said Paul as the Land Rover set off for the palace.

'And leave his head on a spike on Tower Bridge for all to see, no doubt.'

'Or will he end up being pardoned like Colonel Blood?' asked Paul.

'Not if I have anything to do with it,' replied William as he looked out of the window and watched the crowds winding their way slowly back home, while articulated lorries were beginning to pick up the makeshift barriers that had been placed along the Mall.

Even before they reached the palace gates, William could see a grey Jaguar on the far side of the parade ground, parked behind an elite motorcycle escort waiting to be given the order to accompany them back to the Tower in the shortest possible time. William waited for two Guards officers to appear carrying two black boxes that he wouldn't be letting out of his sight until the Resident Governor and two Yeomen returned them to the Jewel House.

• • •

Booth Watson picked up the phone, confident his most important client would be on the other end of the line. Like the Queen, he was never late.

'So far, so good,' said Miles, sounding rather pleased with

himself. 'But the time has come to move on to the next stage of Warwick's downfall.'

'Have you decided which national newspaper you'll leak the story to?' asked Booth Watson.

'As the owner of the *Daily Mail* is an hereditary peer, I think he'll appreciate the irony of the story.'

'But when?'

'Around five this afternoon, which should give the editor more than enough time to clear the front page.'

'Do you think Warwick already knows?'

'No, he doesn't.'

'How can you be sure?' Booth Watson queried.

'He's sitting in the back of a Land Rover at Buckingham Palace waiting for the Lord Chamberlain to join him. Still, it shouldn't be too long before he's enlightened, to use one of his boss's favourite expressions.'

The Hawk, seated behind his desk back at the Yard, switched off the live wire tap and delivered a stream of invective that would have left a Glaswegian docker with his mouth open. Although in truth, he still had no idea what Faulkner's next move would be. However, the words, 'it shouldn't be too long before he's enlightened' rather suggested he was about to find out.

• • •

'What's his problem?' asked Paul as they both watched a young subaltern hurrying across the parade ground towards them.

'No idea,' said William, winding down his window. 'But I have a feeling we're about to find out.'

'Chief Superintendent Warwick?' asked the subaltern even before he'd reached them. William nodded. 'The Lord

Chamberlain wonders if you could join him in his office.' He tried to make it sound like a request rather than a command.

'Of course,' said William, who jumped out of the car and quickly followed the young officer back across the parade ground, catching up with him only as he entered the palace. They climbed a steep flight of stairs, the walls on both sides filled with photos of members of the Royal Family on overseas tours. The subaltern came to a halt at the end of the corridor, knocked on a door and opened it, standing aside to allow William to enter a large comfortable room that felt more like a study than an office. The Lord Chamberlain was seated behind a large antique desk. A painting of the Queen Mother hung on the wall behind him.

William would have enjoyed spending a few moments studying the paintings that adorned the walls and might have done so had his eyes not settled on two familiar black leather boxes that had been placed on a table in the centre of the room.

The Lord Chamberlain rose from behind his desk and walked slowly across to join him. Without a word passing between them, he opened the larger of the two boxes and gazed down at the Sword of State in all its glory. He finally spoke.

'This magnificent piece of weaponry dates back to 1678 and was first used officially by Charles II in 1680. The jewelled hilt reminds us that it was never intended to be raised in anger but only used on ceremonial occasions. This ancient artefact will be returned to the Jewel House where it belongs, but not by you.'

William raised an eyebrow.

The Lord Chamberlain turned his attention to the smaller of the two boxes. He lifted the lid and took out the crown which William had recently seen on television when the Queen addressed both Houses. He placed it in the centre of the table.

'Whereas this imposter,' he said with venom creeping into his voice, 'will not be allowed anywhere near the Tower of London.'

A dozen thoughts passed through William's mind – none of them positive – as he stared down at the crown and waited for an explanation.

'Take a closer look, Superintendent, and you will see a magnificent counterfeit crafted by a modern master, but not, I can assure you, by royal appointment. Her Majesty realized the moment she placed this object on her head that it was not the Imperial State Crown which she wore at her coronation, but a usurper.'

William could feel beads of sweat forming on his forehead and could only just stop his legs from buckling, as he tried to remain calm.

'It was the weight of the crown that gave the game away,' continued the Lord Chamberlain, 'which is why Her Majesty described it as a "lightweight".

'The 1937 Imperial State Crown contains 2868 diamonds, 17 sapphires, 11 emeralds and 269 pearls, which rest on a frame of solid gold. This monstrosity,' said the Lord Chamberlain pointing at the crown, 'is gold-plated. The stones are glass and the pearls certainly weren't found in a shell. I'll spare you the details of the 317 carat Cullinan II Diamond, the pride of South Africa, the St Edward's Sapphire that dates back to 1042, and the Black Prince's Ruby that Henry V is said to have worn in his helmet at the Battle of Agincourt. Not to mention the four drop pearl earrings that were a gift from Catherine de Medici to Mary Queen of Scots when she married the Dauphin.'

William could only hope the Lord Chamberlain had a secret trap door that, with the touch of a button, would spring open and put him out of his misery.

'I have no doubt,' the Lord Chamberlain added, looking back at the crown, 'this is a work of consummate skill but paid for by a rogue who should be banished from the kingdom. And I suspect you know only too well who that rogue is,' he said, placing the substitute back in its box. 'So please take this pale imitation away and display it in the Black Museum where it belongs, or you can replace it with the Imperial State Crown before sunrise. The choice is yours.'

William couldn't think of a suitable reply.

'However,' continued the Lord Chamberlain. 'As the Tower of London will be open to the public at ten o'clock tomorrow morning, I venture to suggest that time is not on your side, so I won't hold you up any longer, Superintendent.'

William grabbed the box, ran out of the office, down the stairs and back across the parade ground. He'd reached the car even before Danny had the chance to open the back door. He grabbed the phone in the armrest and said firmly, 'Put me through to the governor of the Scrubs.'

The few minutes he had to wait felt like hours, but eventually a voice came on the line.

'What can I do for you, Superintendent?' asked the governor.

'Lock up Miles Faulkner in solitary, now!'

CHAPTER 26

'Can I speak to Mr Booth Watson?'

'May I ask who's calling?'

'My name's Tulip. I share a cell with Mr Faulkner, and he asked me to pass on an important message to his brief.'

'I'll put you through, Mr Tulip.'

Tulip kept an eye on the second hand of his watch while he waited.

'Booth Watson.'

'Good afternoon', guv, my name's—'

'I know who you are,' snapped Booth Watson. 'But what I can't work out is why it's not my illustrious client on the other end of the line.'

'He's been banged up in solitary, guv, but he thought that might happen so he gave me a message to pass on to you.'

'Which is?' asked Booth Watson as he opened a yellow pad and picked up a Biro.

'If they haven't released me by tomorrow mornin', let the editor of the *Daily Mail* know where the speckled band is,' said Tulip. 'And tell Mr Dacre, if he doesn't believe you, he can always visit the Tower and see for himself.'

Booth Watson wrote down every word, before he said, 'Well done, Tulip. If you should pick up anything else that might be of interest, don't hesitate to phone me back.'

'I would, guv, but I'm only allowed one three-minute call a day, so I can't—' The phone went dead.

• • •

The commander switched off the tape recorder. 'So, what did we learn from that conversation?' he asked as he looked around the table.

'Since the call came from the Scrubs,' said Paul, 'both of them would be aware it was being recorded.'

'Agreed,' said the Hawk. 'And?'

'Faulkner's mouthpiece will leak the story to the *Daily Mail*, telling them the crown was not returned to the Tower this afternoon,' said William, trying to remain calm, 'and add if they don't believe him, they should go and check for themselves, which leaves us with only a few hours to find out where it is.'

'And if we don't?' Paul chipped in helpfully. 'Booth Watson will reveal exactly where the real crown is. But by then, it will be too late for us to do anything about it.'

'Except resign,' said the Hawk. 'Which is exactly what he had planned for us in the first place. Let's start with you, Jackie. Did you pick up anything useful from the staff you interviewed at the Tower immediately following the robbery?'

'Not a great deal,' admitted Jackie. 'And it wasn't made any easier by the fact I couldn't let anyone know the real reason we were interviewing them.'

'Any recent recruits who could have been planted by Faulkner to assist him on the day?' asked William.

'Two former Green Jackets, both with honourable discharges, have recently been signed up as Yeomen,' said Paul, turning to another file. 'We've checked them both out, but as they'd only just returned from serving a two-year spell in Northern Ireland, they couldn't possibly have been involved.'

'But that doesn't apply to Penny Cummins,' said Rebecca, 'the young woman who's been working part time in the ticket office and admitted texting the words "Colonel Blood" to an unknown contact – undoubtedly Faulkner or Lamont. But she wouldn't have known that, not being a member of the inner team.'

'But how did she find out the password in the first place?' demanded the Hawk.

'The Governor's wife,' said Rebecca. 'When she was stopped at the West Gate and asked by Cummins if she knew the password, one of the children blurted it out.'

'If he hadn't,' said William with some considerable feeling, 'Faulkner couldn't have risked going ahead with the whole operation.'

'Where was Faulkner at the time?' demanded the Hawk.

'As far as it's been possible to trace his exact movements, while I was at the palace picking up the Lord Chamberlain, Faulkner was at the Old Bailey chatting to my father.'

'Your father?' repeated the Hawk.

'All part of an elaborate alibi that would prove he couldn't possibly have been in the Tower when the crown was stolen.'

'And after that?'

'He walked to the House of Lords, dropping in at the Savoy

to book a table in the Grill for lunch, adding several more eyewitnesses to prove he couldn't have been in two places at once.'

'Well, he won't be having lunch at the Savoy today,' said the Hawk, 'because he's locked up in solitary. And we shouldn't be wasting any more of our time on Faulkner, but concentrating on his foot soldiers who appear to have been in on the operation from the start. You can be sure whenever Faulkner's involved, Booth Watson, Lamont and Collins won't be far behind.'

'Although I suspect Harris was the key component in the operation,' said William, 'as he was clearly their inside man. If he hadn't been sitting behind the wheel of the Jaguar, they could never have made it past the East Gate, although what I can't work out is how he and Faulkner ever met.'

'Harris was up to his eyes in debt until about six months ago,' Jackie said while opening another of her files, 'when suddenly his monthly alimony and mortgage payments are paid up to date, and his bank account is no longer in the red. I also found out that Harris was in debt to a leg-breaking bookie, so clearly felt the risk was the better of two evils. I think we can assume his paymaster was Faulkner, and he must have received a large down payment to keep him on side.'

'But while we know where Faulkner, Lamont and Collins are,' said William, 'we still haven't been able to track down Harris.'

'Didn't he leave a paper trail of any sort?' asked the Hawk. 'Plane, boat or train bookings, anything?'

'Not in his name,' came back William, 'but let's face it, that's something else Faulkner could have taken care of, and once Harris had played his part, he wouldn't have hung about. He'd have been only too aware he was the one person who could have been identified by those who work at the Tower so would have had to make a quick get-away while he had the chance.'

'My bet,' continued Paul, 'is having dumped the Jag in the churchyard only minutes after leaving the Tower, he bolted, knowing that within a couple of hours, half the police forces in Europe would be looking for him.'

'But where's he bolted to?' asked Jackie. 'Because—'

'Somewhere where there's no extradition—'

'I don't give a damn where he is,' snapped William, taking them all by surprise. 'Harris is the least of our problems. He won't have any idea where Faulkner's hidden the crown. That wasn't his role in this operation.'

The Hawk had never seen William so rattled, and quickly intervened before it got out of hand. 'But that doesn't apply to Lamont,' he said calmly, 'who could well have been the Chief Superintendent sitting on the back seat of the Land Rover probably wearing his own uniform.'

'He even promoted himself,' said Jackie, 'but as he only got out of the car once and kept his distance, we have no way of proving he was even there.'

'Where does he claim he was at the time?'

'At home with his wife all morning. Says he never left the house, which she confirmed when we interviewed her.'

'Of course she did,' said William.

'CCTV?' asked the Hawk.

'He would have known where every camera was, sir. Don't forget, you trained him.'

'And where are they now?'

'They're sadly still at home, having had to postpone their holiday,' said Paul. 'But we won't be able to hold them up for much longer.'

'Then let's also forget Lamont for the moment,' said the Hawk, 'and hopefully move on to more promising ground. Collins.'

'There's every reason to believe Collins was the driver of the Land Rover,' said Rebecca. 'But if it was him, we're going to find it equally difficult to prove. He was wearing dark glasses and a chauffeur's hat, which someone with their wits about them should have queried at the time as he should also have been wearing a police uniform.'

'And to make matters worse,' said Paul, 'because it was raining, when we checked the CCTV the driver hadn't put on the windscreen wipers so all we have on record is a blurred figure.'

'Any fingerprints?'

'They all wore gloves,' said Jackie.

'What did Collins have to say for himself when you interviewed him?'

'Had his story off-pat,' said William, 'and once he'd told me where I would find Faulkner, he slammed the door in my face.'

'Someone else taking the piss,' said the Hawk, 'which all seems to be part of Faulkner's master plan.'

'You have to admire the man,' said William. 'Not only has he got nerves of steel but the gall to leave his Old Harrovian tie on the front seat of the Jaguar.'

'Well aware that Harrow was also the Lord Chamberlain's alma mater,' added Paul.

'And the Resident Governor confirmed that he recognized the tie and assumed—'

'Time's running out,' said the Hawk, checking his watch. 'So, forget the tie, which Faulkner clearly left to provoke us, and let's start concentrating on the missing crown. Do we think he made a copy or switched it for one that already existed?'

'I don't think he would have had enough time to make something quite as magnificent and detailed as that,' said Rebecca, staring at the replica on the table in front of her. 'Not least because, if he had, the craftsman who made it would also have had to be in on the scam along with several gemologists, as well as their assistants.'

'Agreed. But if we're to have any hope of finding it in time,' said William, 'let's begin by going back over the golden hour and taking it apart minute by minute, starting with the two figures who were caught on CCTV entering Tower Hill underground station carrying a Tower of London shopping bag.'

'Unquestionably Collins and Lamont,' said the Hawk after looking at the CCTV photo yet again. 'However, only one of them – Collins – turns up at Westminster thirty-eight minutes later, still carrying the same bag which we now know contained the replica crown.'

'Which he must have handed over to Faulkner before returning home,' said William.

'Agreed,' said the Hawk. 'But when and where did they switch the crowns?'

'Let's assume both Lamont and Collins remained on the underground for just under twenty minutes,' said Paul, studying a map of the Circle line that he laid out in the centre of the table. 'If they'd gone east, they could have reached Paddington, Baker Street or possibly Kensington. But if they travelled west, Westminster seems their obvious destination.'

'Agreed,' said the Hawk. 'After all, that's where we found the damn man standing around waiting for us to turn up. He's probably placed the real crown on a statue of the Queen to make sure the public can't miss it.'

'I don't agree,' said Rebecca. 'I think he's put it somewhere where the public won't give it a second thought.'

'Buckingham Palace?' offered Jackie. 'The House of Lords?'

'Please God don't make it the House of Lords,' said the Hawk sounding exasperated.

'It's times like this,' said William, 'I wish Inspector Hogan was with us, as he's someone who thinks outside of the box.'

'Angela's been trying to track him down all morning,' said the Hawk. 'But all she got was—'

'He's taking the children on a school trip,' interrupted William, looking at his watch, 'to see the other man who stole the Crown Jewels.'

'Colonel Blood,' said Paul.

'Baker Street!' said Rebecca, still staring at a map of the Circle line.

'What about Baker Street?' asked the Hawk.

'It's nine stops on the Circle line and would have taken them about twenty minutes.'

'Hidden in plain sight,' said the Hawk. He picked up his phone and started to dial.

CHAPTER 27

'NORTHCLIFFE HOUSE,' SAID A CHEERFUL voice. 'How may I help you?'

'I'd like to speak to the editor of the *Daily Mail*.'

'Who shall I say is calling?'

'Booth Watson QC.' He emphasized the QC.

'Hold please. I'll try his line.'

Booth Watson glanced down at his yellow pad and checked his script while he waited, and waited, and waited . . .

'Good afternoon, Mr Booth Watson, Paul Dacre. How can I help?'

'Good afternoon, Mr Dacre. I have an exclusive for you, but before I tell you the details, I need to be sure it will never be traced back to me.'

'That goes without saying,' replied Dacre.

'This morning at the State Opening of Parliament . . .'

• • •

'Colonel Blood was a notorious seventeenth-century scoundrel and the only person who's ever attempted to steal the Crown Jewels.'

'But he failed,' said Artemisia, loud enough for everyone to hear.

'However,' continued the tour guide, 'he might have succeeded if the jewel keeper's son, a soldier on leave from fighting in Flanders, hadn't arrived back . . .'

'Just in time,' said Peter as Ross's mobile phone began to vibrate in his pocket.

'. . . at the same time as the robbery was taking place.'

Ross checked the number on the screen and realized he had no choice but to answer it.

'. . . While Blood was running out of the Jewel House with the crown under his cloak . . .' Ross let go of Jojo's hand and turned away '. . . Talbot Edwards, a captain of the Guard, was walking towards the Martin Tower when he heard the words—'

'Stop, thief!' said Artemisia.

'Stop, thief!' repeated Peter.

Ross touched the green button and said, 'Sir.'

'Now listen, Inspector,' said the Hawk, 'and listen carefully, because you're no longer on leave.'

• • •

'Right,' said the Hawk after he'd put the phone down. 'We're only going to get one chance so we can't afford any more cock-ups. William, I want you to go straight to the Tower and brief the Governor. Warn him that the editor of the *Mail* is likely to phone him at any moment. Advise him not to take the call under any circumstances, but of course the decision is his. However, don't under any circumstances tell him what we're up to, the less he knows the better. Meanwhile, Paul, Jackie and Rebecca will join Ross as quickly as possible. You'll find him standing outside Baker Street tube station next to the statue of Sherlock Holmes. And be sure to take that with you,' he added, pointing at the false crown. 'By the time you get downstairs, I'll have a squad car waiting for you. Paul, the moment you arrive, make sure you hand over the crown to Inspector Hogan and follow his instructions.'

Paul leant forward, picked up the crown and placed it back in its box while Jackie held open the Tower of London bag so he could lower it carefully inside. Rebecca was the first to leave the room and was repeatedly jabbing the lift button as Paul and Jackie followed her out of the commander's office.

As the lift door opened, Jackie dashed past them, down the stairs, and had reached the door just as Danny drove William out of the Yard on their way to the Tower. The promised squad car drew up and took their place.

Jackie was holding open the front door as Rebecca came out of the lift. She shot past her, opened the back door of the squad car and waited. Paul walked out of the lift and headed slowly towards the car, clutching the bag as though it contained the real crown.

Once Paul was seated in the back, Rebecca joined him while Jackie jumped into the front and told the driver where they were going. He already knew, and the moment she'd closed the door, the squad car took off.

• • •

After they'd left, the Hawk sat at his desk waiting for the editor of the *Mail* to call.

But first he needed to brief the Commissioner, who would inform the Prime Minister, who would seek an audience with the Queen to tell her something she already knew.

The phone on his desk began to ring.

• • •

Ross turned off his mobile, bent down and whispered to Jojo, 'I've just got to do something quite important. Shouldn't be too long,' he promised.

Jojo reluctantly let go of his hand and continued to listen to the guide.

'Colonel Blood and his co-conspirators were immediately arrested and locked up in the White Tower . . .'

'But not for long,' interrupted Artemisia as Ross slipped out of the Rogues' Gallery and headed for the Royal Family, where he was greeted by another guide addressing an even larger group.

'The 1937 Imperial State Crown was worn by Her Majesty the Queen at her coronation in 1953.'

'It looks real,' said a young boy standing near the front.

Bright lad, thought Ross as he turned a slow circle and studied the layout of the room. His gaze settled on Princess Diana, and a plan began to form in his mind. One more slow circle before he left the gallery and made his way quickly back to the main entrance. He knew the team couldn't be with him for a few more minutes, so he used the time to buy three tickets from the box office so there wouldn't be any delays.

'You do realize,' said the lady behind the counter, 'that we close at six.'

That should be more than enough time, Ross wanted to tell her, but simply handed over three five-pound notes in exchange for the tickets.

Ross left the museum and was walking towards the statue of Sherlock Holmes when he saw a squad car heading towards him. He raised a hand as if hailing a taxi, and the car screeched to a halt by his side.

Rebecca was first out, with Jackie following in her wake. Paul was the last to join them, still clinging on to the bag. Ross gave them their tickets, while explaining exactly what he expected them to do once they were all in the Royal Gallery.

Paul handed over the Tower of London shopping bag to Ross as Rebecca left them to go in to the museum. Jackie followed thirty seconds later, with Paul not far behind.

Ross was about to enter the gallery when his mobile began to ring. He pressed the answer button while on the move and, when he saw the name flash up on the screen, said, 'Not now, sir,' and cut the commander off for the first time in his life.

Once inside the Royal Gallery, he found his three colleagues as instructed standing apart from each other at the back of the group, looking as if they were listening intently to the tour guide. Ross took his place at the end of the front row. A thick rope barrier surrounded a wax model of the Queen, with the clear warning that if anyone stepped over it, an alarm would go off. Ross had already anticipated that and built it into his plan.

'The Imperial State Crown never leaves the Tower of London,' continued the guide, 'except on official occasions such as the State Opening of Parliament when Her Majesty will wear the crown when she delivers the Queen's Speech to the House of Lords. Look carefully at . . .'

Ross turned around and nodded firmly.

• • •

The Hawk picked up the phone to hear an unfamiliar voice on the other end of the line.

'Good afternoon, Commander Hawksby. My name is Paul Dacre, and I'm the editor of the *Daily Mail*.'

'Good afternoon, Mr Dacre,' responded the Hawk, only too aware he was talking to the most powerful editor in Fleet Street.

'I've just had a call from a reliable source claiming that at the Opening of Parliament this morning, the Queen wasn't wearing the Imperial State Crown, but a replica of little value, and I wondered if you'd care to comment?'

'And who may I ask is your reliable source?' asked the Hawk, even though he knew the answer to that question.

'I'm not at liberty to reveal that.'

'Then neither am I at liberty to comment on your fishing expedition.'

'What I can tell you,' said Dacre before the Hawk could ring off, 'is my source also claims that the real crown should have been returned to the Tower by your deputy this afternoon, a certain Chief Superintendent Warwick, but it wasn't.'

'I have no idea what you're talking about,' said the Hawk as he stared at an empty table where, only moments before, the replica crown had been.

'Then I suggest you read the first edition of our paper tomorrow morning, commander, when you will discover exactly what I'm talking about,' said Dacre as line two lit up on the Hawk's phone.

'I'll be sure to do that,' said the Hawk, cutting Dacre off before answering line two.

'Good afternoon, commander, it's—'

'Good afternoon, Governor,' Hawksby replied, 'I was just about to phone and warn you to expect a call from the editor of the *Daily Mail*.'

'He's already been in touch,' said the Governor, sounding anxious. 'He told me he'll be sending over the paper's royal correspondent with a photographer to take a picture of the 1937 Imperial State Crown. I have several crowns and coronets at my disposal, commander, but, as you well know, that one is not among them.'

'Call Dacre back and tell him the Tower is closed, as I'm confident you'll have the crown back on display by the time you open to the public tomorrow morning.'

'In normal circumstances, I could get away with that,' said the Governor, 'but unfortunately, Dacre anticipated that might be my response and informed me he's already been in touch with the Crown Jeweller, a Mr Thomas, who can verify the authenticity of the crown. However, when Thomas turns up, he'll find there is nothing but a velvet cushion to verify.'

'Tell Mr Thomas he can see the crown like the rest of us at ten o'clock tomorrow morning.'

'I only wish I could,' came back the Governor. 'But unfortunately, because of a certain Colonel Blood, that's not possible. I'll spare you the details, commander, but in 1673 King Charles II issued a proclamation allowing the Crown Jeweller access to the Tower at any time of the day or night, and no one, I repeat no one, not even Her Majesty, can prevent him from carrying out his duty.'

'He could be abroad, out to dinner, at the theatre, even—'

'He's on his way to the Tower as we speak,' said the Governor, cutting him short. 'Dacre has already contacted Mr Thomas and told him he has reason to believe the crown may have been stolen, and that's what he will be telling his three million readers tomorrow morning unless Thomas says otherwise. Frankly, all he'll see now is a large empty display case.'

'Bluff as long as you can,' said the Hawk, 'and I'll get back to you the moment I have any more news.'

The Hawk put the phone down and began tapping his fingers as he waited impatiently for Ross to call back. The phone began to ring. He grabbed it as if it were a lifeline, only to hear his secretary say, 'It's the commissioner returning your call.'

• • •

The editor sat on the corner of his desk, eager to start the early evening news conference.

'There's only one story worth working on, as it's bound to dominate the news agenda for the next few days, possibly weeks,' he began, 'and as we've got the exclusive, the rest of Fleet Street will be chasing our tail.' No one interrupted him.

Dacre began briefing his heads of departments on the conversation he'd had with an eminent QC without once mentioning his name, the stonewalling he'd met when he contacted Commander Hawksby and the unconvincing responses he'd received from the Resident Governor when he asked him to confirm that the crown had not been returned to the Jewel House this afternoon.

'So, Matt, let's start with you,' barked the editor at his royal correspondent. 'Knock me out a thousand words. History of the crown, details of the jewels and, most important, how much it's worth. I don't want priceless, I want as many noughts as possible.'

The small group gathered in the editor's office didn't look up while they continued to scribble away.

'Meanwhile, I'll be writing a leader about the four morons who allowed this catastrophe to happen and calling for their resignations. I need photos of the Resident Governor of the Tower, Commander Hawksby, who heads up Royalty Protection, and Chief Superintendent William Warwick, along with his second-in-command whose name I don't know. And don't forget, we've only got a couple of hours before the first edition rolls.'

'Forgive me for asking,' said the royal correspondent, 'but what if we find the real crown is back in the Tower and Mr Thomas says the one your eminent QC is going on about is nothing more than a replica?'

'Then I need a picture of the replica crown and the most recent photograph we have of Miles Faulkner.'

'Who's he?' asked the head of the picture desk.

'The eminent QC's leading client,' interrupted the chief crime reporter, 'who's currently in Wormwood Scrubs and I'm told will be appearing in court tomorrow, applying for bail.'

'By which time everyone will have the story,' said Dacre. 'So we haven't got a moment to waste.'

'What's our headline if it turns out that Faulkner has been bluffing and only has a replica of the crown?' asked the deputy editor.

'"Throw away the key". Hold the front page until the last possible moment but tell the print room that if Faulkner has got his hands on the real crown, we'll be printing an extra million copies.'

'And if it's the replica?'

'Half a million. Either way, it will increase our circulation and keep us ahead of our rivals,' said Dacre. 'Although I know which one I'd prefer.'

• • •

Rebecca took a pace back and let out a piercing scream. Everyone in the Royal Gallery except Ross and a young boy immediately swung round to see Princess Diana lying on the ground, decapitated. A young woman was kneeling by her side, crying.

Ross stepped over the rope, setting off the alarm, but he'd completed his task by the time the first security guard came rushing into the gallery thirty seconds later.

'I'm so sorry,' said Rebecca, still in tears, with Jackie kneeling by her side trying to console her.

'I know you're not going to believe this, miss,' said the guard, 'but it's the second time it's happened this week. In fact, they're still patching up Prince Charles.'

The three police officers did believe him but pretended to look surprised.

'Mum!' shouted the young boy at the top of his voice. 'That man has just pinched the crown,' he said, pointing at Ross's back as he disappeared out of the Royal Gallery.

A security guard ran across to check, but the crown was still in place. He frowned at the young lad and returned to what was left of Princess Diana.

Paul was helping Rebecca to her feet by the time Ross had reached the Presidential Gallery. He ran past Washington,

Jefferson, Lincoln and Kennedy without giving them a second look. The first thing he saw as he rushed out of the front door was a police car with three elite outriders in front and another two behind. As a back door was open, they were clearly expecting him.

Ross flung himself onto the back seat and hadn't even closed the door before the escort party set off at a speed unknown in London unless you were a member of the Royal Family or a criminal on the run. Ross wasn't sure which he was.

He grabbed the phone in the armrest and immediately contacted the commander to tell him he was in possession of the Imperial State Crown and had left the replica on a waxwork model of the Queen, where it belonged.

'And the rest of the team?' the Hawk asked.

'Trying to put Humpty Dumpty back together again.'

The Hawk laughed for the first time in days, but quickly moved on to his next problem.

'The royal correspondent of the *Daily Mail* and a photographer are already on their way to the Tower and, as they're only coming from Blackfriars Road, they're likely to get there long before you. However, the Governor assures me that he can hold them up until you arrive. Unfortunately, that doesn't apply to the Crown Jeweller, a Mr Thomas from Garrard, who has the right to enter the Jewel House at any time of the night or day and there's nothing anyone can do to stop him.'

'Where's he now?' asked Ross.

'He's already on his way, but he's about to find out every traffic light on the journey will be red, whatever route he takes, while yours will always be green. Despite that, it will still be difficult for you to reach the Tower ahead of him. The press are certain to be there first, but the Governor will hold them up until Thomas arrives. Though if the Crown Jeweller turns up before you . . .'

'Faulkner wins,' said Ross as they sped past Marble Arch and on down Park Lane towards Hyde Park Corner.

The Hawk didn't comment other than to say, 'Keep this line open so I always know where you are and can update you.'

'Will do,' said Ross as he looked out of the front window to admire the polished drill of his colleagues from the Special Escort Group who ensured their progress was unimpeded. Despite their expertise, he still wasn't confident he would make it to the Tower in time.

• • •

The Resident Governor and the Chief Exhibitor were standing beside a large empty display case, that for three hundred and sixty-three days a year was occupied by the Imperial State Crown. They had run out of small talk. The phone rang.

'The two gentlemen from the press have arrived, sir,' said the Chief Yeoman. 'I've explained that they can't enter the Jewel House until Mr Thomas turns up.'

'And even then, try to hold them up for as long as you can,' whispered the Governor. 'Minutes could make all the difference.' He should have said seconds.

• • •

'I'm just circling Hyde Park Corner,' said Ross. 'So far we haven't been held up once. Where's the Crown Jeweller?'

'Mr Thomas is just entering Parliament Square. So he's about eight minutes ahead of you. But there are still eleven sets of traffic lights for him to negotiate, and they will all turn red just before he reaches them and will continue to do so all the way along the Embankment. Once he enters the City, the lights are no longer under my control. But keep going. You're gaining on him with every mile.'

• • •

'Where are you?' demanded Dacre.

'Twiddling my thumbs in somewhere called the Middle Tower,' replied the royal correspondent. 'They won't let us into the Jewel House until Mr Thomas arrives. Any idea when that might be?'

'He's just called to say he's never known the traffic so bad. Every light seems to turn red just as he approaches it. He hopes to be with you in about five or six minutes at most.'

'I get the distinct feeling they're trying to prevent us from getting anywhere near the Jewel House,' said the royal correspondent.

'I'm glad to hear it,' said the editor.

• • •

'Where are you?' barked the Hawk.

'I'm driving down Constitution Hill towards Buckingham Palace,' said Ross. 'Do you think Her Majesty has any idea what we're doing in her name?'

'Tell your driver to go over Westminster Bridge,' said the Hawk, ignoring the comment, 'and head for the Tower along the south side of the river, otherwise you'll end up behind Mr Thomas, in which case he's certain to get there before you.'

• • •

'I've just passed the two griffins that herald the boundary to the City of London,' said Thomas, 'and inexplicably, the traffic is flowing a lot more smoothly, so I should reach the main entrance to the Tower in about five minutes.'

'Where will you park?' asked Dacre. 'It's nothing but double-yellow lines in the Square Mile.'

'Where I always park,' said Thomas without explanation.

• • •

'I'm now south of the river heading along Tooley Street towards Tower Bridge,' said Ross. 'I should be outside the East Gate in about eight minutes. That's assuming I'm not held up.'

'You'll find the East Gate is already open, but you can only risk driving as far as the moat, which is about a hundred yards further on. If five police motorcycles and a police car were seen driving into the Tower, the press wouldn't have to put two and two together to realize everything they've been told by Booth Watson was true. So, when you reach the East Gate, dump your escort and walk across the middle drawbridge where you'll find a contact waiting for you on the other side. You can hand them the crown.'

'I assume it's William?' said Ross.

'No, he's already in the Jewel House with the Governor. It will be—'

'Thomas has just driven past Mansion House,' interrupted a voice, 'but he'll still need to find a parking spot.'

'That should give me another couple of minutes,' said Ross as his little convoy swung left past Southwark Cathedral and headed for Tower Bridge.

'Don't count on it,' said the Hawk.

Ross became distracted by a foghorn blasting three times and looked to his right to see a huge yacht relentlessly heading towards the bridge. He turned back and stared out of the front window and couldn't miss a line of flashing red lights with the traffic ahead of them grinding to a halt.

'Go for it!' shouted Ross but the driver didn't need any encouragement to weave his way in and out of the traffic, ignore the red lights and accelerate onto the bridge as it slowly began to rise. Ross snapped on his seatbelt, clung onto the crown and began to pray to a god he didn't believe in.

The three leading outriders shot over the narrow gap as the driver of the squad car slammed his foot to the floor. When he reached the gap, he took off and, for a few seconds, hovered in mid-air before crashing down on the other side of the bridge, like an aeroplane making a bad landing.

The two follow-up bikes swerved and skidded to a halt as they reached the ever-widening gap, leaving them with no choice but to watch the yacht pass serenely below them.

'Where are you?' demanded the Hawk as what was left of the escort party continued on its way down the other side of the bridge.

'About two minutes from the East Gate,' said Ross, having decided this wasn't the time to tell the commander that another five seconds and the crown would have ended up on the bottom of the Thames.

• • •

The editor stared down at the provisional headline.

EXCLUSIVE: CROWN JEWELS STOLEN
FROM THE TOWER OF LONDON

A colour photograph of the 1937 Imperial State Crown dominated the front page. The editor switched his attention to the alternative headline:

NOTORIOUS CRIMINAL IN BOTCHED
ATTEMPT TO STEAL CROWN JEWELS

'I still need a picture of the replica crown,' hollered Dacre, 'along with an up-to-date photograph of Faulkner.'

'Not easy,' suggested the deputy editor. 'No one knows where the replica is, and Faulkner's currently banged up in solitary.'

'Don't make excuses,' said Dacre, pointing at his crime reporter, 'and knock me up a thousand-word profile on Faulkner and why he should never have been let out of jail in the first place.'

'And if the crown isn't in the Tower and only Faulkner knows where it is?' asked the chief crime correspondent.

'A thousand words on the new Raffles. The Old Harrovian cavalier who's run circles around Scotland Yard's finest, making them look like the Keystone Cops. Either way, I've only got forty-five minutes before I decide which headline I'm running with. So make sure you have both articles ready for me to consider before we go to press.'

Everyone except the editor left the office and quickly returned to their desks. Some began hitting the phonelines while others tapped out opening paragraphs, aware they only had forty-one minutes left before the presses rolled.

• • •

Mr Thomas parked his car on a single-yellow line on Lower Thames Street only a hundred yards away from the Tower entrance. He walked quickly down the slope towards the West Gate where he could see a welcoming party waiting for him, as well as the Senior Yeoman holding a large bunch of keys. He didn't look quite so welcoming. Was it just possible . . .?

Mr Thomas was asked to sign the visitors' book before the Chief Yeoman picked up the phone and dialled the Jewel House. It was some time before the call was answered.

'Mr Thomas has arrived, sir. Shall I escort him across to the Jewel House?'

The Governor stared at the empty display case that housed only a plush red velvet cushion. He accepted he could be the shortest serving Resident Governor in the Tower's thousand-year history and would forever be remembered as the man who handed over the Crown Jewels to a criminal. He could hear Faulkner telling the jury, 'He even accepted an invitation to join the Lord Chamberlain at his club, White's, for lunch.' When he'd warned his wife earlier that afternoon about his possible fate, she had reminded him that three former Governors had been beheaded.

'That might be less painful,' he'd responded.

'Is there anything I can do to help?' she asked.

'Yes, while there is still an outside chance . . .'

• • •

'Yes, please escort Mr Thomas to the Jewel House. I'll be waiting for him.'

'What about the gentlemen of the press?'

'Yes, they can come as well. If I'm going to have my head

chopped off—' began the Governor as a message flashed up on his mobile.

Arrived outside East Gate. Have abandoned the outriders and heading towards the middle drawbridge on foot. Should be with you in less than a minute.

'This, gentlemen,' said the Yeoman, pausing for a moment, 'is the Martin Tower, where the Crown Jewels were stored during the sixteenth century, but perhaps more interesting—'

'I didn't come here for a history lesson,' said Thomas, not breaking his stride.

'Once you've crossed the moat,' responded the Governor, 'you'll find your contact waiting for you on the other side and . . .'

Ross ran across the middle drawbridge and, once he reached the other side, whispered loudly, 'Where are you?'

'Over here,' said a voice he didn't recognize. A figure stepped out of the shadows, grabbed the carrier bag and began running up the slope towards the Jewel House.

Ross would have chased after them if a smartly dressed man, whom he assumed had to be Thomas, hadn't strode past him followed by a Yeoman, a photographer and someone Ross thought must be the *Daily Mail*'s royal correspondent. Ross slipped back into the shadows, a reluctant onlooker.

The four of them were turning the corner at the top of the slope, just as the bag snatcher reached the Jewel House. The heavy door inched open and they slipped inside. The door was slammed shut and a key turned in the lock.

The Chief Exhibitor looked up to see someone he recognized heading towards him. They stopped in front of him and handed over the shopping bag.

'Most irregular,' said the Chief Exhibitor as he lovingly extracted the Imperial State Crown from the bag. He was lowering it onto its cushion when they all heard a key turning in the lock. 'Most irregular,' he repeated just as the Jewel House door swung open.

Mr Thomas marched in followed by the Chief Yeoman and two uninvited guests. The Crown Jeweller strode across to the Governor and even before he could introduce himself said, 'Why is the crown not locked in its exhibition case?'

'I gave orders for the case to be removed when I was told you were on your way from the Middle Tower,' said the Resident Governor calmly. 'I'm only sorry you were called out at such short notice, especially as I was informed you have a special guest for dinner.'

'Had,' said Thomas as he took a loupe out of an inside pocket, polished it with his handkerchief and stepped forward to take a closer look at the crown.

After only a few moments he swung around, stared at the royal correspondent and his photographer and said, 'Which one of you nincompoops was responsible for me having to leave a member of the Royal Family to come over here on a wild goose chase?'

The photographer took a step back, while the royal correspondent stammered, 'But we thought—'

'That's your problem,' said Thomas, 'you didn't think.'

'So are you telling me it's the real crown?'

'And anyone else who's willing to listen,' said Thomas.

'But did the Queen wear it at the State Opening this morning?' he pressed as the photographer began to snap away.

'Yes, unless she's got another one,' barked Thomas, not

attempting to hide any sarcasm. He turned to the Governor and said, 'I'm sorry. But I'll have to leave you in the hope I can get back before HRH departs.'

'I do apologize,' said the Governor, 'if we put you to any inconvenience.'

'Not your fault, old chap. But forgive me, must dash.'

'Of course, Mr Thomas. But before you go, may I introduce my wife, Caroline.'

'Good evening, Lady Faber,' Thomas said, giving her a slight bow. 'I certainly hope we'll meet again when I'm not in so much of a rush,' he added before leaving them without another word.

It was while Thomas was driving back to Chelsea that he couldn't help noticing every light was green. Even more puzzling, what was the Governor's wife doing in the Jewel House at that time of night? And why was she dressed in a black tracksuit, black trainers and holding a Tower of London shopping bag. Could it be possible . . .?

• • •

'That was too close for comfort,' said the Governor once the two disgruntled journalists had reluctantly left the Jewel House without a story.

William stared at the Imperial State Crown as it was placed back in its case by the Chief Exhibitor and couldn't disagree with the Governor's assessment.

'Perhaps you'd care to join my wife and me for a celebration drink back at the lodgings?' he suggested. 'I think we've both earned it.'

'Most irregular,' repeated the Chief Exhibitor as he switched the alarm back on.

'Thank you,' said William, 'but I'll first need to go and rescue my colleague and tell him the good news.'

'Why don't you ask Inspector Hogan to join us?' said the Governor's wife. 'What's his poison?'

'Guinness, ma'am,' said William, stifling a chuckle before he left them to go in search of Ross.

Ross stepped out of the shadows the moment he saw William striding purposefully towards the middle drawbridge. When he suggested they join the Governor and his wife for a drink, all Ross had to say was, 'It will have to be quick. I've got an eight o'clock dinner date with Alice, and she doesn't like to be kept waiting.'

'You're sounding more like a married man every day,' teased William.

'I wish,' said Ross as they headed for the Governor's residence.

William pulled out a mobile phone from an inside pocket. 'But first, I'll have to call the Hawk and bring him up to date.'

'I already have,' said Ross.

'How can you possibly have known what took place inside the Jewel House when you weren't even there?'

'Three clues, Chief Superintendent,' replied Ross. 'I don't think the Crown Jeweller would have left quite so quickly if the crown hadn't been back in place. He might just have hung around and demanded an explanation.'

'Circumstantial at best.'

'Possibly,' said Ross, 'but the resigned looks on the faces of the two hacks who followed him out a few moments later rather confirmed my suspicions.'

'Hardly conclusive,' suggested William.

'My dear Watson,' said Ross as if he were playing a violin, 'they would have both been on their phones and running if they'd nailed their lead front page exclusive. In any case, there was a final clue that would have convinced any jury.'

'Namely?' said William, who stopped in his tracks and turned to face his friend who had clearly decided to keep him in suspense for a few more moments. 'Get on with it!'

'The next person who came out of the Jewel House looked rather pleased with himself.'

'Guilty,' admitted William. 'But I still have to call the commander and ask him to arrange for Faulkner to be released from solitary.'

'Why would you want to do that?' asked Ross.

'Elementary, my dear Hogan,' said William as they headed for the Governor's residence. 'But I'll let you think about it for a few moments while I have a quick word with the Hawk, because he won't need to be told why.'

• • •

No one was more surprised than Miles when a senior prison officer unlocked his cell door and told him he was being released from solitary.

'Why?' Miles asked suspiciously as he followed the PO out into the corridor.

'Don't ask me,' said the PO as he led the prisoner down a long dark corridor back to his cell on the first floor. 'Way above my pay grade.'

'I need to make a call to my lawyer,' said Miles, blinking as he stepped back into the daylight.

'Can't stop you doin' that, Mr Faulkner. But don't forget, only one call per day is permitted and they'll cut you off after three minutes.'

It wouldn't take three minutes for BW to confirm he'd

briefed the editor of the *Daily Mail* to let him know the Imperial State Crown hadn't been returned to the Tower of London following the State Opening of Parliament. However, when he appeared in court tomorrow morning, he would finally reveal where they could find it – for an entrance fee of five pounds. Miles had a feeling he would be playing to a packed house.

'And don't forget, Mr Faulkner,' said the PO, lowering his voice. 'Everything you say is being recorded.'

'Couldn't ask for more,' said Miles as he headed for the phone booth, assuming Commander Hawksby and his team would be listening to every word.

• • •

Booth Watson picked up the phone, knowing exactly who would be on the other end of the line, because only one other person had that number.

'I'm out of solitary, BW, and presumably I have you to thank for that?' were Miles's opening words as he didn't have a moment to spare.

'I'd like to take the credit,' said Booth Watson, 'but no, I suspect it was Warwick who arranged that.'

'But why when I'm about to cause him so much grief?'

'Possibly because the Imperial State Crown is back in the Tower, as the public will discover when they open for business in the morning.'

'How can that be possible when no one else knows where it is?'

'The simple answer, Miles, is, once again, you underestimated your favourite Chief Superintendent.'

'But when I appear in court tomorrow, how will Warwick

explain that I've been charged with stealing the Imperial State Crown?'

'By adding three words to the charge sheet.'

'Which three words?' demanded Miles.

'"A replica of", which you didn't steal from the Tower of London, but from Madame Tussauds.'

'They won't get away with it.'

'They already have,' said Booth Watson. 'Commander Hawksby has given the *Daily Mail* an unattributable exclusive with a photo of the replica crown, which I have a feeling will be their lead story tomorrow.'

'Saying what?'

'That you were arrested outside the Sovereign's Entrance to the House of Lords in possession of a replica of the Imperial State Crown that you'd earlier stolen from Madame Tussauds. He's even given them a recent photograph of you – the one taken in police custody following your arrest.'

'When I give evidence from the witness box tomorrow,' came back Miles, 'Warwick will be laughed out of court.'

'I have a feeling when the presiding judge, not to mention the press, examine the replica crown, it will be you who is laughed out of court and all the way back to Wormwood Scrubs.'

'But the two cars with the false number plates should be proof enough that my team got into the Tower and somehow managed to get back out with the Sword of State and Imperial State Crown.'

'Both cars are gathering dust at a pound in Wandsworth, with their original number plates back in place, and no doubt will be reclaimed by Lamont when he returns from Milan next week.'

'But Bruce will confirm my story.'

'I don't think so, Miles, unless of course he wants to join

you in the Scrubs. No, I have a feeling the ex-superintendent will be happy to pay a small clamping charge before reclaiming both cars and I wouldn't be surprised if he hadn't sold them back to the dealers for a good price by this time next week.'

'Once I'm out on bail, I'll let every other paper know the truth about what really happened.'

'I don't think they'll be letting you out on bail quite that quickly,' said Booth Watson.

'Why not? The fake crown can't be worth that much.'

'The chairman of Madame Tussauds has given the police a written statement which says the crown was made by one of the nation's leading craftsmen, at a cost of over twenty thousand pounds, and he has the bill to prove it. He also pointed out in his statement that it was one of the museum's most popular attractions. He went on to warmly congratulate the police and in particular Chief Superintendent Warwick on its welcome return to the gallery, while reminding everyone that the crown will be back on display when the gallery opens at ten o'clock tomorrow morning. So I think, Miles, given the circumstances, you're unlikely to get away with less than four years, remembering your past record. But I'm happy to take your instructions.'

'I'll tell you exactly what I expect you to do . . .' the phone began to purr. Booth Watson checked his watch. A most satisfactory three minutes.

Commander Hawksby switched off the tape. He also considered it had been a most satisfactory three minutes, and decided to take Booth Watson's sage advice.

He called the editor of the *Daily Mail* and gave him an exclusive, along with a picture of the replica crown and an up-to-date photo of Miles Faulkner. After all, wasn't that exactly what Booth Watson had advised him to do?

The Hawk couldn't make up his mind who was the bigger

villain, Miles Faulkner or Mr Booth Watson QC. In William's opinion, it was a score draw.

• • •

Ross smiled when the Governor's wife handed him a Guinness and William a glass of champagne.

'I've worked it out,' said Ross.

'Worked what out?' asked the Governor.

'Why Faulkner's been released from solitary.'

'Because he's no longer a threat,' said the Governor, 'and we don't need the public to think he ever was.'

'Wouldn't care to join my team, would you, sir?' said William. 'I even know the person you would replace.'

'No, thank you, Chief Superintendent. In fact, I don't want to see either of you again for another year.'

Both men laughed as the Governor's wife refilled their glasses and said, 'May I ask which of you was responsible for preventing my husband from being summarily executed?'

'Modesty prevents me, ma'am . . .' began Ross.

'Caroline, please,' insisted the Governor's wife.

Ross raised his glass in a mock salute. William would have told Ross to stop flirting, but it would be like asking a cat to reprieve a mouse.

'Truth is,' said William, 'the officer who worked it out first was Detective Sergeant Rebecca Pankhurst, a formidable young member of my team.'

'My number two, Caroline,' said Ross.

'Only in rank,' suggested William, 'and not for much longer. But I must confess, Ross did the heavy lifting.'

'Then let's raise our glasses and toast Rebecca,' said the Governor, 'who saved all our lives.'

'To Rebecca!' they all said in unison, as Ross's mobile began to ring.

Ross assumed it had to be Alice asking where he was and he already had his excuse ready.

'Inspector Hogan?' said a voice he didn't recognize. 'I'm the manager of Madame Tussauds. I'm sorry to bother you, but I thought you ought to know that your daughter is sitting on the execution block and refusing to move until you come and collect her.'

ACKNOWLEDGEMENTS

My thanks for their invaluable advice and research to:
Simon Bainbridge, Alain Baron, Michael Benmore,
Jonathan Caplan KC, Kate Elton, Stephen Froggatt, Alison
Prince and Dr David Smith

Special thanks to:
Detective Sergeant Michelle Roycroft (Ret.)
Chief Superintendent John Sutherland (Ret.)